In 1990, **Patricia Cornwell**
while working at the Office o
Richmond, Virginia. An aus
the Edgar, Creasey, Anthony, as well as the French Prix du Roman d'Aventures—the first book ever to claim all these distinctions in a single year. Growing into an international phenomenon, the Scarpetta series won Cornwell the Sherlock Award for best detective created by an American author, the Gold Dagger Award, the RBA Thriller Award, and the Medal of Chevalier of the Order of Arts and Letters for her contributions to literary and artistic development.

Today, Cornwell's novels and iconic characters are known around the world. Beyond the Scarpetta series, Cornwell has written the definitive nonfiction account of Jack the Ripper's identity, cookbooks, a children's book, a biography of Ruth Graham, and three other fictional series based on the characters Win Garano, Andy Brazil, and Captain Calli Chase. Cornwell continues exploring the latest space-age technologies and threats relevant to contemporary life. Her interests range from the morgue to artificial intelligence and include visits to Interpol, the Pentagon, the U.S. Secret Service, and NASA. Cornwell was born in Miami. She grew up in Montreat, North Carolina, and now lives and works in Boston.

ALSO BY PATRICIA CORNWELL

SCARPETTA SERIES

Livid
Autopsy
Chaos
Depraved Heart
Flesh and Blood
Dust
The Bone Bed
Red Mist
Port Mortuary
The Scarpetta Factor
Scarpetta
Book of the Dead
Predator
Trace
Blow Fly
The Last Precinct
Black Notice
Point of Origin
Unnatural Exposure
Cause of Death
From Potter's Field
The Body Farm
Cruel and Unusual
All That Remains
Body of Evidence
Postmortem

CAPTAIN CHASE SERIES

Spin
Quantum

ANDY BRAZIL SERIES

Isle of Dogs
Southern Cross
Hornet's Nest

WIN GARANO SERIES

The Front
At Risk

NONFICTION

Ripper: The Secret Life of Walter Sickert
Portrait of a Killer: Jack the Ripper—Case Closed

BIOGRAPHY

Ruth, a Portrait: The Story of Ruth Bell Graham

OTHER WORKS

Food to Die For: Secrets from Kay Scarpetta's Kitchen
Life's Little Fable
Scarpetta's Winter Table

PATRICIA CORNWELL

UNNATURAL DEATH

SPHERE

First published in the United States in 2023 by Grand Central,
a division of Hachette Book Group, Inc.
This paperback edition published in Great Britian in 2024 by Sphere

1 3 5 7 9 10 8 6 4 2

A CIP catalogue record for this book
is available from the British Library.

ISBN 978-1-4087-2867-3

Printed and bound in Great Britain by
Clays Ltd, Elcograf S.p.A.

Papers used by Sphere are from well-managed forests
and other responsible sources.

Sphere
An imprint of
Little, Brown Book Group
Carmelite House
50 Victoria Embankment
London EC4Y 0DZ

An Hachette UK Company
www.hachette.co.uk

www.littlebrown.co.uk

To Staci—
You make everything possible.

"WAS I, THEN, A MONSTER,
A BLOT UPON THE EARTH,
FROM WHICH ALL MEN FLED
AND WHOM ALL MEN DISOWNED?"

—MARY SHELLEY, *FRANKENSTEIN* (1818)

UNNATURAL DEATH

CHAPTER 1

I STEP OFF THE ELEVATOR on the morgue level, the air foul beneath a cloying patina of deodorizer. A stuttering fluorescent light is enough to cause vertigo, the white tile floor blood-dripped and dirty. Cinder block walls are scuffed and smudged, the red biohazard trash cans overflowing.

It's a few minutes past nine A.M., November first, and yesterday was the deadliest Halloween on record in Northern Virginia. People were busy killing themselves and others, the weather dangerously stormy. I left my Alexandria office late and was back before daylight. We're far from caught up, and I'd be inside the autopsy suite right now if I hadn't been summoned to a scene that promises to be a nightmare.

Two campers have been killed near an abandoned gold mine sixty miles southwest of here. The primitive wilderness of Buckingham Run isn't a place people hike or visit, and I've looked up information about it, getting a better idea what to expect. Virginia's Office of the Chief Medical Examiner hasn't had a case from there in its eighty-some-year history. That doesn't mean there haven't been fatalities no one knows about.

Buckingham Run isn't mapped or accessible by motorized ground transportation, and I wouldn't dare try it on foot. Thousands of acres are riddled with mineshafts and tunnels, among other life-threatening hazards that include contamination by poisons. There's no telling what might live in vast forestland that's been relatively untouched by humans since before the American Civil War.

It goes without saying there are large wild animals, perhaps some that people wouldn't imagine, and I'm not talking about only bears. Images flash nonstop from videos that Pete Marino has been sending since he arrived at the scene. *The nude female body impaled by hiking poles floating in a lake reflecting fall colors. The campsite scattered near the entrance of the abandoned gold mine,* DANGER *and* GO AWAY *barely legible on centuries-old warning signs.*

Marino filmed with his phone while shining a light down a mineshaft, illuminating a body caught in collapsed wooden scaffolding, the bloody face staring up blindly. I can hear Marino's booted feet moving through loose rocks and grit. I see his light painting over rusty iron rails…An ore cart shrouded in spiderwebs…Then he's exclaiming "*Holy shit*," the light stopping on a bare footprint that seems to have been left by a giant…

Leaving the building. I send a text to Marino's satellite phone.

A former homicide detective I've worked with most of my career, he's my forensic operations specialist. Several hours ago, he was airlifted to the scene with Secret Service investigators. Marino is getting an overview before I show up and is excited by *the find of a lifetime*, as he puts it. I'm not sharing his positive sentiments about evidence that's sensational and likely fake. Any way I look at it, we could have a real mess on our hands.

If you want me to bring anything else tell me now. Typing with my thumbs, I push through the ladies' room door.

I feel for the wall switch, turning on the light inside a closet-size space with a sink, a toilet and a plastic chair with uneven legs. By now I'm programmed not to pass up a chance to use the facilities. In the early days I might have been the only female except for maybe the victim. At death scenes I don't get to borrow the bathroom, and where I'm going doesn't have one.

While I'm washing up with institutional soap, my computer-assisted *smart* ring alerts me that Marino is answering my texts to him. Drying my hands with cheap paper towels, I unlock my phone.

Bring bolt cutters, he's written back, and I've already thought of it.

All set. Anything else? I answer.

A snakebite kit.

Don't have.

There's one in my truck.

They don't work, I reply, and we've been through this countless times since I've known him.

Better than nothing.

They're not.

What if someone gets bit? He adds the emoji of a coiled snake.

I answer with the emojis of a helicopter and a hospital before tucking my phone in a pocket. Reapplying lip balm, I brush on mineral sunblock, spritzing myself but good with insect repellent. I pick up my Kevlar briefcase, a birthday gift from my Secret Service agent niece, Lucy Farinelli. Looping the strap over my shoulder, I'm confronted by my reflection in the mirror.

It's as bad as I expected after days of little sleep, eating on the run and too much coffee. When Lucy notified me about the two victims inside Buckingham Run, she said to dress for extreme conditions. The tactical cargo pants and shirt, the boots I'm wearing wouldn't be flattering on most women. I'm no exception. I text Lucy that I'll meet her outside. First, I need to chat with Henry Addams, I tell her, and she'll understand why.

The funeral director is on his way here to pick up a body from an unrelated case, an alleged suicide from yesterday. I texted him that we need to talk when he gets here. He doesn't know what's happened inside Buckingham Run. Nothing has been on the news yet. But he'll realize something is going on or I wouldn't have communicated that I'm waiting for him.

As I follow the corridor, observation windows on either side offer remnants of recent horrors. Air-drying in the evidence room are the bloody clown costumes donned by two ex-cons who picked the wrong home to invade last night. The Bozos (as they're being called) got a trick rather than a treat when they were greeted with a shotgun.

Sneakers with laces tied in double bows were left in the road at the scene of a pedestrian hit-and-run. A shattered wristwatch shows that time stopped at nine P.M. for the victim of an armed robbery in a retirement home parking lot. The paper strip from a fortune cookie reads, *Your luck is about to change*, and it did when a woman fell off her deer stand.

Inside the CT room's scanner, images on monitors are of a

fractured skull. The decomp autopsy room's door is closed, the red light illuminated. Inside is the badly decomposed body of a possible drowning in the Potomac River, the victim last seen fishing almost a week ago.

I'm walking past a supply closet when Fabian Etienne emerges from it. He's holding a box of exam gloves as if he just happened to be in the area, and I know his ploys.

* * *

"Hey! Doctor Scarpetta!" Fabian's voice interrupts my grim preoccupations. "Wait up!" Flashing me one of his big smiles, he's been watching the cameras, waiting for me to head out of the building.

Fabian intends to have another go at me in hopes I might change my mind, and I understand his frustration. I also am keenly aware that he craves drama and is *easily bored and underutilized*, as he puts it. When he was growing up in Baton Rouge, Louisiana, he was earning money giving swamp tours by the time he could drive a car.

His father is a coroner, and Fabian grew up in a *deadly environment*, he often quips. He's not afraid of much, and there's no type of case he wouldn't handle given the opportunity. But he can't be involved with Buckingham Run for a lot of reasons. The Secret Service wouldn't allow Fabian at the scene, and I'm not to discuss the details with him or anyone unauthorized. More to the point, I need him here.

"I've helped Lucy haul everything out to the chopper, and she let me look inside the cockpit." His Louisiana accent is more New York than Southern. "OMG, that thing is *sick*. She says it can go more than two hundred miles an hour. And mini–machine guns can be swivel-mounted. Plus, it can see through fog. You sure I can't come with you, Doctor Scarpetta? I promise I'll be helpful."

His straight black hair would be halfway down his back were it not pinned up under a surgical cap, black with a skull pattern. Black scrubs show off his goth tattoos and a lean body that's whippet strong and fast. People find him sexy. *Dreamy* is what my secretary, Shannon, says, describing him as a combination of Cher and Harry Styles.

"I've never been in a chopper, certainly nothing like that thing in our parking lot. It's smoking hot and straight out of *The Avengers*," Fabian says excitedly. "If you bring me with you, I know you won't regret it."

"I'm not running the investigation or calling the shots." I repeat what I've told him several times now.

"You're in charge of the bodies," he says. "Seems like you could have anyone help that you decide."

"Access to the scene is extremely restricted for safety and other reasons. The priority should be that you help where most needed," I reply with patience I'm not feeling. "We're short-staffed and overwhelmed by cases, Fabian. That's the biggest reason why you're staying here. I can't have you and Marino at the scene with me..."

"So much for on-the-job training," Fabian says. When he gives me one of his wounded looks, I feel like a bad mentor, and that's his intention.

"I'm sorry you're disappointed." I find myself apologizing to him often these days, because he doesn't take no for an answer.

I don't like being put in the position of denying him what he wants and inevitably sparking a drama. My forensic psychologist husband says that subconsciously Fabian sets me up to be the idealized and overly involved mother who's the root of his troubles. We have a parent-child relationship with oedipal overtones, according to Benton. All I know is Fabian can be a holy terror when he doesn't get his way.

"It's important I have some idea of what to expect," he's saying. "Everything's so hush-hush, like something really bizarre is going on. I asked Lucy a few very basic questions and she wouldn't say anything except two people are dead inside Buckingham Run. And obviously, the Secret Service has taken over the investigation. That right there tells me plenty. Whatever's going on must be a really big deal."

"There's not much known yet and it's unwise to speculate." I won't get into this with him. "I need you to look after things here during Marino's and my absence. The semi-trailer needs deconning and setting up. I know the Secret Service is in charge and will be bringing in special equipment. We have to abide by their protocols. And everything must be ready for us when we return with the bodies."

"Why does *he* get to be there instead of me?" Fabian says, and I hope the day comes when he and Marino get along.

After Lucy located the victims, her first call after me wasn't going to be Fabian. She's known Marino most of her life. Lucy told him to meet her at the Secret Service hangar outside of Washington, D.C., in southern Maryland. From there Lucy flew him to the scene as the sun was coming up. He's my boots on the ground until I arrive, and in Fabian's mind that was like winning the lottery.

"I'm the one who needs the experience." He continues

making his argument in the corridor. “Marino grabs all the good cases, leaving me to take care of chicken shit that doesn’t teach me anything new.”

“Gathering the proper equipment and supplies for a complicated scene isn’t chicken shit,” I reply. “If I get there and don’t have what we need, it could be catastrophic.”

“As my mom keeps reminding me, this isn’t what I *signed up for*.” Fabian is fond of making quote marks in the air. “I’m supposed to be *an investigator, not a grip or a gofer*.” More air quotes. “Doctor Reddy pretty much gave me free rein, which is why I took the job to begin with. Not that I’m sorry he’s gone. But I don’t get to do half of what I used to.”

I didn’t hire Fabian. My predecessor, the former chief medical examiner, did, and that’s unfortunate. Elvin Reddy ran the Virginia M.E. system into the ground and would do the same to me given the opportunity. We worked together briefly when both of us were getting started and have an unpleasant history. At first, I couldn’t be sure about Fabian or anybody else working here.

Loyalty hasn’t been a given, and it’s been tricky knowing who to trust. But I don’t want to be unfair. Innocent until proven guilty is the way it’s supposed to work, and I can’t afford for Fabian to quit. We’re down to three death investigators, including Marino. The other one is part-time on the way to retired. As much as Fabian may get on my nerves now and then, I know he’s talented. I feel a responsibility toward him and a certain fondness.

“I have plenty that you can help me with as long as you abide by my instructions,” I reply. “There are always investigations that need following up on.”

"That's what I want to do." His mood is instantly brighter. "Finding out the important details that tell the story is my special sauce. That's why I was such a damn good P.A.," he adds modestly about his start as a physician's assistant. "I'd find out details from the patients that the docs would never imagine. Stuff that was a game changer in terms of a diagnosis. Like my dad's always saying, the big thing is *listening*..." Air quotes again.

"We'll have to finish talking about this later, Fabian..."

"You know, *hear* what someone's saying to you and pay attention. But you know how rare that is...?"

"I certainly do, and I've got to go."

I can see on a wall-mounted video monitor that Henry Addams has pulled up to our security gate. He'll be driving into the vehicle bay any minute.

"Addams Family is here to pick up Nan Romero, the suspected suicide from yesterday morning." I indicate what's on the monitor.

"I'll take care of it." Fabian is in much better spirits. "By the way, that's a weird one. I don't know what Doctor Schlaefer's said to you."

"We've not had a spare moment to talk," I answer.

"The painter's tape bothers me," Fabian volunteers as he walks with me. "I can't imagine anyone wrapping their lower face like that. Especially a woman."

"I expect Investigator Fruge to be calling with further information," I reply. "I'm sure she knows we'll be pending the cause and manner of death until we get the toxicology results."

Fabian heads back toward the elevator as I continue along the corridor. It begins and ends like a morbid conundrum, the receiving area the first and last stop in my sad medical clinic. No appointments are required, our services free to the public. Death doesn't care who you are, everybody treated equally. With rare exception the only thing our patients have in common is they never thought they'd be here.

When bodies arrive, they're rolled in through a pedestrian door and weighed on the floor scale. They're measured with an old-style measuring rod and assigned case numbers before waiting their turn inside the refrigerator. Names are handwritten in what I call the Book of the Dead, the large black logbook chained to the chipped Formica shelf outside the security office window.

On the other side of the bulletproof glass Wyatt Earle's khaki uniform jacket is draped over the back of his chair. The remains of takeout food are on his desk, and propped in a corner is the aluminum baseball bat he borrows from the anatomical division where bodies donated to science are stored and eventually cremated.

We have no choice but to pulverize large pieces of bones; otherwise they won't fit inside the cremains boxes returned to loved ones. Wyatt carries the bat while making his rounds after hours. Unlike me, he's more afraid of the dead than the living.

CHAPTER 2

WYATT IS INSIDE THE vehicle bay, the massive garage door retracting loudly. The silver Cadillac Landau hearse glides in, and he walks toward it as I watch on the security monitor.

The driver's window lowers, and Henry Addams is behind the wheel, the two of them chatting cordially like always. The closed-circuit TV (CCTV) microphones pick up exchanges about business and the weather. The two of them ask about each other's families, and it's the first I've heard that Henry's wife requires full-time nursing care. She doesn't live at home anymore.

The last time I saw Henry was about a month ago, and he didn't mention it. But I thought he seemed tired and preoccupied. I've known for a while that Megan isn't well but had no idea how bad it had gotten. He drives inside as Wyatt puts on his uniform baseball cap and sunglasses. He strides through the huge square opening and into the bright morning.

A curious crowd has gathered outside to gawk at the ominous black helicopter my niece, Lucy, flies for the U.S. Secret Service.

Code-named the Doomsday Bird, it's surrounded by traffic cones and sitting quietly in a distant corner of the parking lot as she loads the back cabin. I'm making sure we have special personal protective equipment (PPE) necessary when there's a risk of exposure to toxic chemicals, and unknown animals and organisms.

"Golly Moses...!" A metal stretcher bumps and clangs as Henry struggles to slide it out of the back of his hearse. He mutters euphemisms in his lilting Virginia accent and seems unusually aggravated. "Oh, for crummy sake...!"

An app on my phone accesses my office's CCTV security system, and I turn off the cameras inside the bay. A section of the video monitor blacks out, Henry vanishing from view. Next, I send Wyatt a note making sure he's aware that it's me doing the tampering. He's familiar with my routine when I need a cone of silence.

Copy that, Chief, he texts me back. *About 30 people out here. I'm keeping my eye on things.*

Nobody gets any closer.

He answers with a thumbs-up emoji. *Already getting complaints as expected,* he informs me. *The devil herself.*

It's assumed that Maggie Cutbush is going to stir up trouble given the chance. When I replaced Elvin Reddy as chief medical examiner, I inherited his secretary, suffering with her my first two years on the job. Not so long ago, both of them were fired and repurposed as so often happens in government. Maggie no longer works for me but remains an unwanted presence like a phantom pain or a haunting.

What I'm about to confront inside Buckingham Run promises to cause the very sort of stink she wants. In fact, it's already happening. That's why she's started her complaints about the helicopter before I've so much as left the building. She knows I'll hear about it. She'd like nothing better than to get under my skin, to interfere with my concentration.

Do not engage. I'll handle later, I let Wyatt know.

I walk out the door, and our vehicle bay is the size of a small hangar. On wooden pallets are cleansers, bleach, biocides, cases of PPE. There are gallon jugs of formaldehyde and embalming fluid marked with skull-and-crossbones warning labels. Walls and floors are sealed with epoxy resin, and easy to hose down. But that's not happened in recent memory, as busy as we are.

The concrete ramp is marred by blood drips and wheel tracks dried reddish black. Flies crawl and alight on trash cans. Sparrows dart about, and that's not uncommon when the bay door is left open, as it is right now. I can see more people wandering into the parking lot, Shannon Park among them. She's wearing an emerald-green dress that looks 1970s.

Her bucket hat is just as old, and she'll be holding on to it soon enough when Lucy and I take off. A former court reporter, my recently hired secretary is a world-class snoop skilled at getting people to talk. Knowing her, she's gathering intelligence, possibly taking notes. I wouldn't put it past her to record conversations of those around her. She's done it before.

"God bless America…!" Henry has pinched his thumb on the stretcher, not noticing me yet.

"Good morning, Henry!" I call out as I reach the bottom of the ramp.

"Oh!" He looks up, startled. "Hello, Kay! Please excuse my manners." He's unusually flustered. "I'm so busy making a mess, I didn't notice you come out of the building."

"Are you hurt?" I ask as I reach him.

"A blood blister. I'll live."

"If not, you're in the right place."

"With all due respect, I don't want you as my doctor." He smiles, but his eyes are distracted and dull.

Tall and distinguished, with pewter-gray hair and a thin mustache, Henry is dapper in a black suit and Scottish tartan vest. In his lapel is a rosebud with a sprig of baby's breath. He's thin and seems bone weary, his demeanor shadowed by sadness.

"What have you been up to besides not eating enough?" It's my way of asking about his personal life. "It looks like I might have to make a house call with some of my lasagna. I believe you're also partial to my cannelloni and panzanella salad."

Since moving back to Virginia three years ago, I've dropped off food to him before when his wife wasn't doing well. But I had no idea her dementia had progressed this rapidly.

"Well, if you must know," he says with a drawn-out sigh, "I've had to move Megan to a place in Fairfax." He goes on to tell me the name of the memory care center and how long she's been there. "It had been coming on for the last few years, as you know, Kay. But it's taken a dramatic turn in recent months compounded by her having a stroke."

"I'm very sorry."

"She can't walk or eat on her own and doesn't know me anymore."

"Not much is harder."

"I go to visit every day. She thinks I work there." His eyes are touched by tears for an instant.

"Biology can be cruel."

"A couple of weeks ago Megan started wearing another patient's wedding ring. She thinks she's married to him. And has been all her life." He clears his throat.

"Are you taking care of yourself, Henry?"

"You're right, I could do better about eating." He tugs the stretcher some more with uncharacteristic impatience.

"Here. Let me help you."

I lean inside the open tailgate, and he's managed to wedge a side-rail against the hearse's faux suede headliner. He's a shade away from ripping it.

"This is so gosh darn frustrating, excuse my salty language." He moves out of the way, wiping his eyes. "But nothing's more aggravating than getting somewhere and finding your equipment is undependable. That's one thing I've never tolerated. As swamped as we've been, we're down to the bottom of the barrel, using things that should be put out to pasture."

"I know what you mean since almost everything we have is like that," I tell him. "Including a lot of hand-me-downs from you, for which I'm always grateful."

* * *

My bread and butter are the rejects from hospitals, funeral homes, rescue squads, and I'm not above begging. I'll take packets of sutures, scalpels, obsolete x-ray and CT scanners, malfunctioning stretchers, power washers and shop vacuums, also computers and vehicles. Whatever someone wants to give us, we're happy to accept.

"One of the side-rails is defective and won't unlock." I diagnose the problem as Henry gives me the once-over.

"You look like you're going on a safari and reek of DEET," he says as I help him lift out the stretcher. We set it down, straightening the legs to the height he wants. "I won't ask what's going on." It's his way of doing exactly that. "But you didn't wait for me to get here because you've got nothing better to do."

"Are you familiar with Buckingham Run?" I ask him.

"I've only driven past," Henry answers. "A lot of mining went on there a long time ago as best I know, but I don't believe it's a place people visit. As I recall there are no-trespassing signs posted, that sort of thing. It's quite foreboding when you drive past."

"The cameras in here are off at the moment," I tell him, and we've done this before. I turn off the CCTV inside the vehicle bay only, ensuring no one is monitoring us. "We have a situation, Henry."

"I had a feeling when you said you needed to see me," he says. "What can I do to be of assistance, Kay?"

"I'm directing two bodies your way if you're willing. I'm afraid we've got something ugly brewing that's just getting going. I'm warning you in advance that I don't know how we'll control fallout that could be considerable. The situation is of serious concern to the federal government. And there are other factors that will cause a public panic if we don't handle these deaths with the utmost care and discretion."

"Judging by what's going on in your parking lot, I figured as much." Henry stares out the open bay door at the helicopter and those gawking at it.

More people are trickling outside, gathering by the tall metal privacy fence. Topped by spikes, it serves as an ugly moat around my four-story building. Until a month ago, I shared it peacefully with the consolidated forensic labs, the anatomical division and Safe Kids, which tracks injuries in children. Then the governor created the Department of Emergency Prevention (DEP) for no good reason, literally.

Redundant and ridiculous, it's a boondoggle if there ever was one. Elvin Reddy has been recycled as DEP's first director. He's now as powerful as ever, installed in a corner suite near the governor's office in Richmond. His deputy chief in charge of operations, Maggie Cutbush, also has reappeared in my life with a vengeance. I didn't see any of it coming when DEP took over most of my building's top floor.

Many of its employees are gathered outside on the tarmac. I can imagine the negative and derisive comments made as they wait for Lucy and me to take off in the helicopter. Maggie and Elvin have poisoned the well, nobody working for them my fan or even civil.

"What do I need to know?" Henry asks me.

"Please be mindful there are far more questions than answers at this point. Lucy's been flying investigators into Buckingham Run where the two victims were camping near the entrance of an abandoned gold mine. Apparently they'd set up a tent and had been living there for several months, basically since late summer."

"That seems awfully strange," Henry says. "Why the heck would anyone camp in such a godforsaken place?"

"There's much that's not making sense yet," I reply. "But the victims were attacked at some point after three o'clock this morning while it was dark and rainy. That much seems indisputable. The tent is flattened, belongings flung everywhere, the scene extremely violent and chaotic based on images Marino and others have been sending. Let me add that we haven't confirmed the identities."

"Who do we think they are?" Henry asks.

"They're believed to be outdoor enthusiasts Huck and Brittany Manson. Lucy says they were under investigation by federal law enforcement for massive cybercrimes involving the Russians, possibly the Chinese. Apparently, the Mansons had retreated deep into the woods where it was harder to monitor everything they were up to."

"What about spying?" Henry asks. "I'm wondering if they were doing that on top of everything else."

"I don't know all the details. Lucy will fill me in further when she's taking me to the scene," I reply. "But she said the Mansons were tied in with very bad people who shouldn't be underestimated. I want to make sure I'm clear about that, Henry. If you don't want any association with this, I'd understand."

It's only fair I warn him of the liabilities, and this won't be the first time we've handled sensitive situations together. Last summer it was the murder of someone who worked for the CIA. Before that it was an FBI-protected witness whose cover was blown after relocating to nearby Arlington.

"What are you thinking?" Henry asks. "Do you have a clue what might have happened to them?"

His eyes are uneasy as we talk by his hearse. Both of us keep glancing out the wide bay door opening, making sure nobody walks in and overhears a word.

"A bear or more than one?" he's saying. "If they're big and riled enough they can do a lot of damage. So can a pack of wolves or even a lone one, especially if it's rabid. I've seen these kinds of fatalities up close and personal, as have you. No open casket in the cases I've had."

"Based on the information I'm getting, I don't believe we're dealing with bears, wolves, bobcats, feral hogs," I reply. "There appears to have been no interest in the food stored at the campsite, none of the usual telltale signs, including the expected tracks or scat. The victims had been living at this same location for months. I don't deal with a lot of wild animal attacks, but one wonders why now?"

"It wouldn't make much sense if food didn't seem to be a motivation," Henry says. "Almost always that's what draws a wild animal close to where people are camping. And bears, wolves and such don't have babies this time of year. So I doubt it was something protecting its cubs or pups. Do we think the victims were asleep inside their tent when attacked?"

"Presumably the Mansons were alerted when their trail cameras' motion sensors were triggered by the intruder," I reply. "Whoever or whatever it was didn't show up on the thermal imaging trail cameras the victims had set up. Lucy says you could hear something trudging along but not see what it was."

"Well, that's bizarre." Henry looks slightly unnerved.

"It also appears to have been bulletproof when fired upon at close range with large-caliber weapons."

"Even more bizarre and what the hello?"

"Deformed slugs on the ground indicate ten-millimeter *bear load* lead bullets hit something and bounced off."

"My Lord, it's all sounding stranger and stranger," Henry says. "What condition are the bodies in? Pretty grim, I have a feeling."

"They've been in the elements for hours, and I don't expect

them to be in good shape. We also don't know what they've been exposed to that might be dangerous to the rest of us, including poisons and microscopic organisms I don't usually encounter."

I explain that I'm treating the deaths like a potential biological and chemical hazard. It's important the bodies are isolated as much as possible. We can't be certain what threats might lurk inside Buckingham Run. I'm mindful that the water and soil likely are contaminated by arsenic, cyanide, mercury, lead and other heavy metals associated with abandoned mining operations.

Of more concern are pathogens in the unlikely event the victims have been exposed to wild animals. They could have been in contact with all sorts of things that can find their way into the human population. Severe acute respiratory syndrome (SARS) is believed to have been spread by bats. Monkeypox is transmitted by rodents. Bears, wolves, bobcats can carry rabies. Armadillos can cause leprosy.

CHAPTER 3

THE SECRET SERVICE IS in charge of the investigation and will be working closely with you as they have in the past," I tell Henry as we talk privately next to his hearse. "If you're willing to help."

"As long as we ensure the safety of our staff and all involved, that's always first and foremost. Especially in this particular situation you're describing," he says. "We don't need our businesses, our client databases hacked into by the Russians, the Chinese or who knows what? And they're capable of doing far worse things than that. You and I both know that anything can happen. Bodies have been stolen and held for ransom. Other unfortunate things have been done to them." Henry places a folded blanket on the stretcher's mattress pad. "Not to mention assassinations."

"The state police will assist in keeping everything secure here and at your place," I assure him.

I explain that the bodies will never be inside my building, and special measures will be implemented in the labs for evidence tested. The examinations will be conducted inside the Remote Mobile Operating Theater Environment, the REMOTE, as we refer to the mobile autopsy facility's fifty-foot semi-trailer. I helped design the government prototype with other experts, including Henry, Lucy and Benton.

We serve together on the National Emergency Contingency Coalition. Better known as the Doomsday Commission, it's a collection of professionals appointed by the White House to help ensure the safety of the planet. We've been involved with the REMOTE's research and development for several years; the Biosafety Level 4 trailer moved into my parking lot in early summer.

It gives me the ability to handle human remains in extreme circumstances such as suspected radiation deaths from a nuclear attack or mass fatalities by an unknown plague. To date, the REMOTE hasn't been needed often. Most recently was a month ago when eleven people were found dead at a tourist motel, overdoses from fentanyl, as it turned out. Before that it was a regional jet crash with twenty-two fatalities, the bodies burned and contaminated by fuel.

"You have similar bio-level capabilities at your mortuary. Otherwise, I wouldn't ask you to handle something potentially risky," I explain to Henry, and technically I'm not supposed to make referrals, doesn't matter the circumstances.

It's considered a conflict of interest for the chief medical examiner to influence the handling of funeral arrangements. But I can't function without a network of experts that I trust. In business since the mid-seventeen hundreds in Old Town Alexandria, Addams Family Chapel & Mortuary is the funeral service of choice for dignitaries, the rich, the famous and notorious.

Henry is accustomed to dealing with the Secret Service, the FBI, CIA, the Pentagon and other enforcement entities. He's buried gangsters, undercover agents, celebrities, four-star generals and former presidents. A sworn peace officer who carries a gun, he holds a high-level government security clearance.

"You're probably familiar with the Mansons' sporting goods store," I say to him as we continue talking by his hearse, no one near us. "Wild World is just down the street from you. Not far from my house, for that matter."

"Oh boy, that's who it is? I didn't know the owners, but I know their store quite well," he says. "I also buy a lot of their things online. You can't beat the prices."

"For good reason, it seems," I reply. "It's likely the retail business is a front for money laundering and who knows what else. I doubt any of us will be shopping at Wild World in the future. Including me, and that's a shame."

The retailer's inventory is on the scale of a Target combined with a sporting goods store. Wild World sells outdoor and athletic gear, automotive supplies, kitchenware, tactical clothing, firearms and all that goes with them. Best of all are cutlery and sharpeners well suited for autopsies. There's an enormous selection of tools, and industrial rolls of butcher paper, tape, string and all sorts of things for a fraction of what I'd pay a forensic or surgical supplier.

"I'm assuming the victims' criminal activities may be connected to their deaths," Henry says. "Is that what the police are thinking?"

"I know it's what Lucy believes. Based on what I'm learning, that's making the most sense," I reply. "Although there are elements to the case that are unexpected and hard to explain, as I've mentioned. A good example is someone trekking deep into a pitch-dark forest in the rainy early morning hours."

"Whoever it was had to know the way and maybe was equipped with night-vision goggles," Henry says. "Unless we're not talking about a human. As we know, many animals can see perfectly fine at night. I remember when my father used to take me camping as a kid. *If you hear a noise in the dark and something's eyes reflect red, it's not a human.* Then he'd ask me what I was going to do about it. My answer was to pick up my shotgun and wait. He taught me not to shoot without knowing what I was pointing at."

"A good rule of thumb," I reply. "I'd like for you to work with me as we have before, Henry. The Secret Service will make sure that happens if you're amenable."

"It goes without saying that I'll help. Do we have any idea how they died? Homicides, obviously."

"If we're talking about humans killing other humans, then yes," I reply. "If an animal did it that's a different story. As I've said, that's not what I'm thinking, but for now it needs to be part of the differential."

In the unlikely event we're dealing with a bear or some other powerful creature, it will be game wardens tracking it down, making sure it does no further harm. In such a case I would rule the manner of death accidental. There would be no police investigation. Lucy and her colleagues would have no further legal interest or jurisdiction beyond the victims' criminal involvements.

"For now, I'm calling the deaths unnatural," I'm explaining to Henry. "But I don't think a wild animal is to blame. I've never heard of one removing every stitch of its victims' clothing, for example. Or spearing them with hiking poles, throwing one body in the lake, the other down into a mineshaft."

"Good Lord. This is sounding only more disturbing, Kay."

"And then there's the not-so-trivial problem of a humanlike footprint, a shoeless one that's abnormally large, if you get my drift," I add. "Marino found it inside the abandoned mine."

"Oh my!" Henry is visibly startled. "Fake, I'm assuming?"

"That's probably the most likely scenario, I'm told. But to answer your question, I don't know."

"Have you seen a photo? Does it look real?"

"Real enough," I admit. "But that doesn't mean much considering the technologies available these days."

I remind him that the sky's the limit when it comes to the mischief and mayhem that can be created with 3-D printing. It's increasingly sophisticated, easy to use and affordable. One can give form to all sorts of nasty thoughts without special training or leaving the house.

* * *

"It's routine for 3-D-printed weapons to end up in the firearms lab," I tell Henry. "Knives, guns and their pieces and parts, you name it. The other week it was a 3-D-printed nine-millimeter pistol carried by a drone. You may have heard the story on the news. An angry neighbor, and that was the attempted solution."

"The world's going to hell in a handbasket," he says.

"A face mask 3-D printed from a scan of another person's photograph can trick facial recognition software." I give him another scenario. "Prosthetic devices might include a glove that has someone else's fingerprints, enabling the wearer to open biometric locks."

"And that's what you think may be the explanation for the footprint," Henry says. "Someone created a fake foot."

"Or just the bottom of one that could be pressed in the dirt," I suggest. "I have no idea except Marino finding the footprint will make working this case exponentially harder."

"I'm not well versed in all things Bigfoot, Sasquatch, Yeti, whatever name it goes by," Henry says. "But I do know that it's a very popular topic around here. A sheriff's deputy I go fishing with swears he encountered this huge shaggy thing crossing the road late one night. It was walking upright like a person, about eight feet tall, its shoulders as wide as his car. I'm not aware of a Bigfoot hurting people. Assuming it's real."

"I have no idea if it is or not. But there are no reliable accounts of such a thing attacking anyone. That much I do know," I reply. "I started looking into it the minute Marino told me about the footprint he discovered between ore cart rails that go back hundreds of years. Secret Service agents arrived at the scene hours before he got there, and it would seem they hadn't noticed it."

"I don't think it's a good thing for Marino that he's the one who found it after the police didn't see it," Henry says. "How can that be explained without making him look like he's guilty of perpetrating a prank?"

"He definitely wouldn't do anything like that, and you know it, Henry."

"It's not about what I know. It's about what the media and others will do with the information."

"Apparently the footprint was left deeper inside the mine

than the investigators had ventured. The shallow impression in dirt wasn't all that easy to see because of the conditions."

"If it wasn't obvious, that might argue against it being planted," Henry considers. "I would think that if you were going to do that, you'd leave it where it was sure to be noticed."

"I don't know what to think, honestly," I reply, and through the vehicle bay's opening I notice Lucy headed this way.

I tell Henry that I'm turning the security cameras back on inside the bay. As if on cue, Fabian opens the door at the top of the ramp. He's cheerfully snapping his fingers while humming the theme song of *The Addams Family* TV sitcom from the 1960s.

"Come on up!" Snap-snap. "She's ready and waiting!" Snap-snap…He holds the door open as Henry doesn't react. He's been hearing the jokes all his life. "One of the best shows ever. Who's your favorite character? I'm partial to Uncle Fester…"

I walk out into the morning's clean-scrubbed cool air. Fall foliage is fiery against skies the polished blue of Murano glass, the colors peaking later than usual this year after a dry, hot summer. Lucy is waiting on the tarmac, keeping her distance from the spectators gathered by the fence, many of them filming with their phones.

Her dropping in from the sky to pick me up at work is a first since we moved back to Virginia three years ago. I'm fairly certain no one has done it before, not even for the governor. There's no helipad or suitable place to land and plenty of people to offend. But that didn't stop her, and we've got quite the audience.

"Nothing like being subtle," I remark as we begin walking through rows of cars.

"You know me," she says. "Subtle is my middle name." Her face is keenly pretty, her short auburn hair highlighted rose gold in the sun.

I sense her preoccupations like a magnetic pull, and what I'm intuiting doesn't bode well. I know when my niece is bothered by something that holds her complete attention.

She looks menacing in a black flight suit and boots, her Desert Eagle .44 Magnum in a drop-leg holster. My gun is locked up in a drawer at home. I don't bring it to work routinely.

But a 9-millimeter pistol wouldn't be my weapon of choice for where we're going. Inside my briefcase is a large canister of bear repellent pepper spray. I have an air horn that could wake the dead were it possible.

"So far so good. No phone calls from the media," I inform Lucy. "And I've seen nothing on the internet."

"Enjoy it while it lasts. Which won't be much longer." She says this as if she knows it without a doubt.

Up close the helicopter looks stealthier and more dangerous with its wide tactical platform skids and multiple antennas. Radomes on the undercarriage conceal lasers and cameras able to "see" in zero visibility. Otherwise, Lucy wouldn't have been able to locate the campsite in the stormy dark.

She wouldn't have known to look had the Mansons not been under surveillance. Their nonworking farm abuts Buckingham Run, and they'd cleared a path to their secret campsite next to the old gold mine on a lakeshore. They'd set up the thermal imaging trail cameras that the Secret Service hacked into early on. This is what Lucy has told me.

She walks around the helicopter, giving it a final once-over while unlocking the doors. Moving traffic cones, I stack them near the fence. I'm making sure they're far enough out of the way that rotor wash won't send them skittering.

"I've sent a few text messages to Benton," I let Lucy know. "I've not heard from him. I'm wondering if you have."

"He knows what's going on and is inside a SCIF."

Benton is my husband and the Secret Service's top threat advisor. He's been inside a Sensitive Compartmented Information Facility for hours. The case is of interest at the highest levels, Lucy says.

"And his opinion so far?" I place my briefcase inside the helicopter's back cabin.

"The victims were targeted, and the degree of violence is meant to send a message." She checks the tail rotor, turning it slowly.

"He's aware of the bizarre footprint Marino found?"

"Benton's initial reaction is that we're being jerked around. Most of all, Marino is. Because if he's disrupted, all of us are. And I wouldn't say this to him but he's the weakest link," Lucy says. "He's a Bigfoot fan. An active and vocal one."

"I'm aware."

"Since we moved back to Virginia, he's been going to festivals and other related events," she says as we step up on the platform skids. "And he's been known to go out Bigfoot hunting with his camera, playing alleged vocalizations on a field recorder, hoping he might get a sighting or the thing to answer him."

"It's unfortunate under the circumstances."

"If people find out, they'll make something of it," Lucy says. "Get ready. Because Marino doesn't take it well when anyone makes fun of him or treats him like he's stupid."

"I don't know anybody who appreciates that." I open the

copilot's cockpit door, and the interior smells new, the air heated up inside.

I've flown with Lucy many times but never in the Doomsday Bird, and I'm glad I'm not wearing a skirt for a lot of reasons. I swing my leg over the copilot's cyclic in a most unladylike fashion.

"I guess the day I'm not spry enough to do this anymore is when I retire on a nice beach somewhere," I comment.

"That will be when hell freezes over." Lucy settles into the right seat.

"With climate change it might."

CHAPTER 4

PUTTING ON FOUR-POINT harnesses, Lucy and I leave our doors open for now. The sun is hot through plexiglass, the breeze almost chilly, and it's my favorite weather. I was looking forward to a bike ride with Benton at the end of the day. While getting dressed early this morning, we fantasized about coming home at a decent hour for once.

We talked about getting in a ten-mile round trip along the Potomac River. Maybe afterward we'd have drinks and cook out on the grill, inviting Lucy, Marino, my sister, Dorothy. But I already know none of that's going to happen. Benton and I have lived a lifetime of interrupted plans and broken promises. We're used to it, as much as that's possible.

"...Seat belts on, flight controls A-okay..." Lucy is going through the Doomsday Bird's extensive preflight checklist as Fabian emerges from the bay. He casts longing glances in this direction, headed to the refrigerated semi-trailer, big and shiny white in the sun.

Our Biosafety Level 4 REMOTE autopsy facility is parked

out of the way against the back fence. He'll check that the generator's working fine and full of propane. He'll wash down and disinfect the interior before anything else happens. He'll make sure that all necessary supplies are there.

"...Throttles are closed. The altimeter is set..."

I send a text to Wyatt. He's watching the crowd, and I let him know we're about to start the engines. His response is to hold out his hand palm-first like a traffic cop, shouting something I can't hear. He's making sure everyone stands back even though no one seems to have the slightest intention of getting closer.

"...Battery going on..."

Lucy continues the start-up, silencing the low rotor horn inside a glass cockpit that reminds me of a spaceship. Blinking on around us are dazzling displays of weather and terrain in moving shapes and vivid shades. The artificial sight picture painted on video screens mirrors the real one out the windshield.

"...Volts are good...We've got the expected caution lights..." Testing the foot pedals, she pushes them one at a time, the actuators making loud metallic clicks.

"...Throttles are good..." She rolls them open and shut. "...We got plenty of fuel, one thousand pounds..."

In the bright sun I can make out the fine lines that show her age, and the jagged pink scar peeking out of her collar. An eighth of an inch closer, and the shrapnel would have sliced through her carotid. I'm reminded that my niece isn't a child anymore. She's not immortal.

"...We're clear to the right," she says.

"Clear to the left." I look out my side window.

"Throttle for engine one in idle. Hitting the start switch."

The first engine fires with a rush and a roar, the rotor blades beginning to turn... Thud... Thud... Thud... faster and faster.

"Throttle in idle for engine two...," she says to another roar, the powerful torque thrumming in my every cell.

Lucy goes through elaborate tests and procedures, menu pages brightly suspended in the ether of the heads-up display (HUD). Checking computers, the hydraulics and other systems, she works switches on and off while moving the controls. She turns on the generator, the avionics. Headsets cover our ears, the mic booms touching our lips, and we're talking over the intercom now. Shutting our doors, we make sure they're latched.

"You all set? Speak now or forever hold your *pieces*, as the king's horsemen said to Humpty Dumpty." Lucy's quirky dark humor can border on corny. "Seriously, Aunt Kay." She calls me that only when it's just the two of us. "I'll be doing some wicked maneuvering in really tight places that even you aren't used to."

"It can't get much worse than where we are." I look around at an obstacle course of fencing, tall light standards and flagpoles, and vehicles parked all over.

"Trust me, it can get worse, as you're about to find out." She twists the throttles open to the Fly position, the rotor blades beating faster. "If it wasn't for this thing's capabilities you can forget it."

"What's our ETA?" I unlock my phone. "And I'll let Marino know."

"About twenty minutes from when I pull pitch. Could be more depending on the interference I get." Lucy turns on the blower and we adjust our vents. "You know how bad traffic is around here anyway. But it's backed up more than usual because of all the flight cancellations before the rain and fog cleared out. And there may be other nuisances we have to deal with."

While she listens to the latest automated weather update, I text Marino that we're about to take off. I remind him to make sure the landing zone inside Buckingham Run is clear. *Hopefully nothing is there that wasn't earlier*, Lucy has me pass along to him.

Just checked and it was 10-4. Will check again, he writes back.

"...Anti-collision light should be on already, and it is. Position lights, landing light on." Lucy flips those switches. "Want to make sure everyone knows we're here."

"I think everyone knows," I reply. "Outer space probably does."

"Truer than you might imagine. Clear to our right." She's constantly scanning.

"Clear to the left." I'm looking out my side window again, the crowd of spectators growing. They're waiting for the warship-looking bird to take off with me in it, and no doubt people are speculating like mad over what must be happening.

"We got the current ATIS," Lucy says. "Weather couldn't be better. But we'll have some mechanical turbulence and loud automated warnings because of all the buildings."

Her trigger finger squeezes the radio switch, and she checks back with the Washington National tower.

"Niner-Zulu departing from present position," she says over the air.

"Niner-Zulu. Ident."

"Identing." She presses a button on the transponder, identifying us on radar.

"State destination."

"Buckingham Run, same as before."

I feel the helicopter getting light on its skids as Lucy eases up on the collective, pulling in power. Then we're rising in a blizzard of colorful leaves swirling crazily, alert tones blaring. The automated voice complains nonstop, trees rocking violently in our rotor wash as we climb above the state government northern district office complex.

"...OBSTRUCTION...! OBSTRUCTION...!"

My building is relegated to five acres that back up to wetlands and a power station. We're an island to ourselves like Alcatraz, nobody eager to be our neighbor. Despite my best intentions our business is antisocial, especially when the crematorium oven is running, and that was on the schedule for this morning. Bodies donated to our anatomical division are returned after medical schools are finished with them.

I told Fabian to hold off on the cremations. We don't need smoke billowing up from our rooftop, my headquarters unwelcoming enough. There's little in the budget for landscaping or anything else that might make the place less off-putting. We have no trash cans or public restrooms, not even a drinking fountain.

"...OBSTRUCTION...!"

Elvin Reddy removed the meditation garden and eternal flame before I took this job. All that's left to show even a modicum of hospitality are two concrete benches painted dark green and often covered with bird deposits. We're down to a skeleton crew of three security guards, only Wyatt trustworthy.

"...OBSTRUCTION...!"

The lobby isn't open to the public, the front doors secured with a heavy chain and padlock. I have no receptionist to answer questions and we no longer allow viewings of loved ones. Cremains and personal effects aren't picked up in person. We send them UPS, and that's a difficult package to find on your doorstep.

"...OBSTRUCTION...!"

I don't have the budget to fix what's been done or I would have by now. Were it up to me I'd ensure that people are as comfortable and respected as possible in their darkest hour. But that's not the world we live in anymore.

* * *

Lucy holds us in a hover five hundred feet above my tan brick building, the crowd by the fence staring up at us. I notice that Henry Addams has driven his hearse out of the bay and is chatting through his open window with my secretary, Shannon. I can't tell much from here, but it seems he's handing her something, and I didn't realize they were acquainted.

"...OBSTRUCTION...!"

"If you want to get an aerial photo of *La Rue Morgue*, now's a good time," Lucy says as the warnings continue blaring.

"May as well while I'm here." I take several photographs.

"You can use them in this year's Christmas letter."

"We look even worse from the air," I decide.

It's the first time I've seen our roof from up here, flat and dingy gray with rusting mechanicals, tilting antennas, stained satellite dishes, the tall concrete smokestack an eyesore. Windows are small or nonexistent, depending on the work that goes on inside. The vehicle bay looks like a sally port, and from this perspective we might be a factory or a city jail.

"...OBSTRUCTION...! OBSTRUCTION...!"

"All right already," Lucy complains as the warnings continue jarringly.

She reaches overhead to pull out a circuit breaker, abruptly silencing a voice that's shrilly female.

"It's like crying wolf," I say to her. "You stop hearing it after a while."

"Artificial intelligence software that talks too much, nothing's perfect, a work in progress."

"Seems less than ideal to pull the plug on your AI assistant," I remark.

"Her software needs tweaking or it's like anything else that will drive you nuts. There's not much choice but to shut her up like I just did," Lucy says. "Or she'll keep going until we get away from all the congestion like I'm about to do. Hold on, because I'm busting a move."

She makes a tight turn, the G-forces pushing me hard. Unfortunately, the course will take us directly over Shady Acres Funeral Home and their cemetery. Set back from West Braddock Road, the sprawling complex is surrounded by a serpentine stone wall, the pillared entrance ostentatious, their billboard across from it advertising HAUNTED TOURS.

"Best you don't go anywhere near them." I remind her that the people who work there don't need much of an excuse to complain.

I'm not high on their list because I don't direct business to them. They're accustomed to being treated with favoritism. For more than twenty years Elvin Reddy, Maggie Cutbush and Shady Acres had a very close and profitable arrangement. They likely still do in some form or fashion.

"Don't worry. I'll be polite." Lucy pulls in power, gaining altitude.

We fly over what looks like a combination family religious retreat and amusement park. Attractions include peaceful sitting areas, an amphitheater, picnic grounds and an artificial lake with swan boats. Workers rake leaves, tending to the landscaping, the rolling grassy grounds groomed like a golf course.

Sprinklers are going, and sunlight refracted by spraying water creates small rainbows as if by design while a backhoe digs a grave. Everybody stops what they're doing as we thunder overhead like a mechanical dragon. The white-painted brick buildings have blue tile roofs and steeples topped by weather vanes that look familiar for a reason.

The architectural design is a deliberate appeal to nostalgia and old-fashioned values. The funeral service says exactly that in prolific advertising. Shady Acres compares its variety of goods and services to the different flavors of ice cream the Howard Johnson's restaurant chain was famous for in the good ol' days.

"Clam strips and a chocolate shake to go." Lucy places her mock order. "Do you dare me to broadcast it over the public address system?"

"Please don't," I reply.

"Because this thing has one."

"Lucy, if we so much as cause the slightest disturbance? There will be hell to pay."

"Twenty-eight tacky ways to be ripped off. Pick your favorite flavor of being taken advantage of and robbed." She overflies the outdoor chapel where folding chairs are being set up. "How 'bout a double scoop of greed in a sugar cone of fake sympathy with plastic-flower sprinkles on top?"

Making another tight turn that pushes me against my door, she heads toward I-395, solid with cars in both directions. She pushes the obstruction alert system's circuit breaker back in.

"The big problem's going to be when we come back carrying our curious cargo," she says. "And by the look of things, Dana Diletti will be there capturing every bit of it. I have a feeling that she's gotten tipped off about what's happened."

I scan around us as if I might see the local celebrity TV journalist and her crew somewhere on the ground or in the air. We pass over pastures dotted with bales of hay, and fields of rapeseed as yellow as road-marking paint. Cannons outside a Civil War museum look like a child's playset, and buzzards sail past like tattered black kites.

"Her chopper's on the ramp, getting ready for action." The "smart" lenses of Lucy's dark-tinted glasses are computer assisted, constantly updating information I can't see. "I think we know what she's up to. The word is getting out."

"Let's just hope she's not been tipped off about what Marino found," I reply. "Although I can't imagine how that could happen this fast unless the guilty party is one of those closest to the investigation."

"I'm not seeing any mentions of Bigfoot, so that's good," Lucy says. "But Dana Diletti's helicopter is being fueled at Dulles as we speak. Passengers are waiting to board. No flight plan has been filed, unsurprisingly. I can't tell you for a fact where they're going, but I think we know."

"That would be most unfortunate if they film us recovering the bodies." I envision the female victim floating in the lake, and how grotesque that would look on the news.

"Their pilot's an asshole."

"You two know each other?"

"Lorna Callis, twenty-five years old, an aviation major in college." As Lucy is saying this, an image of the pilot appears in one of the digital displays. "Her ratings far exceed her experience. She doesn't always execute good judgment, as we're about to find out, I have a feeling."

I've seen her on TV, an unattractive smug-looking woman with short hair shaved close on the sides. In the photograph Lucy's voice recognition software pulled up, Lorna is standing next to the news chopper, a white Robinson R66 with the TV show's logo on the doors.

"But to answer your question," Lucy explains, "we're not friendly."

"Well, I hope she'll stay away from us but don't know what we can do about it."

"If asked, most aircraft will avoid the area."

"What if they won't?"

"I have ways of being persuasive," Lucy says. "The big problem's going to be when we're flying back to your office. Then it will be open season for anybody hoping to film something sensational. Once we lift off from Buckingham Run, we won't be able to disguise what's strapped to the skids."

"I wish there was a way to make it less obvious," I reply.

"There's not. Other than the bodies riding inside the cabin with the rest of us."

"Even if you didn't mind, I wouldn't permit it."

"Niner-Zulu is seven out at one thousand." Lucy checks in again with the Washington National tower as we overfly trees blazing orange, red and yellow.

CHAPTER 5

NINER-ZULU, STAND BY," the tower tells Lucy over the radio.

"Standing by," she answers.

"Seriously?" I look at her annoyed profile as she scans her displays and out the windshield.

"In addition to the earlier flight cancellations screwing up things royally?" she says to me. "There's a temporary restriction north of D.C. because of the vice president's visit to Baltimore later this morning."

"Even so it would seem that you would have special status. You're the Secret Service. I'm surprised they make you wait even a second," I reply. "Air traffic controllers must know you're on official business."

"Unless we're in a pursuit or doing an intercept, I abide by the same rules as everybody else up here," she says. "Well, almost."

"Niner-Zulu, state request." The tower gets back to her.

"Would like to turn on a two-thirty heading...," Lucy answers.

My smart ring alerts me that I have more messages from Marino. As Lucy talks over the radio, I review the latest images he's sending. Unable to resist show-and-tell, he's making sure I'm aware of dangers to be avoided once we reach the scene. Pictures of a huge hollow tree with a honey beehive, the massive spiderweb could be from a Tarzan movie.

A few minutes ago, Marino almost stepped on a bull snake, he makes sure I'm aware. They're not poisonous but look enough like a rattler that he shot first and questioned later. In a selfie, he holds up the deceased reptile and it's over seven feet long and as thick as my arm, *dear help me God*. Marino smiles stiffly, staring wide-eyed at his camera phone. He looks befuddled and startled.

Other photographs are of bloody jackets, pants, sweatshirts, undergarments that have been shredded by something sharp, the victims' clothing cut off them. By all appearances they were outside the tent when attacked.

"Huck and Brittany Manson would have been alerted by their trail cameras, and were dressed and ready with weapons loaded," Lucy says. "They must have wondered what the hell was going on when the intruder was headed toward them. But the thermal imagers weren't picking up whatever it was, as I've explained. Just this occasional flash of yellowish-orange light as you hear heavy footsteps and see dead leaves kicked up."

"I'm assuming that you and the victims were hearing and seeing the same thing simultaneously," I reply. "Since you'd hacked into their trail cameras."

"That's right. The intruder triggered the cameras' motion sensors at three A.M."

She and the Mansons were alerted simultaneously, as were other key people, including Sierra Patron, her investigative partner at the Secret Service. Everyone calls her Tron. Both of them are cyber experts and on permanent loan to the CIA.

"Huck and Brittany prepared themselves as best they could while they heard the something getting closer, we can only assume," Lucy says. "But there's no place to run, as you'll see once we get there. The only way in and out for them was the same footpath the intruder was on. They were trapped."

"Did they try to call for help?" I ask.

"No, and they knew anybody showing up in those conditions would have been impossible."

"Except you did."

"Your typical aircraft couldn't get in to land. This thing could, but I was too late."

She begins a gradual detour around a ranch to avoid startling the horses and cattle. Ahead is the Manassas National Battlefield Park, the site of the Civil War's first major clash between the North and South. I can make out the wooden palings, cannons and monuments of Bull Run. People are jogging and hiking the trails, some out with their dogs.

"The victims could hear the intruder getting closer. Then what?" I ask Lucy.

"Their only hope was to ambush whoever it was," she says. "I would expect they did what they could to get ready, and it's looking like the confrontation happened in the woods near the footpath's entrance. I've not seen anything for myself yet, been too busy Ubering everyone to the scene. Tron's there as we speak with a metal detector."

Lucy says the wooded area likely is where the victims were

hiding with guns ready. When the intruder got to them, they opened fire, bullets bouncing off like it was nothing.

"And clearly that's not Bigfoot. Unless he's wearing body armor," she adds.

"...OBSTRUCTION! OBSTRUCTION...!"

We avoid a cell tower sticking up like a giant pitchfork, the guy wires faint like pencil strokes.

"Were the Mansons connected to any local hate groups?" I ask. "I'm wondering who they might have associated with before they started living in the woods. Did they ever have visitors? Russian or otherwise?"

"For the most part Huck and Brittany were loners, which is one of the reasons they got away with their crimes for as long as they did. I wouldn't accuse them of having any deep-seated convictions or meaningful relationships. They didn't care about much beyond themselves," Lucy says, and we're about ten miles from our destination.

Winds are light with occasional gusts that shove us around as the shadow of our helicopter follows on the ground.

"Maybe you couldn't see anything on the surveillance cameras, but were you able to pick up sound besides footsteps and dead leaves kicked around?" I continue anticipating what I'm about to encounter. "Could you hear anything helpful that might give us a clue what happened early this morning in the pitch dark and rain once the intruder reached the campsite?"

"Mostly I heard the wind blowing. Then eventually gunshots in rapid succession," Lucy says. "It sounded like more than one person shooting semiautomatics. Based on what's been found at the scene, it was Huck and Brittany firing their pistols, possibly having no idea who or what they were shooting at."

"What happened after that?"

"It got dead quiet, no pun intended."

"How long was the intruder at the scene?"

"Long enough to be massively destructive to everything, including the bodies," she answers. "Of course, the sound of that wasn't picked up. An hour and a half after he got there you can hear him leaving, striding past the cameras on the path the same way he did earlier. I'm doing searches of the area and he's not showing up on my thermal imagers. And I'm saying *he* because it's easier. I'm not assuming it's a male. And it's not a bear or a Bigfoot. The monster in question is of the human variety."

"That's what it sounds like," I reply. "How far from the campsite to the Mansons' farm?"

"About a mile."

"That's a lot of brush to clear for a footpath."

"They used flamethrowers and pesticides, not caring what they damaged and killed on the way," Lucy says. "That's what the self-proclaimed nature lovers were like when no one was looking. The footpath is the only way in and out of the campsite. And it's not visible unless you know about it."

"Suggesting the intruder was familiar with them and their setup," I reply.

"Absolutely."

"Would this person know about their cameras?"

"I'm going to assume so."

"And was undeterred."

"Because he knew he had a way of defeating them," Lucy says. "Explaining why we can't see anything on thermal imaging except that infrequent flash of light I mentioned. But you can hear something big and powerful walking loudly, steadily, aggressively."

Lucy could see leaves displaced and kicked along the path. Branches were shoved out of the way and in some instances broken off.

* * *

"It was as if a violent spirit was passing through," Lucy explains as she flies, the sunlight bright and warm through the plexiglass. "Based on the height of damaged foliage, the intruder was between five and six feet tall. He didn't leave any tracks. Just a few scraped areas in mud."

At close to four-thirty this morning, the assailant left the scene the same way he arrived. Following the footpath, he reached the edge of the Mansons' farm at around five, Lucy says. After that he was out of range of the cameras' microphones. But that doesn't mean he wasn't somewhere in the area.

"Maybe he returned to wherever he'd left his vehicle, high-tailing it out of there," Lucy says. "Or it's possible he hung around because of me. If he heard a helicopter flying toward the campsite, that must have come as quite a surprise."

It's doubtful the assailant would have expected anyone looking for the Mansons so soon and in such terrible conditions. When this person heard the approach of a powerful helicopter, I suspect he would have been intensely curious and wary. He might have been lying low, hiding as Lucy lumbered over with lights strobing in the foggy dark.

"This thing's thermal imagers didn't see the intruder any

better than the trail cameras did." She enters a new radio frequency into one of the communication systems.

"A possible explanation?"

"Apparently the assailant has the ability to outsmart the cameras' sensors. But again, I don't know what I'll find when I run forensics with the software," she replies, and I can tell when she's being cagey.

My niece knows things she's not saying, and it won't do any good for me to ask a lot of questions. She's not going to tell me until she's ready, and that might be never. Pressing the mic trigger, she gets back on the air, talking to Manassas Regional Airport.

"...Helicopter Niner-Zulu is five to the northeast."

"Niner-Zulu, state request."

"Would like to cross midfield," Lucy says as a gash in the countryside becomes the airfield with boxy hangars and an air traffic control tower. Planes are flying in the pattern, taking off and landing.

"Call when three out and climb to one thousand, Niner-Zulu. Traffic is an amphibious at your one o'clock."

"Will call at three and have traffic in sight," she answers, pointing out the seaplane to me.

Barely visible below the horizon, it disappears in the trees at intervals. I can make out the canoe-shaped floats on the wheeled landing gear, the red-striped fuselage, and something else that strikes me as unusual.

"I think I'm seeing a radome under the nose not so different from the one you've got on this thing," I say to Lucy. "Maybe the plane belongs to a TV station? Or some other interested party that's filming?"

"It's not the media," Lucy says, and she has information that she's not sharing.

"The police? Maybe it's one of your aircraft?" I probe anyway because I prefer knowing what I'm dealing with.

"It's not ours and has been buzzing around out here since the fog burned off," Lucy says. "As I've been flying back and forth dropping off investigators, I've been seeing it."

"Is that significant?"

"Let's just say it's not unusual for the plane to be flying around here, weather permitting. It's registered to the Mansons' retail business," Lucy replies to my surprise. "They bought it around the time they moved to their run-down farm out in the middle of nothing."

"Why would it be out now flying in the very area where the owners are dead? Or at least we think it's them. What's the plane used for?"

"Wild World customers charter it for extreme adventures. Supposedly. The seaplane is popular with skydivers in particular, people into high-risk activities, according to the website. Also, the plane is used for commercial aerial photography. Again supposedly. The hourly rate is four thousand dollars if you want to hitch a ride. But no one does, even as the Mansons falsely claim an annual income from it to the tune of millions."

"And you can't tell what it's doing or who's in it this morning?" I look for the plane but can't see it anymore.

"Probably it's up to the usual, which is more than one thing." She doesn't answer the question. "No flight plan has been filed, and whoever's at the controls isn't much for making traffic announcements."

"I find it hard to believe that you don't know who the pilot is." I look at her sharp profile, the lenses of her photovoltaic glasses tinted dark green.

"I don't know who's up right now," she replies.

The seaplane flies by visual flight rules (VFR) in uncontrolled airspace, meaning the pilot doesn't have to talk to anyone. The more Lucy elaborates, the less I believe her.

"Could it land on the lake in Buckingham Run?" I ask. "Because that's the first thing to enter my mind. Maybe it's been transporting the Mansons to their clandestine campsite. Maybe it was supposed to meet them this morning to fly them out of there."

"It wasn't. And no way that would happen," Lucy says. "The lake is small and surrounded by tall trees. A fixed-wing couldn't get in. Most helicopters can't either, and after dark, forget it. Like I've said, you'd need something like this." She means the Doomsday Bird.

"How long would it take to get to the campsite on foot, assuming one knew about the path?" I ask.

"It's barely wide enough for one person, and dense woods are on either side," she says. "Should you wander off the beaten track you could get lost and never be found. You could fall through an overgrown mineshaft even worse. Not to mention whatever might be living in forestland that's been mostly undisturbed for the past two centuries."

Trekking to and from the campsite would take the Mansons at least half an hour each way in daylight and good weather. The intruder didn't have either advantage in the rainy predawn, and yet his stride didn't falter. Lucy gets back on the radio again, announcing that we're three miles from Manassas Regional

Airport. Moments later, we're flying over the runways, the Blue Ridge Mountains getting closer.

She directs my attention to colorful hardwood trees, the dark evergreens of Buckingham Run, named after the river flowing through it. When the gold rush started in this part of the world during the early eighteen hundreds, it was big business. Virginia was making more money from it than any other state in the country, Lucy informs me. Then the war broke out between the North and South, and the mines were abandoned, never to reopen.

"I have to wonder if the Mansons realized how dangerous it was to camp out there for extended periods," I say to her.

"They knew enough."

"If they weren't using special heavy metal water filters? If they were eating fish from the lake and showering or washing dishes with water from it? That could have been very bad eventually," I explain.

"They didn't care."

"About a lot of things, it seems," I reply.

CHAPTER 6

THEY NEVER PLANNED ON being out there all that long and believed they were smarter than everyone else. Also, invincible," Lucy says as we fly over the small city of Gainesville, known for its outlet malls. "The only thing they cared about was themselves."

"They had to know what mining did to the environment back in a day when there were no regulations," I reply. "Obviously they were aware that Buckingham Run is a protected wilderness and not a place recommended to the public."

"They were anti-science and anti-fact if the message didn't suit them," Lucy says. "Whether you're talking about elections, vaccines or what might be in the water they boiled at their campsite."

Experienced campers, the Mansons knew how to handle themselves in harsh conditions, she goes on to explain. But they had big egos. They were cocky and didn't thoroughly research everything that interested them. This had gotten worse over recent years as they accumulated more wealth, getting in deeper with their criminal handlers.

"Their choices and arrogance got them caught and are the reason they're dead," Lucy says as if there can be no question.

"Did you ever interview them together or separately?"

"Not that they were aware of."

"What about meeting them, being around them?"

"Put it this way," Lucy says. "If they ran into me somewhere they were none the wiser."

We've reached Lake Manassas, the smooth water mirroring the wooded shore. Nobody is around, no boating or swimming allowed. Fears of contamination and threats of terrorism have kept the huge reservoir closed to the public for decades. Hundreds of acres of prime waterfront land have remained undeveloped and desolate.

"I'm curious if anyone else might have visited the Mansons' secret campsite, including their Russian connections. Who else knew about it?" I ask. "Who might have had an idea where to find them and would have a way of getting out there? Especially after dark?"

"We don't know for sure who might have been aware, but no way what happened to them is random." She flies over the reservoir's massive stone dam. "As I've pointed out, you can't see the footpath unless you know where to look. It wouldn't be visible from a normal aircraft because the tree canopy is too dense."

Over recent months Lucy has been spying as the Mansons hiked to and from their farmhouse. She says they'd run errands in their pickup truck, buying food and other supplies, making sure they were seen by the locals. The couple acted as if all was normal, claiming their Wild World retail business kept them busy, which is why nobody saw them often.

They described traveling regularly, taking clients to remote locations for hiking, camping and wildlife photography. When they weren't doing that, they were home in front of their computers. They were visiting their store and fulfillment center, they explained to anyone who listened.

"All of it lies," Lucy says, the sun bright on her scar again.

The slightest nick to her carotid is all it would have taken. I couldn't have saved her, and I was right there when it happened.

"In truth, they hadn't been doing trips like that for years," she says. "The only people they were ferrying around were themselves until they began to isolate at the campsite a few months ago. Then they didn't go anywhere except to run errands. Always paying in cash ever since they started holing up in the woods. They had a lot of money stashed at the campsite, much of it still there."

When they were done with shopping, they'd move their purchases inside the farmhouse. They'd backpack what they could carry, including bottles of propane they refilled for their portable cooktop stove and hot water heater. They might do this several times a week depending on the need.

"Always returning to the campsite well before dark," Lucy tells me.

To know this much detail, she was doing more than monitoring Huck and Brittany in cyberspace. She must have been showing up in person, tailing them and spying in other ways. It occurs to me that Lucy might have visited their campsite at some point when they weren't there. I have no doubt she could get in and out undetected by trail cameras or anything else.

"They'd set timers inside the house to control the lighting," she's saying. "Their pickup truck was in the driveway, and to the average observer it looked like somebody was home. They knew to be careful about sending out electronic transmissions that could be intercepted. Obviously, any bad guy worth his salt knows that people like me use signal analysis to track what suspects are doing."

"*People like you*?" I repeat. "Did the Mansons know who you are? Did they know your name?"

"I suppose it's possible," she replies, and I detect deception again. "But it's hard to say what they might have been aware of. They didn't email or text information that could be incriminating or give us info about much of anything."

We fly over a winery that Benton and I have visited, the parking lot empty at this early hour. Ahead is the Prince William Golf Course where people are playing and riding in carts, enjoying the beautiful morning.

"It was difficult to know who the Mansons were hearing from or the nature of the information," Lucy continues explaining. "As long as they didn't answer, nothing was detected. They were probably sitting out there in the woods hour on end opening emails, text messages, accessing all sorts of files. It wasn't possible to know what they were doing or with whom. Meanwhile, their software's algorithms are running on proxy servers around the globe, hacking into companies, news services, government institutions."

Lucy could see the couple on their surveillance cameras hiking with backpacks along the path, wearing guns and chatting as if everything was relaxed and routine. They would use the very hiking poles that now impale their bodies, she tells me.

"I could hear what they were saying, and it was obvious they suspected their cameras had been hacked," she explains. "They would have been stupid not to wonder. If nothing else, it could have been their Russian friends spying on them. Or the Chinese for that matter. Huck and Brittany were careful. They knew it was a lot harder for them to be monitored out in the woods, which was the major reason for them being there."

When the Mansons moved from Old Town Alexandria three years ago, supposedly it was to get away from COVID. They were opting for the simple life. That's the story they told when relocating to Nokesville, population thirteen hundred.

"It's the kind of place where people notice everything and nothing," Lucy explains. "There's no real industry, very little going on. It's just a nice quiet spot if you want to get away from modern civilization. A place to hide in plain view."

* * *

The rural community of Nokesville has no passenger train service, police department or major medical care. Downtown is a scattering of businesses along the main drag of Route 652. A Dollar General store, a few automotive places, a 7-Eleven, a coffee shop, I recall from a visit not long ago.

"The farm they bought is close to the abandoned gold mine inside Buckingham Run," Lucy says. "And that was important to them."

"If anything, I would think it made that area of the forest

more treacherous," I reply, looking down at a mobile home park, a church with a cemetery.

"When you're surrounded by thick stone walls in the side of a hill it provides shielding in certain situations..." Something has caught her attention outside the windshield. "Here comes trouble."

She points at a small dot that looks farther away than it is, explaining it's Dana Diletti's helicopter. Lucy gets on the radio, and any pilot on the same frequency can hear what she's saying.

"Request traffic stay clear of police activity in Buckingham Run." In a nice way she's telling the TV chopper to make itself scarce.

"Seven-Charlie-Delta is five miles northeast and inbound. Area in question is unrestricted," Lorna Callis answers, and I don't like her tone.

A live video image of her suddenly appears on a cockpit display. We're watching her at the controls in real time, and Lucy's AI software must have hacked into the news chopper's cockpit.

"Request that unauthorized aircraft avoid police operation southwest of Nokesville," Lucy repeats over the air.

"Negative and no can do. *Area is unrestricted*," Lorna says condescendingly as we watch her every move without her having a clue. "Will stay on present heading while maintaining space and separation. Appreciate you doing the same."

"Oh gee. I think she's telling us to fuck off." Lucy is talking to me. "Well, that's not very friendly or respectful, is it? Not even patriotic, let's be honest. Told you she's an asshole."

"Sounds like you two have something personal." I watch the

helicopter coming toward us at the same time I'm seeing live video of the pilot who's flying it.

"She doesn't like me for some reason. She'd like me less if she knew we were watching her right now." Lucy squeezes the mic trigger again. "Roger that, Seven-Charlie-Delta," she replies over the air, as cool as they come.

"Glad we understand each other," Lorna has the nerve to fire back. "See you there."

"Meanwhile we're seeing her here and now." Lucy is talking to me again. "Such a shame she has to be a bad sport."

"Does she know who you work for? Clearly, she must recognize that what you're flying isn't exactly a civilian aircraft."

"That's a big part of the problem. A wannabe hell-bent on proving herself. She'd be wise to pick on someone her own size. But I guess she didn't get the memo."

"Now what?" I watch Lorna on the display, and she's flying directly toward us with a somewhat maniacal smile.

"Now it's showtime," Lucy says. "And I've got just the thing in mind. She's about to have a new experience to write home about. And Dana Diletti will have a death-defying adventure to brag about all over the news."

Reducing power and slowing down, Lucy scrolls through menus on a touchscreen. She activates the beacons and strobes as the TV chopper gets closer, and we must be flashing like a UFO. Settling into an aggressive high hover, my niece selects what she refers to as a *mood killer*. A signal jammer of some sort, I have a feeling, and instantly Lorna vanishes from the display inside our cockpit.

"And oops! She's lost her avionics," Lucy says. "All the displays went black. Just... like... that. She's trying to use the radio or talk over the intercom right now and nothing's working, including their phones and TV cameras."

"She's not going to crash, is she?" I'm watching out the windshield as the news helicopter flares like a reined-in horse, slowing down.

"She's fine unless she does something stupid," Lucy answers.

I imagine Lorna Callis frantically trying to figure out what's wrong. But we can't see her anymore.

"Her bird is deaf, mute and blind." Lucy holds our position. "Oh boy. What a mess."

We're close enough that I can make out the logo on the door as the helicopter slows into a hover. Lucy keeps us pointed directly at it in an aggressive manner, staring calmly, not the least bit stressed. She reaches for the touchscreen again.

"Lights back on, no harm done," she says. "But Lorna's not sure of that, and unfortunately the cameras are still offline. That must be frustrating." Waiting a beat. "Nope. She's not sure of much. And she's out of here, got no choice. One of those *land as soon as possible* kind of situations. Better run! Hurry back to the barn!"

The news chopper slowly swoops around in a one-eighty, retreating to the north. Lorna radios the Dulles International Airport tower, reporting possible problems with her avionics. The aircraft is acting off-nominal. She's unnerved and unable to keep it out of her tone as she asks permission to reenter the class B airspace.

"Hope you're able to fix whatever it is, Seven-Charlie-Delta," Lucy tells her over the air. "Have a good one."

"You haven't heard the end of this!" Lorna threatens.

Beneath her bravado she's scared and embarrassed. That's a bad combination. It often leads to revenge.

"Can she cause you a problem?" I ask Lucy.

"I'm sure she'll try. She already bad-mouths me to anyone who will listen."

"How long has she been flying Dana Diletti's chopper?"

"About six months."

"And before that?" I ask.

"Why the interrogation?"

"Because the two of you seem to have preexisting hostilities." I look over at my niece's strikingly pretty profile, the stubborn set of her jaw, her glasses tinted dark in the glare.

"Since she arrived on the scene, she's made her presence known to me in various ways that I'd call antisocial." Lucy has a hard time making friends, always has. But enemies come easily.

"Maybe her problem is that she likes you a little too much," I offer, and that's not uncommon when it comes to my niece.

"The feeling's definitely not mutual," Lucy says. "And the good news is we just bought ourselves some time. She'll have to run diagnostics, making sure nothing's wrong, and nothing will be. She won't be back for an hour at least, if at all."

We resume on course, flying over a tire store, a school, a library, the volunteer fire department, downtown Nokesville passing under us in the blink of an eye. Houses give way to fallow cornfields with rusting silos and decaying outbuildings. We pass a Christmas tree farm and greenhouses, then lush fields speckled with bright orange pumpkins.

As we cross Route 646, Lucy reduces power, slowing down. We're getting close, and I recognize the pond surrounded by pastureland. I'm familiar with the long shiny silver sheds, the big brick house and outbuildings near a cemetery. The name ABEL DAIRY is painted on a rusting blue silo, and I tell Lucy about the man who overturned his tractor several months ago.

"It's strange. I didn't realize how close the dairy farm is to where we're going. It's an entirely different perspective from up here," I say to her. "There's never been a good explanation for the victim suddenly driving the tractor erratically. It's one of those frustrating occasions when the autopsy told me what killed someone but not how it happened. I've not finalized his manner of death. It's still pending investigation, which is sticky. You can imagine what the life insurance people are doing."

"A big policy?"

"I can only assume."

"They want it to be a suicide, let me guess," Lucy says. "A lot of policies have special provisions that limit the claims or cancel them altogether if the insured commits suicide."

"I don't believe the victim in this case killed himself. That would be a bizarre way to do it and no guarantee it would work," I reply.

"Unless he wanted it to look like an accident so his beneficiaries would get the payout. If he shot himself or took pills it would be more obvious. But flipping over his tractor?"

"I asked all sorts of questions about the victim's mental health and habits," I reply. "I've never had any reason to think he committed suicide."

CHAPTER 7

FABIAN AND I RESPONDED to the scene at Abel Dairy. That's why what we're flying over looks familiar," I explain.

"And it abuts the Mansons' farm." Lucy points out a patchwork quilt of fields.

Around it is the forestland of Buckingham Run, spreading out like a fiery autumn ocean with swaths of dark evergreens. The Mansons' hundred-acre run-down property is on the same narrow dirt road as the dairy farm. Huck and Brittany might have known the man who was crushed in his cornfield under mysterious circumstances. Now the three of them are gone violently.

"You could see the crazy tire tracks as if he were trying to get away from something when he flipped over." I describe what I found when I got to the scene.

"Get away from what?" Lucy asks.

"The first thought was he ran over a yellowjacket nest or something like that," I reply. "Or maybe he was having a heart attack or a stroke. I found no evidence of any such thing, and police decided something must have startled him."

We've reached the Mansons' farm, and from the air, six black Secret Service SUVs and vans are small like toys on the long unpaved driveway. Investigators are covered from head to toe in white PPE. They look like Ghostbusters as they sweep with metal detectors and signal analyzers while K-9 handlers search with their Belgian Malinois shepherds.

"I'm going to do a high recon, then a low one before we head to the landing zone," Lucy lets me know. "We'll get a bird's-eye view while making sure nothing's in the area that we should be aware of, something predatory that might be hiding, for example. We'll capture video and other data that can be analyzed later."

There are plenty of thickets and woods where someone or something could duck out of view, she says as we begin a slow orbit. I can make out the bones of a red barn, the rusting farm equipment in a field invaded by creepers. The two-story house on a rise predates the Civil War, brick with white columns and in bad repair. The front lawn is crowded by elms and oaks peeking through a chainmail of kudzu.

A tiered stone fountain probably hasn't worked in many decades. The wraparound porch is steeply sloped, the house listing to one side, the tin roof curling up in places like the lid of a sardine can. The backyard is overgrown with shrubs and weeds. Scattered about are a junkyard of tires, a washer and dryer, a refrigerator and other old appliances.

I doubt the Mansons made any improvements beyond installing a backup generator, an antenna satellite dish and a propane tank that Lucy shows me. The couple's white pickup truck is parked in front of a tall boxwood hedge that flanks a sidewalk missing many of its pavers. From the air, the homestead is a languishing shadow of its former self. It looks unloved and belittled.

I have no doubt that during Virginia's gold rush days it would have been considered grand. I can well imagine sitting on the porch, sipping lemonade or something stronger. It must have been peaceful gazing out at cornfields, at cattle grazing by the big red barn against the backdrop of forests and mountain ranges.

"Here's the other thing they did after buying the place." Lucy directs my attention to a grass airstrip tucked between fields and barely visible. "They'd put out the wind sock when expecting their seaplane, and that's the only time it was visible. They wanted to draw as little attention as possible to their comings and goings."

"When did you first get interested in them?" I know how obsessive Lucy can be.

"About six years ago," is her stunning answer.

She wasn't working for the Secret Service then. At least not that I'm aware of, but that doesn't mean she wasn't collaborating with them. She could have been chasing the Mansons to the gates of hell and I wouldn't know. Benton probably would. But that doesn't mean he'd tell me.

"Huck and Brittany were one of my major focuses when I was working with New Scotland Yard and Interpol," Lucy explains as we complete a second orbit of the farm, thud-thudding over it low and slow.

She was a private cyber investigator at the time, or that's what I was led to believe. For several years Lucy kept a flat in London, never discussing the details. She tells me that she brought the Mansons to the attention of the authorities. The couple is tied in with a Russian criminal organization that has stolen billions and is determined to destroy American democracy.

"You'll be hearing more about this later, but we're talking about extremely ruthless people," Lucy says. "The sort who would do the unthinkable to those who dare to cross them. Huck and Brittany got off easy comparatively speaking."

"I'm sure that's not what they were feeling early this morning as they heard something coming toward them in the dark."

We've entered the forestland of Buckingham Run, and Lucy activates the forward-looking infrared (FLIR) thermal imager. Real-time live video of dense trees and underbrush is vivid in displays, the footpath the Mansons burned and hacked through the woods a winding shoelace beneath unbroken canopies.

"The more I hear about the kind of people you've been after, the worse I'm feeling about your personal safety, Lucy." I'm honest while we have a private moment. "You've had enough close calls in recent memory." I stare at the scar on her neck as images, sensations flash in my thoughts.

I'm remembering the crack-crack of gunfire in the produce section, a bin of lettuce spattered bright red. I detected the metallic smell of blood. Only it wasn't me who was injured.

"I know damn well the kind of people we're up against and how dirty they play. I know it better than you think," Lucy says. "That's why we're searching for any nasty calling cards they might have left."

Bomb experts and their dogs aren't visible through the treetops. But in thermal imaging they're chalky white as they search the path for explosive devices, not finding them or other booby traps, Lucy informs me. On the FLIR's video screen deer shapes move gracefully, flicking their bright white tails, their mouths flaring orangish yellow.

I'm reminded of the strange flares of light Lucy described seeing on the Mansons' hacked trail cameras when the intruder was striding along the path. A buck with antlers stares up as we fly over endless acres crisscrossed by creeks and old mine trails that look like scars. Woods becomes wetlands with cypress knees, the rocky river called Buckingham Run emptying into a lake shining dark blue in the sun.

* * *

The female victim barely shows above the surface. Her head and limbs are submerged, her body drifting on the current and a daunting distance offshore. Retrieving her will be an ordeal, and it's not possible to anticipate the dangers. We don't know how deep the water is or what might live in it besides the snapping turtles and water moccasins common in this part of the world.

Marino and I will have to put on Mustang immersion suits, braving the elements as we tow the victim to shore without a life raft or a boat. He'll complain the entire time but will rise to the occasion. We've done water recoveries before. Descending into a tight space belowground is a different story. I knew what to expect from the first moment I started seeing the videos and photographs.

Marino will say he's too big to fit through the collapsing mineshaft's opening. He's over six feet tall and weighs more than two hundred pounds. That's a lot to be hoisting in a harness. It makes sense to pick someone smaller. But that's not the real reason it will be me doing the honors, and I recognize his bodybuilder shape five hundred feet below us.

Wearing headphones, Marino is busy with a metal detector while the Doomsday Bird charges in as loudly as a locomotive. He and five Secret Service investigators are outfitted in HAZMAT-yellow hooded jumpsuits. They've set up a pup tent near the entrance of the gold mine yawning darkly in the rocky hillside. Then the scene is gone, the dense canopies stretching endlessly.

"This is when it starts being fun." Lucy drops lower. "The trick is not to get impatient. No rushing anything." Trees loom alarmingly close, shaking like pompoms as we begin to circle. "Nice and easy…Like I always say, never be in a hurry to die."

She slows the helicopter to a hover, and I don't see the small clearing until it's directly under us, a dry creek bed littered with boulders and deadwood several hundred feet below. There's no room for error, our trajectory straight down like an elevator. Were anyone else at the controls I'd be saying my prayers. I'd be crossing myself mightily, backslidden Catholic that I am.

"Wish me luck." Lucy's gallows humor as we begin our descent.

I stare straight ahead, trying not to get disoriented, trees churning furiously in our mighty wind. They close in like a rioting mob, the ground reaching up, tall grass and bushes thrashing and grabbing. Hunting for a level spot, Lucy touches down on the back of the skids in a confined area that could be from the Jurassic period.

The small bright blue opening we descended through seems a portal to another dimension, and I look around for Marino. Pushing the collective all the way down, Lucy rolls the throttles to flight idle, silencing warning horns. Colorful tree canopies dance wildly in our rotor wash as fallen leaves swarm like panicked moths.

"I hope Marino's okay," I say to her, the blades thudding as we sit in the clearing, and no sign of him.

"He won't come close until we're completely shut down, disliking helicopters even more than he used to." She begins going through her checklist, keeping an eye on the digital clock. "When I dropped him off earlier, he didn't want to climb out while the blades were turning, and I wasn't going to shut down. He ducked his head and ran like someone was shooting at him."

"He's gotten worse," I reply. "More easily unnerved, then makes excuses for why he won't do something."

I noticed a decided shift after his birthday in July, and it had nothing to do with getting older. My sister surprised him by trading in his fishing boat for a newer model. She picked a grander, more expensive one *that you've only dreamed about*, she lovingly wrote in the card. I don't think he's been out on the water more than once or twice since.

"Mom makes him feel bad about himself, and it does no good to tell her. Some things never change. The more she dotes on him the worse he gets," Lucy says, and I predicted this would happen when Dorothy and Marino got married during COVID.

She turned him into a project as she's always done with the men in her life. My sister has a habit of re-creating people in the image she decides. Most times she means well and has a valid point. But inevitably the story ends poorly for all involved. I've never known Marino to be so well cared for, and it's not without a price. Feeling powerless is his kryptonite.

"There's always someone who's going to make him insecure," is my diplomatic response. "Unfortunately, that includes me. Also Benton, and of course Dorothy. And you, Lucy. Marino feels you don't admire him anymore." I'm not telling her anything she doesn't know.

"Not when he acts like a jerk, I don't." She bends down to tighten the friction of the cyclic, keeping it centered as she continues the shutdown while we talk over the intercom.

"It's uncomfortable for him when the roles are reversed. A lot of people would feel that way. It's human nature."

"Our roles have been reversed for a long time." Her voice in my headset. "He can't bring himself to see it." She turns off the strobes and the landing lights. "And I've been dealing with his human nature most of my life, Aunt Kay."

"In his mind, he taught you everything you know. I'm not justifying his behavior, Lucy. But it's important to be reminded of how things started. He still thinks you need his guidance. Or he hopes it."

"As you well know, he's not all that easy to handle when he decides he's the most qualified to do something." She flips off more switches. "Such as casting a foot impression that's going to be the most controversial and problematic evidence in this case. And maybe that's the reason it was there. Exactly for that purpose."

"Maybe."

"The point is to cause a shit show with Marino at the center."

"We don't know that it's evidence or related to the deaths," I remind her. "We don't know the explanation for what he discovered."

"It shouldn't have been him who did the discovering. Tron says he's been acting like he's part of our crime scene unit."

"The difficulty is that in some instances, Marino probably is the most skilled and experienced," I reply.

"He got out the can of hairspray, started mixing up the plaster of Paris, and next thing you know he's doing it."

"As many casts of tire tracks and footwear impressions as he's made, he'd probably qualify as an expert in court," I reply. "But that doesn't mean it's his jurisdiction in this instance. Not to mention aggravating everyone involved and creating an even bigger liability."

"He's so sure he knows what's best, and he doesn't. He mouths off when he shouldn't and throws his weight around, especially with me. It would be helpful if he stopped treating me like I'm ten years old." She turns off the avionics master switch and with it goes the intercom.

We hang our headsets on hooks, saying nothing else for now. Twisting the throttles all the way off, Lucy cuts the engines, the blades beginning to slow. She reaches up for the rotor brake handle. Then the battery goes off, and the sudden silence is absolute. I look around and it's as if we've time traveled or landed on another planet.

I halfway expect a dinosaur to crash out of the forest. Or a pterodactyl to fly over screeching bloody murder. Maybe extraterrestrials will appear to take us to their leader. Scanning woods dappled with shadows, I have the uneasy sense that we aren't alone. I'm not seeing Marino, and the feeling persists. It must be my imagination as fear prickles up my spine for no obvious reason.

Lucy and I unbuckle our harnesses, opening our doors, the

air chilled and as clean as anywhere I've been before. As we step down from the skids, leaves crackle and dead sticks snap somewhere in the woods.

"I hope that's Marino," I comment, the din getting louder.

Suddenly he emerges from the trees like an apparition in bright yellow. He's carrying a white banker's box sealed with red evidence tape. His hood is down around his shoulders, his shaved head and weathered face flushed and sweaty. He has on a tactical gun belt over his PPE. His Dirty Harry 1911 pistol and extra magazines are on his hip, a pump-action 12-gauge shotgun on a paracord sling looped over his shoulder.

"I was getting worried that something might have grabbed you in the woods," I say to him.

"I figured maybe you ran into Bigfoot," Lucy starts in. "And you were asking his whereabouts early this morning at the time of the attack, checking on his alibis. Swabbing him for DNA and all the rest."

"I was waiting until you shut down, playing it safe." Marino's not the least bit amused. "I didn't want to get blasted by this big-ass thing while carrying something fragile." He gently sets down the banker's box on a skid as I continue feeling spied on. "I'm wondering if it was you who blew shit all over the place. As you'll find out soon enough, the scene looks like a twister ripped through."

"I might have blown a few things." She's not worried about it. "I was over the treetops, about a hundred and fifty feet above the ground, when I found the campsite. There was going to be some rotor wash."

CHAPTER 8

I HAVE THE WEIRD SENSE we're not alone. I'm sure it's nothing." I continue looking around as if something is observing us.

"I've been feeling the same thing all morning." Marino's eyes dart everywhere. "I feel something staring. I feel it like a rash."

"Never know. There could be something watching." Lucy looks around, a bland expression on her face. "It's best to assume that wherever you are these days. Never safe to think otherwise."

"Watching us from where?" Marino scans the tree canopies.

"Dunno. Maybe a satellite up there using L-band frequencies that can penetrate dense foliage." She waves at the sky just to annoy him. "*Privet tam!*" she yells. Then to him she says, "That's Russian for *hello up there*."

"You telling me someone could be spying on us this very minute and the freakin' Secret Service wouldn't know?" Marino asks. "I thought that's why you carry a fish finder everywhere."

"It depends," Lucy says. "Some things we'll know about. Not necessarily others."

She routinely uses spectrum analysis to detect rogue electromagnetic signals that might indicate an invisible and unwelcome presence. Her habitats are monitored twenty-four/seven, and that includes the old estate where Benton and I live. The guesthouse she stays in is set up like a cyber lab.

"Something could be watching us right now, and we might know about it but can't do much." Lucy is walking around her dry creek bed landing zone, checking it out. "We also don't have the same absolutes today that we did even a year ago. What was science fiction one month may not be the next."

She offers explanations that are both cryptic and technical while I continue watching the woods all around us. Shapes and shadows are playing tricks on me. I think I see something. But I don't.

"...An example of what one might miss is a transmitted signal the software doesn't screen for because the frequencies are spread out and hopping all over the place." Lucy is unlocking the helicopter's back cabin. "Or maybe one signal is hiding behind another."

"Speaking of spying?" Marino says. "A seaplane's been flying over, white with red stripes, the last time about an hour ago. I thought it might be a TV station but got no clue except it's suspicious. I've pointed it out to your investigators. But they don't seem interested."

"We may have spotted the same plane as we were flying near the Manassas airport," I tell Marino as I open the back cabin to retrieve my briefcase.

"I Googled the tail number. It comes up as an LLC in

Delaware, which doesn't tell me anything helpful," he informs Lucy. "I'm assuming you must know who's been flying around here and why."

"A 2015 Twin Otter worth about seven million. Belongs to Wild World." She passes along the same information she shared with me earlier. "They have several pilots who fly it for them. I don't know who's in it this morning."

"I'm just hearing this?" Marino can't believe it. "We're down here working the scene and the victims' plane is buzzing right over us? And you couldn't bother passing that along?"

"Those who need the information have it." She doesn't add that certain investigative details are none of his business.

But that's what she's saying. It's not the first time she's reminded him that he works for me and not the police. He doesn't have Lucy's authority or power.

"It would have been good to know sooner," he says to her.

"So you could do what about it?"

"More than it seems you have, that's for sure."

Walking around the helicopter, she begins picking up loose branches blown down, and he helps her. They toss them out of the way while pecking at each other the way they always have.

"The seaplane is part of the Mansons' sporting goods business, or that's what they pretended." She moves more sticks and downed branches away from the skids. "Customers charter it for outdoor adventure packages."

"Do you think that's what it's doing this morning? Taking people on adventures?" he asks.

"It's extremely unlikely the plane was taking customers anywhere. It's usually empty." Lucy tosses several large rocks off to the side.

"And how would you know that unless you've been watching it for a while?" he says, and she doesn't answer. "The damn thing has flown overhead three freakin' times since you dropped me off. It was going kind of slow like it might be filming."

"No telling what it's doing. But I strongly suspect it's not what you think," Lucy says.

"I'm wondering who might have a clue that the Mansons are here alive or dead," I ask her. "Who knew they were camping inside Buckingham Run? It's not like a violent person just happened upon their campsite. What was done to them isn't seeming random. In fact, I don't see how it could be."

"That's because it isn't. They were targeted by someone who knows a lot about them." Lucy unlocks the baggage compartment. "Everything done to them was premeditated with the intention of taking them out while creating havoc. And I have a feeling that by now Dana Diletti has an inkling what's happened out here."

I dig in my briefcase for my satellite phone, turning it on.

"The enemy we're up against will make sure to manipulate the publicity," Lucy says.

I pull out the canister of bear repellent. It comes with a plastic holster that I clip to my belt.

"What enemy?" Marino asks. "You act like you might know who it is."

"I don't know who killed these people," she says. "We'll take what gear we can manage, and I'll have a couple agents pick up the rest."

While she and Marino discuss what to bring on our trek to the lakeshore, I send Benton a message. I let him know we've landed without incident but that the situation is perplexing and intense. Next, I text Shannon that until further notice I'm reachable only by my satellite phone, and she responds immediately.

Do you have a minute to call the governor? She's eager to speak to you.

Does she know where I am and why? I write back.

I said you were out of the office, and I didn't know when I'd hear from you next. She's reachable on her cell phone.

I reply that I'll call her now, and I find her private number in my contacts list.

"Roxane, it's Kay Scarpetta," I say when she answers, and my attention is on the woods as I continue to sense a curious and wily presence.

"Thanks for calling and I'll get straight to it. My office has received information that I need to confirm. Or better yet, deny, because I'm hoping it's just some kook trying to get attention." She sounds most unhappy, and so am I.

I'm thinking about the footprint Marino found. The Secret Service knows about it and is in communication with the state police. There's no telling what's been said or if the subject of Bigfoot has come up. I hope to hell Roxane is none the wiser.

"I'm having a hard time getting details. For some strange reason I'm being given the runaround," she's saying. "I assume you'll know whether there's any truth to what I'm about to share since it seems to imply that two people have been killed. Or better put, executed."

* * *

The governor explains that an anonymous caller left her a message on an office line that immediately goes to voice mail. That extension isn't answered by a real person, and staff members sift through the messages.

"'*You're about to see what happens to traitors.*'" Roxane reads what was said in the voice mail left an hour ago. "'*Two of them are inside Buckingham Run where justice was served early this morning. Death to those who defy The Republic. Beware, Governor Dare. It's already begun.*' The voice sounded mechanical," she explains. "The person was using some sort of app to disguise it. That's what I've been told by my IT experts."

Roxane mentions proxy servers and a burner phone *impossible to trace* as I'm startled by a turkey vulture flapping off from a treetop. Dragonflies dart close, some alighting on the helicopter.

"...My state police protective detail is working with the FBI and I don't know who else. For some reason information isn't being shared," the governor reiterates as Lucy meets my eyes, nodding her head.

She's alerting me that she's aware of the anonymous call left at the governor's office. The Republic is a domestic terrorist group that has cells around the country. Their main outpost was only twenty miles southeast of here in Quantico until the feds raided it in July. This was after a string of crimes, including a foiled plot to assassinate the president during a funeral in Old Town.

"I'm just wondering what you've been told. I need to know what's happening and any dangers it might pose to the public." The governor's tone is demanding over speakerphone as Marino and Lucy listen.

"Roxane, I'm with Secret Service investigators inside Buckingham Run, where two people are dead." Sunlight is warm on top of my head, the static of insects unsettled and pervasive. "That much is true. That much I can tell you."

"My Lord! Well, this wasn't at all what I was hoping to hear." She doesn't raise her voice often. "Then the person who left the message must be one of the terrorists taking responsibility for killing whoever the two people are. Suggesting that any threats made are viable."

"It would seem that at the very least the caller has an idea what's happened out here." As I look around, I continue to feel something looking back.

"I'm worried the point is to create mayhem."

"What we're dealing with here could do exactly that, Roxane," I reply, and she doesn't know the half of it.

"Presumably, we can expect something else bad to happen next."

"Considering the violent extremists in question, I'd say that's a real danger," I answer.

"What does your office plan to release to the media?" she asks as Marino looks on with a disapproving expression on his face.

He's no fan of Roxane's since she created the Department of Emergency Prevention, reinstalling Elvin Reddy and Maggie Cutbush for reasons that evade me. Digging in a pocket of his coveralls, Marino pulls out a folding knife and a tactical flashlight, while Lucy begins typing on her phone, her glasses tinted amber.

"Why is it the Secret Service's jurisdiction? Seems to me this is a matter for the state to handle, and not the federal government. What am I missing? Please explain." Roxane asks one question after another, and that's not unusual.

When I was getting started in my career, she was a commonwealth's attorney in Henrico County just outside of Richmond where I lived at the time. We were acquainted in those early years, often working cases together. I'm reminded that she can be a relentless prosecutor. The difference is now she's the governor.

She persuaded me to move back to Virginia after long years away. I was to return the medical examiner system to its glory days. Roxane had confidence I was up for the challenge, and if she doesn't like the job I'm doing, she can send me packing.

"You're inside Buckingham Run right now, Kay," she's saying. "What are you seeing? Are there photographs or videos you could share that might better educate me on what's going on?"

"I've not seen much yet." No way I'm showing her anything.

"I'm wondering if this is a politically motivated stunt to create more conspiracy theories. Now would be an unfortunate time for that kind of distraction."

"It doesn't appear that the two victims are a stunt." I return my briefcase to the helicopter's back cabin, not worried about anybody stealing it out here.

"What was done to them?"

"At the moment I'm calling the deaths unnatural. That's as much as I can say this early on." It's all I intend to tell her.

"Do we know who they are? And why they might have been targeted? And what were they doing inside Buckingham Run?"

"Their identities aren't confirmed. It's best you deal directly with the Secret Service, Roxane," I again remind her, and she's well acquainted with Benton. I suggest she try him.

"The timing is of great concern, and the more I'm thinking about it, I can't help but suspect it's deliberate," she says with conviction. "Less than a week before our next general election, a very important one, especially in Northern Virginia. A sensational case like this will be an unfortunate diversion and deterrent. It could stop some people from getting out to vote for fear they might be targeted."

"Whoever left the message at your office was making sure to create explosive publicity and fear," I agree with her. "I think that much we can say with confidence."

"The instant you find out anything, I want to be informed. I'll expect to hear from you as soon as you have answers." Roxane ends the call.

"She's being manipulated, and is about to make things worse," Lucy says. "That's why the message was left on her office line. The goal was for the governor to create an uproar while using the situation to her political advantage. Because that's what people like her do. They can't help themselves. They've got to spin the situation, turn it into something that gives them a bump in the polls."

"Imagine her reaction if she gets a load of this?" Marino sits down on the skid next to the banker's box. He places it in his lap. "Doesn't sound like she's got a clue. And that's a damn good thing. Pictures don't do it justice. It might be my best so far, and I've done a lot of casts in my lifetime. Never a Sasquatch, though. Not until now."

"I understand why you're excited, but this isn't a good thing for you or anyone," I tell him. "I also realize what's done is done.

But it's going to be difficult explaining why someone from the medical examiner's office made a cast of a foot impression at what's likely going to turn out to be the scene of a double homicide. If you'd talked to me about it in advance, I would have insisted that you were hands-off, Marino."

But he didn't ask, and probably for that very reason. I knew nothing about the footprint until he sent images of it. He didn't mention making a cast until it was a fait accompli.

"What matters is protecting and preserving the evidence. I was the best one to do it." He's not going to back down. "You only get one shot at making a good cast, and I did. The details are crystal clear."

"That's probably because they were made by a fake foot," Lucy tells him. "Probably 3-D printed with something firm but pliable like rubber or silicone, and it's going to leave a realistic impression every time."

"I'm not saying that's impossible. But it sure seems real. When I first saw it, I felt this shock go through me and my hair stood on end."

"If you had any hair," Lucy says, and Marino smiles in spite of himself.

"Obviously, this is new for us," I reply. "And from here on out we're going to treat it like any other evidence."

"We need an expert to look at the cast and photographs of the actual footprint." He begins slicing through evidence tape on the banker's box.

"I don't think the Smithsonian has a forensic podiatrist on staff," Lucy says cynically. "Or a cryptozoologist either."

CHAPTER 9

THERE'S A PROFESSOR IN Charlottesville who's in the news a lot." He says this to me. "You may have heard of Cate Kingston?"

She teaches anthropology at the University of Virginia, and Marino met her at the Shenandoah Sasquatch Festival this past June. It was at Lydia Mountain in Luray, where he stayed in a cabin for the weekend, he explains. I remember him going there while Dorothy was visiting friends in Florida. But he never told me that he was attending a Bigfoot gathering.

"Cate Kingston was the keynote speaker and shared photographs and plaster casts with the audience, pointing out what made them authentic or not," Marino is saying.

"None of this helps your cause." Lucy roots around inside the baggage compartment, finds a can of eco-friendly insect repellent. "Especially if you might have had access to any of the plaster casts or photographs you saw at some festival." She begins fogging the clearing around the helicopter to keep mosquitoes and other unwelcome pests away. "You'd better hope nothing matches the footprint you found."

"Let's take a peek at what you've got." I sit down on the skid next to Marino, and he takes the lid off the box.

He shines the light inside, the colossal white plaster cast covered with transparent cling wrap. It's cushioned like a crown jewel on a bed of folded disposable sheets.

"You've got to admit it's pretty damn impressive." He's excited and amazed all over again, as if part of a miracle.

"Wow, that's impressive." I have to give him credit. "I guess there's a first for everything."

"Like we say in aviation, don't fly through a sucker hole." Lucy looks inside the box, trying not to show her reaction while continuing her cynicism. She's surprised. She might even be startled as she warns Marino about being distracted and using poor judgment. "Be careful what you trust. Ask yourself why someone might want to mess with you in particular."

"*Me* in particular?"

"That's right."

"You got someone in mind?"

"I have a feeling the list is long," she replies as I continue sensing that she's not telling us something important.

Inside the box is a six-inch ruler used as a scale in photographs. Marino carefully lifts out the cast, holding the ruler next to it. The humanlike bare footprint is a mind-boggling eighteen inches from the heel to the tip of the five toes. It's nine inches at its widest, and I can imagine the uproar it would cause.

"Talk about creating a shit storm," I say to them.

"Consistent with a Sasquatch at least eight feet tall or more that could weigh half a ton. Obviously, something that size would be a male," Marino says as if it's common knowledge. "We know from prehistoric fossils found in caves how big they could get and that they mostly ate plants, in case you're wondering."

"The fossils you're talking about are teeth and bone fragments discovered in China," Lucy says to him. "Not in North America."

"Looks like you've been Googling," he says sarcastically.

"That's not what my data mining is called. But yes, I'm seeing the information. In fact, I'm seeing it as we're talking." She indicates her computer-assisted glasses.

"Point being, we know for a fact that Bigfoots used to exist," Marino replies. "And there's nothing to say that a remnant of them isn't left in places where they can avoid people. Like out here, for example."

"Science says differently," Lucy answers. "The species known as the *Gigantopithecus* was wiped out hundreds of thousands of years ago during the Ice Age."

"We don't know that for sure," he says.

He explains that ice forming caused the levels of the oceans to drop, and land was uncovered between continents, connecting them for a period of time. The theory is that some of the huge primates may have migrated from China. They may have walked here the same way early humans did across the Bering land bridge between what's now Siberia and Alaska.

"We're talking only a couple hundred miles depending on where they crossed. And if humans did it, why not Bigfoot?" Marino makes his argument.

"Except there's no evidence the *Gigantopithecus* species has ever lived here in North America," Lucy repeats.

"The hell there isn't. The Native Americans have depicted

them in artwork and stories for more than a thousand years," Marino answers. "You can't say for a fact that these huge humanoids are gone from the entire planet."

"Maybe they're not. And now they're killing campers about to be arrested, saving taxpayers the cost of a trial and incarceration," Lucy replies. "Imagine that."

"I didn't say I thought a Sasquatch killed anyone, including the two victims out here." Marino is getting more defensive. "Finding the footprint could be completely unrelated to them being whacked."

"Remember what I said about sucker holes." Digging inside the baggage compartment again, Lucy pulls out the long red nylon straps used to tie down the rotor blades.

"There's a couple of hairs right there stuck in the plaster, kind of blackish silver." Marino shines the light, and I lean closer. "And as you can see, there's no arch, the foot completely flat. All of it consistent with a Sasquatch."

"Sucker hole." Lucy says it again.

"No telling what we might see microscopically." He's not listening to her. "Best of all would be if we get lucky with DNA."

"Wouldn't that be something if we get a hit on a Bigfoot in CODIS." She's referring to the FBI's Combined DNA Index System database. "Maybe we'll finally catch the Abominable Snowman while discovering the true identities of Grendel and King Kong."

Slinging a tiedown strap over a rotor blade, she gently bends it down, fitting the tip with a red nylon cover. She clips the strap to a cross-tube under the skids.

"You can even see where one of the toes is bent." Marino shows me on the cast. "Like maybe he broke it once."

"Only once?" Lucy begins tying down the next blade. "It's amazing you can tell all that."

"Look at the ridge detail, Doc." Marino shines the light, showing me fine looped and whorled lines, bits of dirt and dead vegetation stuck to areas of the plaster. "It's good enough that we could make a match."

"A match with what?" Lucy isn't going to relent.

"Another footprint. Saying another one is found out here," he answers her.

"And if it is and then another one is found after that? I'm sure they would match, all of them made by the same Sasquatch," she says. "In other words, faux, fake, a hoax, someone's idea of fucking with us. Most of all, fucking with you."

"The only one fucking with me is you," he snarls.

* * *

"Listen, Marino. I'm just giving you what you're about to get from a lot of other people." Lucy surveys her work, the four main rotor blades held in place with the bright red straps. "It would have been better if someone else had made the cast. That's the takeaway from all this."

"Well, someone else didn't. We're just lucky I did," he snaps.

"I'm sure that was the plan."

"What plan? What the hell are you talking about?"

"Even if someone else had found the footprint before you did, the story would end the same way," Lucy says. "That's what happens when there's a fanatic in the crowd. Next thing, plaster of Paris is being mixed up in a bucket."

"At least I thought to bring it."

"And someone might ask why? Were you expecting to find something special?"

"Because I always carry it in a scene case. And I'm not a fanatic." He glares at her. "It's no different from you thinking UFOs are real."

"That's because they are. We just aren't sure *what* they are or from where."

"Tell me how it is that you found the footprint," I say to him as I get up from the skid. "I need to know the details. If people find out about this, you and our office are going to be in the hot seat any way we look at it. Lucy's right about that."

"As soon as I got here and suited up, Tron took me into the gold mine." Marino digs in a pocket of his coveralls, pulling out a roll of evidence tape. "We were talking about how best to get the male victim's body out and I was shining my light all over the place while hearing weird noises."

"Such as?" I feel compelled to ask since it will be me putting on a harness and descending into the mineshaft.

"It sounded like something moving somewhere deep down in the dark." He begins taping the lid back onto the banker's box. "As I was looking around, I noticed disturbances in the dirt near an opening that leads into another tunnel."

Scuff marks, maybe the partial shape of a heel, and some distance away Marino found the intact footprint between the ore cart rails, he says.

"How far from the mineshaft where the body was dumped?" I ask him.

"Maybe thirty feet inside, which was pretty deep considering what a hellhole it is," he reports, and the location continues to bother me.

"Assuming the footprint was planted," I say to them, "one might expect that whoever's responsible would make sure it was discovered. What if it hadn't been?"

"We wouldn't have missed something like that," Lucy says.

"Bullshit," Marino retorts. "Your investigators had already missed it."

"That doesn't mean we wouldn't have found it."

"And it doesn't mean you would have, either. If you have no experience in something like this, you might not know what you're looking at." Opening the helicopter's back cabin, he sets the banker's box on the floor. "Even if you did, some investigators might choose to walk right past it pretending they don't see it. Why? Because they don't want the very shit I'm getting."

"Someone anticipated that you'd say all these very things and act exactly as you have," Lucy tells him. "In other words, you're being played."

"By who? You act like you know."

"Real or not, we don't know how long the footprint had been there," I remind them. "At least I'm assuming we don't. If a foot impression was left in a protected area like an old mining tunnel, I suppose it could have been there for a while."

"That would suggest it's real," Marino answers. "Unless the killer planted it days, weeks, months, even years ago? Or maybe the Mansons did it as a joke. Which makes no sense."

"You do realize how you're sounding," Lucy warns him.

"Finding a footprint where I did doesn't surprise me. It's believed Bigfoots live underground in abandoned mines and deep caves." He returns the knife, the roll of tape to his coverall pockets. "When Luray Caverns were being excavated, workers came across these huge creatures living deep inside. Some of the men fled in holy terror and never came back. It happened more than once, and there are similar accounts all over the world."

"And I suspect a lot of people who report these experiences are telling the truth as they perceive it but are mistaken." I'm pulling out two wire rescue baskets from the back cabin.

"Or maybe they're not," Marino says. "We don't know what might be out there deep in the forests, just like we don't know what might be at the bottom of the ocean. I thought you're the ones always lecturing about keeping an open mind."

"We're giving you a dose of what you're going to get from everyone else." Lucy helps him lift cases of water out of the baggage compartment, setting them on the ground. "I don't want you going off on a tangent. Especially when you've been known to swear that you believe Bigfoot is real. You've posted stuff about it on Facebook."

"I've been hearing about Bigfoot all my life," Marino replies. "When I was growing up in New Jersey, people would tell stories about sightings and encounters. Like Bobby O'Reilly, the guy I used to train with at the boxing gym. He came face-to-face with a Sasquatch, a smaller one, probably a juvenile with long black hair everywhere. It jumped out of a tree and ran off on two legs while Bobby was hunting in the woods on his property. He saw it clear as day. He said the eyes were humanlike and something told him not to shoot it."

"Maybe don't tell that story to a lot of people," Lucy says as we unload the rest of the equipment, lifting out Pelican cases that hold PPE and additional forensic supplies.

I also included an insulated bag of snacks and drinks, and a few other conveniences such as a camping toilet and a twelve-pack of Charmin. Then Lucy is locking the cabin doors when a strange knocking noise starts deep inside the forest. It sounds like a hard stick hitting a tree slowly, rhythmically from far away. Then it stops.

"Shhhh!" Marino shushes us as we look around.

I see dense woods dappled with light and shadow that become impenetrable. Then the noise starts again as my pulse picks up.

"Holy shit! It's answering us!" Marino's eyes are wide as he stares in the direction of the sound. "It's like it heard us talking about it!"

We've stopped what we're doing, waiting to hear the noise again. But nothing.

"Have you heard this before since you've been here?" Lucy asks him, and she has a strange look on her face.

"Nope." His eyes are moving everywhere, and he's about as spooked as I've seen him. "But I've heard wood-knocking in the past when I've been treasure hunting and something's warning me to keep my distance."

"Like a big woodpecker doing its thing," Lucy says to him.

"What we just heard wasn't a woodpecker." He casts about, his face startled.

"Or a beaver having fun. Or maybe somebody messing with us."

"I can't imagine there's anybody out here who might mess with us," I reply. "But I don't know what that was. It's not one of the investigators at the scene, because it's not coming from that direction. I don't know who else might be out here."

"I'm going to guess it was coming from at least half a mile away," Marino says tensely, excitedly.

"If something's out there in the woods watching us, we're going to know soon enough." Lucy picks up a hard-sided case, placing it on a skid.

Clasps snap loudly, and she lifts out a drone that has gimbalized cameras and four carbon fiber propellers. Unfolding the arms, she places the quadcopter on the ground.

"He answers to *Pepper*, no remote control needed," she explains. "I have an app on my phone for that. His voice recognition capabilities aren't bad but have a way to go. He's also been in and out of Santa's workshop as we've tried to remedy problems that I won't bore you with."

Holding her phone close to her lips, Lucy tells Pepper to *wake up*. The drone's lights turn on and begin flashing red and green.

"*Pepper, start.*"

The propellers begin spinning fast, with a whiny hum.

"*Pepper, hunt...*"

The drone lifts up...up...up...a hundred feet, two hundred and more. Clearing the trees, it levels off, sailing away.

CHAPTER 10

HE HAS HIS DESIGNATED orbits in the area for while we're working. Anything big out there and I'm going to know," Lucy says. "I'll see it on the display." She holds up her phone to show us what Pepper is flying over. "And I can see it in the lenses of my glasses."

Like the Doomsday Bird, the drone has a lidar laser scanner and L-band GPS capabilities that can penetrate dense foliage. If someone or something dangerous is lurking about in daylight, Pepper will see it.

"But nothing yet. No lions, tigers or bears so far," Lucy tells us as we shoulder rucksacks and pick up hard cases. "Most of all, no humans. Nobody who might have come out here to teach a lesson, to do a hit Russian style." We set out with our gear, and the woods smell like fall, sunlight filtering through the bright leafy canopy.

Our boots rustle and crackle through a thick carpet of leaves still soggy from last night's downpour. Pushing branches out of the way, we're careful not to snap them back into each other's faces. When we bump into trees, we're sprinkled with rain-water, followed by swearing. As I look around, I can't shake the feeling that something is looking back.

Marino leads the way, with Lucy following, and every other second I'm glancing behind me. I tell myself I'm being silly. All this talk about footprints and wood-knocking have fired up my imagination. I'm on edge as I scan light and shadow, and leaves ruffled, branches rocking in the breeze. A squirrel scampers up a tree. A rabbit hops through bushes, creatures stirring now that the invading helicopter is quiet.

Marino points out an indented mossy area square-shaped and no bigger than the diameter of a phone booth. It would be easy to miss in the fog or dark. Even if you noticed, you might not recognize the significance.

"That's where the ground closed over an old mineshaft, and it's not the first one I've come across," he explains. "From what I understand they're all over Buckingham Run, these deep holes in the ground. There's no record of how many there are or where. Imagine if you drove your ATV over something like that? Or walked on it...?"

As he warns us to be *careful where we step at all times*, I'm reminded that Lucy's not seen anything here from the ground. When she dropped off personnel and their gear, she didn't shut down the helicopter until now. As I walk behind her, I'm aware of her laser attention probing, her hand close to the holstered .44 Magnum strapped to her thigh.

"...Like falling through a trapdoor or being buried alive," Marino is saying, and I'm trying not to listen. "Except you might not die right away. Maybe not for days, and nobody would ever find you..."

His graphic descriptions are enough to send most people into a tizzy, and I'm doing my best to block him out. We make slow and painful progress trudging along, avoiding deadwood, boulders, poison oak and briars. The bags I'm carrying bump into my legs, making it harder to stay balanced, the straps digging into my shoulders, my muscles beginning to burn.

I better understand the problem with finding footwear impressions or animal tracks. We aren't leaving them either, the forest floor of dead vegetation deep in places, and other areas are rocky. There's very little exposed dirt or mud, and I can't tell what might have been passing through.

"I'm detouring us around the humongous beehive and spiderweb I told you about," Marino announces. "They're over thataway." He points. "Just follow me and you'll be fine."

"We're right behind you," I assure him.

"It's like something you'd expect in Africa," he says. "I'm talking about a spider as big as my palm with bright yellow legs. I don't know what it was and didn't want to spend a lot of time looking at it."

But he did take a video, making sure I saw that too, and I push the images out of my head. As he continues the tour, pointing out other dangers, I get increasingly uncomfortable. I routinely deal with unpleasantries that the average person can't fathom. But I'm not fond of slithery critters and creepy crawlers.

Of course, he's going to point out the sun-splashed rocky area, the thick rotting stump where he encountered the snake. I notice pellet holes and a lot of splintered wood. The dark stains probably are blood.

"...It was coiled and looked as big as a damn fire hose," Marino is saying as I envision the images he sent. "I didn't see it until I was close enough that it could have bit me. Blew its head off with the shotgun before I realized what it was."

"A case of *mis-snaken* identity." Lucy ducks under low-hanging branches of a fir tree that smells like Christmas.

"It was damn scary to almost step on something like that, enough to give you a heart attack," he says.

"Some people have bull snakes as pets," she replies. "The one you shot may have been twenty-five or thirty years old judging by the size. And that's too bad because they aren't dangerous."

"The hell they aren't. They kill things by strangling them, and the one I'm talking about could have taken out a deer or even a person. Where there's one, there's others." He glances back at me. "So, keep an eye out, Doc."

"What did you do with it?" I explain that I'd prefer not happening upon the carcass unexpectedly.

"I tossed it off the beaten path. But like I said, while Tron and I were searching inside the mine you could hear stuff moving around in the dark. Something scraping along, knocking into loose rocks. God only knows what lives in there."

* * *

We've reached the edge of the forest, the lake shining deep blue between trees. Emerging on the rocky shore, I'm startled by dozens of hundred-dollar bills floating in the water with dead leaves. The sight is bizarre, like something from a dream.

"When I was told the Mansons kept a lot of cash here, this wasn't what I expected." I indicate what's gently drifting on the current.

"Hundred-dollar bills were scattered all over the place like a money piñata exploded," Marino replies. "We've collected over forty grand so far, the only ones left in hard-to-reach places like up in the trees and in the lake. You and me will grab what we can from the water while we're recovering the female victim."

Her body is at least fifty feet out, her buttocks and torso showing above the surface. I can see the two hiking poles speared through her back, the handles sticking up, V-shaped like a peace sign. She's been in the water long enough for marine life to do plenty of damage, I have no doubt. But the body in the mineshaft is my priority. It's most at risk for being irretrievably lost.

From the shore I take in the destroyed campsite next to the collapsed wood-framed entrance of the gold mine. Clothing is strewn about, some of it caught in tree branches with paper money, and I find that peculiar. I understand Marino thinking the helicopter might have done it. As I'm looking around, I can't come up with a different explanation.

Shattered electronic equipment, batteries and solar panels litter the churned-up dead leaves, and it's as if something huge and heavy went on a rampage. The camouflage tent is flattened, and Secret Service investigators are collecting evidence. They're taking photographs and video. One of them cuts something out of a poplar tree that has flaming yellow leaves, the cordless electric saw whining and grinding.

"C-notes were all over the place, along with credit cards, driver's licenses," Marino continues to explain. "Passports are ripped up, the pages torn out like a person did it. No tooth-marks I've seen, by the way."

"Why would a bear or any other animal go through wallets and tear up passports?" I point out.

"It wouldn't but an assassin might," Lucy says. "Not the typical hit person, but a bad guy taking care of a problem while leaving a strong message."

"The Mansons pissed off the wrong people," Marino replies. "That's what this is about."

"They won't need passports or anything else anymore," Lucy adds. "Their days of moving around freely are over. They aren't going anywhere ever again. That's the message."

"I worry what's next." Marino continues looking all around us. "Because something is. I feel it like a big storm coming. Like bad juju in the air."

"More like a bad energy field you're detecting." Lucy continues with allusions that she doesn't explain. "It's called hatred and has the pull of a black hole."

A myriad of tiny yellow evidence flags mark the helter-skelter landscape. I imagine what Benton might say about emotions left behind like an echo or an odor. Contempt, rage and arrogance come to mind. A need to annihilate and degrade, I'd add to the list. Also, to shock, to terrify, and I know what Lucy means about hatred. That's here too. I feel it like an undertow.

We follow Marino to the open-sided pup tent investigators set up on the lakeshore. It shields personnel and equipment from the sun but doesn't offer much in the way of privacy. Placing our scene cases and bags inside, we begin to unpack and make plans. I hand out bottles of water and snacks, reminding them we need to stay hydrated and fed.

"Any money you find goes in here." Marino points out a large paper bag where investigators have been placing the hundred-dollar bills. "Most are wet because of all the rain. I figured they were fake the minute I started seeing them everywhere. But I'm not so sure after holding a few of them up to the light and seeing the watermarks. They look damn real."

"Our labs will make sure they're properly preserved and analyzed." Lucy answers in a way that reminds him who's in charge. "If they're counterfeit, we'll know it and hopefully find out the source."

"Were the Mansons into funny money?" Marino and his old-fashioned expressions.

"They were into whatever was profitable that they thought they could get away with," Lucy says.

"That might be why the assailant didn't take the cash." Marino continues speculating as if he's the expert, moving around inside the pup tent, red-faced and sweaty. "Maybe he knew it was fake and that it would be really incriminating if he tried to pass any of it." He's already chugged down the water I gave him, tossing the empty bottle into a trash bag.

"Maybe the money wasn't important. That's what enters my mind based on what I'm hearing." I take a bite of a granola bar as Lucy takes off her drop-leg holster. "Maybe the point was to kill Huck and Brittany Manson. It certainly seems that someone wanted them dead. Assuming that's who the victims are."

"I just don't understand how the money got scattered all over the place." Marino gives Lucy an accusing look. "You're sure the helicopter didn't cause some of the mess out here? It's okay if it did. Shit happens."

"As I mentioned, I would have blown some things, mostly

leaves." She places her .44 Magnum on top of a hard case, sitting down next to it.

"Well, I'm not the only one who's been wondering about it. I heard a couple of your own investigators saying something." Marino hands her a pair of yellow coveralls like the ones he's wearing. She begins pulling them on.

"Everything I fly over is captured on video," she says. "When I review it later, I'll be able to show you what the scene looked like and how much I disturbed it, if at all. We'll re-create exactly what happened."

"I assume we can't know what was here originally, including cash, other valuables, weapons and electronic devices," I reply. "We don't know what the assailant might have made off with...?"

"Uh-oh..." Lucy is distracted by her phone. "Dammit, not again. Well, that's too bad."

She shows us the video image on the display, a lot of dark green pine needles and brown branches with blue sky shining through. Pepper the quadcopter has crashed high up in a tree. He won't be surveilling Buckingham Run further. He might not fly over anything ever again.

"*Pepper, return home*," Lucy says to the app on her phone. "Three of the four blades are spinning, but no bueno," she tells Marino and me. "He's not budging."

She commands Pepper to *fly away*. He doesn't.

"Recently, we've had a bad run of Pixhawk flight controllers that without warning tell the drone to take a nosedive," she explains. "And that's what happened about a mile from here, and I don't know how we'll retrieve him. As you just saw, he's not responding to flight inputs."

While Lucy details her latest technical woes, the investigator with the cordless electric saw is walking this way carrying plastic evidence bags. Removing her face shield and mask, she pushes back her hood.

"How's it going, Doctor Scarpetta?" Tron never calls me by my first name even when she's at the house for supper. "I feel bad inviting you to this party. It won't be fun, and I apologize for that in advance. But we're very glad you're here."

Exotically pretty, with dark eyes and hair, Tron is covered in PPE like everyone else. Her quick smile and gentle disposition belie how fierce she can be if confronted, and I couldn't ask for my niece to have a better investigative partner.

"Pepper bit the dust," Lucy informs her. "Did a swan dive into a pine tree."

"Not again. That's what? Five now? Why does this keep happening?" Tron looks at the video image on Lucy's phone. "How are we supposed to retrieve him?"

"Good question. He's stuck more than seventy feet off the ground, and it's not like we could get a fire truck out here or sling-load someone into the trees." Lucy's frustration flashes. "The only hope is my hovering as close as I can, blowing him down when I take off next. Except it probably would just get him stuck somewhere else. And I don't want to crash the chopper over a drone."

"I'd say that's a wise decision," I reply.

"Well, we need to figure out something, because we can't leave it out here for others to find," Tron says, and I would expect Pepper to have special features that should remain secret.

"I'm going to power him off for now, no point to burning up the battery." Lucy does it while she talks. "If we don't find a way to recover him, I'll have to reformat, returning him to the factory settings, so to speak."

"No eye in the sky while we're working," Marino says. "That's too bad since we don't know for sure what's roaming around out here. I hope we're safe, and I'm not kidding."

"At least we'll still be alerted about anything in the air that might be headed in this direction," Lucy says.

"Like what?" Marino wants to know.

"Drones that aren't ours and other aircraft," Lucy says. "The media, for example."

"And that will happen soon enough. The quicker the bodies are recovered, the better." Tron returns the cordless saw to its plastic case.

"I don't guess any other footprints have showed up," Marino says to her, and she shakes her head.

CHAPTER 11

WHAT'S YOUR ASSESSMENT ABOUT what went on out here?" I hand Tron a bottle of water as we continue talking inside the pup tent.

"Whoever's responsible wants to make this as difficult as possible," she says.

"Making it hard while making a mockery." Lucy defogs the goggles of a full-face respirator. "The ultimate rush these days is creating headline news, and what's happened out here will do it."

"Here's the latest." Tron shows us what's inside the plastic evidence baggies without opening them. "I just collected these."

The four mushroomed copper-jacketed lead slugs and a myriad of fragments were near the entrance of the footpath, she explains. The Mansons were waiting with their guns early this morning in the rainy dark.

"These and other spent rounds were just lying there in the leaves." She places the baggies inside a manila envelope that she begins to label and initial with a Sharpie. "We've recovered ten intact slugs and countless fragments so far. And then I found this just a few minutes ago."

Inside another clear plastic bag is a copper-jacked bullet tarnished brown like an old penny. The large-caliber slug has a pointed nose that's only slightly flattened and oddly painted yellow.

"Armor-piercing." Lucy takes a close look, and I catch a flicker of anger.

"Probably, depending on what it's made of," Marino says as he and I continue getting ready inside the pup tent. "Obviously not lead or it would have been deformed or fragmented when it hit the tree."

"If it's what I think it is, the core is hardened carbon steel," Lucy says.

"You've seen this type of bullet before?" Marino gives her a distrusting look. "What else aren't you telling us?"

"I'm going to conjecture it was fired by a rifle and not a handgun, but it's too soon to say. The labs will have to examine it." That's as much as she'll explain.

"Is this what you were cutting out of the tree when we got here?" I ask Tron.

"Yes. It hadn't penetrated very far. The metal detector led me to it."

"And it's the only one found?"

"That's correct. But it doesn't mean there aren't others."

"The question is how long it's been here," I wonder. "And did the Mansons have a variety of guns? Maybe at some earlier time they were shooting a rifle in the area? Or a handgun that could fire armor-piercing ammo?"

"Based on our surveillance, Huck and Brittany weren't out here target practicing. They drew as little attention to themselves as possible," Tron says. "But at the moment we can't say who shot the bullet or when. Or from what location."

"And usually, bullet penetration tips are plastic and not painted. They're not yellow." Marino holds up the evidence baggie, looking at the slug inside from every angle, feeling the weight of it. "A hefty two hundred and fifty grains, maybe more, I'm betting."

He takes photographs of the projectile through the plastic, and I know what he's doing. He's sending images to firearms examiner Faye Hanaday. He's doing it right under the Secret Service's nose. If Lucy is aware, she doesn't indicate it. Since she doesn't miss much, I'm assuming what he's doing is of no concern to her for some reason.

"What I can say for sure is it tumbled, keyholing the tree, taking a decent-sized chunk out of it," Tron informs us.

"A heavy round like that tumbling through a target would have a lot of stopping power and do a lot of damage," Marino replies. "Maybe whoever took them out makes his own reloads."

"Unlikely," Lucy says as if she has a reason to know.

"If it tumbled, that might suggest it struck an intermediary target first." I take the evidence bag from Marino.

Studying the crude-looking projectile, I note the clearly defined lands and grooves made by the gun barrel that fired it.

"There may be other reasons why it tumbled," Lucy says.

"The damage to the tree appears to be fresh." Tron tosses her soiled gloves into the trash. "But it doesn't mean the bullet is from this morning's attack."

"And I'm guessing there's no cartridge case," Marino says. "Because that would tell us a lot. Maybe everything we need to know."

"Nope," Tron answers. "No gun to go with it either."

"There won't be," Lucy says. "The bad guy's too careful for that. But maybe not as careful about other things."

"The two pistols we've recovered weren't shooting ammo like this, I think it's safe to assume," Tron explains. "At least not during the attack earlier this morning."

She says that the Mansons opened fire with their 10-millimeter Glocks, each with a fifteen-round capacity. Based on the number of cartridge cases found so far, they shot at the intruder at least ten times.

"One of the pistols has seven rounds still in the magazine, the other has ten," Tron says. "Both guns had a round chambered."

"Possible they jammed?" I suggest.

"I don't think so," she says. "The labs will confirm, but it appears the victims stopped firing. Most likely because they were incapacitated."

"Was anything picked up by the cameras' microphones? Screaming, for example?" I ask.

"What I heard sounded like a rapid burst of gunfire at around three-thirty A.M. It went on for maybe half a minute total. Then nothing," Lucy replies. "But I've not analyzed and enhanced the recordings yet. Maybe there will be more I can tease out."

"The killer must have some pretty impressive body armor if he was hit multiple times and not even slowed down," Marino says.

"I can't think of another explanation," Tron agrees.

"Even so?" he adds. "Getting shot while wearing ceramic, steel or even high-tech composite plates is like getting hit with a hammer. He might have kept on coming but he should have been hurting like a mother and knocked off balance."

"This individual was well equipped, possibly with military-grade equipment. He was fearless if not maniacal as he continued toward the campsite," Tron theorizes. "Based on the blood pattern, it looks like the Mansons were brutalized near the entrance of the path, probably where they were waiting in the dark."

"Quickly incapacitating two strong adults at once wouldn't be easy necessarily," I reply. "Is there any indication they tried to run away?"

"Not that I can tell."

"There was nowhere to run," Lucy says. "The only hope was to shoot first."

"The question is how he killed them," Marino replies. "They're shooting at him and what did he do?"

"We've only gotten but so close to the bodies. I don't know what was done to them, except it's brutal," Tron says. "At some point they were dragged or carried and dumped in the mineshaft, the lake."

"Spearing them with their hiking poles was the parting shot," Lucy adds. "By then they were dead or close enough, I'm betting."

"For their sake, I hope so." I pull Tyvek covers over my boots and stuff pairs of gloves in a pocket. That's as much as I need for an initial walk-around.

"How do you want to do this, Doctor Scarpetta?" Tron asks.

"And again, I apologize that the conditions are damn awful. Because we can't bring vehicles in here, we had limited ability to carry what we usually would. Such as gas-powered generators so we could set up auxiliary lighting where appropriate."

"I want to take care of the victim in the mineshaft first," I reply. "We'll harness me up and get him out, hopefully quickly and without too much trouble. Based on video I've reviewed, the opening has caved in over the years and is a tight squeeze."

"Five feet at its widest," Tron tells me. "One whole side is caving in."

"We don't want it collapsing further," I reply. "Do we know how deep it is?"

"Deep enough that when you shine a light down you can't see the bottom," Marino replies as I block out a creeping sense of dread.

"You don't need to go in there," Tron says to me. "Lucy and I are the ones with high-angle rescue training. We can take care of getting him out while you guide us from above."

"No question you're more qualified. But the victims are my responsibility. Something goes wrong, and the buck stops with me."

"No way I could fit, as big as I am." Marino begins with the expected excuses about why it won't be him doing the honors. "We're better off if I'm helping with the ropes."

I don't let on that he can't tolerate the idea of tight spaces. I never assumed it would be Marino descending into a collapsing hole in the ground with nothing but nylon lines to hold him as he dangles over what could be a bottomless pit for all he knows. We've been through this before in confined scenes like burned-down, caved-in and exploded buildings.

Also, elevator shafts, and sewer and steam tunnels. Not so long ago it was a dried-up well where a murder victim's body had been discarded. Marino is claustrophobic. He can't even have an MRI scan without taking a sedative.

"I'm going to need plastic trash bags, rubber bands and the bolt cutters," I explain to everyone. "Once we have the male victim out, Marino and I will deal with the body in the lake."

Before I do anything else, I need a quick overview to get the lay of the land. I direct this at Tron, explaining that I want to see things for myself, starting with how the assailant accessed the campsite. I'd like to be shown the location of the closest trail camera.

"While you do that, I'll give Lucy the nickel tour," Marino says.

* * *

Between the pup tent and the woods are clusters of evidence flags accompanied by numbered markers. A laser scanning station has been set up, and investigators are taking photographs.

"You need any help?" one of them calls out as Tron and I walk through.

"We're not going very far, just to where the closest camera was set up," she says. "If you hear me shooting at something, come running."

The footpath begins next to the mine's entrance with its faded DANGER and GO AWAY warning signs. As we get close, I can see burned and withered foliage caused by flamethrowers and herbicides. I imagine the Mansons in the woods with their guns as an intruder they couldn't see closed in on them.

"It must have been shocking to hear bullets hitting something that isn't stopping," I say to Tron.

This is the first chance we've had to talk alone. I intend to ask a few questions that Lucy isn't answering.

"They knew their time was up," Tron says. "That's for sure."

"Then what?" I ask her. "It was two against one, and it sounds like the Mansons weren't exactly shrinking violets."

"Obviously, they were completely overpowered."

"How?"

"I couldn't tell you," Tron says. "I guess it depends on what you find. I don't know how they died, only that it must have been unpleasant."

"Do we know if they had any of their lanterns or flashlights turned on at the time of the attack?" I ask. "What have you been able to reconstruct?"

My thoughts continue returning to the yellow-tipped bullet she dug out of a tree. It would make sense if the intruder had been armed. Assuming he knew much about the victims, he would have expected them to have their guns out and ready. It's hard for me to imagine an assassin showing up empty-handed. And as Marino likes to say, *don't bring a knife to a gunfight*.

"The camping lanterns we've found are shattered," Tron explains. "But it doesn't appear they were turned on at the time. The switches are in the *off* position."

"As overcast and foggy as it was, I'm going to assume it would have been as dark as outer space," I reply. "One or both of them would have had their phones, I would expect. They probably were watching the livestream from the trail cameras and could hear something big and aggressive headed in their direction."

"I'm fairly confident no lights were on. More analysis has to be done, but that's the way it's looking," Tron says. "You wouldn't want to make yourself an illuminated target. If there was no way to escape, your instinct would be to hide. You'd sit tight in the dark waiting with weapons loaded and ready, hoping and praying you survive."

"Did they have night-vision capabilities? Do we know?" I ask.

"We found a thermal imaging scope that's broken like everything else. But it wouldn't have done any good," Tron says. "The bad guy wasn't going to show up on it just as he didn't on the trail cameras or the helicopter's FLIR."

"Your theory about that?"

"Some type of technology involving sensors."

"And why so much was destroyed?"

"An attempt to ruin the evidence while giving us the finger," she says. "That's my guess."

"I wonder if the Mansons had any idea who or what was coming after them."

"They should have, considering the company they kept." Tron holds up a holly branch heavy with blood-red berries, and we duck under. "It's like I've heard you say. People tend to die the way they lived. And Huck and Brittany ran with the wrong crowd even if it was remotely."

Sunlight filters through the trees as we pass through a small clearing littered with deadwood. A branch snapping somewhere in the shadows nearly sends me out of my skin. I have the feeling again. I sense a presence, my pulse kicking up, a chill touching the back of my neck and raising the hair on my arms.

"Is it just me sensing something weird?" I can't help

but remark. "I keep getting this creepy feeling we're being watched."

"It's not just you. If nothing else there are animals living here undisturbed until now. The biggest thing I worry about is bears. I do *not* want to have a bad encounter with one of those. Or a mountain lion, even though they say we don't have them in Virginia anymore. I know people who beg to differ." She glances back at me, eyeing the canister holstered on my hip. "I don't mean to ruin your day, but as fast as lions and bears move, you'd better be a quick draw. Even if you are, there's a good chance it won't work."

Pepper spray might deter a curious bear or wildcat but not necessarily a predatory one. Even if it runs off, that doesn't mean it won't be back, Tron lets me know as I follow her through kicked-up leaves made slippery by the rain. I've worked my share of deaths by large animals that include amputated extremities and crushed heads. She doesn't need to paint the picture.

"Not much farther," she says as I notice broken branches that are recent.

"Have you taken this path all the way to the Mansons' farm?" I inquire.

"No. Other investigators are searching that area. Nothing much they're finding except a red plastic cap caught in the leaves of a bush. Square-shaped, like the cap from an inhaler, is the first thing that comes to mind."

"Where was it exactly?"

"About midway along the path. It could be important."

"Depending on who lost it," I reply. "Maybe the Mansons did at some point when they were back and forth running errands. I wonder if either of them had allergies or asthma."

"No prescriptions for anything like that, but we can't know what they bought over the counter. They were clever about tossing their garbage, hauling it to different Dumpsters in hopes that people like us weren't given a chance to go through it. I also don't think the plastic cap had been out there very long. Otherwise, the earlier downpour and strong winds would have knocked it to the ground, I suspect."

"Have you noticed anything similar at the campsite?" I ask. "An inhaler or parts of one? Any meds for respiratory inflammation? Did either of the Mansons have COVID at some point, for example? Might they have developed health problems?"

"By all accounts they were very fit," Tron says.

CHAPTER 12

THE FOOTPATH WINDS THROUGH underbrush and woods that block out much of the light, and we hear the distant knocking sound again. Like a heavy stick slowly striking a tree, and Tron records the eerie noise with her phone. We stand still for a moment, listening. Silence. Nothing stirring.

"I'm sorry, but that's just weird as shit," she says.

"We heard it earlier when we were unloading the helicopter."

"I heard it too," she says as we resume walking single file.

I'm noticing more broken branches on either side of the path. They appear to have been made by someone about my height or taller moving foliage out of the way, damaging some of it.

"When did you get here?" I ask.

"I was with Lucy when we started searching for the victims in the helicopter. As it was getting light, I was dropped off with the first group of investigators, and she went back for the others, including Marino."

"Take me through what had happened from the start," I

reply. "I understand that you and Lucy were alerted at the same time when the cameras indicated an intruder at around three A.M."

"That's correct," Tron says. "It appeared the Mansons were in imminent danger, and we headed out to our cars, knowing it wasn't likely we could get there in time."

Lucy and Tron met at the Doomsday Bird's hangar and they were taking off within an hour. When they located the campsite, they couldn't be sure if there were multiple victims.

"From the air, all you could see was the female's body in the lake, the belongings strewn everywhere, the tent flattened," Tron says.

"What did you think might have happened to the husband?" I ask. "You knew from having them under surveillance that Huck and Brittany were out here together."

"We assumed he was dead." Tron steps over a rotting log. "If so, he was in the water somewhere, we decided at first. We searched the lake and along the shore from the air, not seeing any sign of him. But we also didn't know for a fact that he wasn't involved in Brittany's death. That maybe it was Huck we were hearing on the footpath on his way in and out."

"It's certainly a consideration that he might have staged something like that to get away while getting rid of her," I reply. "Meanwhile, we continue looking for his body, not realizing he's fled the country."

"Their rosy relationship was bullshit like everything else about them," Tron says. "They'd screwed around on each other before, almost getting divorced a few years ago. We didn't know everything going on with them. I've even entertained the possibility that the bodies aren't the Mansons. That they faked all this so they could flee, and while we're out here in the woods, they're on a private jet headed to Moscow or Dubai."

"Is that what you seriously think?" I ask. "Because we'll know soon enough about the identities."

"Look, just us talking? I've got no doubt it's the Mansons. I really don't see who else it might be," she says. "But we're also not dealing with the usual offender. I think that's pretty obvious already. I have a feeling you're sensing that there's a lot going on we can't be open about."

"Why would a bullet have a yellow-painted tip? I'm familiar with color coding like black, red, purple. But not yellow. And not painted."

"It's not something I've seen before now. Not for armor-piercing," she says. "Usually when someone refers to a yellow tip, what they mean is the observation bullets that flash and create a lot of smoke on impact. Similar to tracer bullets and used in training. That's not what I dug out of the tree."

"I'm wondering if that's what the assailant was shooting. Possible he showed up with a firearm?"

"I know I would have," Tron says.

We round a bend in the path, colorful leaves drifting down through motes of light shining through canopies. I detect the sharp scent of pine mingled with the pungency of decaying vegetation. Mosquitoes whine around us like kamikaze bombers.

"When Marino got here, you escorted him inside the mine as I understand it," I then say. "When did he find the footprint?"

"Within minutes. No one else had noticed it yet."

"Where were you when he discovered it?"

"I was just inside the entrance, scanning with a metal detector. The other agents were outside doing other things."

"Let's just put our cards on the table, Tron," I say to her bluntly. "Do you have any reason to think Marino planted the footprint?"

"No way."

"Or that anybody else here might have done something like that?"

"Absolutely not."

"Because you must know that the accusations will fly fast and furiously if and when the word is out. There will be suspicions about Marino being responsible."

"Believe me, I know. Some of the other agents are already wondering it, to be honest."

"Why did he decide to make the cast himself? Did he say he was going to do it? Or did it simply happen?" I ask. "Technically, he was out of bounds. It's not up to us to collect that type of evidence."

"Bottom line?" Tron says. "Marino had plaster of Paris in one of your crime scene cases. We didn't bring anything that could be used for casting, and it's not something we typically handle. He seemed to know what he was doing."

"He does know what he's doing and wouldn't mean to cause a stink. But I'm worried," I reply.

"I'm afraid the stink has already started." The way she says it is ominous. "I don't want to distract you, Doctor Scarpetta."

"It's a little late for that. Sounds like you have an update. May as well tell me."

"As it's turning out, the governor isn't the only one who's gotten an anonymous voice mail allegedly from The Republic, claiming two traitors are dead," Tron says. "Also, several TV stations and newspapers, including CNN and the *Washington Post*. And of course, Dana Diletti is having a field day talking about her *dogfight with the chief medical examiner's military-looking helicopter*."

"People must think I have a very generous budget," I reply.

* * *

Tron points out an oak tree along the Mansons' footpath. The trunk is marked with an evidence tag some four feet off the ground where the bark is scarred. She tells me this is where the closest trail camera was found.

"From here we're more than fifty yards from the campsite," she explains. "No sound was going to be detected unless it was loud like gunshots."

"How many cameras did the Mansons set up?" From here the path continues through the woods for as far as I can see, dissolving into shadows.

"A dozen strategically placed. None are inside the campsite itself, and none inside their house," Tron says. "They made sure they weren't going to be spied on by their own surveillance devices during private moments."

"Have other investigators found anything significant inside the house or anywhere else so far?" I ask as we start walking back. "I'm wondering about any sign of a break-in. If the Mansons were taken out by someone, then I should think the person responsible would be interested in what might be inside their home, their store or anywhere else they frequented."

"We've got agents inside Wild World even as we speak," she

says. "Also, at their fulfillment center. I doubt we'll find much in any of those places. When Huck and Brittany isolated in the woods, they took their most valuable belongings with them, such as wallets, passports and other important documents. All of which were scattered and deliberately destroyed, as you know."

She continues telling me the details of what's been found at the campsite, and the Mansons weren't roughing it as much as one might imagine. They had bedrolls, linens, an electric fan and space heater inside a tent that was watertight and spacious. A cooler with bear-proof locks was filled with steaks, chicken and other foods. There were snacks and all sorts of creature comforts including booze.

"Also, Wi-Fi hotspots for high-speed internet, and backup power sources for laptops and satellite phones," Tron says. "They have a water filtration system. Solar panels they set up could generate enough power to stay out here for weeks as long as their food held out."

We've reached Marino and Lucy near the entrance of the path. Off to one side of it are huge fir trees, the forest floor crowded with evidence flags and markers.

"This is where it happened. They were probably hiding behind the trees when the bad guy showed up." Marino says this to all of us. "It's where we found the spent cartridge cases, the slugs and frag. As you can see, there's a lot of blood and I've made sure we collected more than enough samples."

I bend down to get a closer look at what he's pointing out, flies alighting and crawling on coagulated blood and bits of drying brain tissue. From here I can see the tree where Tron dug out the rifle slug. Nearby is the flattened camouflage tent, big enough to sleep six, and Tron says that when investigators first got here this is what they saw.

"The tent was on the ground where it is now," she explains. "It's like something big and powerful went on a rampage, intent on destroying everything."

"Considering the footprint I found, I'd be careful with descriptions like that," Marino says.

Back inside the pup tent, Lucy hands me a blaze-orange Mustang anti-exposure suit with built-in boots, gloves and a watertight hood. Spreading it open on the ground, I sit down because it's not possible for me to suit up in a Mustang while standing. I cover my boots with plastic bags, making it easier to pull on the neoprene legs. Then I'm on my feet again, working my arms into the sleeves and zipping up most of the way.

I tuck a flashlight, plastic bags and rubber bands into pockets, grabbing a respirator that I'll put on later. Gathering equipment, we head to the entrance of the mine, framed in old logs and planks of graying wood. Flashlights on, and we duck our heads as we pass through the opening, the air instantly chilled and damp on my face. I smell dirt and rotting wood.

Then the space opens considerably, enough that Marino can stand up straight without bumping his head. Tree roots from above ground have grown through the ceiling, dangling and twisting like claws. When they touch me it's unnerving. I recognize the mining tools, the spiderweb-shrouded ore cart from the videos I've reviewed. Our lights cut through the pitch darkness, finding the narrow opening of the mineshaft.

The timber supports around it are broken and halfway collapsed. Evidence markers and flags dot the rocky floor where

Marino discovered bloodstains. Likely from the victim being dragged, he explains. I shine my light over the dirty, gritty area, not seeing much blood.

"There was very little," he says. "I collected most of it."

"If there wasn't much it's probably because the victim was dead by then," I reply.

"You want to see the real McCoy?" Marino says. "I'll show you what's left of it."

He directs his light at a tunnel's black opening beyond the mineshaft, the stone and dirt sparkling with shiny flecks of what I suspect are gold. Leading me to an upside-down banker's box, he picks it up. The outline of the huge foot in the dark gray dirt would be easy to miss.

"Obviously, it was a whole lot sharper before I poured in the liquid plaster." Marino explains why all that's left is a bloblike shape, the details mostly obliterated. "I was masked, gloved, the whole nine yards, making sure I didn't contaminate anything."

"I wonder if this area floods," I reply. "Because it seems relatively dry considering last night's storm."

"Exactly what I was thinking, and you're right, Doc. We don't know how long the footprint has been here." He again covers it with the banker's box.

"I wonder if the Mansons ever came in here for any reason."

"No sign of it if they did," Marino says. "But it's not like I've been beyond where we are right now. It wouldn't be safe going in any deeper."

Returning to the entrance, we unfold two heavy-duty black vinyl body pouches, tucking one inside the other to form a double barrier. Marino spreads them out while Tron and Lucy assist with my harness. They clip carabiners on sturdy nylon ropes, a belay rappelling device on the main line.

I step close to the edge of the mineshaft's opening, my light illuminating the caved-in wooden scaffolding. A ladder is rotted and missing rungs, vanishing into the abyss. Shining my light on the male victim's nude body caught in crisscrossed logs, I calculate how I'm going to do this.

"There's not much supporting him except the hiking poles he's impaled with, and they're bent," I say to Marino. "If it wasn't for them, he probably would have dropped all the way down, however far that might be. It makes me wonder if the killer intended on the bodies being found."

"I've been wondering the same thing." Marino shines his light down the shaft and I can't see the bottom. "This one in particular is hanging by a thread and he might not have been noticed. This won't be easy and don't feel bad if it doesn't work out, Doc. If his body gets jostled or other things do, gravity's gonna win. If he falls, just don't go with him."

"I'll try to remember that." I will myself to block my emotions completely before he succeeds in freaking me out.

"If he tumbles down out of sight, it won't be us getting him out," Marino lets me know. "I'm not sure anybody could. Let's hope we don't lose him, because it will be hard as hell to explain."

CHAPTER 13

WHEN YOU'RE CLOSE, WE'LL ease the tension on your chest rig, making it possible for you to flip over facedown." Lucy starts giving me the details, our lights dancing and casting shadows along the mine's stony walls and floor. "You've got a safety line on your back, a personal anchor system that will keep you suspended. When you're stabilized, you'll put this on him. And that should do it."

She attaches an additional rescue harness to another line as I put on the full-face respirator, hearing the loud sound of my breathing as if scuba diving.

"Ready?" Lucy asks me.

"As I'll ever be." My answer is muffled through the respirator's speaking diaphragm.

I crouch by the edge of a black hole in the earth that reminds me of a toothless mouth. Sitting down in the rocky dirt, I inch-worm myself closer, dangling my legs over the opening, trying not to look down. Grit and small rocks fall in, clicking against whatever they hit. I ease off the edge, the open shaft yawning under me as I gently swing.

Coarse granite walls sparkle in my light as I slowly descend in a seated position, the straps tight under my arms and around my upper thighs. Careful about banging into scaffolding and rocks, I steady myself by touching my feet to the opposite wall. The opening above is getting smaller and more out of reach. I'm fifteen feet down, I estimate. Then it's closer to twenty.

"EVERYTHING OKAY?" Tron peers over the edge, shouting.

"AFFIRMATIVE." I give her a thumbs-up.

"YOU READY FOR US TO LOWER THE HARNESS?"

"AFFIRMATIVE. AND I'M GOING TO NEED AS MUCH LIGHT AS YOU CAN SHINE DOWN HERE."

Then the harness is descending, followed by the bolt cutters. Keeping my feet planted on the wall, I walk down it until the body is inches below my back. I'm going to need both hands, and I turn off my flashlight, tucking it into a pocket. Working in a chiaroscuro of glare and dark shadows while suspended in the harness, I'm mindful of not losing my balance or bearing.

I'm trying to adjust my position without starting an oscillation that could slam me into jagged rock walls. I don't want to knock into wooden scaffolding that's partially collapsed and treacherous with exposed rusty nails. The victim is snagged and partially held in place by the protruding hiking poles. One false move and I could send him tumbling out of reach forever.

Carefully... Carefully... I turn myself over, suspended by the vertical line attached to my back. I grab the harness hanging nearby as I'm aware of a noise in the void below. Rocks knock together, something moving. Then I hear a huff and a deep quiet growl that send a thrill of fear running through me. Something squeaks past that I suspect is a bat, followed by more huffing and growling that sound closer.

My face mask is inches from the dead man's head. I can see part of the skull is missing in back, brain tissue avulsed, blood slowly dripping on my sleeve from a flap of scalp. Digging in a pocket, I pull out a black plastic bag, shaking it open. I work it over the head, securing it around the neck with a rubber band. Arranging the harness under the arms and across the chest, I fasten quick-connect buckles, my hands awkward in thick gloves.

The leg straps are harder, the victim muscular and slippery, blood oozing from his injuries when I move him. Rigor mortis is well on the way to being set, and he's difficult to maneuver. Should the body start spinning, that would be disastrous. The hiking poles are some five feet long. He was stabbed through the back, the lower part of the shaft protruding from the chest. I notice other perforations.

Using the bolt cutters, I snap through the hollow aluminum, freeing him from the scaffolding. I place sections of the hiking poles inside a bag that I clip to a rope. Another low growl and what sounds like something mumbling as I'm being pulled back up to the surface. I can't get there fast enough. Turning on my flashlight, I'm startled by pairs of round orange eyes in a rocky recess.

Owls, I decide. They don't blink as I ascend, leaving them behind. Tron and Lucy help me climb out while Marino begins hoisting the body with a handheld battery-powered winch. For a moment I'm weak in the knees but don't show it, and if I never do something like this again, I'll be most grateful. Then the bag-covered head rises from the darkness to the whirring of the electric motor.

The victim sits froglike in the harness. Arms and legs are bent at awkward angles, the hands wounded and covered with dried blood. The dusky discoloration to certain areas of the body and the pattern of rigor mortis tell me he was in this position when he died or soon after.

"What I'm seeing so far is consistent with him having been dead at least eight hours in somewhat chilly conditions," I decide, and it's now almost noon.

"Which is consistent with the time we think they were attacked at about three-thirty this morning when the gunfire sounded," Tron says as we lift out the body and Marino grabs the back of the harness.

He lifts it up without any help from the rest of us, and I get a better look at abrasions and lacerations. They're from being dragged over rocks and dropped into the mineshaft, I explain. The left leg is fractured, the jagged femur protruding through skin, and animals had begun their damage. The left foot has been raggedly amputated, the other one badly mangled.

"I have no doubt this happened postmortem, perhaps the culprit of a bobcat, a puma, a bear. But the linear wounds to the wrists and hands weren't caused by tooth or claw. They're incisions." I point them out. "Inflicted by something sharp like a knife."

"Defense injuries?" Marino suggests.

"I seriously doubt it." I help him place the body inside the sheet-lined double pouches. "They aren't random like you'd see when someone's flailing, trying to ward off a knife or some other sharp instrument. These cuts are more uniform, and I see no evidence the victim was moving at the time they were inflicted."

"That's weird. Why would someone do that?" Tron asks me.

"At the moment, I have no idea, but suspect the injuries are postmortem or were inflicted close to death."

As Marino takes photographs, I use a lighted magnifying glass to examine a gaping perforation in the front of the neck that might correlate with an irregular wound in the upper back that's as big as an orange. Rolling the body on its side, I examine what I suspect is an entrance wound, blood seeping out and dripping. The perforation exits through the large wound in the upper back, I tell Marino, and he tosses me a towel.

"Entrance and exit." I point them out. "The wound through and through."

"Maybe from being stabbed with a hiking pole?" he suggests.

"It wouldn't look like this," I reply. "The structures of the neck have been destroyed, similar to what I see in wounds from assault rifles."

"Maybe explaining the copper slug I cut out of the tree," Tron says.

"Could be," I reply. "And a bullet might have caused the damage to his head, part of his occipital skull missing in back."

"Or maybe in their panic Huck and Brittany shot each other accidentally," Marino says as we zip up the pouches.

"Their clothing should have something to say," I reply. "Where is it?"

"Bagged already," he says as we place the pouched body into a rescue basket. "Both victims appear to have been fully dressed in sweatsuits, boots, socks, coats, all of it bloody."

"It appears to have been cut off them after the fact and flung all over the place," Tron says. "Which is weird like everything else. Why cut off the clothing to begin with?"

"We need to make sure it goes back on the helicopter with us," I tell Marino.

"I think the killer fucking hated these people." He helps me pick up the rescue basket.

"That and maybe he was looking for something," Lucy says.

"Did you notice bullet holes in the clothing?" I ask. "Anything else that might give us important information about how their injuries were inflicted?"

"As slashed up and bloody as everything is, it's hard to tell much," Marino replies.

* * *

We leave the rescue basket outside the pup tent in the shade for now. I decontaminate myself with distilled water and disinfectant while Marino sprays down his yellow Tyvek PPE. He takes it off, his field clothes underneath similar to mine. Next, he finds an immersion suit, spreading it open on the ground and sitting down the same way I did.

"You going to take your gun?" Lucy watches him clip his pistol to his belt.

"Yep. I'll wear it inside my Mustang suit. That way if there's a problem? At least I've got a chance."

"A good idea. Because where there's a Bigfoot? There may also be a Nessie," she answers.

"We don't know a damn thing about what lives in the lake. At least it's stream fed." He pulls trash bags over his boots.

"Fresh water in other words. So we don't have to worry about sharks. But there's bound to be other nasty stuff swimming around in there that we don't want to encounter. Which is why I told you to bring the snakebite kit." He says this to me.

"A waste of time."

"Moccasins are the biggest threat, and you don't necessarily see them until they're way too close for comfort." He feels the need to add, "You get bit by one of those and it's curtains. One gets anywhere near and I'm blowing it the hell out of the water."

"Just don't hit me by mistake," I reply.

Pulling on the legs of his Mustang suit, he fusses and fumes as he struggles with the neoprene. He works his hands into the gloves attached to the sleeves, his mood worsening by the moment. We gather more body pouches, a rescue basket and a bright orange lifeguard float attached to a tether.

"...Muskies can get to be six feet long." Marino continues ruining my mood as I clip a flotation bag to a ring on the side of my suit.

We trudge across the narrow rocky shore. Awkward and Gumby-like in bright orange, we pull on our hoods, zipping up all the way. We don't have snorkels or scuba gear. The goal is to float on our backs, keeping our faces out of the water.

"...Catfish can get huge too," Marino persists as we wade in. "And they'll eat pretty much anything, including dead bodies. Nobody's been fishing here or hunting either one, I'm assuming. So you can imagine how big things have gotten."

"I prefer not to imagine anything you're talking about," I reply, the water now up to our waists.

Blowing into tubes attached to our suits, we inflate the neck pillows attached to the collars. The neoprene is buoyant as we float on our backs, paddling with our hands and feet, the lake smelling musty and pungent.

"Could be a Chernobyl effect too," Marino goes on, and I wish he wouldn't. "Because of all the contamination, animals mutating after centuries of mercury, lead and shit like that. For sure, that would change the DNA of things, right?"

"Heavy metals can cause birth defects, among other serious problems," I reply.

"Meaning we might see a two-headed snake or some other freak of nature."

"You're not making this any easier, Marino."

As I back-paddle, my head supported by the neck pillow, I'm staring up at blue sky and bright sunlight. I've sweated off much of the sunblock I put on earlier and can feel my skin beginning to burn. I'm mindful of what's below that might be attracted to our bright movement. I keep up my scan for anything swimming along the surface.

"I'm seeing cash ahead, Doc." Marino speeds up, lunging for several hundred-dollar bills.

We begin grabbing what we can reach without going too much out of our way. I tuck the soggy money into the flotation bag attached to my suit, and within minutes we've collected thousands of dollars.

"There must be another twenty grand floating around out here at least," Marino marvels. "No telling how much cash they had and what might have sunk to the bottom or washed downriver."

The female victim is barely drifting with the current just ahead, a hundred-dollar bill caught in her long brown hair fanned out on the lake's surface. I gently grip the rubber handle of a hiking pole impaling her torso from back to front. There are two of them, the tips sharp like arrows. As I move her closer, she bobs in the water, the shadows of fish darting.

Placing the lifeguard tube under her, we clip the strap in place, turning the body onto its back. She stares up with empty eye sockets and bared teeth, her lips, earlobes and other delicate body parts nibbled off.

"Jesus." Marino blows out a big breath. "Some things I never get used to, and being fish food is one of them."

"She's been facedown in the water since death or soon after it," I reply.

Rigor mortis is fully set, her limbs stiffly fixed in the position they're in, bent as if she's crawling. Her face and posterior trunk are suffused dusky red from noncirculating blood settling with gravity, a postmortem change called livor mortis.

"By all indications," I explain, "she and the male victim were killed at least eight hours ago."

"I'm betting within minutes of each other," Marino says as we swim backwards, towing her to shore.

Both of us are holding the rope when something starts tugging it, pulling the body under the surface. Then it bobs back up.

"What the fuck!" Marino cranes his neck as we feel it again, like a large animal striking bait. "I don't know what that is but it's not good...!"

I look back at the shore getting closer, thank God. More tugging, and Marino curses loudly.

"You guys doing okay?" Tron calls out.

"Something huge is following us and trying to eat the body!"

he shouts, and a prehistoric-looking reptilian head the size of a football breaks the surface close enough to touch. "HOLY FUCK!" Marino paddles frantically, splashing loudly.

Just as quickly the creature slips under again, the large shadow of it vanishing into the deeper darker water. Another tug, and we keep backstroking while towing the body like a grotesque float.

"A snapping turtle, the biggest I've ever seen!" Marino lets me know in a near panic, wide-eyed, his face scarlet. "Even bigger than the one I saw earlier."

"Well, don't go rooting around for your gun," I reply as he fumbles with his zipper. "Let's just get to shore."

"That thing could bite off your hand! Maybe your whole leg!" he exclaims, and we're paddling as fast as we can. "You imagine how old it is? Probably been living in here since the damn Civil War!" He's breathless and won't shut up.

CHAPTER 14

AT LAST, I FEEL the rocky lake bottom beneath us again, and we wade the rest of the way in. As we reach the shore, I grab the body under the back of the knees while Marino lifts it from the armpits. The palms and the soles of the feet are shriveled, a phenomenon called *washerwoman's skin*. I smell the foul odor of decomposition, the flesh slippery and cold as we carry her.

It's not possible to know at a glance if she's Brittany Manson, thirty-eight years old with brown hair and eyes according to the Department of Motor Vehicles and her passport. The dead woman is slender and of average height, with well-defined musculature, her hair brown. Without knowing anything, I would estimate she's in her thirties or forties.

Her wounds remind me of those sustained by the male, and I'm increasingly suspicious the two were shot while hiding in the woods. Afterward their bodies were mutilated and discarded angrily, contemptuously like garbage, and I wonder if they had any idea who was after them. Possibly what Marino suggested is true, and the victims shot each other accidentally.

But that wouldn't explain the rest of what was done to them, the damage far beyond ensuring someone is dead or difficult to identify. Vinyl pouches are spread open inside the rescue basket and we set down the body. Tron and Lucy also thought to bring the bolt cutters, and I'm not touching anything until I'm decontaminated. I close my eyes and hold my breath as I'm fogged from head to toe with what smells a lot like Lysol.

Unzipping my immersion suit far enough that I can take off the hood, I work my hands out of the attached gloves. I free my arms from the sleeves, leaving them to dangle and drip as I unclip the bag of soggy cash, handing it over to Lucy. I pull on exam gloves and a face mask, picking up the bolt cutters, spraying them with disinfectant.

"I sure do hate cutting through the hiking poles. But it's the only way we can close the pouches," I explain. "Make sure we capture it on video as we continue to make a record of what we do. And the goal is to avoid inflicting additional injury."

Marino steadies the body on its side while I cover the hiking poles' rubber grips with plastic cling wrap. I snap through the shafts front and back. The hollow composite sections quietly clack as I place them in a bag that Tron holds open.

"Just like the other ones," Marino says as we zip up the pouches.

He explains that the four hiking poles impaling the victims are tactical and the same brand. They're lightweight, telescoping into a small size one can fit in a carry bag. They also can be used for self-defense, and Wild World sells them.

"I bought a set of them a while back for when I treasure hunt," Marino says. "Usually, there are different tips you can screw on, including ones that turn it into a weapon. It would be easy to spear someone through and through as long as you don't hit bone."

"I'm going to guess that was the final violent act, and meant to horrify," I reply as we pick up the rescue basket, collecting our gear.

"Gratuitously cruel," Lucy says as we return to the pup tent. "The work of a sadist who wants to scare people into submission. Someone who gets off on it, even finds it amusing."

"Creating a sensation seems to be the goal." Tron doesn't react emotionally to much, but I can tell she's unnerved.

"A need to completely overpower and mutilate, an effort to intimidate and make a mockery of us. To goad and taunt," Lucy adds as if she has insight we don't. "Payback."

"For what?" Marino asks.

"Some people seem to be born seeking revenge," she replies. "They arrive on this planet ready to punish. And if you give them a reason, they'll never get past it. And whatever happens? It's your own fault if you ask them."

"Also known as a psychopath," Tron adds. "That's what we're up against."

"Which psychopath?" Marino keeps pushing for answers.

"Unfortunately, there's more than one," Lucy says.

"It will be helpful to hear what Benton thinks," I reply.

"I don't need fancy degrees to know that what was done to the Mansons feels personal," Marino answers.

We set down the rescue basket next to the other one in the shade of a red maple, its leaves vibrant when touched by sunlight. The time is now half past two P.M., and the temperature is dropping as the sun dips lower. Another front is headed in our direction, this one leaving heavy snow. But the storm is expected to blow out to sea before reaching this area.

"Bottom line if these two people were taken out? This isn't how a hit goes down." Marino unzips his Mustang suit. "Usually, the killer is in and out like a shadow. He doesn't draw attention like leaving anonymous phone messages taking credit and bragging about it. Whoever did this was familiar with the victims and probably resented the shit out of them."

Pulling off sopping wet neoprene, he and I clean up and disinfect some more, and I'm grateful there's no mirror. I must be quite the wilted sight, my hair plastered to my head, my nose sunburned. It's important to stay hydrated and fed, and I pass around more bottles of water and snacks. We take care of other necessities before ferrying the rescue baskets and supplies through the woods.

Marino is in the lead, Lucy right behind him. Tron and two other investigators bring up the rear. It's slower going with our unwieldy cargo, bumping and banging into trees, getting snagged in bushes. Trudging through wet leaves, we wait as a black rat snake sizzles into a thicket ahead of us. A red-tailed hawk watches from the high perch of a dead tree bleached pale gray.

A white-tailed deer bounds through brush, and there are other noises, other signs of life stirring. I'm aware of the canister of pepper spray on my belt, trying not to think about a massive bear or wildcat suddenly charging us. The forest is much more restless than before, and as we reach the dry creek bed clearing, I sense something wrong before I realize what it is.

* * *

"What the hell?" Lucy stops in her tracks.

The helicopter's four main rotor blades slowly turn in the gusting wind. I notice the red tiedown straps some distance away. They're piled on top of a large flat rock where Pepper the drone quietly awaits as if he flew here on his own. His lights are out, the power off.

"Fuck." Marino's hand drops closer to his gun.

"Nobody move." Lucy sets down the hard cases she's carrying. "Stay right where you are."

She slides her .44 Magnum out of the holster. Walking closer to the Doomsday Bird, she again tells us to hold our position.

"I'm making sure we don't have any unexpected company." She has her gun in both hands, the barrel pointed up.

Walking closer to the tiedown straps piled on the rock, Lucy announces that they aren't damaged.

"Nothing's bent or torn that I can see. They've been unclipped and not forced." She walks around looking for a possible explanation.

"How could this happen? What idiot would take it upon himself to untie the rotor blades?" Marino directs this at Tron. "Who was near the helicopter besides your people?" He means the two investigators with us.

"No way we did this," one of them answers.

"We helped haul supplies when asked, and it wasn't like this then," the other volunteers. "The drone wasn't here. Last we heard it was stuck in a tree."

"None of us have been near the helicopter in the past couple of hours. After Pepper crashed, we couldn't necessarily see what might be in the area," Tron says. "I just know that none of us tampered with anything and I have no idea what that means."

"It means that something else is responsible. Something with opposable thumbs," I reply.

"Let's load up and get the hell out of here," Lucy decides with a resolve I recognize.

I can tell when she feels threatened. All of us are on high alert as we set down what we're carrying. We begin securing the rescue baskets to the wide composite platform skids, attaching straps to fast-roping hardware. Slowly walking around the helicopter, Lucy makes sure nothing has been tampered with, checking the radomes and the landing gear.

Using handrails and footholds, she climbs up to open the cowling. She examines the main rotor blades, precariously holding on like Spider-Man.

"So far so good," she says when back on the ground. "Everything looks the way it should. Nothing to make me think sabotage such as explosive devices planted or anything else that could cause a major problem."

"I know I'm feeling better about the flight back," Marino snarks. "Getting here was bad enough."

Pulling on nitrile gloves, Lucy picks up Pepper the drone and begins inspecting it while Tron records everything with her phone.

"He's powered off, has a broken prop and his parachute didn't deploy when he started his nosedive," Lucy lets us know.

"Almost like he was trying to commit suicide," Tron explains. "We've seen the same thing with other drones that malfunctioned."

"Like I said, I think you're being hacked. Maybe the Russians are doing it," Marino replies. "It can happen to the best of us," he adds for Lucy's benefit.

"I'm not going to do anything further now." She unlocks the baggage compartment. "We'll look at everything in the labs."

"You sure Pepper couldn't have started working again and was able to fly back here?" Marino is crouched by an open scene case, getting out several large plastic bags. "I mean, the battery's not dead, right?"

"It's fine, almost fully charged," Lucy says.

"So, maybe Pepper picked up some rogue signal that powered it back on?" he proposes. "I don't guess it could remove the tiedowns. I assume there's no drone that could do that."

"Not without grippers of some sort, and Pepper's not equipped with those," Lucy tells him. "He has a *Return To Home* feature, but that's not what happened. The power can't turn back on magically."

"Maybe it could if it was hacked into?" Marino helps her package the evidence, the tiedowns in one plastic bag, the drone in the other.

"Even if that happened somehow? It wouldn't explain how he unsnagged himself from the tree and flew back here with at least one inoperable prop. And he didn't." Lucy opens the app on her phone that controls Pepper the drone, showing us a red screen that reads *Offline*.

"I know that none of us climbed up seventy feet in a pine tree to retrieve him," Tron replies. "I've got no idea how this happened."

"There's an answer somewhere, but for now we need to get the bodies out of here," Lucy says as we continue looking around us uneasily.

For the next little while we lash the rescue baskets to the wide platform skids, the black body bags morbid cocoons that will be obvious to anyone looking. Then Lucy is opening a cabin door. She shows Marino where to sit, and the helicopter shifts under his weigh as he climbs in. I return to the copilot's seat as Tron and the other investigators dissolve into the woods, keeping their distance while we get ready to take off.

"Like the doc said, you'd need humanlike hands or some type of robotic gripper to unclip the tiedowns," Marino says as we put on our harnesses. "A bear or coyote couldn't do something like that. And we don't have gorillas or orangutans in this country. Not even chimps or monkeys except in zoos. I don't guess this fancy helicopter automatically films everything around it when turned off and just sitting?"

"You'd have to try to break in to trigger the cameras," Lucy answers as we shut our doors. "Or mess with the cowling, the radomes, the fuel cap, that sort of thing. Pepper was supposed to be our watchdog, and unfortunately that's not worked out very well."

* * *

Warning horns blare as Lucy turns the battery on, rolling the throttles, starting the engines. Moments later, we're lifting off in a blizzard of autumn leaves swirling crazily. Trees are frenzied, the engines roaring like a tornado as we rise straight up into a bright sky streaked with clouds that portend a change in weather.

"Yikes, that's too close for comfort," Lucy says for the effect. "Gotta remember to update my will."

Marino doesn't answer and probably has his headset off for the time being. He's out of sight behind the partition separating us from the back cabin. No doubt he's closed his eyes, clutching an airsick bag while Lucy makes a tight turn, leveling out of the steep ascent.

She's back on the radio, contacting the Manassas tower, and we're cleared through their airspace. I unlock my phone, and it auto-syncs to the helicopter's Bluetooth. I call my secretary. While we're headed back to the office, she can give us an update.

"We're on our way," I say right off when Shannon answers.

"Hello, Doctor Scarpetta, I'm very glad to hear from you," she says, and her Irish brogue is a comfort. "There's a lot going on, as you might imagine."

"Please check on Fabian and make sure the REMOTE is ready. The tarmac in front should have been cleared so we can land right there and get the bodies inside the trailer as quickly and discreetly as possible."

"I don't believe you'll be able to keep much off camera no matter what," Shannon tells me. "The media is parked along the road outside our building. I understand there's a drone zooming about. And I can only imagine what it will be like if certain other details get out."

"What details?" I have a sinking feeling.

"I suppose I shouldn't ask."

"About what?"

"If it's true about Bigfoot," Shannon says.

"What are you hearing?"

"Faye told me about a footprint found at the scene," she replies, and I know what Marino has attempted.

Faye Hanaday is the top forensic examiner in the tool marks and firearms lab inside my building. I'm aware that he's sent her images of the yellow-tipped bullet. Apparently, he's shared more than that with her, the two of them buddies.

"Faye said Marino's bringing in a plaster cast he made. That he wants her to meet him at the helicopter so he can give her the box," Shannon explains. "Faye said to let her know when you're a few minutes out so she can head to the parking lot."

"Nice try, Marino." Lucy speaks up.

"Shit," he replies from the back cabin. "Faye wasn't supposed to say anything."

"Oh, she hasn't to anyone else. You needn't worry about that," Shannon answers in our headsets. "Faye's told only me. She assumed you knew what was going on, Doctor Scarpetta."

"Not about that."

"She figured Marino had told you what he's doing." What she's really saying is that he should have.

"Hadn't had the chance," he says, and that's baloney.

"I see. Oh dear, I hope I've not caused a kerfuffle," Shannon says, and I know her chess moves.

"I just wanted Faye to take a look," Marino explains. "I don't see any harm in it."

"Except it's not our evidence," I reply.

He's attempting an end run around the Secret Service, worried that the cast might disappear inside their labs forever. He's been saved from himself by my secretary. Sounding as innocent as the day is long, Shannon knows exactly what she's doing.

"You're well aware that the cast and other relevant evidence are our jurisdiction, Marino." Lucy sounds scary stern, but the expression on her face is amused.

"You don't need to tell me about jurisdiction as if I just fell off the potato truck."

"I don't know what truck you fell off of," she says. "But I've got no problem with having your labs taking a first look. Footwear, tire tracks, tool marks usually aren't our focus. And Faye Hanaday is one of the best. I won't argue with that."

"Absolutely, and she's nice to boot," Shannon says.

"What else should we know before we get there?" I ask her.

"The state police are here, which is a good thing. Otherwise it would be poor Wyatt holding down the fort by himself."

"Wyatt's still there? I thought Tina Downs was taking over at noon."

"She called in literally at the last minute. Claimed she took a rapid COVID test and was positive. What a shock."

"The third time in two months," I reply, and it's one of those things you can't say much about.

"Tina didn't come in and won't until she tests negative," Shannon explains. "That's what she said, and there was no one to cover her shift…"

My secretary goes on to tell me Buckingham Run is all over the news. The phones are going crazy about those deaths and others, everything happening at once. Shannon goes on to inform me that Blaise Fruge needs to discuss the Nan Romero case. The Alexandria police investigator has troubling information about the dentist who allegedly committed suicide the day before yesterday.

Also, FBI Agent Patty Mullet needs to speak to me ASAP, and I know how pushy she can be. I don't like her. I never have.

"What does she want?" I ask.

"She has questions about a number of things, including the two ex-cons killed in last night's attempted home invasion," Shannon says. "Such terrible people, and I know I shouldn't say it, but they got what they deserved, dressing like clowns."

"What questions?" I inquire.

"She said it was confidential."

"Thanks. I'll have to deal with all this later." I end the call as Lucy points out an aircraft on the distant horizon.

"Guess who's back for more?" she says. "Two miles at our ten o'clock."

CHAPTER 15

I'M MINDFUL OF THE unfortunate optics of the Doomsday Bird lumbering across the sky with body bags strapped to our skids like Santa turned Grim Reaper. The black vinyl pouch below my door ruffles in the wind, the morbid payload vibrating with the thrumming engines.

"Now what happens?" I stare out at Dana Diletti's helicopter small and bright on the horizon.

"I'm betting on history repeating itself." Lucy's voice sounds in my headset. "I'll ask nicely that they go the other way, and they won't. Amazing how some people don't learn, and Lorna Callis is one of them. Oh well, no one can say I didn't give people like that fair warning. It's not my fault if they come back for more."

Settling into a high hover that I'd describe as predatory, she finds the menu she wants on the heads-up display. I don't understand the acronyms that are her choices. Hieroglyphics might be easier to interpret, but I can guess the threat level by the color coding.

"Manassas traffic, helicopter Niner-Zulu requests aircraft in the area avoid police operation in Buckingham Run," Lucy announces over the radio.

Lorna doesn't bother answering. She remains silent and on course, boldly getting closer.

"Helicopter Seven-Charlie-Delta, what's your intention?" Lucy addresses the news chopper directly, and still no response. She releases the mic trigger with a shrug.

"Be careful, Lucy. I think you're being goaded into doing something newsworthy," I tell her. "They want a bigger story. Please don't give them one."

"As they say...? *Have it your way, hold the pickles, hold the lettuce...*" She begins singing the Burger King jingle over the intercom, displaying another screen on the HUD.

"Is this really necessary?" I take in the determined set of her jaw, the twitch of anger. "Lucy? Are you okay?" I know when something is troubling her.

"What do you mean, *is she okay*?" Marino's disembodied voice sounds worried over the intercom.

Lucy's answer is to touch an option illuminated red on a menu. "Uh-oh! They've lost their avionics again. What a bummer."

She explains that the pilot and crew can't talk to the tower or each other. They can't capture anything on film or use electronic devices, including phones. The map displays are dark, no GPS to guide, no alerts to warn. All Lorna Callis can control is the helicopter itself, flaring into a quick stop, slowing into a hover again.

"What the hell did you just do? Because it sounds like a crime." Marino's voice is alarmed in our headsets, and he's not enjoying anything about this ride.

"I'm giving us a little lead time, which usually wouldn't be necessary. This thing is as fast as a Chinook when I put the pedal to the metal," Lucy says. "But I can't do that now."

She explains that what we're carrying on the skids creates drag, slowing down the speed among other potential problems.

"I'll give us a minute before undoing the special effects," she adds.

"What special effects are you freakin' talking about?" he insists as Lucy tracks northeast, heading toward Alexandria.

I'm reminded of her teenaged years when she and Marino constantly sparred with each other even as they were best friends. He was the uncle, the father figure she never had. He also was bigoted and backward, the two of them everything that threatened the other.

"... All I'm doing is temporarily shooing off a nuisance without causing permanent damage. Also, tough to prove it happened or that anything did." Lucy is pleased with herself. "Poof! And they don't know what hit them."

"Hit them with what, for cripes' sake? What kind of weapon?" Marino's voice is increasing in volume.

"The bug zapper with its insane range. I can knock out your lights with surgical precision from a hundred miles away. Basically, it's the same thing as a UFO signal-jamming a fighter jet that gets too curious."

"I'm serious!"

"So am I."

"I can't see the chopper anymore. Jesus, you didn't shoot them out of the sky, did you?"

"Too much paperwork."

"What you just did isn't funny!"

"They're fine."

"Well, you won't be after pulling a trick like that."

"Apparently they had intermittent avionic problems while interfering with a federal police investigation." Lucy gives Marino the sound bite.

She flies us over heavy traffic on the Capital Beltway while reaching for the HUD display again.

"And presto!" she says. "Like magic! Everything's up and running just fine after all. How lucky is that? Mission aborted, and they'll be diverting back to Dulles for the second time today."

"You're going to have hell to pay," Marino replies. "They'll probably report you to the FAA, getting you violated so you can't fly anymore."

"Don't make me laugh."

"Or sue."

"Good luck suing the Secret Service," she says, and we're five minutes from my office.

* * *

The George Washington Masonic National Memorial soars from a hilltop like an austere granite cathedral or a lighthouse from the ancient world. People on the ground are aware of the powerful helicopter churning in low and slow with its grotesque payload on the skids. Cars pull off the road, the drivers climbing out to stare.

Multiple news choppers are deploying throughout the greater Washington, D.C., area, and stories have gone viral on the internet. Lucy passes along the latest information she's seeing in the cockpit's HUD and the lenses of her wearable computer glasses. Out of necessity she's developed an ability to multitask that's uncanny. But it's not easy getting her undivided attention.

"*...Violent extremists who call themselves The Republic claim responsibility for the deaths of outdoor enthusiasts Huck and Brittany Manson.*" Lucy reads from the headlines as she flies. "*The owners of a successful retail business had been camping in Buckingham Run throughout the fall. Sources close to the investigation said the couple was ducking federal law enforcement while planning to flee the country...*"

"Where the hell is all this coming from?" Marino asks.

"There are mentions of me piloting the chief medical examiner because we're family," Lucy says.

"Unfortunate, but I'm not surprised." I think of the crowd gathered in my parking lot when we took off this morning.

"I'm betting the leak is someone in our building," Marino decides.

"It might be," Lucy answers. "And it might be more than one person. Almost any assumption you make in this situation likely will be wrong. Be careful."

"What are you telling us?" Marino sounds exasperated.

"I'm reminding you that we're tangling with very dangerous people who shouldn't be underestimated."

"How did the Mansons' names get out, and who would be so reckless as to release their presumed identities?" I ask Lucy. "We've not confirmed anything or notified next of kin. I've not even examined the bodies yet."

"We're talking about someone who has reason to know as much as we do. Maybe more. Probably the same person who made the anonymous phone calls," she says.

East of us is the historic district of Old Town Alexandria, its colonial buildings and pricey high-rises clustered on the Potomac River. I spot my modest old estate overlooking the waterfront, the two tall brick chimneys and slate roof peeking above trees.

I send Benton another text, giving him a quick update. I mention strange sounds and other inexplicable happenings at the scene. As we're flying back to my headquarters Lucy is having aerial confrontations with the media, I tell him. This time he answers.

On a quick break at HQ and following events as they unfold. You ok in all this chaos?

He's letting me know that he's been sequestered inside a Sensitive Compartmented Information Facility at Secret Service headquarters in Washington, D.C. He's aware of everything going on and closely involved.

Almost back at my office, I answer.

See you soon, he replies, and if only that were true.

In my fantasies when I land, he'll be there waiting. But that's not going to happen. I'm not looking forward to what I'm about to confront when we set down in my parking lot.

"Roxane Dare is scheduled to give a press conference within the hour," Lucy tells us the latest.

"This early on and with so little information, it seems more about politics than informing the public," I reply. "It's a bad idea."

"The governor should keep her piehole shut. She's dumping gasoline on the fire." Marino offers his diplomatic opinion from the back cabin.

"The goal was to cause exactly what we're seeing, with more

disruption on the way," Lucy says. "And to recruit. This is how The Republic and other threat groups attract new members. It's how they get funding and heightened visibility."

"Wait until the footprint gets leaked. I'm expecting that next," Marino says.

"I'm surprised it hasn't already happened," I reply. "If the goal is to create frightening publicity, then why leave out that detail?"

"Because maybe the footprint has nothing to do with anything," Marino says. "Maybe it just happened to be there, and the killer has no idea."

"Sucker hole," Lucy reminds him. "A diversion that prevents you from seeing what's really going on. That's the danger. Not whether it's real or not."

"Except if it's real?" Marino's voice. "What the hell does that tell us?"

"Focus on the two people who are dead," Lucy says. "Just keep telling yourself that, Marino. Unless Bigfoot wears body armor, carries a rifle and has a way of defeating thermal imagers, we don't need to be worrying about him."

We're flying along West Braddock Road now, and I can make out the strobing blue and red nimbus of emergency lights. My building is surrounded by Virginia State Police vehicles securing the perimeter. News vans and trucks have raised their dish antennas outside our privacy fencing, and more spectators than before are gathered in the parking lot.

"Traffic off our nose," Lucy says, and a target on the HUD is flashing red.

I look out the windows and don't see what she's talking about. Then she points at a speck that turns into a drone speeding straight at us. It swoops aggressively close, darting around like a crazed insect.

"Good God, you don't think it's trying to hit us, do you?" I look over at Lucy, and her face is unreadable.

"What the hell?" Marino pipes up in alarm.

"Not very neighborly getting in my airspace like that," Lucy says. "Especially when I'm inbound for landing over a crowded terrain, putting a lot of people besides us at risk should we fall out of the sky."

"Shit," Marino says.

"Don't worry, we won't." Lucy is calm, almost peaceful, the two of us wired differently.

I don't like fights, rarely start them and wish they weren't necessary or inevitable. My niece is fired up when challenged, daring someone to take her on. Her attitude is *make my day* as she ruins yours.

"It's big enough to do a lot of damage, and that's the intention of whoever's piloting it remotely," she's saying as a matter of fact. "Six props and probably weighs more than fifty pounds depending on what it's carrying besides various cameras and a lidar mapping scanner. I'm picking up its transmissions on spectral analysis and this isn't someone's cheapo hobby drone."

"That's way too close." I watch it fly under us, and it wouldn't take much to destabilize the cargo tethered to the skids.

I halfway wonder if that's the objective, to send bodies tumbling to the earth for all the world to see. Or maybe someone is trying to do far worse.

"Is it filming us or are we being attacked?" Marino asks, and I imagine him looking out the windows in back. "Fuck! I just saw it go by, heading toward the tail boom. What if it hits the blades?"

"We've got a special kind of bug repellent. Otherwise, it would have hit us already. And then there's our friendly zapper that I told you about." Lucy makes another selection on a menu. "You're about to be the property of the U.S. government. Bye-bye, birdie."

CHAPTER 16

INSTANTLY, THE DRONE HAS vanished from my side window. The flashing red target on the display has been replaced by an X, and we begin circling my parking lot.

"Where did it go?" Marino asks. "You vaporize it? What did you do?"

"As simple as yanking a plug out of the wall." Lucy lines up the landing zone near the REMOTE's semi-trailer against the fence. "Looks like our invasive visitor fell out of the sky, setting down hard a couple blocks from here on top of a Catholic church. A good thing since it's going to need last rites, as will the asshole who was flying it. Can't wait to take a look at it in our lab."

"How are you going to recover it?" Marino asks.

"As we speak it's in the process," she says as we're coming in to land. "Now I need to pay attention."

"Glad to know you weren't doing it before."

Fabian and Wyatt are waiting next to the refrigerated

tractor-trailer where stretchers and surgical carts shine like polished silver in the sun. Four uniformed Secret Service officers stand guard, their black Tahoe SUVs parked nearby. People shield their faces from our rotor wash as we hover-taxi in, traffic cones rolling and skittering. I barely feel the skids touch down, then the helicopter's weight settles, the engines cut to flight idle.

I can sense Fabian's excitement as I watch him out my window, and I'm tired of being the bad mother. Once again, I'm about to disappoint him. It's simply not possible for him to assist me inside the REMOTE. The autopsies will be done in isolation, no staff allowed except Marino. The only spectators are those the Secret Service decides, and I think about Fabian's and my conversation early this morning.

The best remedy is to keep him busy with something that he feels matters, and I know just the thing he can do to be helpful. Lucy finishes the shutdown, and we open our doors as he pushes a stretcher across the tarmac, the noise reminding me of roller skating. I climb down from the cockpit, and Wyatt is waiting.

"How are you doing?" I ask him. "You must be exhausted."

"Wyatt's like the walking dead," Fabian volunteers as he trots back for the second stretcher. "As usual, Tina never fails to be a C-U-Next-Tuesday no matter what day of the week it is!"

"I won't lie," Wyatt says to me. "This is getting old."

"I'm very sorry Tina left you and all of us in the lurch, and not for the first time. You should have headed home anyway or taken a nap in the on-call room."

"I couldn't do that, Chief." He stares at the body pouches in their rescue baskets lashed to the skids. "It's a good thing we've got police everywhere. But someone from our office has to protect our interests. No way I was going to leave. Especially with the devil sticking her nose into everything."

He shows me a string of text messages on his phone from Maggie Cutbush. She's demanding information about what's going on at my office, and he's wise not to answer.

"I'm sorry she's harassing you. I'm sorry for all of this," I reply. "You're always getting the short end of the stick because you're a responsible and unselfish person, Wyatt. You care."

Former military, he's in his early sixties with bad knees and his phobias of the morgue. But he doesn't abandon his post, complain or make excuses for the most part. He'll pass out from pain and fatigue before walking off the job or letting me down. Certain parties use this to their advantage, knowing he'll cover for them when they don't show up.

"I'm glad you're still here, because I don't know what we'd do. Thank you for staying. I'm sorry Tina didn't give more advance notice." My diplomatic way of letting him know I'm aware that she screwed us.

No doubt she'll be out of work the rest of the week, if not longer. She'll be on paid sick leave, waiting for at least two negative test results. This has been going on in one form or fashion since I moved back to Virginia early in the pandemic. What I'd like to do is fire her. But I'd be in for a world of trouble with the Department of Labor, and that's what she counts on.

"I'm not sure how much more of this I can take." Anger shows on Wyatt's tired face.

"You have every right to be upset," I reply.

"She gets paid while I'm here covering for her bad behavior.

Not sure you know, but Tina's been escorting Maggie Cutbush to her car as if she's got her own security detail," Wyatt then offers.

"How long has this been going on?" Marino carefully lifts the banker's box out of the back cabin.

"A few weeks," Wyatt says. "That's not a good thing when there's only one of us on duty at a time."

"It's not a good thing for any reason I can think of," I reply, and Maggie may not work in my office, but she's anything but gone.

"Like I said, she's asking questions that are none of her business," Wyatt replies, and I detect helicopters in the distance, probably the media. "She wants to know what you're doing." He again eyes the rescue baskets with their pouched bodies.

"She's been pestering me too." Fabian rolls up a second stretcher. "Claiming she's got a right to the details since she's in charge of the Commonwealth's safety."

"She's certainly not in charge, and the Department of Emergency Prevention isn't an enforcement agency," I clarify. "Their focus is compiling statistics and they have no legal right to medical examiner records. The less said to Maggie and her staff the better."

I restrain myself from adding that I don't know what Roxane Dare was thinking. A watered-down version of the Health Department's division of epidemiology, DEP is a needless redundancy and waste of taxpayers' money. It's nothing but a place to park political hacks, suck-ups and empire builders who won't go away quietly.

"Maggie was asking all sorts of stuff about what was done to the victims," Fabian continues. "Are there signs they were bitten or clawed, maybe partially eaten by bears or something? Why is it they're not visually recognizable?"

"And how would she know a detail like that?" I ask.

"It's all over the internet," he says. "But hey, how would I know whether it's true or not? Since I've not been included in any conversations?"

"You don't need to be included," Marino says, walking off.

I notice Faye Hanaday waiting some distance away from the helicopter, her lab coat over jeans and sneakers. She's wearing earbuds, no doubt listening to music, her hair blond with hints of blue and purple. Last week it was cotton-candy pink with touches of lavender. She takes the banker's box from Marino without a word, and they start signing paperwork.

"Will check with you later," he calls out as she walks back toward our building, and of course she can't hear him.

* * *

"What's in the box you just handed off?" Fabian asks when Marino returns to the helicopter.

"Blackbeard's treasure," he says.

"Seriously."

"Seriously, none of your business, and don't go bothering Faye about it even if she's your girlfriend. She knows how to be professional and not run her mouth." Marino scowls up at three helicopters hovering high over us with cameras mounted under the noses.

"Nothing is shared without my authorization. I don't care who asks." I pull on gloves, raising my voice above the din. "And everyone needs to refrain from speculating or perpetuating rumors. Things are bad enough with all the disinformation on the internet. We don't want to add to it."

"I saw the Mansons a couple of times when I was inside their store running errands. Most recently was in June when I'd stopped in to pick up some cleaning supplies," Fabian says. "They were filming a commercial, dressed up like Indiana Jones, pretending they were camping in a jungle. My impression was that they were really stuck on themselves and rude, bossing around their staff disrespectfully. I could see why somebody might have had it out for them if that's what happened."

"I could see why somebody might have it out for a lot of people, but that doesn't mean shit," Marino says.

Reaching inside the helicopter, I lift out large paper bags sealed with red biohazard labels. Inside is the victims' bloody clothing, and I hand the bags to Fabian.

"Under no circumstances are you to open them, and they go directly to the DNA lab," I instruct. "I'm treating all evidence in this case as a potential biohazard. We also have to worry about toxins."

"You got it." He unclips a pen from a pocket of his scrubs, initialing the evidence forms taped to the bags. "And I hope everything goes okay." He indicates the trailer, a steel ramp attached to the back and leading to the closed cargo door.

"Hopefully everything is ready for us?" I ask.

"I have no idea what it's like inside right now." Fabian doesn't like his turf invaded. "I can't vouch for everything done by the feds in and out with their geek squad. They've not let me back inside since they started storming the castle. I couldn't set up for you the way I usually would."

He stares at the four uniformed officers carrying MP5 submachine guns on slings across their chests.

"As you can see, we have limited control over how things are done in a situation like this." I explain it will be only Lucy and Marino inside the trailer with me.

"I'm sitting out the game again . . . ?" Fabian starts to protest.

"We don't have much choice about who's inside the trailer. And it's close confines, as you know." I collect my briefcase from the helicopter's back cabin. "But there's something I could use your help with."

Fabian wants to investigate, and I'm going to let him in a limited way. I bring up the Nokesville case from three months ago, the dairy farmer crushed to death after driving his tractor erratically. Fabian was at the scene with me. He transported the body in one of our vans and assisted while I did the autopsy.

"A weird one, right?" he replies too enthusiastically. "I'll never forget rolling up on the field he was plowing and seeing the tire tracks all over the place. I thought for sure we'd find he was under the influence of alcohol or drugs. Either that or he had a heart attack, maybe a stroke."

"I'd like you to pull the records we have and also anything that's been in the media about it." I swap my satellite phone for the one I usually carry.

"Are you're thinking it might be connected to these two people?" Fabian indicates the pouched bodies in their rescue baskets. "The dairy farm's really close to Buckingham Run. Weird to think if they all knew each other, now that we're talking about it . . ."

"Nope, we're not talking about it," Marino butts in again as he unfastens the straps of a rescue basket.

"Eventually I'm going to have to finalize the manner of death in that case anyway," I explain to Fabian. "Ideally, I don't want to leave it pending indefinitely."

"For a while the life insurance company was calling," he says. "But I've not heard anything in weeks."

"What I need you to do is to reach out to the investigator and ask if there are any updates. His name is Wally Jonas and he's with the Prince William County P.D. Tell him I'd like to finalize the manner of death on Mike Abel's autopsy report and death certificate but can't until we've answered more questions."

"I'm on it!" Fabian walks off, glancing up at the helicopters every other second.

"You cut him too much slack, Doc." Marino is unfastening the straps and bungee cords lashing the second rescue basket to the skid. "If the tractor death might have anything to do with the Mansons? You shouldn't want Fabian anywhere near it."

"It can't be just you and me doing everything. And what if people hadn't given us a chance when we were getting started?"

"I got no problem with Fabian," Lucy says. "And you know me. I've got problems with most people."

Marino and I lift one of the pouched bodies as Lucy begins humming the wicked witch theme from *The Wizard of Oz*.

"Flying broom at our three o'clock and closing in," she says sotto voce as I detect heels clicking toward us aggressively.

Maggie Cutbush is headed our way like a heat-seeking missile, her haughty face masked by designer sunglasses. She's buttoned up in a tight skirt suit the bright red of danger, the stiletto heels of her shoes weaponlike.

"Doctor Scarpetta? Please explain what you think you're doing." She has a London accent that I'd find charming if I didn't know her. Since I fired her last summer, she's more pinched than pretty, her hair dyed as black as tar and cut severely short.

"In case you didn't notice, we're busy," Lucy says to her. "You need to leave."

"Not so fast." She says it like an order.

"What do you want, Maggie?" I ask.

"People are most upset with you roaring in here like this and placing the safety of everyone in jeopardy." She starts her litany. "We don't have a helipad or any suitable place for an aircraft to operate safely. You had no right to authorize such a thing. I'm sure people will file all kinds of complaints."

"I have no doubt you'll encourage it." I'm helping Lucy carry empty rescue baskets and straps off to the side where they won't get blown when she takes off next. "And I'm not the one who authorized anything. I'm not the pilot."

"The Secret Service doesn't need your permission," Lucy adds.

"There's no precedent for anyone else daring to do such a thing. No one's ever landed here before," Maggie argues. "I made sure to check into the matter when I heard your niece flying in earlier to give you a ride as a favor. Nepotism, I believe it's called."

"We don't have to tell you shit, in case you've forgotten," Marino replies.

"You always have such a way with words." She smiles condescendingly at him. "What's so bad about these cases that you're doing autopsies in the parking lot?"

"Go away, Maggie," Lucy warns her.

"I understand that Shady Acres is complaining about you flying over this morning and deliberately blowing things around. Including Halloween-themed decorations." Maggie places her hands on her hips like a stern headmistress, giving Lucy the evil eye. "As you likely know, they have haunted events this time of year for disadvantaged children. I'm hearing that you ruined thousands of dollars of landscaping, and flying rocks damaged some of their hearses."

"I have video recordings of what their place looked like as I flew over." Lucy locks the cockpit doors, and Maggie's not going to get a rise out of her. "If they want to file false reports, fine by me. I'll make sure it's worth the price of admission. Up to five years in prison."

"I've been on the phone with Elvin Reddy several times already, and he's most concerned." Maggie stares at the pouched bodies. "Why are they being isolated out here in a trailer as if they might be contagious or radioactive or something else dreadful?"

CHAPTER 17

MAGGIE IS RIGHT BEHIND us as we push the stretchers across the tarmac toward the trailer's ramp.

"What are you keeping from everyone? Doctor Scarpetta? I insist you answer my questions." Her demanding voice follows us.

"I'm not at liberty to discuss an active investigation." I'm professional, even polite, while thinking *go fuck yourself.*

I envision her walking into my office without knocking, acting as if she were the de facto chief. And she was much of the time she worked for my predecessor, Elvin Reddy. He has no passion for people or forensic medicine. The two of them are just alike, their relationship symbiotic.

"What is it you don't want the public to know about?" Maggie asks in an imperious tone, holding up her phone, outrageously recording us now.

"What the hell do you think you're doing?" I tell her angrily. "Put down your phone and leave."

"You heard her. Clear the area." Lucy blocks Maggie from

filming or getting closer. "You're interfering with a police investigation."

"That's twice you've threatened me," she replies.

"Don't make it three times."

"Now you're trying to intimidate."

"And you're obstructing justice."

"I'll make sure Doctor Reddy is aware of our conversation." Maggie stalks off as she gets on her phone.

"Well, I tried...," she is saying, probably to Elvin Reddy. "...Not even a glimmer of cooperation..."

Then I can't hear her anymore, and Lucy helps Marino and me roll the stretchers up the REMOTE's diamond plate ramp. I open the cargo door, closing it behind us, the vestibule brightly lit and clad in polished metal. It's where we leave shoes, coats and other belongings before passing through airlocks connecting the four self-contained compartments.

"Maggie's a rabid dog with a bone right now," Marino says, and I'm fuming inside but he wouldn't know it. "She sees an opportunity and this is just the beginning. I still can't believe it. How is it possible we ended up with her again? And whatever she's up to, she's not going to quit until she gets what she wants."

"I don't know what she's up to beyond her usual bullying." I set my briefcase on top of a steel desk that reminds me of prison. "We've got enough to distract us." The steel chair grates loudly when I move across metal flooring. "We don't need anything else." I sit down and begin unlacing my boots, resisting anger that's hard to control once it gets going.

"Distractions are one of the most effective offenses," Lucy says, and I can't understand why Roxane Dare would put me in a position like this.

The governor terminated Elvin Reddy and Maggie Cutbush last July, only to repackage and reinstall them three months later. In some ways it's worse than it was before, and I thought Roxane and I were friends. Were it not for her I wouldn't have taken this job, and now I'm left to wonder why she hired me.

"...Also known as psyching someone out so they do themselves in." Marino continues talking about Maggie. "That was the point of her accosting us in the parking lot..."

I'm suspicious she and Elvin have utility to the governor that wasn't a factor when she appointed me. Or maybe it's dirt they've threatened her with somehow. It's been rumored for months that Roxane plans to run for the U.S. Senate. I've heard from people I work with that her attorney husband has been shopping for condos in Washington, D.C., where he's interviewing with big law firms.

It's said that unless something unforeseen happens, she's expected to win. I'm not surprised by her ambitions, especially in Virginia, where the governor isn't allowed to serve consecutive terms. Roxane has a year left in office, and I imagine that soon enough her Senate campaign will be announced. It will get into gear, overriding everything else no matter what she or anybody pretends and promises.

"...Maggie's taking advantage of the situation to score political points." Marino places his pistol, its extra magazines inside the vestibule's gun locker. "Then if she's lucky, she convinces the governor to fire the doc and me." Banging the door shut, he pockets the key. "It's been in the cards from day one..." He takes off his boots, the three of us moving around in our stocking feet.

On carts are boxes of PPE, and we put on Tyvek booties,

the metal floor cold through the thin polyethylene. Lucy isn't locking up her gun or staying for the duration, her face somber and preoccupied. Something haunts her that she's not saying. I've been catching her flares of temper, her angry glints. I feel as if we've not looked each other in the eye all day. It's not just because of her tinted glasses.

"...Her goal is to run us out of town," Marino continues venting about Maggie. "She and Elvin both won't stop until that's what they do. Maybe at the end of the day the joke's on us. Maybe we got moved here so certain people could throw us to the lions."

"Way too much trouble," Lucy says. "Maggie and Elvin are a problem, but not our biggest one."

"And talking about them is exactly what they want," I add.

"After not even three years, we'll have to uproot all over again," Marino launches in. "Only where the hell do we go this time? And no way I'm throwing in the towel and retiring."

"Don't worry so much," Lucy says to him. "It gives the enemy power."

"Easy for you to say. Try telling Dorothy we're moving," he replies, and I can predict her reaction.

She loves their townhome on the Potomac, my sister the happiest I've seen her in many years, maybe ever. Should that change, I know who she'll blame, and it won't be Marino. But it might be the end of them as a married couple, and not because of moving or even the location. It's about him following me as he has since we left Virginia decades ago.

"Nobody's running us off," Lucy says to Marino.

"You got no idea the grief I'll get at home if things turn to shit...!"

"Of course I have an idea. She's my mother..."

As my niece and Marino go back and forth like they always have, I'm texting with Wyatt. I've asked him to enter our two new cases into the morgue office computer. They're John and Jane Doe for now, the location Buckingham Run, their deaths unnatural, I let him know.

Then he's sending me the newly accessioned numbers: *NVA023-1898* and *NVA023-1899.* My office is nearing the two thousand mark for cases so far this year in Northern Virginia alone.

* * *

On top of the vestibule's metal desk is a tray filled with stiff paper toe tags that I label with a Sharpie. I tie them to the zippers of the body bags, a throwback to habits from the old days. Now we print bracelets and stickers embedded with radio frequency identification (RFID) chips.

I can walk inside the coolers, the freezers, with a handheld scanner and find what I'm looking for quickly. But inside the REMOTE I've had no choice but to keep things as simple as possible. Nothing electronic is permitted unless it's stand-alone like our x-ray machine. I can do autopsies just fine in a low-tech environment, and that isn't what bothers me about working inside the trailer.

It's the restrictions, the severe oversight. Everything we do must be approved by the federal government. I can't so much as bring in a set of battery-powered forensic crime lights without checking first. Worse than that, I have no control over what's done to the facility without my knowing. The REMOTE doesn't belong to the medical examiner's office, and we're not the only ones with keys and combinations.

"It would be a good idea for you to inform Faye that Maggie Cutbush isn't to come anywhere near her lab, and we know she will, given the chance," I tell Marino. "Should Maggie see the plaster cast, that will be the end. Especially if she realizes you're the one who made it. I can't think of a worse person having access to our building right about now."

"If she tries to poke her nose where it doesn't belong, I'm going to cause her real trouble," Lucy says.

"I made it clear to Faye that everything is hush-hush," Marino reiterates.

She's examining the cast even as we speak, he tells us. Alone inside the firearms and tool marks lab, she has the door locked, and the blinds are closed in the observation windows.

"She'll keep to herself, making sure no one comes inside while the cast is out and in view," he's saying. "And she knows what to do with the swabs I receipted to her when we met in the parking lot."

"Swabs?" Lucy inquires.

"Clark and Rex are expecting them and will get on it right away." More of his feigned innocence. "They know not to say anything to anyone."

Clark Givens and Rex Bonetta are the heads of the DNA and trace evidence labs. I trust them completely, and what Marino did is manipulative. But I'm not sorry that certain experts in my building will be involved in examining the evidence. I can tell Lucy isn't surprised by this latest ploy. She knows Marino. She might know him better than anyone except perhaps me.

But what strikes me as unusual is I sense she doesn't

care. Or maybe he's doing exactly as she's scripted even as he's unaware. Lucy can predict his behavior. She's skilled at maneuvering him.

"What swabs?" she asks him again.

"The ones in evidence baggies," Marino replies. "I had them protected under layers of folded sheets inside the box Faye picked up."

"On the bottom and covered so I wouldn't see them, in other words." A bemused smile is playing on Lucy's face as we continue this discussion inside the trailer's vestibule.

I'm realizing that she doesn't want the Bigfoot evidence. She wants nothing to do with it and is happy to let us help ourselves.

"It's smart to keep everything together since the swabs in question are from the cast and also the actual footprint." Marino continues rationalizing.

"Is there any other evidence you've squirreled away that you might want to tell me about?" Lucy asks him.

"Bloodstains I collected, but those are for us to handle."

"Depends on the source."

"The bullets and frag are with your guys at the scene."

"As they should be," she says. "What else?"

Marino took pictures of the lands and grooves and other identifying features from spent rounds collected inside Buckingham Run. He says he emailed them to Faye, coming clean about that too.

"And just so you know? She thinks the footprint cast I made is amazing," he brags as I decide that we need someone who's dealt with this sort of thing.

I think about the University of Virginia professor he met at the Shenandoah Sasquatch Festival. It would be helpful if we could work with an expert locally and quietly.

"I'm wondering if Cate Kingston can be trusted with sensitive information," I say to Marino and Lucy. "Is there any reason you think we should stay away from her?"

"All I can say is she impressed the hell out of me," he replies. "She wasn't full of herself and didn't talk out of school. She could look at a plaster cast and tell you all kinds of stuff about it that was mind-blowing. Such as whether the Sasquatch was walking, running, slipping in mud, looking over his shoulder or had an injury. She could show you how he was moving at the time he left the footprint. You know, things you can't fake."

"There's not much you can't fake," Lucy reminds him. "It's getting harder to know what's real and what isn't."

"What I found doesn't look fake, and I've seen my share of bullshit Sasquatch footprints, videos, photographs, hair, scat, you name it. I've got a gut feeling about what I found." Marino isn't backing down. "I'm betting it's the real thing and we just happened to come across it because it was in a place we wouldn't normally go. I mean, who in their right mind would go spelunking inside that old gold mine?"

"Real or not, we've got to do our best to prove or disprove it," I reply. "We can't pretend the footprint doesn't exist, as much as we might wish otherwise. And if it's fake and was planted, then obviously we need to determine who did it and why."

"Cate Kingston is thirty-one, born in Boise, Idaho, got her Ph.D. from Idaho State University." Lucy is reading information displayed in the lenses of her AI-assisted glasses. "She's well respected in the fields of evolutionary anthropology and primatology. Studied under Jeff Meldrum, regarded as the world's foremost Sasquatch expert."

"He's the Jane Goodall of the Bigfoot world," Marino is quick to inform us. "I've seen him on TV when he gets called to places when there's a sighting. Or where footprints and other evidence have been left."

"And the enthusiasm you're showing right now isn't good for you," Lucy reminds him. "Try to keep a lid on it, Marino."

"All I'm saying is Doctor Kingston learned from the best."

She began at UVA a year ago, her course "Tales of the Cryptid: The Reality of Bigfoot" the most popular on campus. She's also worked with the police on various cases involving skeletal remains, Lucy continues to inform us.

"Not around here but in Idaho while she was still living there," she says.

"That would explain why I'm not familiar with her," I reply.

I regularly work with area forensic anthropologists, including those at the Smithsonian Institution's National Museum of Natural History in Washington, D.C. I know experts in almost any specialty one might imagine. But there's no one I would approach about alleged Sasquatch evidence.

"If you feel Doctor Kingston is worth the risk, we can ask what she thinks," I say to Lucy. "She's worked with the police and should understand discretion. I'll let you reach out if you feel that makes sense."

"She's got to see the cast I made," Marino replies.

"I'll talk to her, and if there are no red flags, we'll see what she can do to help," Lucy says. "We need to figure out everything we can, and no one in the Secret Service labs is qualified to examine that kind of footprint."

"Or any footprint." Marino can't resist giving her another stick.

"We also don't need the public thinking that we're trying to determine if Bigfoot exists and left a footprint somewhere," she says, and that might be the biggest reason she's not fighting Marino over the evidence.

Rumors and misinformation about such a thing aren't what the Secret Service wants all over the news.

CHAPTER 18

LUCY OPENS THE REMOTE'S wall-mounted steel Faraday box that blocks all electromagnetic signals and has a combination lock. Tucking her phone, her computer-assisted glasses inside, she tells us to do the same with our electronic devices.

"You know the routine," she says, and Marino's and my phones go in next.

I take off my nickel-plated smart ring, essentially a fitness tracker that alerts me of messages, among other things. I place it inside, and we're in a communication blackout except for any electronics the Secret Service may have installed.

"Ready?" Lucy closes the Faraday box, spinning the dial.

"Ready as we'll ever be." Gripping the handle of a stretcher, I use my foot to unlock the wheels.

We push the bodies out of the airlock, entering the first compartment to loud fans blowing. I can see my breath, the sharp odor of disinfectant making my eyes water. Racks of empty steel trays are stacked to the ceiling where I spot a small white dome that's a new addition. The security camera isn't ours, and I worry there might be one inside the vestibule.

If so, I didn't see it. But we were talking freely, and I wouldn't have if I'd known about cameras that weren't installed by us. Marino and I had no idea anyone might have been listening, and I ask Lucy about it.

"Cameras are in every compartment, not all of them easily spotted," she answers as if it's no big deal.

"I need to know if we're being monitored." I'm thinking of every word I've said so far, especially about Bigfoot evidence and Maggie Cutbush.

"You've got nothing to worry about," Lucy assures me.

"And we're supposed to just take your word for that?" Marino says.

"Yes. By now, you should know you can trust me."

"I hope you know what you're doing, Lucy," I reply. "Considering the problem with leaks we're having? This makes me very nervous. God forbid we get hacked."

"No shit," Marino replies. "Cameras, microphones in here are a bad idea. No matter what, it creates a huge liability. Not that you guys care what I say. It appears you just did whatever the hell you wanted like you own the joint."

"We sort of do own the joint. And the point of the REMOTE is we can deal with sensitive cases *remotely*," Lucy says. "Ultimately, it's for this very type of situation."

I'm well aware of the purpose. One of my tasks on the Doomsday Commission has been to help design the mobile facility and test it at my headquarters. But when I've performed autopsies in here, they were unwitnessed. It was only Marino and me with Fabian or my deputy chief, Doug Schlaefer. Cameras hadn't been set up, the cases of no interest to the federal government.

We can see our breath inside the cooler as we park the bodies on the floor scale one at a time. We measure them, deducting the weight of each stretcher. The male victim is five foot eight and 160 pounds, the female five foot five and 125 pounds. That's inconsistent with information Lucy gave me when she first called about the deaths.

"Weight can dramatically fluctuate," I say to her. "But one's height doesn't change significantly under normal circumstances. The information I have is Huck Manson was five foot ten. Brittany was five foot seven."

"That's what they have on official documents requiring a physical description," Lucy says. "In some instances, they also list tattoos and scars that are nonexistent."

"Making it more confusing when someone's trying to identify them alive or dead," Marino supposes.

"I don't think there was any one reason for their chronic lying. Assuming they could tell the difference between that and truth anymore," Lucy replies.

"Who do you want to do first?" Marino asks me.

"I'd leave both of them in here for now," Lucy answers before I have the chance. "You need to get the lay of the land." She says it like a directive. "That's going to take a little while."

"Huh?" Marino replies. "It's a damn fifty-foot trailer. How much time can it take. What the hell did you do, add an addition?"

"What's going on, Lucy?" I ask her.

"I'm about to show you." She opens the next door, and we leave the bodies behind. "You're about to see a lot of things that it's best others explain."

Inside the trailer's hygiene compartment are a shower, a sink, a toilet and an emergency eyewash station. Shelves are stocked with towels, PPE and supplies.

"You'd better not be monitoring us when we're cleaning up in here later," I say to Lucy.

"It's right there." She points to a camera on top of a cabinet. "When you need a little privacy just throw a towel over it."

Leaving our field clothes on, Marino and I cover up in heavy-duty Tyvek, finding full-face respirators that we won't put on yet. Through the next airlock, we enter the decontamination chamber. As the name implies, it includes an autoclave, chemical sprays and ultraviolet cleaning. The mandatory stop on our way in and out prevents cross-contamination.

I clamp various forms and body diagrams to a clipboard that has a ballpoint pen attached by a spiral plastic string. I spritz all of it with Lysol, and we pass through the final airlock.

* * *

Inside the autopsy compartment I'm pleasantly startled by the sight of my husband on multiple wall-mounted video screens that weren't here earlier. The volume is turned off, and I have no idea what he's saying to those sitting with him around a conference table.

My mood lifts as if the sun just came out even as I realize that what I'm looking at doesn't bode well. Benton is with Secret Service Director Bella Steele, her press secretary Aiden Wagner and other high-ranking officials I've worked with before. It's obvious they can't see us yet, my husband talking while turning pages in a legal pad, jotting notes.

He looks especially good in the charcoal suit he put on this morning while we were having coffee in our bedroom. The blue-striped shirt, the silk tie are the perfect accompaniments, and when I watch him from a distance, I'm reminded why I fell for him. The first time we met was during my earliest days in Richmond. The FBI's star criminal profiler, he was the head of its Behavioral Science Unit, as it was called then.

He'd been summoned to assist the police with serial murders in Richmond. They'd begun soon after I became the chief medical examiner in a part of the world that didn't seem far removed from the Civil War era. The first time Benton Wesley walked into the room I felt the air shift. He didn't look so different then, tall and lanky with premature silver hair and fine features.

I remember he was wearing a pin-striped suit, his initials monogrammed on the cuffs of his crisp white shirt. I found him strikingly handsome, keen and mysterious. He also was married, and the instant we began working together, we knew we were in trouble.

"We're seeing them on camera," Lucy explains as I take in the details of what's been changed in my absence. "But they don't know we're here yet. I'll let you know before I connect you."

The autopsy compartment is the size of a one-car garage, and the Secret Service has turned it into an operating theater. They've installed computers, video equipment and special lighting. Set up next to the downdraft dissection table is a mobile 3-D scanner that will laser-measure and map wounds and other physical features. Everything is covered with anti-microbial plastic film like in a doctor's office.

"Being briefed is one thing," I say to Lucy. "But I wasn't expecting to do the autopsies in front of a crowd. Can you explain the reason this is necessary? Because it's not my preference, and that goes without saying."

"Transparency. Creating a record should anything be questioned." She gives the party line.

"I'm aware the Mansons were suspects in serious crimes, but even so?" I'm not happy about this.

"Certain people involved want the chance to witness what you're finding and ask questions directly." She offers the more likely explanation. "There may be suggestions about what to look for based on information we have."

"For example?" Marino opens a new box of nitrile gloves.

"You'll be informed as we go along. That's for others to do," Lucy says. "You'll be told some things, and you should. It's time."

"I've had enough of your Secret Squirrel talk," he says to her. "Informed of what?"

"It's not my job to brief you. Others will do that."

"We don't have time for a damn briefing by a bunch of suits." Marino glowers.

"When you realize what it's about, you'll listen."

"How do we know that this video *record* you're creating won't get out somehow?" he continues to challenge her.

"Basically, this is one SCIF communicating with another. Only approved PEDs allowed."

She's talking about the portable electronic devices the Secret Service decided to implement, and prior to this none were approved for the REMOTE. Nothing Wi-Fi–enabled has been allowed. We've had to resort to a refurbished 35-millimeter Canon camera that's vintage and approved. I retrieve it from a cabinet, making sure it has film and the battery is good.

"I'm going to get you started." Lucy picks up a computer

tablet I've never seen before. "Then I'm headed back to Buckingham Run, making sure everybody's out before dark."

"Maybe I'll see you later tonight?" I ask her.

"Not sure when I'll get home."

Lucy living in our guesthouse doesn't mean Benton and I see her daily or even often, as busy as she is. There's much about her private life that I don't know. And I'm careful not to pry. I give her the space she needs.

"I'm not sure when I'll be getting home either. But I'll throw together something to eat no matter the hour," I tell her. "I'll leave supper in your refrigerator if you'd like. Whenever you come in, you'll have it. And I'll check on Merlin, make sure he's fed and fine." Merlin is her Scottish Fold cat, a rescue who's a handful.

"He should have plenty of dry food to tide him over, but I won't say no to your offer," Lucy replies. "I'll probably have Tron with me. Unless something else happens, we'll be working through the night reviewing videos, running software."

"I'll make sure there's plenty for both of you to eat. Be careful, please," I reply, and this would be a good time for a hug.

But we won't when on the job and can't be sure who's watching. Lucy, Marino, Benton, all of us are conditioned to shield our personal lives as much as possible. If the wrong people detect what you care about most, it gives them power.

"Let's see what everybody's saying." Lucy selects an option on the computer tablet, and the volume turns on. "We can hear them, but they won't be able to hear or see us yet." We catch Benton mid-conversation.

"... The temptation is to focus on certain details when it's the emotionality of the act that matters most. That's the true north in this case." He's talking to Director Bella Steele on the video screens. "What was the killer feeling? Emotions are what drives the bus. From them, we can have a shot at predicting."

"Hatred and rage." Bella is fond of power pantsuits and scarves in bold colors. "That's what I see when I look at the photographs," she adds while shuffling through a stack of them.

In her midfifties, she's the first female director of one of the oldest federal law enforcement agencies, its inception a cruel irony. The Secret Service began at the end of the Civil War when as much as a third of American currency was counterfeit. The head of the Treasury Department convinced President Abraham Lincoln that an enforcement division was critical.

Executive protection wasn't the reason. Saving the nation's financial system was, and on April 14, 1865, Lincoln signed the bill creating the U.S. Secret Service. That night he and the first lady had no bodyguard while attending a raucous comedy at Ford's Theatre less than a mile from the White House. As the audience laughed uproariously, Lincoln was shot to death inside his private booth.

"Our sound is going on and we're up on the monitors," Lucy announces. "Hello, hello?" She greets everyone remotely. "How are you reading us?"

"Loud and clear," several people answer, the mood heavy with tension.

"Roger that." Lucy opens the airlock's outer door. "I'll leave you guys to it." She looks at me before vanishing as if beamed to another place.

"Welcome and thanks for being here on such short notice," my husband begins in his measured, pleasant way. "I'm Benton Wesley, in charge of threat assessment for the Secret Service.

We're grateful for the participation of Virginia Chief Medical Examiner Kay Scarpetta and her head of investigations, Pete Marino—"

"I sure as hell hope all this crap you set up is leakproof," Marino interrupts with his typical diplomacy. "I don't want to wake up tomorrow and find videos of the doc and me all over the freakin' internet."

"That would be disastrous," I agree.

"There's way too much stuff on it already about these damn cases," he complains.

"With more on the way, and that's one of the payoffs for the enemy we're up against," Benton promises. "But before we get into this any further let me make quick introductions."

He goes around the conference table, and most people I've met. Several I know well. I'm informed that key counter-terrorism and other experts will be witnessing the autopsies internationally. I have no clue who's out there in the ether. It could be five people. It could be fifty.

"Today is Wednesday, November first, and it's three-forty-five P.M. East Coast time," my husband begins for the record, and I'm seeing him on all three video screens the Secret Service has set up in here. "Approximately twelve hours ago two people were killed inside Buckingham Run, a heavily forested wilderness several miles southwest of Manassas."

He goes on to say that Huck and Brittany Manson were under investigation for cybercrimes and domestic terrorism. It's believed that the couple was targeted by an assassin before they could be arrested.

"This isn't an isolated incident, the enemy only getting started," Benton says with a certainty I find unsettling.

CHAPTER 19

MY HUSBAND EXPLAINS TO whoever might be listening that he and his colleagues are inside a SCIF at Secret Service headquarters in Washington, D.C. They're connected by a blockchain-protected link to my Biosafety Level 4 trailer here in Alexandria, what we refer to as the REMOTE. Or a SCIF that's *operational*, Benton can't resist the pun.

"The United States and our allies are under attack on multiple fronts, and this is about to worsen exponentially," he says. "The biggest threat is Russia's invisible influence over those in our own backyard who buy into disinformation without having a clue where it's coming from. American citizens turning violent as we saw on January sixth when the Capitol was under siege."

"Neighbors, friends, colleagues, even family members. It could be anyone who becomes radicalized," says the Secret Service's director of counterterrorism. His name is Bart Clancy, in his forties and as physically imposing as Marino.

"The power of propaganda," says Aiden Wagner, the press

secretary. Young and intense, he's a former journalist, and I'm getting an uncanny feeling.

They're pulling us into something, and we're not going to have a choice about it.

"Words can hurt," Aiden is saying. "They might even wipe out our planet if we're not careful..."

This isn't good. A warning begins flashing in my head.

"The goal is the destruction of democracy by a shadow army that for years the Kremlin has sworn doesn't exist. We now can be certain of the driving force behind it," Benton says, looking directly at me, and my bad feeling gets worse. "The Kremlin's mastermind in its secret private military, the psychopathic wizard behind the curtain."

He informs us that yesterday a video was posted on the Dark Web, an encrypted network used almost exclusively by criminals. As he's talking, his eyes are intensely on me alone.

Something is very wrong.

"The timing's not coincidental. And regrettably, what you're about to learn won't be pleasant. But you need to know the truth for your own good," he adds. "These cases and other events are connected to something much bigger."

"What truth? And what the hell do you mean, *for our own good*?" Marino places a plastic bucket under the autopsy table. "What's this got to do with the doc and me...?"

"Just listen, and all will become clear soon enough." It's the CIA's director of clandestine services, Gus Gutenberg, talking in his quiet voice.

He's somewhere in his fifties, with thinning gray hair and a neatly trimmed beard. Colorless like a moth, he's dressed in a gray suit, a white shirt and gray tie. He knows how to draw little attention to himself while taking in everything around him like a dish antenna. Often in meetings I forget he's present.

"Doctor Scarpetta, it was but a few months ago when you had cases related to the domestic terrorist group known as The Republic." He polishes his rimless glasses with a cleaning cloth.

"That's correct." I'm busy finding syringes and hypodermic needles in a cabinet, setting up my surgical cart the way I like it.

"Proxy terrorism," Gus says. "The Russians, other enemy nations don't need to step foot on U.S. soil to recruit Americans. And there's nothing more effective than another American luring them. Someone who understands the way Americans think and feel. Someone who's completely indoctrinated in all things Russian."

"I'm assuming you're going to tell us the Mansons were involved with this psychopathic wizard you're talking about." Marino sprays down every surface with disinfectant.

"Unbeknownst to them, yes. It's one of many reasons we didn't arrest the Mansons sooner," Benton answers. "They were giving us important intel without realizing it, as cocky and self-focused as they were. And in return, we were able to manipulate them in certain ways."

"It's sounding like this might be why they got whacked." Marino places a stack of towels on a cart. "The bad guys decided Huck and Brittany were a problem that needed solving."

"That's part of it." Benton is making notes in his legal pad.

"What I call urban renewal," Marino says to our pantheon of federal officials on the video screens. "Good riddance is what I say. It's really disgusting to think of all the times I've been shopping at Wild World, not knowing my money was going to dirtbag assholes."

"The Mansons were doing the Russians' bidding by helping fund domestic terrorism," says Elena Roland with the National Security Agency.

In her thirties, she's always smartly dressed and wearing makeup. When I'm in meetings with her I feel like a frump by comparison.

"They were supplying equipment that includes camping and hunting gear, firearms, ammunition, tools," she's saying. "The very things they sell through their retail business. Wild World is a supply depot for domestic terrorism and a front for money laundering. That's its real purpose."

"Damn, I hate that we ever got an account there," Marino remarks, and I couldn't agree more now that we're hearing the details.

"This type of assistance has enabled The Republic to grow at an alarming rate," Benton says as I continue wondering why.

We're being set up for something we'll have no say about.

"It's been creating satellite camps within a two-hundred-mile radius of Washington, D.C.," Benton goes on. "Chatter picked up by intelligence agents indicate the threat group is planning a major attack that will make January sixth look like a meet and greet."

"They promise that this time they'll finish what they started," Elena with the NSA explains. "They're going to storm not just the Capitol but the White House, Camp David and Senate and congressional office buildings."

"No place will be spared, including private residences," Gus of the CIA explains without a trace of emotion or an accent.

"They plan to publicly execute political figures and others who are traitors to the cause. Before they're done, The Republic's flag will fly over every government institution, including *the Federal Reserve and fucking Pentagon*. Pardon my language. I'm simply quoting."

As he's saying this a video screen has filled with the image of men in ballistic gear, their faces covered as they stare into the camera. They're brandishing M4 carbines, holding up a black-and-red-striped flag featuring a white Punisher skull.

"Obviously, they're threatening a second civil war, only with modern weapons and technology." It's rare Benton is so intense. "This is what's hurtling toward us invisibly, silently like an Armageddon asteroid. The Mansons knew what they were doing and the consequences. They didn't mind helping to facilitate a coup that in our worst nightmares none of us ever want to see happen. They assumed by the time it did, it wouldn't impact them. They'd be out of the country living the good life."

* * *

Benton tells us remotely that Huck and Brittany were brazen enough to visit The Republic's outpost in Quantico. It wasn't far from the FBI Academy and the Marine Corps base. The couple was there several times before federal agents raided it this past summer. Many of the members have since been arrested, and others are feared to have reconvened elsewhere.

"Loading a rental truck, the Mansons would show up with gear and supplies," my husband is saying. "They were hanging out with these people and sympathetic. Huck and Brittany encouraged, aided and abetted. At the very least they're indirectly responsible for the crimes these people have committed. Burglaries, robberies, even murder."

I envision the mob of extremists marching around my building last summer, many dressed in camouflage and tactical garb. Angry over my testimony in an ongoing trial, they made their feelings known at my workplace and also my home. These people were armed and violent, making as much noise as possible, spewing hatred while flaunting their weapons.

It turned out that they were members of The Republic, the threat group we're talking about. Driving around in trucks with gun racks and Confederate flags, these homegrown folks call themselves the real patriots. The true Americans. All the while they're doing the bidding of the Russians and other enemy nations.

"Were the Mansons aware of how dangerous their so-called handlers could be?" I fill a plastic quart jar with formalin, a diluted version of formaldehyde that's extremely toxic. "Did they understand the magnitude of what they were meddling with?"

"That's the problem and the point," Benton explains. "Their offshore accounts are overseen by Russian cybercriminals they'd never met whose real names the Mansons didn't know. They had no idea who they were associating with overseas. It was a remote relationship they didn't question or investigate."

"Which is what's wrong with everything these days. You don't know who or what the hell you're dealing with because of the internet." Marino pulls down an electrical cord from an overhead reel. "Sometimes I'm not sure the person online is even real." He plugs in the Stryker saw.

"The Mansons connected with the Russians in cyberspace,

never meeting face-to-face at any time as best we know," Gus says. "They didn't talk on the phone unless their handler was using a voice scrambler."

"Like the individual who left the voice mail on the governor's phone." I cover a countertop with disposable sheets.

"Exactly like that," Gus replies. "I suspect we'll find the call was placed in Russia, and we have an idea by whom."

"The psychopathic wizard, let me guess," Marino says.

"The Mansons trusted blindly and were cavalier while stealing a fortune they'd never get to spend." Benton continues a briefing we didn't request, his attention locked on me. "They didn't anticipate something like this would happen when in fact it was inevitable. They believed they were going to spend the rest of their days in Dubai and Switzerland, where they had luxury apartments waiting when they fled the country."

As a rule, when I deal with federal agents the information is a one-way street. I pass along what I know while they barely answer the most basic questions.

"I have to ask. Why are you telling us all this?" I stop what I'm doing, giving Benton and his colleagues my full attention. "It seems dangerous considering the sensitive nature. And it's not typical, which is the bigger point."

"Nothing about this is typical, and you should know the truth for a number of reasons," Director Bella Steele answers. "Not the least is your safety, Kay. But also, we need your help. We need to be in lockstep."

"All of us are going to have to work together closely and with complete trust," her press secretary, Aiden, says. "We need you to collaborate with us about information released to the public, when and how."

"I would do that anyway," I reply.

"Yes, but it would be very helpful if not everything comes from us," he explains. "In other words, when needed it would be best if some of the information comes from the medical examiner's office. As long as we control the narrative."

"Oh, I get it," Marino says cynically. "We're supposed to say whatever it is you want the public to think."

"Not you personally, Marino. You won't be talking to the media at any time," Aiden replies bluntly. "Your role is to assist Doctor Scarpetta, to be mindful that both of you are in a dangerous situation. She can't be in this alone. Neither of you can be."

"What situation?" Marino asks. "You're starting to freak me out."

"The Mansons had no idea who was pulling the strings," Benton says. "They didn't care that it might be the Kremlin."

"More specifically, someone protected by it," says the head of Interpol's National Central Bureau in Washington, D.C.

His name is Lucas Van Acker, and he speaks with a heavy French accent. We became acquainted at Interpol's headquarters in Lyon earlier in the fall, both of us there for a meeting. We lunched on local sausages, cheeses and crusty bread at an outdoor café on the Rhone River. Watching the *bateau mouche* tour boats motoring by, we discussed the latest threats to humanity and whether our planet would survive and be worth inhabiting.

He said that Interpol was extremely concerned about international prisoner swaps, many of these political transactions never revealed to the public. Some of the world's most dangerous criminals end up back in circulation. These people often go underground for years as they plot and plan. "They're infinitely worse than before," I remember him saying.

"An example is the Taliban leader American politicians helped release from a Pakistani prison as part of a deal. Now he's in power again and worse than before," Lucas explained as we drank a very nice Côte-Rôtie from the region.

"There's nothing more dangerous than dictators and other despots who've been locked up and then return to power." He's saying this now remotely from a SCIF at Secret Service headquarters. "They're more ruthless and will have scores to settle."

As he's talking, a gruesome image has appeared on one of the video displays set up in here.

"What you're seeing is a Black Notice." Lucas refers to unidentified bodies Interpol believes are connected to international crime. "He washed up on a beach in Monte Carlo at the height of the tourist season this past August. To clarify, I should say that parts of him washed up. You might have seen something about it in the news."

The victim's decomposing head is in a nest of seaweed crawling with flies and crabs on a beach crowded with sun-polished beautiful people. They're looking on in horror, the Monte Carlo opera house looming in the background. A colorful hot air balloon floats over a casino, huge yachts bright white on the harbor's sparkling blue horizon.

As Lucas is talking, I'm hearing the Doomsday Bird's powerful engines firing up on the tarmac outside the REMOTE. I envision Lucy turning on switches, going through the preflight checklist. I don't like her returning to Buckingham Run and hope she doesn't get into any other aerial showdowns. It would be good if she avoided further news headlines. Most of all I want her home safely.

"…Estimated to be in his late forties, early fifties," Lucas explains. "To date, we don't know who he is, but have an idea who he worked for. He was a *serviteur*, a minion, a means to an end just as the Mansons and others were."

That image is replaced by one of an eviscerated nude body on a wet sidewalk. In the background, the ornate Byzantine turrets of St. Basil's Cathedral are like something out of a fairy tale. Pedestrians in dark clothing have stopped to gawk beneath a moiling overcast Moscow sky as city police cars pull up with lights flashing.

"A man who allegedly fell or jumped from the tenth-story fire escape of a hotel in Red Square. The temperature was around forty degrees, and it was raining at the time," Lucas says. "This was just two weeks ago."

"Why the hell would someone naked be out on a fire escape in weather like that?" Marino asks. "Or any weather? Sounds like bullshit to me."

"The more likely story is he had some help hurtling to his death," Lucas agrees. "He was staying under an assumed name, and based on tattoos, likely an American. There were vodka bottles inside his room, also drugs, as if to imply he was impaired and didn't know what he was doing. Or maybe we're supposed to think he committed suicide."

"Toxicology should tell you something," I reply. "Also, any injuries that might indicate a struggle."

"Nothing suspicious according to the Russians. They reported that the victim had been behaving oddly, as if he might be suffering mental health issues," Lucas says. "This is according to witnesses staying in the hotel, what they allegedly told police."

"And the autopsy results?" I ask. "What did they have to say?"

"An accident due to a high alcohol level and presence of opioids including fentanyl," Lucas summarizes. "Of course, we're talking about Moscow. We can't trust the information to be accurate."

"Understatement," I answer.

"This is what happens when people become inconvenient and expendable," Lucas continues. "They're made examples of, and I could tell you about others. Those who mysteriously go out windows. They die on park benches after being poisoned. Their cars blow up or they're shot while walking their dogs."

CHAPTER 20

THE DECAPITATED HEAD WASHED up barely a mile from where an oligarch's superyacht was anchored in the Monte Carlo harbor. The next day it was a severed arm. Then another one, the hands missing, Interpol's Lucas Van Acker explains on the autopsy compartment's video screens.

Based on the tides and other information, the authorities have a good idea where and when the victim's remains were dropped into the Mediterranean. It's no accident they ended up on one of Monte Carlo's most glamorous strips of beach at the height of tourist season.

"The goal is to terrify and destabilize the public while inspiring those vulnerable to being radicalized," Lucas says. "We have an idea who was on the superyacht at the time. Many of these examples have the same common denominator."

That was the wording he used when we were together in Lyon not so long ago. He repeatedly mentioned a *common denominator*. I had the sense that he was alluding to something

I would be hearing about soon enough. I remember feeling puzzled by the way his demeanor changed when he talked about it. He looked away from me and was almost apologetic.

"...We believe this common denominator is a ruthless terrorist known as the *Prizrak*, the Russian word for ghost," Lucas explains. "This individual is the most dominant figure in the Kremlin's shadow army, a transnational criminal organization with the goal of universal dominance."

"This common denominator is someone we're familiar with, unfortunately." Benton's attention continues to fix on me. "I apologize in advance that what you're about to see is upsetting."

A paused video appears on a display, and I recognize the person in black. A shockwave runs through me even as I've been waiting for the boom to drop.

"Holy shit," Marino drawls in disbelief. "Please tell me this is a sick fucking joke."

I don't react visibly or say a word as I'm ambushed. I feel furious and betrayed in ways hard to fathom. If I were alone with Benton this moment I'm not sure what I'd say. I don't know if I'd cry or yell. Possibly both. Or maybe I'd just sit there and stare at him as I'm doing right now.

How could you not tell me?

"...Carrie Grethen, the expat from hell...," my husband says as I'm confronted by the image of someone who I believed was dead.

She was never gone, and he's known it all along.

"Holy fuck," Marino mutters.

How could Lucy not say something?

"...As violent as ever but now on a mission and with

tremendous wealth and power…," Benton is saying, and I trusted him. I trusted Lucy. I believed what I was told and have been misled.

I understand why they couldn't share top secret information. There's much I don't discuss with them either. We often have little choice but to lie by omission. Knowing that doesn't make me feel any better. Had the roles been reversed, I would have found a way to warn them.

"This video was posted yesterday at six P.M. East Coast time. Halloween, as the sun was setting," Benton says, and Lucy's cryptic remarks are making more sense.

You'll be told some things, and you should. It's time. I hear my niece's voice in my head.

I can tell by the sound of the helicopter's engines that she's lifting off from the tarmac in front of the trailer. As she pulls in power, the roaring and thudding get louder and change pitch. Of course, she's aware of what Marino and I are learning. She's been dropping ominous hints all day and can't feel good about any of this.

No doubt she's known the truth from the start. That's why she began working with New Scotland Yard and Interpol when she did. It had to do with Carrie Grethen. Attempting to track her and everything she's involved in likely led Lucy to Huck and Brittany Manson. Carrie has continued to be Lucy's major preoccupation, and that's the truth of the matter.

"…A recruitment video and the first time the *Prizrak* has shown herself. Let's take a listen," Benton says, and the video begins playing.

* * *

Dressed in a tactical jacket, cargo pants and boots, Carrie Grethen holds a submachine gun in her graceful hands. She's facile and sinewy strong, in her early fifties and aging well. The younger woman with her carries a large metal ammo box.

Physically imposing with dyed red hair and Slavic bone structure, the younger woman wears camouflage, her affect oddly vague. Her gait is stiff and slightly jerky as if she has bad knees or a prosthetic limb. She and Carrie walk along berms on a windswept firing range in slanted sunlight, their shadows elongated on dead grass.

Then Carrie stops and turns around, staring directly into the camera. Her piercing stare runs right through me like an electrical current, my mouth dry, my heart pounding.

"*... Greetings from one of my favorite places to train in the beautiful region of Yarosavl Oblast...*" Carrie's voice sounds the same but with a Russian accent, and it penetrates my soul to hear her again.

I stare at scars on her once pretty face, the deformation of her once perfectly shaped nose and ears. I can hear the long blade of a stiletto hissing out and see the look in her eyes as she strode toward me intending to end my life. Then blood was flying everywhere as I was knocked unconscious.

"*... Let me give you a brief tour of what is in this area,*" Carrie says in the video, her garish blond hair short with rose-gold highlights as if she's my niece's parody. "*Who knows, you may want to visit someday and avail yourself of the very special and elite training we offer...*"

I first met her at the FBI's Engineering Research Facility (ERF) on the same Quantico campus as their famed academy. Lucy was a senior at UVA, a computer genius, a magician at AI coding. I'd managed to get her an internship with the FBI and will regret it for the rest of my life.

Living in a dorm with new agents in training, she was assigned to ERF. Her supervisor was Carrie Grethen, an outside contractor twelve years her senior. Lucy had no idea what she was up against. None of us did.

"*...Just over the berms and beyond the trees is Lake Nero and the majestic Cathedral of the Assumption...*"

I'd be disingenuous if I said I hadn't found Carrie impressive. Together she and my niece were creating an AI network. They were talking about quantum computing before most people had heard of it, their entanglement intensely competitive and obsessive. Carrie became a constant presence in Lucy's FBI Academy dorm room, and I didn't approve. But I understood the attraction.

"*...Also, the whimsical Princess Frog Museum. A reminder that it's not the Russian people who are uncivilized and brutish...*"

Carrie gave me an uneasy feeling from the start, but she had a security clearance in a classified facility. She was brilliant and charming. I couldn't possibly know she was evil. It seemed nobody did, including the very FBI personnel she worked with daily. At the time her hair was long and dark. She was statuesque and graceful, the sort to turn heads and command respect.

"*...We have peaceful monasteries in the area where we are welcome to stay while we train very hard, and that is appropriate. We serve the highest of causes with the devotion of someone in a religious order...*"

Benton says the original sin in all this goes back to an abusive childhood malignant with religious judgment and sexual perversion. She's projected her self-loathing onto Lucy. Added to that is a pathological need for Carrie to possess what she can't have. She envies Lucy and is obsessed with her. While that might make sense, I'm beyond giving a damn about the reason.

* * *

"... *This is where we train the most precise snipers, the most valiant of warriors in the world...*," Carrie says on the video, and it's as if she's in the room with Marino and me.

Her eyes lack warmth like a reptile even as she smiles arrogantly. She seems to know something that's amusing. I try to block out the memories of our last encounter when she came close to killing all of us while we were living in Massachusetts.

"... *Today I will introduce you to a very special AR-nine rifle...*"

She showed up at the house while Dorothy was visiting. My sister didn't realize who she'd been friendly with earlier on the commercial flight. She inadvertently led Carrie to our door.

"...*I'm going to demonstrate its capabilities. This is how we combat the infidels. Death to America...!*"

"Unbelievable!" Marino blurts out angrily. "Why the fuck would you not tell us this before now?"

Smacking an extended magazine into the submachine gun, Carrie racks back the bolt. She loads a round as I watch the video in astonishment.

CLANK-CLANK-CLANK-CLANK-CLANK...

She mows down a row of metal targets, the spent cartridge cases grabbed by a bag called a brass catcher that's attached to her weapon's folding stock. She switches her AR-9 to fully automatic, blasting away at a military truck. Next, she's inside a *kill house* constructed of tires filled with sand.

The video cuts to her companion emptying the brass catcher into a bucket, the cartridge cases clinking. She trades loaded magazines for empty ones, playing the role of armorer.

"*This is Yana.*" Carrie introduces her with a hint of flirtation, and I suspect they're more than just colleagues.

Yana smiles into the camera, her eyes unblinking, and she gives me an eerie feeling. Her front teeth are badly discolored, as I often see when someone was on a medication like tetracycline as a child.

"*Yana, how do you like serving with our group?*" Carrie asks her.

"*It is a cause I will happily die for,*" she says in a heavy accent, her English awkward. "*It is my honor and my privilege to defend my country from the infidels in the West. And to work with such a great soldier as yourself.*"

"*You sound proud.*"

"*I'm very proud. This has given me the purpose I've always wanted.*"

"*Why is that important, Yana?*" Carrie continues their stilted, propaganda-driven conversation.

"*Without a purpose there is no motivation to exist. There is nothing but disappointment and meaninglessness.*"

"*Which is something the infidels don't understand and why they will fail ultimately,*" Carrie says with contempt. "*They are spoiled and weak.*"

The video cuts to a scene in the woods where Carrie takes out an invisible tactical unit with an explosion of firepower.

"Holy shit...," Marino keeps saying.

Then Carrie is back on the range shooting a round into a ballistic gelatin torso wearing body armor that Yana removes. The bullet has penetrated Kevlar, causing terrific damage. Embedded inside the transparent gelatin is a copper bullet that looks like the one Tron cut out of the tree.

"*... See? Very special and unique...*"

Carrie shows us a hefty live round in the palm of her hand. The cartridge case is dark green, the pointed copper nose painted yellow.

"*... The nine-by-thirty-nine SP-Six two-hundred-and-fifty-grain armor-piercing is copper-clad with a hardened steel core. It trucks along at a thousand feet per second, tumbling like a tomahawk...*"

"Meet the Kremlin's super recruiter for its mercenary shadow army," Benton says.

"*... It will penetrate eight millimeters of steel at one hundred meters,*" Carrie explains on the video. "*Because of the air pocket deliberately built into the tip, the bullet tumbles its way through flesh, creating a devastating wound channel. All to say, tremendous stopping power...*"

"How is this possible?" Marino stares at the video, his face livid.

"We're sorry to ruin your day," Lucas answers sincerely in his French accent.

"You've ruined a lot more than that!"

"*... I'm often asked why the bullet's penetrator tip is yellow.*" Carrie talks directly into the camera, her eyes digging into mine. "*The answer is simple. It is my favorite color.*" The video stops.

"Holy shit, I'm not believing this!" Marino erupts again.

"I thought she died while she was locked up at Bridgewater. What the hell else have we been lied to about?"

Seven years ago, Carrie Grethen was incarcerated in a hospital for the criminally insane outside of Boston. A month later, she died suddenly. I recused myself from the case. For every reason imaginable I couldn't be the medical examiner. Marino and I were told that she suffered an anaphylactic reaction to an antibiotic while alone inside her maximum-security cell.

Her airway closed, her cause of death asphyxiation. Not an easy way to go, but far more humane than what she'd done to others. We were informed that her body was spirited away by the federal government and examined at Dover Air Force Base in Delaware. I never saw the reports, and that's the way it was supposed to be. It made perfect sense that Carrie's autopsy would be handled by the military.

I wasn't told what became of her remains or if she might be buried somewhere. I didn't make any attempt to learn the details. After decades of her violence and destructiveness, she was out of our lives finally and forever. In retrospect it's making sense that Benton had a different reaction. He didn't relax or seem relieved, reminding me we should never let our guard down. If not Carrie, there will be another enemy, he said.

I remember his words struck me as oddly prophetic. About this same time Lucy began working with New Scotland Yard and Interpol. She rented the flat in London, and her partner Janet and their son Desi moved in. When COVID started, their lives were forever upended. Now I'm left to question the truth about everything.

"Carrie Grethen was traded for two high-value Americans held prisoner in a Russian penal colony," says Gus with the

CIA. "They were in very poor health due to harsh conditions that included torture. There was nothing in the news about it, their identities protected out of necessity."

He explains that Carrie was flown by private jet from Hanscom Air Force Base in Massachusetts to the Abu Dhabi International Airport in the United Arab Emirates where the exchange was made. From there she went to Moscow. This happened the night before her faked death was made public.

"I'm not believing this crap! That's like turning over bin Laden," Marino complains loudly, accusingly.

"Close enough, and gives a sense of Carrie Grethen's high value," Benton replies. "She'd spent a lot of time in Russia by the time she was locked up in Boston. The Kremlin was willing to do a lot to get her released to them, and our government had an opportunity that was hard to resist. I didn't think it was a good idea. But I wasn't in charge."

CHAPTER 21

I APPRECIATE KNOWING THE TRUTH," I say to everyone on the video screens. "Bad news that it is. Maybe the worst in a long time. But I'm just going to keep asking. How is it okay to be discussing a top secret investigation, a secret prisoner swap, with us? I have a security clearance. But Marino doesn't."

"That's already been taken care of," answers Gus with the CIA. "I thought you knew that when you were briefed," he adds, and I don't believe him.

"What are you talking about?" Marino looks baffled.

"The minute you stepped foot inside the REMOTE we granted you an OTRI," Gus replies. "I assumed Lucy discussed this with you as you were getting ready."

What he says is another misdirect. More bluntly put, a lie. If they're monitoring us, then they know the subject of classified information didn't come up. That's how they wanted it, and now we've been exposed. We can't unknow what we've been told. And if either of us don't play by the rules, our careers will be over. We could suffer consequences far worse than that. I'm used to this, but Marino isn't.

"What the hell is an OTRI?" he asks with growing aggravation.

"A one-time read-in granting you a temporary top secret clearance," Gus tells him.

"No thanks."

"It's not an option."

"I don't want anything to do with all your spooky stuff."

"You're already here and the information has been shared. You've been exposed to our spooky stuff," Gus says. "And now you're held to a higher standard. This is out of necessity."

"Yeah, and the higher standard you're talking about could land me in jail."

"Up to ten years if you share top secret information with someone unauthorized," Gus says. "Of course, if you get charged with treason, that's a different matter."

"How long have you known that Carrie Grethen is on the loose?" Marino is doing his best to hold his temper. "Seems like it would be a good thing to pass along to those of us she's tried to kill more than once."

I screw a ten-gauge needle into a syringe that's big enough for a horse as everyone continues the discussion. We're reassured that Carrie is in Russia. That's where she was when she filmed the video two days ago with her associate Yana Popova, a mercenary sniper.

"As far as we know, Carrie hasn't been back in this country since she was transported to Moscow seven years ago in the dead of night," Gus says. "Russia's shadow army is notorious for scooping people out of prison and forcing them into military service. Only Carrie didn't need coercing. And she's too valuable to send to the front."

"*As far as you know* she's not been back here since you gave her a private jet ride to freedom?" Marino echoes. "I sure as hell don't like the sound of that. How could you not track her?"

"Once someone is in Russia and protected by the Kremlin, it's not so easy. Especially if the person is shrewd enough to stay off the radar." It's Bart Clancy, the head of counterterrorism, who answers. "She dropped out of sight until yesterday. We have no reason to think she's been in the U.S. It would be far too risky."

"But that doesn't mean she hasn't traveled across the border, moving freely throughout Europe." Gus from the CIA again. "She has the means to get around."

"You're telling me you've had no idea what she's been doing all this time?" Marino doesn't believe it.

"We've suspected she's involved with the Kremlin's mercenary army. We believe she's the *Prizrak*, the Ghost mentioned in chatter on the Dark Web. But she hasn't shown herself until now," Bart repeats.

"Are we one hundred percent sure she isn't in the United States? Maybe here in Virginia? Are we positive she didn't take out the Mansons herself with her fancy yellow-tipped bullets?" Marino is getting more bent out of shape, confronting our hosts on the video displays. "Because nobody's safe when she's in the area. I can't believe we're hearing all this now...!"

"She didn't personally take out the Mansons, but that doesn't mean she isn't behind it. I believe she is," Benton says. "And I agree with you, Pete. Her not being in the country doesn't mean we're safe..."

As I'm listening, my mood is worsening, the thought of who we're talking about surreal and enraging. I won't be distracted by her. I won't give her my emotional energy. Even as I'm telling myself this my fury borders on the homicidal, and I resent anyone having that much power. I try very hard not to hate. It disturbs me that I can imagine putting a bullet in Carrie Grethen's head.

I was beyond relieved when I heard she was dead. It was like finding out a terrible scourge had come to an end, and I felt no remorse about injuring her badly, permanently. I'd come home to discover her in the backyard with Dorothy and nine-year-old Desi. There wasn't time for me to get my gun, and I regret that I wasn't able to end Carrie forever.

"...She doesn't have to be here to cause tremendous destruction and chaos," Benton explains. "She has boots on the ground..."

Just the thought of her pulls at my very soul, and I'll take up all of this with Lucy and Benton in private when I see them. We'll have to talk about how we live going forward. But for now, I must focus on what's in front of me. I tell Marino we need to get started on the female victim, and he leaves the autopsy compartment, making his way back to the cooler.

* * *

"I don't know how many of you have witnessed a postmortem examination," I say to our remote audience, and several heads nod affirmative.

I explain that what they're about to see isn't for the faint of heart. It's important not to fixate on any single detail of what

I'm doing. I begin giving them a quick primer about what to look for and how to prevent getting sick or fainting.

"If you find yourself staring too long at any one thing, avert your gaze," I'm saying. "The trick is not to fixate while keeping your mind on the reason for all this. It's not about the gore. It's about finding the answers."

By the time I've outlined what to expect, Marino is bumping and clanging his way through the airlock. He rolls in the stretcher, parking it next to the autopsy table. We put on our respirators, from now on talking through rubbery speaking diaphragms.

"First what I need to do is draw blood from both victims," I explain to our remote audience as images of Carrie flash disturbingly in my head.

Old files reopen in my memory, one after the next. I can't make them stop. I never could while I knew she was alive. My first impression of her was shadowed by something I couldn't identify at the time. When we met, she was willowy tall and gracefully pretty in a lab coat, her chair pulled up close to Lucy in front of a computer screen.

My niece was barely out of her teens when she got involved with Carrie, and I realized the truth early on. I spotted them passing a lighted cigarette back and forth, intimately talking in quiet voices. This was after dark in the academy's picnic area, and I slipped away before they saw me. Or I assumed I did, but that's not what I believe anymore.

Carrie wanted me to know about the two of them. She made sure I did, her every action intricately calculated. I continue to blame her for seducing Lucy while exposing her to the darkest of energies. I suppose I've held Carrie responsible for every bad thing that's ever happened to my niece.

"Rapid test DNA can give us results in less than two hours," I hear myself explaining. "But the profiles won't help if we have nothing to compare them to. I'm hoping investigators have collected potential sources from the Mansons' home, for example. Such as their toothbrushes, their clothing."

"Your DNA lab has what we found inside their Nokesville farmhouse," Bart answers. "I remind you that the Mansons hadn't been arrested yet. Their fingerprints and DNA aren't in law enforcement databases."

But that doesn't mean investigators such as Lucy didn't get the evidence other ways. She's the sort to tail a suspect, waiting until the person discards a coffee cup, a food wrapper, a cigarette butt, a vape cartridge.

"Hopefully, we'll be able to confirm identifications quickly," Benton says as Marino unzips the double pouches.

I pick up the large syringe from the cart. The dead woman's legs are cold and stiff through my gloves, and she's difficult to manipulate. Inserting the needle into the upper inner thigh, I'm pretty good at finding the femoral artery on the first try. Blood no longer oxygenated is dark red as I fill a test tube preloaded with a fluoride preservative. I place it inside a cardboard mailer for safe transport.

I explain to those watching that this might be a good time for them to take a break. Changing my gloves, I pass through the airlock, returning to the cooler where the male victim awaits cocooned in his body bags. Unzipping them, I draw a tube of his blood that I label and box like the other one. These go inside the vestibule's evidence refrigerator, and every reflection on shiny metal, every sound startles me.

I'm jumpy as hell, expecting Carrie to suddenly appear out of nowhere, and I've not felt like this in seven years. I worry what damage she's caused during the interim as my thoughts continue drifting back to what happened to Lucy's family. What if her partner Janet and their son Desi didn't die from COVID as we've been led to believe? What if they were poisoned or killed by some other means, and I wasn't told the truth about that either?

Deconning again, I return to the autopsy compartment. I remind everyone that Marino and I don't have our phones.

"We're unable to contact our labs or anyone." I direct this at the video screens as people return to the conference table with coffee and bottles of water.

I tell them that someone needs to alert Clark Givens. The tubes of blood are waiting in the vestibule refrigerator, and he has the codes for getting inside the trailer and collecting them. He needs to do this right away. The sooner we can confirm the victims' identities, the better.

"Also, Henry Addams of Addams Family Mortuary should be notified that the bodies are here. He'll be called when they're ready for pickup," I'm saying.

"We'll take care of it," Benton promises.

"Normally, I would draw vitreous fluid from the eyes." I work my hands into a pair of fresh gloves. "It tells you whether the drug and alcohol levels were on their way up or down at the time of death. It's the most accurate measure of how impaired someone might have been at the time of death. But that won't be possible with the female victim because of damage done by aquatic life."

"Consider yourselves lucky," Marino tells everyone "It's no fun watching a needle being stuck in someone's eye even if they're dead."

"Sexual assault is unlikely in this case." I retrieve a physical evidence recovery kit, a PERK, from a cabinet. "But I'm not about to make assumptions. What I'm going to do now is swab her orifices, clip her fingernails, checking for evidence that might be from an assailant."

Opening the box, I remove the PERK's contents, a simple black plastic comb, swabs, test tubes, small paper bags, fingernail clippers. I also rely heavily on Post-its. Their adhesive backing is ideal for collecting hairs, fibers and other trace evidence. Arranging everything on the paper-covered countertop, I walk my audience through the process.

I explain the same way I do when it's a demo autopsy for rookie cops. Peeling the wrapper off a plastic speculum, I put on a lighted magnifier headset. I sense the discomfort of those watching as I swab orifices while checking for any sign of recent sexual activity, consensual or otherwise.

"She has significant postmortem injury to soft tissue from being preyed upon by animals living in the lake." I explain her appearance. "If you didn't know what you're looking at, you might think her genitalia, her breasts, her face were mutilated. But that's not what happened."

Her jaw is clamped tight, the muscles fully rigorous as if she's being stubborn. I have to pry open her clenched teeth with a thin metal file. Wedging my fingers inside, I force her mouth open wide.

"Her front teeth are chipped, one of them in half," I explain while looking for foreign objects. Swabbing the inside of her cheeks, her throat, I notice she's bitten the side of her tongue.

"Obviously, she was still alive at the time," I tell Marino as we lift the body off the stretcher.

We set it down on top of the autopsy table, and she's looking worse by the moment. Her abdomen is marbled green and bloating as decomposition advances. Her empty eye sockets and bared broken teeth, the damage caused by aquatic predators, are more startling than before.

"Holy mother of God," Secret Service Director Bella Steele mutters at she takes it in.

"I warn you that the victims are in bad shape and what you're about to see won't get any easier." I continue telling everyone what to expect as I roll the digital x-ray machine close to the table. "If you've never watched an autopsy, these aren't good ones to start with."

CHAPTER 22

I REPOSITION THE C-ARM around the table, x-raying the body from head to toe. Images appear in quadrants of the hard-wired video display on a cart. I point out two linear objects flaring bright white inside the torso, what's left of the hiking poles impaling the victim. I describe cutting through the metal shafts so I could close the body bags.

"With both victims, the hiking poles were stabbed all the way through, the shaft protruding front and back," I'm saying.

I begin sliding them out of the body, careful not to further damage the surrounding tissue. I place the two sections of bloody aluminum tubing inside a large paper bag that I label and seal.

"We'll check for DNA and trace evidence," I explain. "I can say with a fair amount of confidence that she was already dead by the time she was impaled. The hiking poles perforated her liver and pancreas, and I'm not seeing any tissue response."

"Unnecessary violence and degradation are limbically driven," Benton says. "There was no logical reason to strip the bodies, to degrade and mutilate them. The motivation was purely emotional and also to send a message."

"Maybe this is a dumb question," Bella says, "but can you tell whose hiking poles impaled whom? I'm assuming they belonged to the victims."

I explain that both pairs are the same brand and advertised as tactical. Black with sharply pointed tips, they're designed for self-defense in the wilderness should one be confronted by an adversary, human or otherwise. There's no mud basket, the plastic-cup-like barrier near the tip that helps prevent the pole from sinking in mud or snow.

"Similar to what you see on ski poles," I describe. "If the hiking poles had those it would have been impossible to stab them all the way through a body. You can adjust shafts to different lengths depending on preference, and the victims had done that. One set was extended to five feet long, the other four inches shorter."

"I think we can safely guess that the longer poles were the male's," Benton says. "Do you recall who was stabbed with what?"

"Yes. And it would appear they were impaled with their own poles. The shorter ones were used on her, the longer ones on him," I reply.

"Could be a coincidence," Aiden the press secretary says.

"Unlikely," Benton answers. "A taunt meant to hint that the assailant knew his victims and is showing contempt."

"Intentional or not, chances are the assailant did this last, perhaps right before he dumped her body in the lake and his in the mineshaft," I explain.

"Overkill. Rage and frustration," Benton says. "This isn't

typical. To be successful, assassins are coldly calculating. They're detached emotionally, feeling nothing. It's just a job. That's not what happened with the Mansons. I'd call everything about what we're seeing emotionally out of control and sloppy."

"Frustrated about what?" Marino thinks forensic psychology is mostly mumbo jumbo.

He's always been skeptical when experts appear on the scene and start predicting the age of the killer, his ethnicity, the car he drives, how he feels about his mother. It's been my experience that very often the profiles are wrong. They can be destructively misleading.

"Things didn't go as planned and it made him very angry," Benton says, his intuition rarely off the mark. "This is someone who has an insatiable need to overpower. Someone who gets off on it. And the more he's resisted by his victim or doesn't get what he wants, the more the violence is going to escalate."

I continue moving the x-ray machine's C-arm around the table, images changing on the display. The victim has multiple skull fractures that I point out. She has a broken jaw, clavicle and left arm.

"All of it caused by severe blunt force trauma," I explain.

"Let me make sure I understand. At some point she was beaten?" Bella asks.

"Very badly, yes."

"What about the male? Were the same things done to both of them?"

"Based on what I saw at the scene, some of their injuries are similar. Others aren't," I reply. "He's missing part of his head, very possibly from being shot. He has a compound fracture of his left femur, possibly from being dropped more than twenty feet into a mineshaft. We'll know more when I get him on the table."

I explain that the female has multiple blunt force trauma injuries, and the question is whether they were inflicted before or after she was shot. I draw attention to the radio-opaque shape of a projectile in her abdomen.

"I can tell you right now that's not from their ammunition." Marino looks at the x-ray image. "They were shooting ten-mil Hydra-Shok hollow-points that expand on impact. The bullet casing is scored to open like a razor-sharp metal claw so it can do the most damage. That's not what this is."

"Possibly a rifle round," I reply. "Probably the same thing Tron found at the scene. And there's something else in her left hip."

It's too small for a bullet, the cylindrical shape too regular to be shrapnel. There's no correlating injury, no entrance wound.

"Whatever it is, we'll get there soon enough. I try to do things in a certain order, so I don't forget anything," I explain. "Next I want to look at her hands."

* * *

Rigor mortis has continued to advance, requiring considerable effort to break the stiffness in the arms, allowing me to manipulate them. I hold up the hands, turning them front and back while explaining that missing fingertips and other areas of flesh are from marine predation. As I pass along the gory details, I'm envisioning the massive turtle head surfacing, the shadow of it under the surface.

"These injuries are what's known as postmortem artifacts,

normal changes that occur after death," I explain to the video screens. "The exception is the hiking poles. I'm all but certain those were a parting gesture."

"They were a weapon of opportunity," Benton says. "That's not what the killer brought with him to take out the victims. He came prepared for a one-sided battle in which he planned to completely overpower them. He knew they didn't have a chance."

"To play devil's advocate," Bella Steele asks, "are we absolutely certain an animal didn't kill them? I can't imagine a bear stabbing someone with hiking poles, but we need to explore every possibility. God only knows what accusations and theories will be flying around. We'd better be able to address them."

"It would seem that a bear or bobcat might inflict injuries similar to some of what we're seeing." Bart of counterterrorism speaks up. "You know, if you put your hands out to protect yourself?" He defensively raises his arms as if about to be mauled. "And something big could have dragged the male down into the mineshaft. We don't know what lives in there."

"If claws or teeth were involved, I would expect to see the associated gashes and puncture wounds." I pick up a magnifier from the surgical cart. "The injuries to this woman's hands front and back are incisions. You can see the clean edges made by a sharp blade. The male victim has the same type of injuries, their hands, fingers, wrists cut in an organized manner and for a purpose."

"In your opinion, why would someone do that?" Bart asks me from the video displays.

"The assailant was trying to find something." It's Benton who answers. "I'm guessing that's the purpose and not mutilation.

He also was enraged, his system in overdrive. It's important to remember there can be more than one reason."

Benton explains that surveillance video footage from a variety of sources indicate Huck and Brittany Manson had injected RFID microchips beneath their skin. They purchased the necessary equipment off the internet and did it to themselves. As he's informing us of this, I open a cabinet, finding the old-style handheld RFID scanner.

It's the same thing used in a veterinarian's office to read a chip that's been injected into your pet. Only this scanner, like our camera, is obsolete and cumbersome. It's used only in here and must be plugged into an electrical outlet. People injecting microchips into themselves isn't as uncommon as it used to be. But we know to look and have found them in the past.

These days injected RFID or near-field communication (NFC) microchips can be located by scanner apps available for your phone. It's what I use to track bodies and evidence throughout my building.

"Huck and Brittany had chipped their right hands," Benton says. "You can see them on their security cameras releasing electronic locks they'd installed at their store, the fulfillment center, their house. A wave of a hand and they could open doors." He shows us with an abracadabra gesture. "They could pay for things without physical credit cards if they wanted. Only someone close to them or spying would know this."

"A typical location for those types of chips is in the web of the hand between the thumb and the forefinger," says Gus with the CIA.

"It wouldn't be possible to cut such a thing out of a body without knowing it was there and having a means to find it," I reply. "This would be especially challenging in the dark, suggesting to me that the assailant had some sort of night-vision enhancement."

"I think you can count on that," Benton says.

"If a chip has been injected, it's going to light up when syncing with the scanner. You can see it glowing under the skin," I reply. "So, it wouldn't have been difficult to find a microchip if you knew about it in advance and had a scanner app on your phone."

"The assailant had to have known to look, that's absolutely true," says Lucas from Interpol. "But why make so many cuts? Why slash up both hands?"

"Frustration and rage. He didn't find what he'd come for," Benton repeats as I scan the lower arms and hands.

"Well, I'm supposing he found something. The microchip isn't here now. The same may be true with the male victim. We'll know soon enough." I continue to tell them what I'm finding.

"I wouldn't be surprised if the assassin took them," Benton says. "But they weren't going to be helpful. It wasn't what this person was looking for."

"If you don't know who the killer is, how can you be so sure what he was after?" Marino asks skeptically. "Maybe he just hated the Mansons and that's why he tore the hell out of everything, including them."

"I'm going to venture a guess that he found the microchips implanted in Huck's and Brittany's hands," Benton replies. "And he realized that wasn't what he was looking for. This was when he started smashing up everything, impaling the bodies and all the rest."

I move the cumbersome RFID scanner over the left hip where the small object shows up on x-ray. Nothing happens.

"Am I to assume that what you're looking for isn't a normal microchip with a radio antenna?" I ask.

"It's not," Gus says.

"I don't want to get your hopes up. But whatever this is inside her left hip, it's not syncing with the scanner. Nothing is lighting up under the skin." I continue moving the scanner around, to no avail.

"So we know it's not an RFID or NFC chip," Gus says.

"Unless it's embedded too deeply for the signal to be picked up," I reply. "But I don't think so. It's barely six millimeters under the skin, not even a quarter of an inch, about five millimeters in size."

Using x-ray images to guide me, I find the spot in an area the assailant apparently didn't know to check. Otherwise, I imagine he would have made more cuts.

"Even if he had?" I tell everyone. "There's a good chance he wasn't going to find what he was looking for without an x-ray machine."

Blood oozes darkly as I make exploratory incisions. Digging my gloved fingers into the wounds, I feel around, finding nothing. I continue cutting, hitting something small and hard.

"Maybe this is what the assailant was after." Digging it out, I wipe off a glass capsule. "Bigger than the typical microchip but still small enough to implant with a low-gauge hypodermic needle. I don't know what this is, but I don't think it's for unlocking doors."

"Thank God you found it," Bella says.

"Why the hell would anyone chip their ass?" Marino asks.

"It's a fleshy area where something tiny could be concealed." That's the best I can suggest.

"This is very good news," Gus replies.

"A glass capsule with a tiny black square object inside." I'm looking at it with an illuminated magnifier. "This is what the killer was after, I assume?"

"Think of it as a micro hard drive holding data we don't want the enemy anywhere near," Benton explains, and he's talking about Carrie Grethen and her Russian comrades.

"You're thinking that's why she had someone whack the Mansons?" Marino asks. "To get this micro hard drive?"

"It's not the only reason," Benton says. "But Carrie, the Kremlin, want it. And she expected that the assassin was going to deliver it."

"Uh-oh, I wouldn't want to be the one who goes home without it," Marino says. "A good way to have your head wash up on a beach somewhere."

I seal the glass capsule inside an evidence button that I'm instructed to enclose in a Faraday bag. There should be one inside the vestibule locker, and I expect the chip will be spirited away without further explanation. I may never know its purpose or why the U.S. government and Russia are after it.

"Be back in a few," Marino says.

Changing his gloves, he takes the evidence button, heading through the airlock. I pick up the scalpel and make the Y-incision from clavicle to clavicle, down to the pubic bone. Reflecting back tissue, I cut through the breastplate of ribs, removing the bloc of organs, setting it on the cutting board.

It doesn't take long for me to find the projectile that I expect was her initial injury. I hold up the bullet, copper-clad with a yellow-painted tip like the one Tron cut out of the tree.

"I believe we've seen this before." I show it to our audience.

"Carrie's Grethen's special AR-nine ammunition," Bart says.

Using a steel ladle, I fill a large measuring cup with more than a liter of blood pooled in the abdomen.

"The bullet ripped through the iliac artery and vein, shredding her colon," I explain. "She hemorrhaged and would have died in a matter of minutes. Exsanguination due to a gunshot wound is going to be her cause of death."

"A blitz attack in the dark," Benton says.

"Lucky for her it was quick," Bart comments.

"Not quick enough." I feel a sudden rush of anger that surprises me with its intensity. "She would have felt the gut shot. She may have felt it when she was struck in the face hard enough to break bones and teeth. But she wouldn't have felt anything for long."

CHAPTER 23

I PACKAGE THE BULLET FOR evidence that will be examined in the Secret Service labs. Returning to the cutting board, I pick up a pair of surgical scissors, snipping through the stomach, smoothing it open, and it's wrinkled like wet sand. Nothing is inside but a small amount of brownish fluid that I collect for toxicology.

"She'd not eaten anything close to the time she was killed," I say as Marino returns.

"What do you think they did when they heard this invisible thing coming for them?" Bella asks Benton as if he's a psychic.

"The footpath is almost a mile long. They knew they had a good twenty or thirty minutes before the intruder reached their campsite," he replies. "They would have done everything they could to get as ready as possible."

"You think they had any idea who it was?" Marino puts on fresh gloves and the respirator.

"I doubt it," Benton says. "But even if they did, they were caught completely off guard, and that was the intention."

He paints a picture of them turning on camping lanterns inside their tent as they monitored the intruder's progress over the surveillance cameras' microphone. Scrambling to collect guns and ammunition, they loaded extra magazines. They grabbed the thermal imaging nightscope that wasn't going to work any better than their trail cameras did.

As paranoid as they must have been, it surprises me they had no body armor, not even a bulletproof vest. What that tells me is they weren't expecting an ambush. It never entered their minds that something like this could happen until their cameras alerted them to the intruder on the footpath. Huck and Brittany got dressed and ready. They waited inside the tent as a steady rain fell in the foggy dark.

"They would have talked and planned while inside the tent." Benton continues explaining what he thinks happened. "They could calculate how long it would take for the intruder to reach them. I'm going to guess that they stayed sheltered until he was about ten minutes out, and then turned off the camping lanterns."

They ventured outside, positioning themselves in the woods near the entrance of the footpath. Likely they had their phones with them and were monitoring the trail cameras.

"Adrenaline is pumping, and they're in fight and flight mode simultaneously because they're cornered," Benton describes. "The impulse is to run. But they can't go anywhere, their only hope to take out whoever it is."

He theorizes that Brittany and Huck were hiding in the pine trees where most of the blood was later recovered. When they could hear the intruder getting close, they put away their phones so he couldn't see them glowing in the pitch dark. Then the Mansons opened fire, but to no avail, and Brittany was shot. Probably Huck as well, the yellow-tipped bullets ripping through his neck and taking off the back of his head.

"It's very possible they never got a look at their assailant," Benton says. "Obviously, he had night-vision capabilities, as I've mentioned. He could see his targets, but they couldn't see him because he was utilizing some type of technology that can defeat thermal imaging."

"How might that be possible?" Bella asks.

"Thermal imagers can detect fluctuations as minor as a fraction of a degree." It's Gus who explains. "These differences paint the picture instead of light and shadow. But in this case, there was no heat signature, no images."

"Sensors were fooled into perceiving that the intruder was the same temperature as the air he passed through," Benton adds. "What that suggests is the gear he had on was constantly making the most subtle adjustments, the sensors reading the surrounding air and sending signals to defeat thermal imagers. There's no other explanation unless we're dealing with a killer that's paranormal."

"What you're describing sounds absolutely terrifying," Bella says as I'm sectioning a lung, the blade hitting something hard. "Imagine hearing this thing coming but you can't see it."

I dig out a piece of broken tooth. Then I discover another one.

"She aspirated them." I explain what I've found. "The blunt force trauma was inflicted soon after she was shot. She was still breathing, perhaps gasping, when she received powerful blows to the head, breaking her front teeth, fracturing her jaw, her nose and other facial bones."

I spend the next few minutes sectioning the rest of the organs, all of them healthy and unremarkable. I cut along the hairline, reflecting back the scalp, exposing a skull fractured by multiple hard blows. Turning on the Stryker saw, I press the oscillating blade against bone, and we don't talk over the infernal grinding.

Weighing the brain, I place it on the cutting board. I begin sectioning with a carbon-steel knife that has a long wide blade. It also came from Wild World, and I can't help but think of the irony. The badly contused and lacerated left frontal lobe shows little vital response to the injuries. Everything I'm seeing confirms she was killed brutally but quickly.

"The longer somebody survives, the worse they look." I drop sections of brain into the jar of formalin tinged dark pink from blood. "She was already dead or almost dead when she was hit in the head. The question is with what. On gross examination I'm not seeing pattern injuries that might have been caused by a weapon."

"Maybe she was banged against the ground?" Bella suggests, an unpleasant expression on her face.

"I would expect abrasions." I extend the Y-incision up both sides of the neck, all the way to the ears. "Often dirt and bits of rocks are embedded in the wound, and I'm not seeing that."

Undermining the skin, I expose the torn strap muscles and neck organs. I remove the tongue, the crushed larynx, windpipe and hyoid. I rinse them with water I squeeze from a sponge, patting them dry with a towel.

* * *

Marino takes photographs, winding our obsolete camera each time to advance the film. At intervals he steps over to a countertop, writing down organ weights and other details on forms attached to the clipboard.

"I can't say when she bit the left side of her tongue, but obviously, she was alive when that happened," I continue. "It's a significant injury with hemorrhage, likely occurring around the time she was killed."

I describe a deep laceration on the inside of her upper lip, and blood at fracture sites in bony structures of the neck. All of it indicates she still had a blood pressure for a brief period.

"Sounds like she had the hell beaten out of her," says Elena with the NSA.

"What we're seeing here isn't typical," I reply. "These injuries aren't."

I explain that the bones of the neck are broken in a pattern that's unfamiliar. I've handled a lot of strangulations in my career but never seen one like this.

"First, she was shot in the abdomen. After that, the assailant confronted her physically," I say to the video displays. "He struck her hard enough to break her teeth and the bones in her lower face. He fractured her skull."

This is when she bit her tongue, I suspect. Her neck was crushed as she hemorrhaged internally from the gunshot wound. At some point she was impaled with the hiking poles, but by then she was dead or close to it.

"Although her eyes and some areas of her face are missing, we're not seeing any sign of petechia, the pinpoint broken blood vessels I would expect if she'd still had a blood pressure when she was throttled," I'm saying. "That's one of the hallmarks of manual strangulation."

"Overkill." Benton keeps saying it. "Sexualized aggression."

"The injuries to her neck go all the way around, and I've not seen anything quite like that before." I continue to explain. "Something gripped her with extreme force."

"Which brings us back to a huge animal," Elena suggests. "Is that possible, Doctor Scarpetta?"

"Not unless it has hands."

"That's not good considering the footprint I found," Marino reminds everyone. "A Sasquatch can crush an alligator's skull with its bare hands. Imagine what it could do to a person."

"These two victims weren't attacked by a Sasquatch, assuming there is such a thing," I reply. "They were brutally killed by a human." I move out of the way as Marino takes photographs, using a plastic ruler as a scale.

"But how do we know this for a fact?" Bella plays devil's advocate again. "If there's an ongoing debate about whether Bigfoot is real, then I suppose it's possible it is. And if so, we can well imagine the damage something that huge and powerful could do if enraged or threatened."

"The assailant who killed these two people didn't show up on thermal imaging. This person was bulletproof and armed with an assault rifle," Benton says to everyone. "The female victim was shot by an armor-piercing bullet. Then she was beaten and manually strangled, which is personal. Often, it's sexual. The violence itself is the turn-on, the source of the offender's fantasies. It's the ultimate power rush to rip someone's life from them."

"She has what appears to be fingertip bruises, also consistent with manual strangulation." I adjust the overhead surgical lamp to get a better look. "And yet they're not. They're wider and go all the way around the neck, as I've mentioned. This is most unusual."

"Do you have an explanation?" Bella asks me. "Beyond someone with very big hands."

"I don't think a normal person could have the strength to inflict these injuries. I've never seen a neck crushed like this unless the victim was run over by a car or something similar."

"I hate to keep saying it, but that brings us back to Bigfoot," Bella replies. "I'm just asking the same questions the public will if word of that footprint gets out."

"For what it's worth, the injuries don't fit with a primate attack," I reply. "In journal articles I've read, the target areas are the face, hands, feet, the genitals."

"Like that poor lady whose face was ripped off by someone's pet chimp," Aiden the press secretary says. "She may have lost her hands too, as I recall."

"I've never heard of a chimp, gorilla or other primate strangling anything or anyone. That's not how they kill, as best I know," I explain.

"And a Bigfoot wouldn't be bulletproof or invisible on trail cameras," Marino offers as he collects the plastic bucket, setting it on top of the autopsy table.

Inside are sectioned organs and festoons of entrails that he'll place inside a plastic bag. The chest cavity is open like a tulip. Everything I've removed will be returned to the body except for tissue requiring further analysis. I close the Y-incision with long sweeps of the surgical needle.

Returning broken pieces of the skull cap to their proper position, I pull the scalp back over it, suturing the incision along the hairline with the very string I buy in bulk at Wild World. And what a strange feeling. I tell everyone watching that I'm about to start the second case. It's a good time for them to take another break.

"We'll see you in a few minutes," Benton says to me as he and his colleagues get up from the conference table. "And we won't need to watch much longer, I'm sure you'll be happy to know. I think we've got what we need, and for that we're grateful. We're fortunate some things weren't found by others."

He's referring to the micro hard drive I recovered from the female's body. Marino helps me lift the body off the table. He wheels the stretcher back to the cooler as I pick up a Sharpie from the surgical cart. I jot the date and other information on jars of sectioned organs and test tubes of fluids that I place inside a refrigerator for Fabian to collect later.

Stepping inside the decontamination compartment to disinfect, I spray down my PPE. I drink water and eat a protein bar before returning to the autopsy compartment. When Marino wheels in the second victim, we unzip the double pouches and I'm startled by a trilling chirp. Then a cricket hops out. It flies off the stretcher, landing on the floor.

"Looks like someone hitched a ride," I say to Marino. "See if you can catch it in a carton and we'll figure out what to do with it when we leave."

The cricket stares up at us as Marino finds a transparent plastic container we use for tissue and organ sections.

"Come here, Jiminy... Hold still. Nobody's gonna hurt you."

It hops away as Marino tries to block it with his Tyvek-covered foot. For the next few minutes, he makes considerable noise moving things about while the cricket artfully dodges him.

"... Stay! Crap... ! Almost... Dammit... !"

It hops behind the x-ray machine, and Marino finds a flyswatter.

"Don't you dare," I warn him.

"It's just to herd him." Marino squats down. "Come here, little fella." He gently guides the cricket with the flyswatter. "Got him! Now we're talking." He sets the plastic container on a countertop, using a scalpel to stab air holes through the lid.

I find another PERK in the cabinet, and we put our respirators back on. I swab the male victim's orifices and collect other evidence the same way I did with the female. Extracting the segments of hiking poles protruding front and back, I place them in a bag. We lift the body, setting it down on the autopsy table, and I conduct the external examination, taking x-rays.

Nothing lights up in his hip or elsewhere. I find no computer chips of any description. Extracting sections of the hiking poles perforating the liver, I place them in a large paper bag that I seal and label. It's obvious by the absence of tissue response that he was stabbed after death. By the time Benton and his colleagues are back on camera, I've answered the most important questions.

"He has no evidence of blunt force trauma and would have died quickly from massive injuries to his neck and the back of his head," I inform everyone. "I suspect these were caused by bullets that passed through and kept going. I can't know if anything such as a chip might have been removed. But if there was one embedded in the right hand, for example, it's not there now."

"While we were on our break the DNA lab was in touch confirming the victims are Huck and Brittany Manson," Bella says. "We won't be needing anything else for now and will leave you to your work." She and her colleagues have begun collecting paperwork. "Doctor Scarpetta, Investigator Marino, we're very grateful for your time and trust. Of course, you'll let us know if you discover anything else important."

"If someone could contact Addams Family Mortuary," I reply. "Henry can start heading this way."

"I'll take care of it," Benton says, his eyes meeting mine, and our video session has ended. "Cameras and microphones are going off inside the REMOTE. We won't be recording anything further, your privacy restored." Just like that the screens black out, everybody gone as if never there.

CHAPTER 24

MARINO AND I FIND ourselves suddenly alone inside the trailer's autopsy compartment, surrounded by gore and off-line video screens. Now that we're longer distracted by our formidable audience, the reality of what we've been told comes crashing home.

"I don't know what we're supposed to feel right now except pissed." Marino breaks the silence while I make the Y-incision.

"I'm weirdly numb." I reflect back tissue. "It's like being hurt and not knowing it at first. Until there's blood everywhere." I pick up the rib cutters. "And the nerves along the edges of the wound start screaming. And suddenly you realize you're about to pass out."

"I got to ask you something, Doc, and you've got to swear to be honest. Did Benton or Lucy in any way indicate that Carrie might still be around?"

"Never. I'm as stunned as you are." I cut through ribs, and the loud snaps sound sadistic. "I hope it's as Benton said and they aren't listening to us right now. I hope at least that much is true."

"If they are, they're about to get a damn earful. Talk about feeling screwed." Marino grabs the empty plastic bucket out of the sink with pent-up fury. "How could they keep this from us, as dangerous as she is?" He bangs down the bucket under the table. "I'm not believing this shit!"

"I think we understand the reason." I remove the breastplate and accompanying section of ribs.

"If nothing else? Where's the fucking respect?"

"It's not like Benton and Lucy had a choice." I lift out the bloc of organs, placing it on the cutting block. "This is nothing new when dealing with classified information."

"Well, it's new to me, and it's wrong."

"It's not personal, Marino." Using a scalpel, I cut through connective tissue.

"Hell yeah it's personal when I've got something hanging over my head for the rest of my life."

"No gastric contents except a small amount of brownish fluid," I report, and Marino jots it down on the clipboard.

"If I'd wanted to live like a spy, I would have gone to work for an intelligence agency," he continues to vent. "But I didn't. Because I damn well don't want to live like that, worrying about what I say. Especially when I live with somebody who has to know everything."

"You can't tell Dorothy." I place the liver in the hanging scale. "Seventeen hundred and fifty grams." I begin sectioning it with a chef's knife.

"I didn't ask to be involved in top secret anything and don't appreciate the exposure."

"Beefy red and within normal limits except for the two perforations caused by the hiking poles," I dictate.

"These past seven years I haven't given Carrie Grethen a damn thought. Benton and Lucy should have found a way to let us know."

"They couldn't talk about it any more than you can." I weigh the lungs one at a time. "Right is six-sixty-one grams, left is five-eighty." I pick up the knife.

Moments later I'm sawing open what's left of the skull. The brain weighs barely one thousand grams, a large chunk of the occipital lobe, the cerebellum missing. Huck's spinal cord was severed by the wound to his neck, and he was alive when he received those catastrophic injuries. Afterward, he wasn't moving or talking anymore. He would have died quickly.

"He has hemorrhage and contusion, the damage consistent with him being shot with a high-powered weapon, most likely at the same time Brittany was," I explain. "The bullets exited his body, and soon after he was either dead or well on the way."

There's no sign of blunt force trauma. It doesn't seem the assailant physically confronted Huck. He has superficial injuries from being dragged inside the mine and dropped down the shaft. Shallow puncture wounds likely are from nails in the wooden scaffolding.

"I suspect the fall is what broke his leg, but it's the head injury, the severed spinal cord that killed him and did so quickly," I say to Marino as he returns the bag of dissected organs to the chest cavity.

I thread a curved needle with cotton twine. Replacing the pieces of the shattered skull cap, I pull up the face and scalp. I begin suturing the incision around the hairline, and I can feel Marino's dark mood like a magnetic pull.

"Maybe when we have a chance to talk to Benton and Lucy, we'll feel better," I say to him. "I'm sure there was much they couldn't tell us with everybody sitting there."

"Nothing they can say will make me feel okay about this." He yanks off his bloody gloves and slams them into a biohazard can. "And it's not fair. I don't like the way they tricked me into it, waiting until they'd already spilled the beans. Suddenly I'm threatened with prison if I breathe a word."

"Things are at a different level now, the consequences nothing to trifle with," I reply. "It doesn't matter that you didn't ask for it, Marino. The fact is you've been exposed to sensitive information. You absolutely can't talk about it except to those of us authorized."

"The rules shouldn't be the same when it's Carrie Grethen." He covers the stretcher with a new pouch.

"But they are."

"I swear if I ever see her, I'll make sure she's dead this time."

He helps me lift the body, and I zip it inside the pouch. Marino collects the plastic container from the countertop, and I'm happy to see the cricket still moving around.

"Come on, little fella. We're going for a ride." He sets the container on top of the stretcher, and we push through the airlock as the cricket starts chirping.

Inside the decontamination compartment, Marino places the container out of harm's way on a shelf before spraying down the body pouch and stretcher. We take off our soiled PPE, our field clothes underneath wrinkled and sweaty. We return to the cooler where Brittany Manson's pouched body waits for us.

"Thanks," I tell Marino. "I'd hate to be on my own in this. Somehow, we'll manage."

"Hell yeah we will, Doc."

We wheel both stretchers into the vestibule, and he places the container on the metal desk. He checks on the cricket, its dark eyes staring through clear plastic. Marino taps the lid with his finger, and Jiminy takes several frantic hops.

"I think he's really stressed," Marino says.

"That makes three of us."

"Be right back."

Moments later, Marino pushes through the airlock, returning to the vestibule with a small cardboard pill box, the ends of it torn off. Lifting the lid of the plastic container, he places the box inside.

"Bingo." He's pleased with himself. "They like to have something to hide in. That should calm him down."

"Maybe I need one of those." I watch the cricket crawl inside his new cardboard quiet place.

"I'm not putting him outside when it's supposed to snow. I don't want him freezing to death all by his lonesome."

"Of course we're not going to let that happen, but I'm not a cricket expert, Marino. What would you suggest we do with him?"

"I don't know. But it's like he's a sign. Maybe he's been sent to us for a reason," he says, and this is how I know Carrie has loosened his moorings.

Marino has to focus on something he can control. He needs to fix things, making them better, even if it's for a cricket. He feels robbed of power and I understand completely.

"A sign?" I ask.

"Maybe from above, like it's a message to us."

"Saying what?"

"I don't know, but how he got in the body bag to begin with is weird," Marino says. "He must have hopped in before we zipped it up. Then he survives being airlifted here and left in the cooler, and for what? To dump him outside so he can freeze to death?"

"We'll leave him in here for now," I reply, and the cricket begins chirping again like a smoke detector with a low battery. "In a while we'll carry him to my office and figure out what makes sense." He chirps some more as if pleased with the plan.

"I think Jiminy understands what we're saying," Marino says.

"Maybe he does."

"We got anything in here he can eat?"

"Hold on."

I rummage inside my briefcase, pulling out a bag of trail mix, realizing how hungry I am. I try not to think about the Scotch, the dinner in my future, preferably in front of the fireplace with Benton.

"I don't know if this will work, but it's salt-free, so I don't think it will hurt him." I lift the perforated lid enough to drop in a few raisins and sunflower seeds. "He's also going to need water, but that will have to wait. And we're going to need actual cricket food, whatever that might be."

"They'll eat pretty much anything, including dog biscuits," Marino says. "Don't ask me how I know."

"I won't." I open the trailer's back cargo door, cold air rushing in.

"I used to raise them for fishing," he tells me anyway. "I

didn't do it for long. It was too much trouble. But I've caught some pretty big catfish and bluegills with them."

"A detail I could have done without, and maybe this is your penance," I reply. "Jiminy is giving you a conscience. Maybe you can try fly fishing or using lures in the future."

We trundle the stretchers outside to the sound of TV helicopters, bright like small planets in the night sky. News trucks are still parked along the street, and then a drone is zipping in our direction, a quadcopter with lights, its camera livestreaming, I have no doubt. Reporters realize we've emerged. They start yelling through our privacy fence.

"*Doctor Scarpetta, what did you find out...?*"

"*How did they die...?*"

"*Were they murdered...?*"

We wheel the stretchers down the metal ramp attached to the back of the trailer, and there's no way to be quiet. The reporters know what we're doing, and the bombardment of questions continues in a nerve-racking din, people shouting on top of each other.

"*Did a bear do it...?*"

"*Is it true they were about to get arrested...?*"

"*Have you ever shopped at Wild World...?*"

The temperature is dropping, a sharp wind gusting, the moon a waning crescent behind haze. Clouds are rolling in like a tarp, and I feel snow in the air as Marino and I ferry the bodies to the black van waiting for us, the engine running. Henry Addams is wearing gloves, a face mask and a winter coat. He's unfolding two stretchers that work better than the one he struggled with this morning.

"I hope we've not kept you waiting," I say to him.

"I've been here only a few minutes. What a carnival." He points at the drone orbiting. "I'm betting it belongs to one of the TV stations. My God, I don't know how people stand putting up with this all the time."

Marino and I lift the pouched bodies, transferring them to the stretchers that Henry brought. We help him slide them into the back of the van.

"I'm not sure what you've been able to keep up with over recent hours, but the news has gone rabid." He shuts the tailgate as the shouting behind the fence continues.

"Doctor Scarpetta…?"

"Why did your niece pick you up in a helicopter…?"

"Why are you using the trailer for the autopsies…?"

"Conspiracy theories range from the Mansons were killed by a huge bear to they were murdered by someone who'd been stalking them," Henry is saying.

"Possibly we're being recorded." I'm keenly aware of the drone whining loudly like a huge mosquito. "I don't know if it can pick up what we're saying, but we should assume it. We should be careful."

"Damn, I wish I had a fire hose right about now." Marino stares hatefully at the quadcopter hovering maybe a hundred feet above our heads.

"I think enough things have been shot out of the air for one day," I reply.

"If you don't need anything else from me right now, I'm going to clean up since only one of us can do it at a time." Not waiting for an answer, Marino returns to the trailer.

His feet thud up the ramp as two state police SUVs drive toward us with emergency lights flashing. Parking near the van, the officers climb out, a man and a woman, both of them young. They let us know they'll escort Henry to his funeral home, ensuring that nobody follows or tries to interfere with the transport.

"We certainly appreciate your help," I say to them. "More than you know."

"I think things will be quiet here once the bodies are gone," says the male officer.

"The TV trucks are relocating to the funeral home," says the female. "Hopefully everybody will leave you alone now, Doctor Scarpetta."

"Can't you do something about that?" Henry points at the persistent drone, now hovering considerably higher.

"Not unless it breaks the law," the male officer answers.

"It's trespassing," Henry says.

"It's one of those modern-day problems there's not much of a solution to yet," says the woman. "I had one hovering over my backyard not all that long ago. Took it out with the power washer and then stomped the hell out of it. But I wasn't in uniform. And I'd had a few beers."

"Why don't we sit inside the van," Henry suggests to me, scowling up at the persistent drone.

"Good idea."

CHAPTER 25

OPENING THE VAN'S PASSENGER'S door for me, Henry climbs into the driver's side. He turns the heat to low, and now we can talk privately.

"As you mentioned earlier, we have to entertain the possibility that someone might attempt to snatch the bodies," I say to him. "As crazy as that may sound, in this case it's a distinct possibility."

"People don't realize that thousands of bodies are stolen every year," Henry says as we talk with the heat blowing. "Remember when grave robbers dug up Charlie Chaplin and held his body for ransom? They demanded six hundred thousand dollars from his widow, if you can imagine anything so disgusting. It happens more than people would imagine."

"We need to be prepared for just about anything." I'm thinking about the micro hard drive I dug out of Brittany Manson's hip.

If that's what the Russians are after, they aren't aware we've found it. They don't necessarily know the evidence is secure and that before the night is over the bodies will be incinerated. As I'm thinking this, I'm seeing Carrie Grethen's scarred face and mocking smile. I felt she was looking at me through the camera.

She was reminding me that revenge is best served cold, and it's on the way. I have a bad feeling it's been in the works. I just didn't know it. After our last encounter seven years ago, I expected there would be consequences. I would pay the ultimate price. All of us would. But we were spared because she died. Except she didn't.

"Whoever's involved may not realize we recovered something they were looking for," I tell Henry without saying what it is. "These bad people would do anything to get what they want. The police will make sure nobody comes to your place looking."

"What about you, Kay? Who's taking care of you?"

"Certain evidence isn't here, and now the bodies won't be." I stare out at my building, most of the windows dark at this late hour. "But the damage has been done. Because of what's on the news we've got to worry about all sorts of things. Not just the media but anyone who wants to cause trouble."

"That's how the next of kin found out. From the news," Henry replies. "The Secret Service talked with the parents, and I've spoken to them as well. They were relieved not to fool with the arrangements, didn't want to spend a penny or waste a moment of their time. Nobody's local, and that's probably best. I wouldn't call them nice people."

Henry says we don't have to be concerned about family showing up and trying to delay what needs to be done. Huck's parents live in Texas. Brittany's are in Florida. It doesn't appear the families were in contact often with each other or their son and daughter. They seemed more surprised than sorry to learn of the brutal deaths.

"I got the impression the parents had no idea what the couple was up to beyond owning a lucrative retail business." Henry continues telling me about his phone conversations. "They didn't know Huck and Brittany had been camping in the woods for months. Or that they might be involved in illegal activities and were about to be arrested. The parents rarely saw them. The last time was before COVID."

The bodies will go directly to Addams Family's crematorium, the oven fired and heating up as Henry and I talk inside his van. Tomorrow the ashes will be shipped to Florida, where they'll be buried in a Vero Beach cemetery, he explains. Huck Manson's family in Texas didn't want the couple's remains. Nobody was interested in any kind of funeral service.

"Truth is, none of them seemed to care about much except what might be in the will," Henry says. "And I'll be surprised if there is one."

"Sounds like the apple didn't fall far," I reply. "I want you to promise you'll drive with your police escort directly to your funeral home. I don't want you alone for even five minutes."

I envision Carrie Grethen shooting her submachine gun. I see the decapitated head that washed up in Monte Carlo, and the man eviscerated on a Moscow sidewalk.

"I'll be fine, Kay. I'm told there's quite a police presence at my funeral home, several officers also standing sentry at our crematorium," Henry says. "Most members of my staff are gone for the day. Those of us left will take care of the cremation immediately, and that will be the end of it."

"I wish it were the end," I reply. "But I wouldn't count on it."

"I'm here to help anytime."

"Promise that when you're ready to go home tonight, no matter the hour, you'll have the police escort you. It's not negotiable."

"I promise." Reaching in front of me, he opens the glove box, lifting out his Glock 9-millimeter pistol. "And I'm not without my own resources."

I climb out of the hearse, and I watch him drive off, the police flanking him front and back, their lights going full tilt. I return to the trailer, and Marino is inside the vestibule, seated at the metal desk. He's wearing scrubs, his pistol on his hip, and I can smell the cheap soap he used in the shower.

"Hey, little buddy. Look who's back." Picking up the cricket container, he stares through the plastic. "The nice lady doctor responsible for your rescue." He lightly taps the perforated lid, Jiminy out of sight inside his evidence box hideaway. "Come out, come out, wherever you are." But he doesn't. "I don't think he likes me, Doc." Marino sets the container back down on the desk.

"He might not."

Chirp! Chirp!

"He's trying to tell us something," Marino says. "What is it, Jiminy? What do you want us to know? That you're a fan of mine? You're just shy?"

Silence.

"Told you he doesn't like me."

"He may have heard about your past behavior with other crickets," I reply, and Jiminy chirps again.

"Bet he knows who the bad guy is. Bet he saw the whole thing, didn't you?" Marino talks to the cricket the same way he does to puppies. "He could pick out the bad guy in a lineup, what do you want to bet? He and Bigfoot both could. No telling what all you know, isn't that right, Jiminy?" Marino taps the lid again but the cricket's not stirring.

"Is he okay?" I ask. "If one more thing dies today, I don't think I can stand it."

"I'm sure he doesn't know what the hell is going on. Must be what it feels like when you're abducted by aliens."

"I don't believe you can say that word anymore."

"Yeah, I can't say half my words anymore. Which sucks when you don't have that many to begin with."

"I'm going to clean up. No coming back there until I let you know I'm done. I won't be long."

"Nope, I'm pretty sure you won't. There's not much hot water," Marino warns, and that's his way of telling me there's none.

Inside the hygiene compartment, I toss a towel over the video camera on top of a cabinet. I don't care what Benton said about our no longer being recorded. I don't trust anything or anyone at the moment, and I hurry out of my clothes. Turning on the hot water, I discover it's tepid at best. I yank the plastic curtain across its rod.

* * *

I have goosebumps and am shivering as I dry off with placemat-size towels inside the hygiene compartment. I put on scrubs, stuffing my soiled field clothes in a garbage bag.

Drying my hair, I realize how cold the REMOTE is when I'm not covered in PPE. I return to the vestibule in my stocking feet, shaking inside, my fingernails blue as I retrieve my belongings.

"I'm letting Fabian know we're on our way." Marino is typing on his phone. "He'll gather up the evidence from inside the autopsy compartment. Are you okay, Doc? You look pale."

"Just cold." My head has started to throb. "It's not even sixty degrees in here."

"No lab coats, no blankets, no nothing," he says. "And it's going to be a bitch walking through the parking lot, dammit. I didn't bother with a coat this morning."

"Neither did I," I reply, and we begin putting on our boots. My fingers are stiff, my teeth about to chatter.

"I told Fabian to lock the tissue sections, the test tubes and all the rest inside the morgue's evidence refrigerator," Marino tells me. "He's to let DNA, trace, the tox labs know what's there so they can get it upstairs as soon as they're able."

"Good." I blow on my hands, trying to warm them.

"It's not that cold, Doc." Marino watches me with a worried look.

Digging inside my briefcase, I find the trail mix, offering the bag to him. Both of us have a handful. But low blood sugar isn't my only problem. A part of me knows I'm stressed as hell. The rest of me won't admit it.

"This place needs hosing down, but I told Fabian that cleaning it can wait," Marino says.

"Absolutely. I don't want him out here in the parking lot alone at this hour," I reply. "Considering all the attention we've been getting? And everything else we know? I'm impressed he's still here. Maybe our little talk this morning did some good."

"What little talk?"

"He said that he was hired to investigate and we're not letting him. I agreed that we'd do better."

"Elvin Reddy hired him," Marino says nastily. "That alone is enough to make me not trust Fabian."

"Try not to be so cynical," I reply. "Maybe if you give him a chance, he'll do the same with you."

"I don't need him giving me a fucking chance."

"We're going to have to trust him enough to let him do his job. If he screws up, then that's another matter," I tell Marino as we collect our bags of clothing.

He picks up the cricket container, and there's not a soul in sight when we step outside the trailer. As the police predicted, the news trucks left when the bodies did. There's no sign of the drone that accosted us earlier, and Marino shuts the cargo door behind us, making sure it's locked.

At a few minutes past seven hardly anyone is here. Shannon's Pepto-Bismol–pink VW Beetle is in its assigned spot, as is Faye Hanaday's silver Tacoma pickup truck with its mud flaps and gun rack. Maggie Cutbush's Volvo is gone. If only for good, I can't help but wish. I don't see Fabian's El Camino and I suspect I know where it is.

I'm chilled to my core in my thin cotton scrubs, the specter of Carrie Grethen all around us, the parking lot unevenly lit by tall light standards spaced far apart. The air pressure is heavy, seeming to press down on me with the weight of water. I feel the way I did at Buckingham Run. Unnerved. Jumpy. I don't know what to expect while sensing an invisible threat.

Dead leaves skitter across the pavement. The wind gusts and moans, the moon covered by thick clouds settling lower. I halfway except someone monstrous to emerge from the shadows, shooting us with yellow-tipped bullets and crushing our necks.

"Here." Marino's breath smokes out as he hands me the plastic container, and the cricket chirps. "You carry Jiminy." He chirps some more. "He likes you better than me."

"You're just saying that to manipulate me into taking care of him," I reply to more chirping as I keep glancing around.

"Right this minute I need my hands free since I'm armed and you're not," Marino says. "How many times do I need to tell you to start carrying your gun? You shouldn't leave the house without it. Especially now, knowing what we do."

"Hopefully we won't have to shoot anybody between here and our building," I reply, holding the container close, trying to shield it from the cold.

"All these times we've walked through this parking lot like we're doing right now," Marino says. "And she could have been waiting."

"Unfortunately, she's not the only one to worry about."

"She's the worst one."

"Let's hope so."

"Lucy and Benton could have found a way to tell us the truth about her. They could have given us a hint without actually saying it. You know, acting it out, showing us something so we connect the dots."

"We don't get to play charades or Pictionary with classified information," I remind him. "No idle talking. You don't need that kind of trouble, Marino."

"Carrie Grethen's flown away in a fucking private jet, not even a slap on the wrist," he retorts angrily. "And we're the ones who will get in trouble?"

"Nobody said there's anything fair about this."

"What if she'd come looking for us when we didn't know she was still alive? We had our guard down just like we did seven damn years ago when she showed up at your house. We would have been easy pickings."

"I trust that Lucy and Benton would have done something to intervene." I can see the silhouette of the cricket moving inside the container. "And we don't know that they haven't in the past."

We've reached the back of our building, the massive door rolled down. Parked next to my take-home Subaru is the black Suburban belonging to security officer Norm Duffy. A rideshare placard is in the back windshield, and that's the job he cares about. Not this one. Marino unlocks the pedestrian door, flipping on the overhead lights, and we begin walking through the vehicle bay.

As I suspected, Fabian has parked his El Camino inside, black with red undercarriage lights and fat brake calipers. I've heard the story many times about his parents surprising him with the vintage pickup truck after he graduated from Louisiana State University cum laude with honors in chemistry. The El Camino was a special gift from his proud parents.

It was parked behind the coroner's office, a big black ribbon around it and black balloons tied to the bumpers. An anatomical skeleton was in the driver's seat, and Fabian comes by his interests, his flair for drama honestly. His father, Arthur Etienne, would be a hard act to follow. A family doctor in East Baton Rouge, he's been the coroner there for decades, running uncontested at each election.

Fabian must be watching our arrival on the cameras. The

door at the top of the ramp opens, and he emerges dressed in his usual black scrubs, his long straight hair loose and as shiny black as patent leather.

"Welcome!" he calls out to us cheerfully while holding the door.

"You know you're not supposed to park in here." Marino can't resist reprimanding him loudly and from a distance.

"There's plenty of room," Fabian replies.

"What's to stop others from doing it?"

"At this hour? What *others*? Hardly anyone's here," Fabian says as we walk up the ramp. "And I didn't move my car inside until it was getting dark. No way it was safe leaving it out there. Especially with the drone that's been buzzing around, obviously up to no good."

"Fortunately, it's gone," I tell him. "Or at least we didn't see it when we were walking through the parking lot just now."

It pleases me that the epoxy-painted concrete is damp from being hosed off. The trash cans have been emptied and I don't see traces of blood anywhere. Fabian's been busy.

"Everything looks much better than it did this morning," I tell him. "Thank you."

"At least somebody notices."

"Speaking of cleaning things up. Make yourself useful." Marino hands over our bags of clothing to be laundered in the morgue's industrial machines.

"This is what I've been talking about," Fabian says as we enter the intake area, and he closes the door behind us. "Ask nicely, Marino."

"This is me being nice."

"You want help with your dirty laundry, then don't be a jerk."

"Remember, no bleach. Not even a whiff or I break out in hives."

"Which is what you deserve. It's probably your own body rejecting you." Fabian sets the bags of laundry on top of an empty gurney.

"And if I insulted you that way?" Marino is enjoying himself. "You'd be going after me with all your *woke* bullshit."

"Don't say that in public unless you want to get canceled..."

I tune them out, walking over to the chipped Formica ledge outside the security office. Opening the morgue log, I begin skimming the lined sheets of pale green acid-free paper. I get an idea of bodies in and out in recent hours. A motor vehicle fatality. Someone hit by falling construction debris. A suspected suicide by gunshot. A possible overdose on prescription opioids.

CHAPTER 26

THE MORGUE LOG'S HANDWRITTEN entries are initialed by Fabian. He's been running the show with no help from Norm, and I feel a wave of annoyance. On the other side of the security office's bulletproof glass are no signs of recent occupation, and I get more irritated.

Unlocking the door with my master key, I look around, feeling the emptiness. The stale air is tainted by fast-food wrappers that have been in the trash since Wyatt was here hours earlier. I don't detect Norm's pervasive musky aftershave. There's no sign of his uniform coat, his car key or paperwork generated while meeting with anybody who has business with us.

"I suspect you've been on your own dealing with the funeral homes and removal services?" I say to Fabian.

"That would be a correct assumption," he replies. "And I hate to be a snitch, but Norm showed up an hour late for his shift. It was supposed to start at four sharp and he rolled in around five. When I said something to him about the importance of us always having coverage? He gave me a dirty look as if to say, *What are you going to do about it, punk?*"

"He said that or you assumed it?" Marino asks.

"Norm didn't say it but calls me a punk behind my back. I had to cover for him so Wyatt could go home."

"You can't be doing that and everything else, Fabian," I reply. "And you're not security."

"I'm better security than two out of the three." He means Tina and Norm.

"I'm afraid that's probably true," I agree.

"Where is he?" Marino scowls up at the intake area's wall-mounted security video screen. "His Suburban is here. Otherwise, who the hell would know? I'm not seeing him anywhere. You notice how good Norm is at avoiding the cameras? It's like he was a burglar in another life."

"He's bitching about all the money he's losing because of the weather." Fabian rolls an empty gurney off the floor scale, parallel parking it against a wall. "I don't know if you've been following the forecast. But the big winter storm front that was supposed to blow out to sea, didn't. It's going to start snowing within the hour. We could get six inches or more, and that's one thing we don't have in Louisiana. I'm so psyched!"

"I'm very sorry about any fares Norm might miss. But he has a job here and gets a state paycheck, such as it is," I reply, and the cricket starts chirping again.

"What the heck?" Fabian stares at the plastic container I'm holding. "I was wondering why there were holes in the lid. Figured you were air-drying something. Where'd he come from?"

"The scene at Buckingham Run," I reply.

"Entomology evidence?" He takes the container from me, holding it up to the light. "You're not going to hurt him, are you?"

"He caught a ride with us. It's too cold to leave him outside," I reply as the cricket ventures out of his hideaway box. His big dark eyes stare through plastic.

"Hello there," Fabian says to him. "It's not the Ritz but nicer than most things around here, tiny friend. Way better than being in the snow. And you need anything? I'm your guy." He returns the container to me. "When I was a kid, one of my girlfriends used to have pet crickets. She'd give them names like Banshee, Zombie, Voldemort. All of us would watch horror movies together."

"That figures." Marino is typing a text. "Let's see if Norm answers. He probably won't. If we don't get decent security around here pretty soon, something really bad is going to happen."

"It's top on my list to discuss with the governor," I reply.

"Only the males chirp, by the way," Fabian says. "They can be *watch crickets* and very protective."

"Sounds like bullshit," Marino replies.

"What else has gone on in our absence besides the trespassing drone and all the rest?" I ask Fabian. "Did you hear from Fruge about the dentist? What about any luck with the Nokesville case?"

"I haven't talked to Fruge. But I did spend time on the phone with the Prince William County investigator, Wally Jonas," Fabian explains.

"Talk as we walk," I reply, and the three of us head down the corridor.

"I don't think the Mike Abel death is high on the list of priorities," Fabian explains. "I get the impression that mostly it's been a squabble between insurers and lawyers. Wally told me there's nothing new to report, but any questions you have, Doctor Scarpetta? He recommends you talk to the widow.

She's going to be your best source. Bonnie Abel, forty-three years old—"

"Talk to her about what?" I interrupt.

"About her son and what might have happened on August fifth when he supposedly wasn't home. Wally said he's suspicious the kid is hiding something. Possibly, he was home after all. Maybe he witnessed what happened and for some reason has kept it to himself..."

"What the hell are you talking about?" Marino is visibly annoyed that I'd have Fabian looking into anything.

"The tractor death in Nokesville three months ago," I answer, and Marino wasn't with me on that occasion.

He and Dorothy were spending their anniversary weekend at a resort on the Chesapeake Bay. Fabian was the death investigator and transported the body to the morgue in one of our vans. We were told the victim's wife was out of town visiting family when the three-ton tractor flipped over, trapping Mike Abel under it from the neck down.

His injuries were devastating, and he died quickly at the scene. I was there when rescuers hoisted the tractor off him. He was still warm and limber as in life, and I could smell his sweat when I examined him in the cornfield. I remember the weather was hot and humid. He was wearing overalls with no shirt. His sunglasses were still on, his Bass Pro Shops baseball cap not far away in the dirt.

* * *

"For a while I heard from lawyers, insurance claims adjusters, an investigator from the Department of Agriculture. But never the widow," I tell Marino and Fabian as we follow the corridor, passing labs and workrooms, the observation windows dark.

"I've not gotten any calls about the case from anyone in the past month or two, I'm pretty sure," I explain. "The tractor death didn't enter my mind until we were flying over the dairy farm this morning and I realized how close it is to the Mansons' place and the scene inside Buckingham Run."

"The widow, Bonnie Abel, is an accountant. Her son, Ledger Smithson, is from her first marriage." Fabian continues telling us what he knows.

"As in a *ledger* book?" Marino asks. "That's what an accountant names her kid? Guess she wanted to make sure he got picked on in school."

"The biological father was a financial advisor," Fabian says. "Bonnie handled his firm's bookkeeping until the office building burned to the ground with him in it eight years ago."

The fire started while he was working alone at night, drinking bourbon, possibly falling asleep with a lit cigarette, Fabian explains. This was in Williamsburg where Bonnie and Ledger were living at the time. Next, she moved in with an attorney whose Piper Cub crashed into the ocean not long after. Two years ago, she interviewed for the bookkeeping job at Abel's Dairy in Nokesville.

"Mike Abel, forty-nine, dated a lot of women but never married and no kids," Fabian tells us. "It didn't take long before Bonnie and Ledger were living in his house."

"She must have a way with the guys," Marino says. "What does she look like?"

"Pamela Anderson pretty based on photos I've seen. She has *endless legs* and *big ideas*, as my mom would say," Fabian replies with air quotes. "Based on some of what I've seen on her social media, she's got some extreme ideas. I don't believe we vote for the same kind of people."

"Did Wally Jonas indicate whether Bonnie and Mike Abel might have been acquainted with the couple one farm over? Brittany and Huck Manson?" I ask Fabian as we near the elevator. The ceiling light that was flickering this morning has been fixed, and the floor has been mopped, not a drop of blood anywhere.

"It's hard to imagine they didn't at least run into each other from time to time," Marino adds.

"I asked Wally about it," Fabian replies. "He said he has no idea and was personally unfamiliar with the Mansons."

"What do we know about Ledger?" Marino asks.

"Nineteen years old and dropped out of college."

"In college where? Did he drop out before or after the tractor incident?"

"It was after that. He was home this past summer and never went back to UVA. This would have been the fall semester of his junior year."

"Studying what?" Marino asks.

"I don't know what he was majoring in. He may have mental health issues. At least some of his reported behavior might cause you to wonder that."

"Such as?"

"Extreme introversion. Signs of depression. Bouts of what the mother calls *his loony talk*," Fabian explains.

Refusing to return to UVA, Ledger started spending most of his time at the local animal rescue instead of with people.

"Again, this is what Wally told me," Fabian says. "He's talked to the mother, and I haven't. He's not talked to Ledger, and somebody should. I wish I could. I feel bad for him, and he might open up to me. A lot of people do."

"Don't get any bright ideas about calling him," Marino says rudely. "Or showing up on his damn doorstep."

"I don't see the harm in asking a few questions. Unlike some people? I don't judge, and I'm betting he'd level with me," Fabian says. "Ledger saw something. I want to know what it was. His stepfather suddenly started driving his tractor like he was tripping on hallucinogens, and there's a reason for it."

"I agree that there's a reason. We need to figure it out. I'd like to finalize his case at the very least so people can go on with their lives," I reply.

"What the crap is wrong with this thing?" Marino presses the button repeatedly, the elevator stopped on the fourth floor and not moving for some reason.

"That's weird," Fabian says. "There shouldn't be anybody up there. Maggie and all her flying monkeys left a while ago."

As he's saying this, the elevator suddenly begins to descend. Then it stops on the third floor. Next it stops on the second floor as if people are getting on and off.

"My notes and everything you need are on your desk," Fabian tells me. "I'll grab my coat from the locker room and head out to the trailer now to collect the evidence you've left."

The elevator finally arrives, and Marino and I step inside. I press the button for the third floor.

"Why all of a sudden do you give a shit what he thinks?" he says to me as the doors shut, and his jealousy is palpable. "Why are you discussing a case with Fabian as if he's a real investigator?"

"I care what everybody thinks. As should you. And he is a real investigator."

"Why would you involve him to begin with, Doc? The last thing we need is him poking his nose into everything like he's Sherlock. He's not much for asking permission."

"Maybe he learned that from you," I reply as the elevator slowly creeps up in fits and starts, stuttering a little. I hope it doesn't get stuck again, and I don't dare say it or Marino will freak out.

"Dammit!" He jackhammers the illuminated button. "Does anything in this joint work worth a damn?"

We've had trouble lately, the elevator being original to the building and more than forty years old. The other day it stopped mid-floor without warning while Marino and I were inside. Just as suddenly it started moving again, and as claustrophobic as he is, it was a bad several minutes.

"Fabian feels you're unnecessarily tough on him," I'm saying as the elevator shudders.

"The hell I am," Marino retorts. "He doesn't begin to understand the meaning of *tough*, and believe me, I know what he *feels*. He makes sure all of us know about his every damn feeling." The elevator lurches to a stop with an off-key ding, the doors stammering open. "Speaking of people who get on my last nerve? I'll go check on Norm."

Walking off in a huff, Marino ducks inside the breakroom, the TV news loud enough for me to hear it in the hallway. Norm is watching Dana Diletti, and I pause to catch the upshot.

"*...Just unbelievably scary. Twice while I was being flown to Buckingham Run, this military-looking helicopter accosted us with extreme aggression. You can see it in the video as we're getting closer...*"

"Norm, how's it going?" Marino's voice booms inside the breakroom. "It's not helpful if you're sitting in here watching TV all the time..."

"...*The nose is pointed right at us, and then suddenly we're attacked with some type of weapon that turned off everything, including our cameras...*"

"It's not right dragging me here at the last minute because of some bogus COVID test..." Norm has started his griping.

"...*Mind you, not once but twice...*," Dana Diletti is saying on TV. "*And the plot thickens. Now get this. Sources close to the investigation say the top secret experimental helicopter is called the Doomsday Bird...*"

"...At the last minute she decides not to show up on a night when I wasn't scheduled to work?" I overhear Norm saying loudly and in a threatening tone. "How's that my problem? You got any idea all the business I'm missing? Nobody around here can drive worth a damn in the snow..."

"...*And the test pilot? Well, you'll never guess. It's Secret Service Agent Lucy Farinelli...*" Dana Diletti continues on the news playing in the background.

"...Guess what, Norm? You're here now just like you're paid to be," Marino is saying. "Make the best of it..."

"...*Who happens to be chief medical examiner Kay Scarpetta's niece! I mean, what is going on here, folks...?*"

"Oh, for God's sake," I mutter under my breath, having heard quite enough.

CHAPTER 27

WALKING AWAY FROM THE breakroom, I check my phone. Benton is leaving his headquarters in a few minutes, he says in a text as my heart constricts and feels heavy. I'm reminded of what I wish wasn't true. I don't look forward to facing him. It's going to hurt. I don't know what I'll say, and I don't want to fight.

Any word from Lucy? I write back while thinking about the two of them lying.

She's safely down, the chopper in the hangar. When are you headed home?

Shouldn't be here much longer. What would you like for dinner? I envision Carrie's scarred face staring into the camera.

Dorothy insists on dropping it off. She didn't say what she's making.

I reply with a question mark. What has possessed my sister to be helpful? What's on her mind? I ask Benton as I feel a touch of anger. He and I have a lot to talk about. We need to do it alone. Dorothy should have asked first. But she never does.

Probably everything in the news. She wants to be included as usual, Benton writes, and of course that's the answer. My sister hates being left out. Doesn't matter what I want.

Walking into my office, I hear my secretary, Shannon Park, through the connecting open doorway. She's on the phone talking with an edge, and that's not like her. I can tell she's aggravated, and as good-natured as she is, it doesn't happen often. It seems an oppressive mood has rolled in like the sudden weather front.

"...I wouldn't know, and as I've said, she's not available. But I'll pass on the message...I suppose it will have to be good enough, as busy as she is...," Shannon says as I look around to see what might have changed since morning.

It's a reflex for me to make sure nothing is out of place, stolen or otherwise violated. While Maggie worked for me, I never knew what I might find. I didn't feel safe and hadn't fully moved into my office until several months ago. A part of me didn't want to cut the tether between my new life and old. I wasn't convinced I would stay in Virginia.

Until recently, most of my professional possessions were taped up in boxes in the basement at home. Then after Maggie walked off the job and was fired, Shannon said she'd like to leave the Virginia court system for good. She wanted to come work for me, and together we unpacked belongings that have moved with me throughout my career.

"...You can complain all you like, and I'm still not at liberty to share that or anything else you're rooting around for like a truffle pig...Not an insult at all...," Shannon declares over the phone.

Together we hung antique anatomical drawings I've found

in antique shops, junk stores and at yard sales. We crowded the bookcases with tomes I don't use much anymore. *Gray's Anatomy*, *Cecil Textbook of Medicine*, *Robbins Pathology*, *Code of Virginia*, *Black's Law Dictionary*, to name a few. They're early editions and not what I rely on when I want current information.

"...Hello? Hello? Well, if that doesn't take the prize...!"

These days, I'm going to look up journal articles on the internet or call an expert I know. But I can't bring myself to get rid of textbooks filled with folded-down page corners, coffee stains and my scribbled notes. I'm touched by memories of when I looked last and why, remembering who I was at the time and what I felt.

"...I sound worked up because I'm more than a little miffed...No, not at you, dear. Not today, anyway...!" Shannon is on with someone else now, a smile in her tone. She's a touch coquettish, possibly talking to Marino. "I thought it best to give you fair warning..."

Setting my briefcase and the plastic container on top of the conference table, I survey my plants and trees, worried about an appropriate habitat. According to Google, direct sunlight and temperatures below fifty degrees Fahrenheit are dangerous, possibly deadly, for crickets. I don't want him too close to the windows. I need a better habitat than an evidence carton.

The cricket should have something with a little room to move around in. I open a cabinet of crime scene supplies that I always have on hand, not seeing a box or carton that will work better than what I've got. I do another Google search on my phone, and Amazon sells cricket pens. Who knew? I may as well, and I order one. I add bags of high-calcium cricket food, topsoil and vermiculite to my shopping basket.

Ducking inside my office bathroom, I'm unwilling to leave the building in surgical scrubs. It feels like I'm wearing pajamas while inviting unwanted attention. Now more than ever I wish to stay off the radar, preferring no one realizes who I am. After what happened in front of me at Old Town Market six weeks ago, I don't feel the same about appearing in public.

For the longest time my focus was COVID. Now it's violence, and no place is immune. It's my nature to find potential dangers wherever I go anyway, and Lucy is the first to remind me of that. I'm always coming up with worst-case scenarios. But nothing I've witnessed tortures me like the naked fear I saw on her face when gunfire exploded. Just as quickly, her eyes steeled over while she drew her pistol, blood dripping as she pulled me to the floor.

"...No worries, Herbie does fine and dandy in the snow," Shannon explains over the phone, talking about her pink VW Beetle. "The few times I've gotten stuck, I just put him in neutral and he's light enough that I can push him..."

An eighth of an inch closer, and I couldn't have saved her.

"...Well, yes, figuratively speaking. I mean that *someone* can push my car," Shannon is saying mirthfully. "At this stage of things, I don't expect it will be me doing it...!"

I've never felt so helpless. Tearing open my backpack where I kept a windbreaker, I was using it to apply pressure on Lucy's neck when the rescue squad rolled up.

You're going to be fine, I kept saying out loud as I thought to myself, *Please don't die*.

Closing my bathroom door, I put on the pantsuit I wore to work early this morning, having no idea what the day would bring. I've been robbed of trust and peace in a way I haven't in a very long time. Maybe ever, and I imagine my old friend Anna Zenner.

How do you feel, Kay?

She was the only psychiatrist I ever listened to, and I can see her intense face. I hear her firm voice, her heavy German accent.

How do you feel, Kay?

The oldest question in the book, and the biggest cliché coming from a shrink.

Not what you think, Kay. But how do you feel?

Anna wouldn't stop asking those simple words all the years we knew each other. If only she were still here. When I think of her funeral in Vienna, Austria, it's a blur of rain and black umbrellas. I still have the impulse to reach for the phone. I would say things to her I won't to anyone else, including my husband.

I decide on a pair of Uggs that are warm, with a rubber tread for slippery conditions. The snow may look fluffy and festive, but black ice lurks beneath it. Next thing you know, your feet are out from under you. Maybe you break your back. Or end up with a head injury. Closing the toilet lid, I sit down to pull on the tall leather boots, tucking in my pants cuffs.

* * *

Washing my face again, I spritz myself with cologne that triggers memories of plush antiques and sumptuous linens inside a room overlooking the Spanish Steps in Rome. When I walk through my front door tonight, I'd prefer not smelling like the antimicrobial liquid soap my office orders by the fifty-five-gallon drum.

Another spritz above my head, and I feel the mist touching my skin. Closing my eyes for an instant, I inhale a deep fragrant breath before facing myself in the mirror over the sink. My limp blond hair could use a color touch-up and styling. My eyes are bloodshot, my nose and cheeks red from sun and wind.

Rubbing Carmex into my chapped lips, I imagine my sister describing my appearance the minute she lays eyes on me. *Death on a cracker* or *something the cat dragged in* come to mind. I try a dash of lipstick, a little gel in my hair, not seeing much improvement. It's nice that Dorothy is bringing dinner, and I'm sure she has good intentions overall. She'd swear to it if asked. She'll tell you she's selfless and would pass a polygraph.

Except it isn't true. She means no harm, but her behavior is predictable. Timing her arrival as she always does, Dorothy will make sure she's at the house when I get there. She'll be in no hurry to leave, which is further complicated by the weather. Of course, I'll invite her to eat with us and to spend the night if she wants.

It goes without saying that Benton and I won't allow her to drink and then drive home in a snowstorm. I'll be gracious and attentive, all of it disingenuous. I was looking forward to making a simple pizza Margherita and opening a bottle of wine. Maybe a French burgundy that's complex while not drawing attention to itself. I'll start with a green salad, tossing it in unfiltered olive oil and a Tuscany red wine vinegar, crumbling gorgonzola cheese on top.

My mouth waters at the thought. I've not had much to eat since a predawn breakfast of Greek yogurt and fat-free granola. I don't know what Dorothy is bringing but don't have high hopes. She adores hearty fare and fine cuisine if someone else is cooking and cleaning up. Almost always that ends up being me when she and Marino visit. I'll tell him to join us after he picks up his truck.

He can drive straight to the house even though we've spent the entire day together. Selfishly, I don't want to see anyone when I get home except Benton. I have questions that I expect him to answer, and I don't like feeling this way.

Feeling what way, Kay? Anna's voice in my head.

Hurt. Enraged. Naïve. Even stupid. And shaky inside. When I discovered that Carrie is alive, I experienced the same fear I saw on Lucy's face when she realized she'd been shot. Now I can't stop seeing her blood spreading through her shirt even as I was terrified that I couldn't save her.

I can't stop seeing Benton on video screens explaining lies I've been hearing for the last seven years. He looked perfectly put together and unflappably in control while I choked on betrayal I'm not supposed to acknowledge or even notice. I'm expected to be fine with the rules somehow.

I'm not this time!

He should have put me first. It may not be logical or right, but I'm not married to the goddamn government.

You should have told me!

"Hello in there?" Shannon knocks on the door adjoining her office with mine.

I clear my throat, dismayed that I'm about to cry. I don't know why. Probably I'm just tired, and I blow my nose.

"Come in!" I emerge from the bathroom in my navy-blue pantsuit and Uggs. "Who are you giving *fair warning* to? Who was that on the phone a minute ago?" I sound stopped-up and keep clearing my throat.

"Marino." Shannon's blue eyes linger on my face.

"I had a feeling."

"Are you upset, dear? Because I wouldn't blame you…" She studies me carefully. "I can't imagine the ordeal you've had."

"Allergies. And it seems you've had ordeals of your own, based on what I overheard."

"If I was raging…"

"Oh, you were."

"I apologize, and it's because of Maggie Cutbush. I was on with her before Marino."

"I suspected as much."

"I was telling Marino that she's clearly on a mission. Stirring the pot."

"When is she not?" I walk over to my desk where paperwork awaits.

"She's making a bloody stink about our expense account with Wild World." Shannon has a habit of talking politely from the doorway. Unlike Maggie, who would boil inside without warning.

"I could have told you that was coming." I begin initialing finalized autopsy reports that Shannon transcribed and printed. "At risk is anything she learned during her previous time in this office. You name it, and she's going to weaponize it."

"Then she hung up on me to boot."

"After you compared her to a truffle pig, I believe."

"We're lucky if that's the worst thing I call her. On a happier note, and something you rarely hear me say around here? Such a lovely fragrance." Shannon sniffs the air. "I can't remember when you've had on perfume, Doctor Scarpetta."

"Generally, I try not to subject others to my choice of

fragrances. But tonight I indulged out of self-defense after showering in the trailer."

"I'm detecting tuberose, maybe a bit of sandalwood." She sniffs again. "A little lemon, maybe vanilla?"

"It's called Amorvero. From the Hotel Hassler in Rome, where Benton asked me to marry him. He gets it for me every Christmas."

"If I could have found someone like him, maybe I wouldn't be all by my lonesome. I didn't mind it as much when I was younger. But it would be nice to have some company at this stage of things, especially if he was like that husband of yours." She sighs dreamily.

"I know how lucky I am."

"Someone who has his own life and is fine with me having mine," she says. "A force to be reckoned with yet thoughtful. And interesting and fun. Not to mention easy on the eyes. I always thought the two of you were perfect together. Even back in the day."

Back in the day is Shannon's code for when Benton was married and we were having an affair. We snuck around for years, and she knew when others didn't.

"We go back a long way, and I can tell when you're out of sorts," she says. "No point in trying to hide it."

"Sometimes we learn things we wish we didn't know, and yet it's for our own good." Collecting a spray bottle of distilled water from a bookcase, I begin misting my potted orchids and trees. "In fact, there's really not a choice because ignorance isn't bliss if it gets you hurt or killed."

"I couldn't agree more." Shannon nods her head from the doorway.

"Some information we're not allowed to share. That's not always easy," I add.

"I understand better than you know. I have things that will go with me to the grave. I wish I didn't know them. But at the same time, truth is what it is. If you don't mind me doing a little mothering?" Shannon's eyes are kind on me. "My advice is to go home straight away and get some rest, dear."

"Mothering is probably what I need right now."

"A shot or two of whisky would be just what the doctor ordered," she says. "I suspect that's in my future as well, a bit of Black Bush neat, and I believe I'll warm up the beef pot pie I made the other night."

"That sounds heavenly." Plastic rustles as I cover my microscope for the night.

"What we mustn't do is give way to discouragement. That's the poison."

"Nothing this day has been much to cheer about."

"Well, it was thrilling to watch you take off in that big helicopter Lucy was flying. You must be so proud." Shannon opens the spiral notebook she's holding. "I had such a grand time listening to all the comments. Some of them favorable. But certainly not most. I wrote them down if you care to see them."

"No thank you. Speaking of poison. Probably half of Maggie's people were loitering out there. I can well imagine the sorts of things said."

CHAPTER 28

I ONLY THOUGHT OF IT because you mentioned *ignorance not being bliss*." She puts on her zany reading glasses, pink like most things she owns. She turns pages in the notebook. "And not only Maggie's people loitering. But Maggie herself. She didn't linger. Was there long enough to make choice comments. I'll share just a few."

From our connecting doorway, Shannon begins reading comments she overheard. It doesn't matter that I don't want to hear them. She's going to make sure of it anyway:

"*It's political. The governor making sensational cases all about herself.*"

"*She's trying to convince us how powerful she is by sending in Black Hawk Down.*"

"*Another stunt at the taxpayers' expense.*"

"*Anyone who wastes money like that isn't fit for office.*"

"*It's just like a woman to do something so stupid...*"

"In other words," Shannon explains to me, "Maggie was

telling everyone that the governor sent the helicopter to pick you up."

"That's patently false," I reply.

"The implication is that Roxane Dare can't properly handle an emergency. And obviously she's a spendthrift. All fitting the sexist stereotype," Shannon concludes.

"Roxane had nothing to do with Lucy transporting people back and forth to Buckingham Run," I repeat.

"Those are just some of the comments Maggie made," Shannon informs me. "I have pages of what she and other people said, mostly implying that you're always creating a spectacle, making sure you draw attention to yourself. And that the governor is weak and showed poor judgment appointing you—"

"Thank you, that's enough," I interrupt. "It's like being on the playground in grade school and hearing kids making fun of you and your friends."

"Yes indeed, it's exactly like that. Everything seems to be the schoolyard all over again." Shannon closes her notebook, clipping the pen on the cover. "It's just surprising that Maggie would be so openly ugly about the very person who got her this job. One has to wonder how the governor would react if she knew the things Maggie says about her?"

"And Maggie said all this right in front of you."

"There was quite a crowd, no one paying me any mind, which was my intention," Shannon says. "It's amazing what people say if they don't take you seriously. I've always been good at putting on the odd duck act."

"Thankfully it's just an act," I reply ironically, because she's the definition of a true eccentric.

When I was starting out in Virginia, she was a fixture in the judicial system. I would hear stories about this tiny Irish woman in crazy outfits she'd buy for a song at thrift shops and outlet malls. Always in a hurry, Shannon was never without her pink hard case containing stenography equipment, her lunch, a paperback novel. She'd go out of her way to be friendly and funny when we'd run into each other.

"Fabian mentioned he had a good chat with you this morning," Shannon is saying from our connecting doorway. "He's certainly made a turn for the better. At least there's some good news I can report."

He's been more industrious and cordial than usual. Instead of looking sullen he's been upbeat and working at warp speed, "like the Energizer Bunny." She tells me that when she retrieved her lunch from the breakroom refrigerator, he was making chicory-laced coffee in his French press.

"He insisted on fixing me a cup, and I can see why he has his mother send it from Louisiana," Shannon says. "It was delicious, and he couldn't have been more pleasant."

She watches as I return to the conference table, retrieving the plastic evidence container. I place it inside the fiddle fig tree's big terra-cotta pot on wheels, giving Jiminy a view of greenery and rich soil. Maybe he'll think he's outside. Maybe he'll feel at home until his new pied-à-terre and other creature comforts arrive in twenty-four hours or less. He chirps a few times as if reading my mind. Or maybe he's lonely.

"It appears you've made a new acquaintance, now isn't that lovely. Might I ask where he came from?" Shannon inquires.

"Hitched a ride in a body bag."

"The things we consider normal around here."

"I'm no longer sure what normal means," I reply as Shannon comes closer to take a good look at our guest. "Abnormal seems to be the status quo. Whatever we think can't happen probably will."

"Poor little dear. I hope he's not missing his family." Shannon bends down, peering through plastic, the cricket ducked out of sight.

"I'm afraid he might. Possibly it's why he chirps," I reply. "I'm sure he would have been better off staying put out there in the woods with all the other crickets."

"Clearly, he didn't think so. Let's see if we can make Jiminy a wee bit more at home."

She helps herself to a bottle of water on my desk. Removing the cap, she fills it while walking back to the fiddle fig tree.

"There we go. Now he has a proper bowl." She removes the container's lid, setting the cap of water inside. "I'm noticing a few peanuts and raisins. Probably not ideal, but we'll leave them where they are for now." She returns the lid, making sure it's sealed.

"I hope he'll be all right here," I say to her. "I can't take him home with Merlin around."

Lucy's cat is what I call a mouser. He'd consider a cricket great entertainment.

"Most assuredly not." Shannon's been in Merlin's company often enough to know. "I think it best to leave him right where he is. Give him a chance to adjust."

"You do realize we sound a little crazy."

"Not at all," she says. "If something ends up in our care, it's the universe testing us to see if we do the right thing. Like Mickey inside the on-call room several months ago."

We captured that mouse and several others in a Havahart humane trap. Marino let them go in a field as we do the occasional squirrel or chipmunk that ends up inside the building. Not so long ago it was a bat inside the anatomical division. This goes on when doors are left open too long at all hours as bodies are dropped off and picked up, especially when the weather is nice.

Critters end up in the morgue the same way they do every other place. We take rescue missions seriously on the infrequent occasion something might be saved at our hospital for the dead. I'm sure Benton could give a psychological explanation for why we declare an emergency when a bird can't find its way out. Or baby raccoons wander into our parking lot as they did last spring. Or a lost dog does.

* * *

I begin walking window to window inside my office, closing the blinds, and it's begun snowing. The large flakes are illuminated by streetlights. Cars and pavement are frosted white, the parking lot unmarred by tire tracks. The view from my third-floor corner office looks like a Christmas card, as if all is peaceful on Earth. As if people have goodwill toward one another and all creatures big and small.

"What else have you got for me before we head out?" Ducking inside my bathroom, I open the closet as I continue to talk. "Both of us need to do that sooner rather than later, Shannon. But especially you. I have all-wheel drive and you don't." Sliding clothes along the rod, I find a tactical jacket with a zip-in winter lining.

"Blaise Fruge has called several times, and you know how insistent she can be. She has information she's not sharing with anyone but you. That's what she told me," Shannon says.

"Information related to what?"

"That poor dentist found dead in her office yesterday morning. I have to agree that there's something peculiar about it."

"Is that what Fruge said? She thinks the death is suspicious?"

"I sensed she does."

"The person she needs to talk to is Doctor Schlaefer. It's his case." I put on my jacket.

"She insists on speaking to you. Just like she always does." Shannon says this as I walk out of the bathroom. "If you ask me, it's time she stops acting as if she has a special claim on you that other investigators don't."

"She feels that way because long ago and far away in my Richmond days I used to work with her toxicologist mother."

"*Tox Doc*. I remember her very well. Quite the showboat."

"Still is. Back in the day, we worked some big cases together. Blaise would have heard a lot of stories while she was growing up. She feels like she's always known me." I collect the files Fabian left on my desk as my office extension starts ringing.

"Should I get that?" Shannon asks.

"If you don't mind."

"Doctor Scarpetta's office...," she answers my phone. "Oh, hello there, dear, you're working long hours. I'm so glad you called, because I haven't had a chance to thank you yet for the generous wedge of Halloween cake you dropped by yesterday. And I do mean *wedge*, as opposed to a normal slice. So unusual, orange marmalade icing with white chocolate ghosts, and a licorice witch flying on a butterscotch candy broom. Positively divine..."

I'm standing by my desk, looking through the files Fabian left for me. He's transcribed his conversation with Wally Jonas, and that's impressive. Except I notice right away that the police investigator mentions he's also been talking to the FBI. Early in his phone conversation with Fabian, the Prince William County detective mentions that Patty Mullet is sniffing around.

"...Of course, I shared it with the chief. Otherwise, I'm afraid I would have inhaled every crumb...," my secretary is saying over the phone, and I suspect she's talking to firearms and tool marks examiner Faye Hanaday.

Probably because the dairy farm is right next to where the Mansons lived. Wally is quoted in the transcript. *If what I'm hearing on the news is true, they were wanted by the feds for being traitors, working with the Russians...*

"...Oh. I see...Well, you timed it perfectly because she just walked in...," Shannon is saying on the phone.

...I told Special Agent Mullet that the one to be looking into is the kid. His behavior has been off-the-charts suspicious since his stepfather was killed. The FBI is concerned he's become radicalized..., the transcript reads.

"...Yes indeed, the day from hell sums it up nicely," Shannon says. "Hold on. Let me ask."

Instead of muting the call, she cups her hand over the receiver as if it's the 1980s, confirming that Faye Hanaday is on the line. She's wondering if I could drop by her lab. There's something I should see, and she wouldn't bother me at this hour and after the day I've had if it wasn't important.

"It sounds rather urgent," Shannon informs me in a stage whisper. "I get the sense it's not good news, I'm sorry to say."

The first thing that comes to mind is the plaster cast Marino made. Maybe Faye has figured out that the footprint is fake. Or maybe it isn't. I'm not sure which would be worse.

"Tell her I'll do it now on my way out," I reply, and Shannon passes along the message.

"You're not driving home alone, are you, Doctor Scarpetta?" She looks disapprovingly at me as she hangs up the phone. "I'm most unhappy the police left. I didn't mind having them parked around our building. It would be fine with me if they did it all the time."

"The bodies are gone from our facility and are Henry's problem now. He's the one who needs police protection most of all. But that doesn't mean we're out of the woods with the media or anybody else interested." I envision Carrie's disfigured face, her cold eyes. "I won't be ready to leave for at least twenty, thirty minutes because I need to see what Faye wants. But if you don't mind waiting, I'm happy to give you a ride, Shannon."

"It's out of your way and I wouldn't think of it. I'll be fine and don't want to be stranded without my car any more than you do."

I don't like the thought of her alone in our parking lot right now, and I can't count on Norm. I send a text to Marino asking him to make sure Shannon gets to her car safely. I tell her that's not negotiable and to let him know when she's ready to leave.

"Once you're home please text me." I check the latest weather update. "The wind chill is supposed to drop below zero, and I don't want any of us stranded on the roadside."

"You have a good night, dear," Shannon says. "Be sure to drink a toddy or two and eat something delicious. It will do you a world of good."

Locking my office door, I follow the deserted hallway, no one left inside the building except a few of us. I'm reminded of how I felt when COVID was at its worst and most people were working from home or not at all. My medical examiners came in on a staggered schedule unless they couldn't.

Two from this office were sick, including Doug Schlaefer, and others had family members who were hospitalized. I remember the surreal sensation of being the only human left on the planet except for our patients in their nondescript cheap body bags. I'd walk the empty hallways, trudging up and down the deserted stairs while avoiding the elevator. God forbid it should quit when nobody else was here.

Our building has thick concrete floors and walls, some reinforced with steel. There are plenty of dead spaces when I'm trying to use my mobile phone. I had existential thoughts about being trapped for days. Maybe that's how my life would end, inside an elevator going nowhere. What was supposed to last months stretched on for the better part of two years, and at times it seemed I was living in a virtual reality.

The TV is still playing inside the breakroom as I walk past, and I don't hear anyone talking. Marino's no longer there. Maybe Norm is doing his job and making the rounds, but I'm not counting on it. Beyond the elevator, I take the fire exit stairs, emerging on the second floor, where work areas and offices are locked up and dark. Around a corner in a wing by itself is the firearms and tool marks suite of labs.

First stop is the indoor range where we shoot at targets, clothing and ballistic gelatin from different distances to reconstruct shootings. There's a two-hundred-gallon water tank for recovering spent rounds from guns connected to violent events. The police bring in an astonishing array of weapons for us to examine, most of them locked up inside a vault the size of a two-car garage.

When the range is in use, I can hear the dull thumping from the hallway as bullets are fired into water or the metal trap. But it's quiet now, the light green outside the door, nobody home.

CHAPTER 29

FAYE HANADAY'S WORKSPACE IS next door in a big open room where evidence is processed and analyzed. I can't see inside because the blinds are drawn, and I knock.

"Faye? It's me!" I call out while opening the door, no one inside but her at this hour.

"Glad you could stop by." She barely looks up amid clutter you might expect to see inside a workshop or a torture chamber.

I catch glimpses of hammers, saws, knives, machetes, shanks, brass knuckles, stun guns, tactical batons, a weaponized drone, a booby-trapped mailbox, pistols and their components, including 3-D-printed ones. The variety is endless and depressing, spread out on paper-covered tables where the examiners work with forensic light sources and fluorescing chemicals.

Propped against walls are damaged windows and doors sooty with fingerprint dusting powder. Stacked in corners are tires. On shelves are tread patterns and footwear impressions cast in white plaster, everything tagged with case numbers.

"What's going on?" I close the door behind me.

"Lock it." Faye is surrounded by large computer displays inside a cubicle that's open on one side.

"I know you don't have a view." I walk past empty computer workstations, each equipped with a comparison microscope and ring lighting. "But it's snowing and sticking."

"Which is fantastically wonderful," Faye says. "Fabian and I plan to go sledding tomorrow. If there's enough snow, we'll build an igloo and camp out in it, which is so much fun if you've never done it."

In her midthirties, Faye brings to mind a funky rock star, decorating her clothing with embroidery and sequins, her rainbow-tinted hair short and spiky. A savant when it comes to recognizing patterns, she's not the gun enthusiast one would expect. The few she owns are only for self-protection.

"Especially sleeping out in the woods where you can't hear a sound." Faye has poetic sensibilities and a reflective nature. "Just the quiet splashing of a creek, and the wind rocking the trees. Pretending the world's civilized for just a little while, that nothing wants to hurt you."

"I'm not sure I'm able to pretend that anymore," I reply. "I feel like everything wants to hurt me, including the desserts you keep bringing Shannon, knowing she'll share."

Taped to the partitions of Faye's workstation are photographs of her latest prizewinning decorated cakes. The Garden of Eden. Stonehenge. Dinosaurs lumbering through a forest. A Picasso painting. My favorite is Mars with its rover *Perseverance* and rotorcraft *Ingenuity*. The planet's red velvet surface is scattered with red rock candy and looming with red chocolate volcanoes.

"I'm always amazed." I look at the pictures of her elaborate baked creations. "I don't know how you stand making something so perfect and then destroying it."

The lemon cake she surprised me with on my birthday was covered with colorful icing wildflowers that looked real enough to pick. I almost couldn't cut into it.

"I think of them as sand art. Here, then erased with the sweep of a hand," Faye explains. "I enjoy beauty when it visits, but it doesn't have to stay."

"If only ugliness wouldn't. What is it you need to see me about?" I ask her.

"I shouldn't be telling you this," she begins. "What you're about to hear from me is the truth. The evidence doesn't lie. But people do. God only knows the spin that will be put on things. In fact, it's already happening."

"That's quite a preamble," I reply.

"I'm talking to you as a friend, Doctor Scarpetta."

"Tell me what?" I can't help but think of Lucy and Benton misleading me about Carrie.

"Something that involves you personally," Faye says. "I'll probably catch hell for this despite our best intentions. The FBI made it clear not to release information without their permission. Or better put, Patty Mullet did. She's called three times in the past four hours, most recently just a few minutes ago."

"It seems she's turning up like the proverbial bad penny again," I reply.

"Come closer." Faye rolls her chair to one side, giving me a view of what's on the video screen attached to her comparison microscope.

The two bullet fragments displayed are from a test fire and an active criminal investigation, she explains. She's placed the copper shards on the microscope's two separate stages. The pair of objective lenses connected by a prism make it possible to do a side-by-side comparison on the split screen.

"A match," she says. "Thanks to the NIST Ballistics Toolmark Research Database. More popularly known as the NBTRD. *Nib-Tired*, as I call it. Marino has another pronunciation that I won't repeat. I got a hit in minutes after running the ballistic fingerprint of a weapon I examined earlier this afternoon."

The lands, grooves and other striations are identical. The markings known as rifling were imparted by the gun barrel that fired the two bullets.

"A shooting from which case? And what does this have to do with me?" I ask.

"Earlier today I conducted test fires with an AR-fifteen that was in the possession of the two ex-con assholes dressed like clowns." Faye is talking about the attempted home invasion in Old Town last night at around nine P.M. as it began to rain.

The police found the assault rifle and other guns inside the *Two Bozos'* truck, as Faye refers to them. The would-be assailants had parked several blocks from the targeted Georgian-style white brick house, designated as a historic site with a plaque in front. The ex-cons left the firearms behind, apparently assuming the victim was an easy mark. And it seems they were interested in a more intimate encounter.

Armed with military-style knives, they had duct tape, zip ties, surgical gloves and condoms. They'd brought an electric livestock prod, a shock collar and box cutters, Faye explains as I think, *The fucking monsters*. Shooting the victim wouldn't be as much fun as what they had in mind. It's an example of what can happen when you don't do your homework.

Had the ex-cons bothered to so much as Google the person who lived at that address, they might have thought twice. It's possible they knew nothing beyond her being older and living alone in an upscale neighborhood where she does her own yardwork. Had they researched her even a little they would have discovered that she's a retired rear admiral who'd served as a senior intelligence officer in Afghanistan and Africa.

When they pried open her kitchen door, she welcomed them with both barrels of a 12-gauge shotgun, dropping them in their tracks. They probably didn't see it coming and never knew what hit them.

"They had it easy compared to what was in store for her and whoever else they planned to victimize next. What had they been in prison for? Do we know?" I'm wondering what this has to do with me personally beyond the location. The house where it occurred isn't far from mine.

"Their rap sheet includes armed robberies, burglaries, assaults, stealing cars," Faye says. "They're suspected of torturing and murdering an entire family in New Jersey before burning down the house. This is according to Blaise Fruge."

"Thank God they won't be hurting anybody else."

"And they would have," Faye says. "The AR-fifteen recovered from their truck was used in at least three previous crimes. Ones considered terrorist acts."

Most recently, it was an electrical substation that someone tried to take out in Hampton Roads in early October. The same thing happened again a week later just south of Baltimore. Shots were fired but little damage was done.

* * *

"This is the new thing violent extremists are up to, as you know. Using high-powered rifles to shoot up electrical grids, hoping to cause entire cities to lose power," Faye explains. "Targeting the infrastructure, in other words, to destroy the lives of innocent civilians."

"You said the assault rifle was linked to three previous crimes," I reply as I'm waiting for her to tell me why she's summoned me to her lab. "The substations are two so far. What's the third?"

"This is why I wanted to talk to you in private, Doctor Scarpetta. The third one is the drive-by shooting at Old Town Market six weeks ago while you and Lucy were there. The same assault rifle was used. I'm supposed to examine the evidence, and it's not my place to say what I think. Had you both been critically wounded or worse? Imagine what a coup for the pieces of shit behind all this."

"Which pieces of shit?" I ask.

"The ones who've been doing a lot of bad things around here."

"You think we were targeted." I stare at the frag shining like rose gold on the video display, the metal twisted and razor sharp. I wonder which piece sliced into Lucy's neck.

"It's not my place to say," Faye answers. "But yes, I believe you were targeted. And I don't know how Lucy can't be thinking it right about now."

"You've talked to her?"

"I told her that the frag taken out of her neck at the hospital is connected to these dead terrorists. In other words, the shooting wasn't random."

"Who else knows?" I ask.

"Blaise Fruge, since the Old Town Market shooting is her case. I also informed the FBI, didn't have a choice about that.

Not even five minutes later, my phone rings and Patty Mullet starts bombarding me with questions," Faye explains. "She asked if the ex-cons would have known who you and Lucy are and what you look like. What was their connection to Lucy or maybe to both of you?"

"They had no connection," I reply. "The suggestion is absurd. And why would Patty ask *you* these things?"

"She assumes Lucy and me are tight because Marino and I are. And because you and I are friendly. That's all I can figure," Faye says. "She asked me how someone might have known you were shopping at Old Town Market six weeks ago at two-fifteen in the afternoon. Was it a routine, a habit?"

"I can tell you that it definitely wasn't," I reply. "Unfortunately, Lucy and I don't shop together very often, as busy as we are."

That Saturday we'd invited Marino and Dorothy over for a cookout last minute. It promised to be a beautiful mid-September day, and I mandated that all of us should find time to enjoy it. I'd keep it simple, grilling beef and vegan burgers, making sour cream potato salad and mixing up margaritas.

"Lucy and I ran an errand to pick up a few things. We decided it only a couple of hours in advance," I explain to Faye. "I don't see how anyone could have known what we were doing unless there was a tracking device or we were under surveillance by other means."

"Who drove?" she asks.

"We rode our bikes. I have a backpack for groceries as long as it's not much. We were out on the Mount Vernon Trail, riding to Daingerfield Island. On the way home we stopped at the market."

"Stupid question. But nobody posted anything on social media about your plans, did they by chance? Nothing was tweeted or whatever?"

"Absolutely not."

"If you were targeted, then obviously someone knew what you were doing," Faye says, getting up from her desk. "Possibly the person was spying." She prints a photo of the matching bullet fragments.

Handing it to me with no explanation, she's making sure I have proof of the ballistic evidence should I ever need it. She can say truthfully that I didn't ask for it and she didn't offer. Before she became a forensic scientist, Faye was a crime scene investigator and instructor. She doesn't miss much and asks a lot of questions.

"It would seem somebody was monitoring us," I say to her. "Assuming your suspicions are correct, and Lucy and I were the target of the drive-by shooting."

"What did you do before you went out on your bike ride? That was in the afternoon. What about earlier?" Faye asks.

"Now and then I go to the office on Saturday mornings to take care of cases that can't wait until Monday. Or if we're overwhelmed and trying to catch up," I reply. "It was one of those occasions when I needed to do this, and I was inside the autopsy suite by seven A.M."

"Who else was here?"

"Doctor Schlaefer, Marino and Fabian," I reply. "Norm was working security. Although he mostly stayed in the breakroom as usual."

"What about police?"

"Fruge stopped by to check on a case. Also, a couple of state police investigators dealing with motor vehicle fatalities."

Then I remember something I haven't thought about since it happened.

Patty Mullet appeared at the morgue midmorning while I was finishing the autopsy of a sudden infant death. Doug Schlaefer was working on a bank robber shot to death by police. The FBI labs were handling the evidence, and Patty stayed long enough to collect the bullets removed from the body.

"Did she say anything to you?" Faye asks.

"No. She was talking to Doug, asking the usual questions. Cause of death. What position was the victim in when the shooting occurred. Patty wasn't there longer than fifteen minutes," I explain.

"Is it normal for her to pop in like that?"

"She's not much for giving advance notice."

I see the FBI investigator in my mind swathed in PPE and a face shield. She was taking photographs, peppering Doug with questions.

"She didn't stop by my table, and I assumed she didn't want to be anywhere near the examination of an infant," I explain. "Doctor Schlaefer couldn't handle it either, which is why I'd come in on a Saturday to begin with."

"You're saying you didn't speak to Patty Mullet." Faye makes sure.

"She avoided me like the plague."

"Then she had no reason to know about your plans for the day."

"Didn't so much as say hello or look in my direction," I reply. "I was home by noon, and Lucy and I headed out soon after that, riding for about an hour before we stopped at the store."

"While you were doing autopsies that Saturday morning," Faye says, "where was Lucy?"

"In her cottage working."

"The entire morning?"

"That was the impression I had."

"And after she was wounded she went to the hospital. Then what?" Faye asks.

"I'm not sure. Why?"

"I want to show you what was filmed by a local TV station in front of Old Town Market approximately three hours after the shooting." Typing on her desktop keyboard, Faye pulls up the file, clicking on Play.

CHAPTER 30

THE VIDEO BEGINS WITH a sea of red and blue emergency lights flashing in the parking lot of the upscale Colonial-style Old Town Market. The front windows are shot out, shattered glass on the brick sidewalk. Police are collecting evidence as Patty Mullet appears, walking with purpose toward the entrance.

The TV crew begins bird-dogging her, the reporter firing questions that she waves off while ducking under the crime scene tape. Dressed in a khaki pantsuit, a gun on her hip and waving her creds around, she looks like a caricature of an FBI agent. In her late fifties, she has short gunmetal-gray hair and a leathery face marred by deep lines from too much sun and scowling.

"But here's the important part and the problem," Faye is saying. "Patty's out front talking to Blaise Fruge, who of course is going to respond to anything that goes down in Old Town if she's on duty. And she was. Now look what happens next."

Lucy walks into the frame, her shirt dark with dried blood,

the side of her neck bandaged. She approaches Patty and Fruge, saying things to them that I can't hear. Lucy gestures at the shattered windows in the produce section. That's where we were when two men wearing ski masks opened fire from a stolen car later found abandoned.

"Lucy must have gone back to the market straight from the E.R.," I explain, and I was most unhappy when she left me at the hospital.

Refusing a ride home, she stalked out before Benton came to the rescue. I didn't know where she went or how she got there. Later, when I checked her stitched-up injury and changed the bandage, she didn't want to talk about what had happened. I didn't push. I know better.

"Who brought this video to your attention?" I ask Faye. "Because I've never seen it."

"The part with Lucy wasn't made public for some reason. I wouldn't be surprised if she convinced them to leave it on the cutting room floor. Patty emailed the clip to me. I guess she got the original footage from the TV station. She said that Lucy showing up after the fact is like a criminal returning to the scene of a crime."

"What a reckless and idiotic thing to say." I feel my anger building like a thunderhead. "Why did she show you this video, Faye? Why was she sharing such detailed investigative information? I think you'll agree that it's not appropriate. It's alarmingly indiscreet and treacherous. Doesn't matter that I trust you."

"She's hell-bent on making a big thing out of what she perceives as a vulnerability, that's my guess," Faye replies. "She kept saying that a normal person wouldn't return to the market just hours after being shot. It's what people do when manipulating the police while getting off on watching the crime scene being worked."

"This isn't a game or a movie. She's playing with people's lives," I reply sharply, and it's not the first time we've had trouble with Patty Mullet.

During Benton's tenure with the FBI, he had the misfortune of working with her when she was fresh out of the academy. Desperate to be part of his criminal profiling unit, she wasn't the right stuff, to put it kindly. Her interest in him went beyond the professional, and he became the embodiment of her every rejection. She punishes him and those he cares about, given the opportunity.

"She was asking if I had any idea whether Lucy was personally familiar with those who've claimed responsibility for the Mansons' deaths," Faye tells me. "The violent extremists who call themselves The Republic."

Maybe my niece had been working undercover and was associating with them. Patty started tossing out criminal profiling jargon like *Stockholm syndrome*, *identifying with the aggressor*, Faye explains. As if Lucy might have gotten too close to the bad guys and started sympathizing with them.

"Vandalizing electrical grids, the shooting at Old Town Market create attention and destabilize the public while recruiting other extremists to join the cause," Faye goes on as I get more offended. "Patty said that *people like Lucy* are especially vulnerable to changing sides and sleeping with the enemy. *And unfortunately, she's done it before*. I'm quoting."

"Patty should be careful," I reply. "She's falsely implicating another federal agent in a very serious crime. Worse than that, she's blaming the victim."

I can see Lucy bagging Bibb lettuce and Vidalia onions while I picked out heirloom tomatoes. Suddenly, an enormous explosion, the crash of glass shattering, and she grabbed her gun, clutching her bleeding neck, yelling at everyone to get down. Several shoppers were badly hurt, people running and screaming.

"I don't think Patty Mullet or a lot of people realize how close Lucy came to being killed," I'm saying as someone starts pounding on the lab door, trying the knob.

* * *

"Hey! Open up!" Marino thumps on the door some more, and Faye leaves her workstation. "Anybody home?"

"Hold your horses already." She lets him in. "For a minute I thought it was Bigfoot about to break down the door, looking for his evidence."

"It's a damn good cast, right?" Marino's attention is everywhere as he searches for his handiwork.

No longer in scrubs, he's changed into jeans and a hooded sweatshirt. Draped over his arm is a waterproof shell jacket. Like me he keeps spare clothing in his office, never knowing when we might have a wardrobe emergency.

"You've not taken a bad cast that I've seen, whether it's footwear or a tire track," Faye is saying to him as I glance again at the weather report on my phone.

The temperature is below freezing, the winds light and variable. The snow is several inches deep already and predicted to be heavy at times until tomorrow midmorning when the front moves out. State government offices and area schools are announcing their closings. People are asked to stay off the roads tonight, Roxane Dare already declaring a state of emergency.

"Back in the day, you had to learn the basics. You had to be able to do anything." Marino loves to tell everyone that he came along the hard way. "Whether it was lifting prints with tape, making comparisons without a computer. Doing scene sketches using a measuring tape. Or mixing up plaster of Paris and pouring casts of footwear impressions, tire tracks, including in awful weather, the whole nine yards."

"Your good ol' days are before my time, Detective Flintstone," Faye says, and the two of them are close.

They spend hours on the range conducting test fires together. He goes with her to gun shows, and for him it's a candy store. For her it's research as she does what she can to keep up with the latest weapons and their components.

"What are you talking about with the door locked and the shades down?" Marino's attention is all over the lab.

"I'll let you fill him in about Patty Mullet," Faye says to me as she sits back down in front of her microscope. "It's a long and ugly story."

"Always is when it has to do with her." Marino moves closer to shelves of plaster casts as if his might be among them. "She's a whack-a-mole always popping up when big cases go down."

"Causing her usual interference, only worse," I reply.

"Okay, I give up. Where is it?" Marino wanders over to us. "Someone didn't take it, did they? Like the FBI, for example? I sure as hell hope not! Because Patty freakin' Mullet would love to get her hands on something like this. They'll use it to make all of us look like morons..."

"Stop getting worried over nothing. Your cast is locked up as it should be," Faye answers sternly with a hint of affection. "Do you need to see it for some reason? Because I'd rather not open the vault. More paperwork."

"I'm just wondering what your opinion is after examining it."

"I'm thinking this is beyond my pay grade. But I see nothing that screams fake to me."

"I knew it!" he says happily.

"No imperfections or artifacts that might make me suspect the impression was made by a prosthetic, perhaps one 3-D printed," she explains.

"Even if it was?" Marino replies. "Then where's the original image? You can't just print something without a photograph, a scan of something."

"I never thought I'd hear myself utter these words," Faye says. "But you need a Bigfoot expert."

"We're working on it," I reply. "And I never thought I'd say that, either."

"I walked Shannon to her car, making sure she's safely on her way," Marino lets me know. "I told her to go straight home and stay put. Speaking of?" This to Faye. "You should get the hell out of here while the getting's good. How about I escort you along with the doc?"

"I'm staying until Fabian's ready to call it a day." Faye turns off her microscope and its video screen. "He'll leave his car here and ride with me. My truck has snow tires and four-wheel drive. No problem. But I think we're going to hang out for a while. We like it when no one else is around. A good time to catch up, and where I live we're prone to get power outages. Fabian's old place isn't much better. Charming but drafty as hell even when the electricity is working."

"You're always welcome to stay in the on-call room," I tell her. "Fabian just restocked the refrigerator in there yesterday. The TV is working and the linens are clean. If you get chilly, the space heater is in the closet. Make yourselves cozy and at home."

"Truth is, it would be helpful having you around," Marino says. "I'm here only a few minutes longer, and I don't have confidence in whatever Norm ends up doing. Which usually is nothing."

"Do you mind if I move my truck inside the bay?" Faye walks us to the door.

"Help yourself," I reply. "I'd do it now if I were you."

Marino and I head back toward the elevator, and I'm seething inside even as I don't show it.

"What Patty Mullet is doing has gone too far." I pass along details I shouldn't have been told.

"It's really dangerous for her to be saying shit like that to someone who works in the labs," Marino says.

"Or to anyone."

"Loose talk like that can spread like wildfire," he says. "At least Faye can be trusted. But who else is hearing that Lucy might be involved with terrorists? The answer is, a lot of people, I'm betting, and then they tell everyone else. Next thing you know, the FBI is at Lucy's door with a no-knock warrant. This is how people end up dead for no good reason..."

As he continues painting the grim scenario, I'm envisioning agents in ballistic gear raiding the guest cottage on my property. My niece has guns in every room, and there would be a tragic outcome. I don't know who would get shot, but somebody would. Maybe everyone. I don't want Lucy dying the way she lives, always in danger and on the edge of the abyss.

I can't help but worry about the choices she's been making from day one, wondering how much of it is my fault. I've never stopped questioning the influence I've had while raising her as my own. I know some of what she's absorbed and emulated is positive. But not all of it. How many times have I heard my sister blame me?

She'll say that Lucy would have turned out differently if I were a teacher, perhaps the head of a biology department in a graduate school. Perhaps I'd be a better influence if I were a physician whose patients weren't dead. Or a research scientist in a commercial lab.

"Doc…?"

What if I helped invent cures instead of chasing after killers? But what bothers Dorothy most is that Lucy chose to be nothing like her.

"Earth to Doc…?"

"I'm sorry." I tune back in to what Marino is saying. He puts on his jacket, zipping it up to his chin as we follow the second-floor hallway.

"It's like you were in a trance." He puts on a plaid hat that has Elmer Fudd built-in earflaps. "You've been halfway beamed out ever since we got abducted by the intelligence community."

"I'm somewhat preoccupied as a result."

"You and me both. I hate being lied to. It's all I can think about."

"Plus, I'm a little sleep deprived. Both of us are," I say to him, and we've reached the illuminated EXIT sign. "I could use some real food. As could you, I'm sure. Everything seems to be crashing in at once. Tomorrow will be better."

"I wonder if Lucy knows what's being spread about her all

over the place," he says. "I hate to think what she might do about it. I wouldn't want to be Patty Fish Bait."

"I wouldn't want to be her for any reason," I reply.

I open the door and we head down to the ground level, our feet scuffing on metal-edged steps.

"I wouldn't be surprised if Lucy's gotten word of it," I add. "She has a knack for finding out things. And if she hasn't, she's going to hear it from me as soon as I see her. I'm going to pass along everything that Faye told me. I'll relay everything Patty Mullet is saying, the rumors she's starting."

"Unlike how we've been treated these past seven years, right? Lucy, Benton and Tron lying to our faces," Marino says, the air dusty, our voices bouncing off concrete. "Meanwhile we don't hesitate filling them in when there's something they should know. Even when we're told not to? We tell them. And they can't return the favor."

"Hopefully we'll have a better understanding once we have a chance to talk to them without a host of other people around."

"How are we supposed to trust them after this?"

"The same way we always have. Nothing's really changed. It just feels that way."

"At the end of the day it's you and me against everybody. Always has been," Marino says, and a part of him wishes that were true. Another part of him believes it.

CHAPTER 31

WE'RE NOT ALONE," I say to Marino. "We really aren't. We have people who care about us." I open the stairwell door at the morgue level.

"What I want to know is how come you're not fucking pissed at them." He can't keep the hurt out of his voice as we set out along the corridor. "It's one thing if it's colleagues not telling us stuff. But we're talking about your niece and your husband, the people you live with."

"I don't think you have any idea how pissed I am," I reply, and the first room on our left is the anthropology lab.

It's out of the mainstream of traffic in the far reaches of the lower level where the odor is rancid and elevator traffic doesn't venture. Through the closed door I can hear the quiet clacking of skeletal remains defleshing in a ten-gallon soup pot of bleach and boiling water. Most of our commercial kitchenware is from Wild World, I'm unpleasantly reminded for the umpteenth time.

"Hold on a minute." Opening the door, I'm greeted by a waft of foul humid air.

I avoid inhaling the steamy acrid stench while I approach the electric stovetop, old with a chipped avocado-green enamel finish. I lower the heat to simmer, my heart pounding furiously. Bits of tissue float on top of the scummy bubbling water, two femurs knocking against metal. The bones belong to the partial skeleton laid out on a paper-covered table, a puzzle missing important pieces.

The remains turned up at a construction site, the victim a young male whose mother was African American, based on the mitochondrial DNA. The police haven't a clue about identity but suspect the homicide is mob-related. Possibly it goes back decades to when that area of Loudoun County was popular with Colombian drug traffickers known for executing snitches and rivals.

"We don't want to leave the pot boiling overnight. Especially when no one's likely coming in tomorrow if we're buried in snow. All the water will evaporate and imagine the fucking mess. Not to mention showing a total disrespect for a victim we still can't call by name. But he mattered to someone, goddammit." I don't mean to be this upset. "Why don't people think? Do they assume I'm always going to clean up after them?"

"Fabian should have noticed. He takes the stairs all the time and walks right past the anthropology lab." Marino can't resist finding fault with him. "He has his lunch in here when Doctor Milton's around. The other week I walked past and the two of them were chowing down on Domino's pizza. Meanwhile, bones are clanking inside the pot like lobsters trying to get out."

"Doctor Milton shouldn't have left the damn lab with the damn burner going full blast." I'm adamant and out of sorts. "God knows how many times he's done it before."

The consulting forensic anthropologist is a professor at James Madison University. Our office has been using him since long before I moved back to Virginia, and he typically shows up on an as-need basis. He must have visited today while I was out, and it's a good thing he's not here right now. I'm afraid of what I might say to him.

"What are you doing?" Marino asks as I use my phone to take a video of the bubbling water simmering down, the bones rattling quietly.

"Maggie's making a thing about our account at Wild World," I reply. "I thought she might like to see how we utilize some of what we buy."

"As much as she hates all things disgusting?" Marino replies with a hint of glee. "Maybe add a few pics of our Wild World autopsy knives in action."

"An excellent idea." I close the lab door.

"And what we do with all the string and butcher paper we buy," Marino says. "You talk about squeamish. She has a hard time picking up after her corgi, has to wear a face mask and gloves."

"I'm feeling more inspired by the moment," I reply, and my former secretary was never one to walk inside the autopsy suite.

Maggie rarely ventured downstairs looking for me unless she was being nosy. Even then she kept her distance, not disguising her disgust. In the main, she wanted nothing to do with the morgue and those we care for alive and dead. During Elvin

Reddy's reign, she spent her time inside her office or his. That's when she wasn't going to meetings and traveling, accompanying him as if she was his wife.

"It's not a good idea mentioning the footprint cast to Doctor Milton," Marino says as we follow dingy off-white linoleum flooring that's supposed to be non-slip. I know from experience that it's not if it's wet. "Even though he's an anthropologist it would be a really bad idea."

"I wouldn't think of it," I reply. "I'd be the first to tell you that he's not a foot anatomist."

"He goes to one of those churches with *Primitive* in the name," Marino says, and he can't stand the anthropologist. "He doesn't believe in evolution, thinks we're exactly the same as we were in the flippin' Garden of Eden. So you can imagine his attitude about a huge hairy humanoid that might be an earlier version of ourselves. I'm just telling you that he thinks Bigfoot is bullshit if not sacrilegious and is the last person we want to talk to about it."

"Doctor Milton is old-school and has been around for a very long time," I reply. "Age, race, sex, and that's about as much as we can depend on him for when we deal with bones. The rest of the time we use our folks at the Smithsonian and other experts, none of whom are appropriate in this situation. Perhaps Cate Kingston can be helpful, depending on what Lucy thinks of her."

Next is the room where we store what Shannon calls posterity pots. The door is cracked open, and I'm getting increasingly agitated.

I scan metal shelves where hundreds of plastic quart containers are filled with sections of organs and other tissue from autopsies. Each has a toe tag inside that's labeled with the case number scrawled in waterproof marker. I can tell the fire deaths and others involving carbon monoxide, the tissue cherry red in its bath of formalin. I shut the door, making sure it's locked this time.

"This is what I mean," I say to Marino. "Carelessness. People getting too damn comfortable."

"I guess when it's as busy as it's been, there's a lot of traffic in and out and doors get left unlocked or open..."

"Remember the formalin spill when someone ran into the shelves with a gurney because the door was left wide open? Back in the day when the jars were glass?"

"Yeah, we lost hundreds of people. Pieces and parts of them, at any rate. But that was in Florida. Not here, Doc."

"My point is that the door should stay locked, especially at this hour. And I'm tired of picking up after everyone. I'm not a damn den mother."

"It's a good thing because you'd scare away all the Cub Scouts right now," Marino says. "You're sure in a shitty mood all of a sudden."

"It's not all of a sudden."

* * *

Ahead is the autopsy suite, and I can hear rock music from the eighties drifting out the open double doors. The Police are singing "Every Breath You Take," and it's ironically appropriate.

"...*I'll be watching you*...," and I feel like something is as I step inside to tell Fabian I'm leaving.

The old-style boom box is turned up loud on a countertop,

and I can smell the sharp odor of hospital-grade disinfectant. He's polished the four steel autopsy tables attached to sinks. He's set up the surgical carts, getting ready for the next cases, because there will be more. That we can always count on. I notice the walk-in cooler door isn't closed all the way.

"Fabian?" I call out, looking around. "Who's in here? Hello?"

I pull open the cooler door, a fog of condensation rolling out to the loud noise of blowing air. Pouched bodies on stretchers are parked side by side with barely enough room to walk between them.

"Fabian? Tell me if you're in here?" I don't see him, and he doesn't answer.

What is wrong with everybody? The cooler door isn't supposed to be left open. I walk out, shutting it hard behind me. *Dammit!*

"Hello?" I duck inside the locker room next, and Fabian has been in here recently.

The old industrial washer is loud in the spin cycle, thudding at top speed as if the machine will explode. Connected to the locker room is the anteroom where we keep surgical scrubs, gowns, PPE and other supplies. I hear someone moving around. Footsteps, then the door opens, and it's not Fabian, I realize with uneasy surprise.

"Didn't mean to scare you." Norm the security officer steps out with a bold smile. He's holding a box of shoe covers. "Can I help you with something, boss?"

"Maybe I should ask you the same thing," I reply.

"Nope, I'm good considering."

Built like a stone column, Norm has an intense gaze, his thick neck tattooed with an eagle. His khaki uniform is badly wrinkled, his shirt halfway untucked, and he needs a haircut. I'd be very happy if he'd trim his beard, but I stay away from making comments about his hygiene or appearance.

"Hope you don't mind if I keep a supply in my car." He indicates the box of shoe covers, and I do mind. "It's important I protect myself. And I wouldn't have to worry about what I might track into my personal car or residence if I didn't work here. It's a job-related hazard. Meaning it should be covered by the employer."

"You can't help yourself to PPE for your personal use. I'm sorry. I thought you understood that," I reply, and of course he knows. "You've been working here almost as long as I have, Norm."

"It's not that I don't understand. I don't accept it, boss."

"I don't make up the rules in state government. And I've asked you before not to call me boss."

"It's meant as a compliment."

"It's not one and I don't believe that's how you mean it," I reply.

"Sorry you took offense, ma'am." Brazenly holding my gaze, Norm makes me feel the way I did when I was getting started in my career.

Some of my male colleagues would look at me as if I were good for only one thing. Their smiles were meant to shrink me into compliance. Not a day went by when I wasn't reminded of my place, and I feel the slow burn of an old anger that I don't want roused. It's been a long day and my resistance is low. Some of what I'm upset about has nothing to do with the here and now.

"The same rules apply to everybody." I return Norm's stare,

refusing to back down. "You've been told before. You can't take gloves, disposable sheets, sticky mats, booties, face masks, nothing out of this building for personal use. Not even a roll of toilet paper if the state paid for it."

"You have PPE in your car." Norm digs in a pocket of his uniform pants, pulling out a stick of beef jerky that he peels open in front of me. "Marino has PPE in his truck." Talking as he chews, reeking of garlic. "All your doctors have crap like that. Even Fabian does."

"For when we respond to scenes," I reply. "Not for our own personal use."

"Like I said?" Norm takes another odiferous bite, smacking loudly as we talk inside the locker room. "Anything I don't want to track into my personal vehicle or my residence is the result of my working here. I shouldn't have to cover the expense."

"We'll have to take this up another time." I have no intention of talking to him again if I can help it. "I just ducked in looking for Fabian."

"Got no idea," Norm says with a rude shrug.

"I assumed he might be nearby since the cooler door was left open," I reply pointedly.

"I don't supervise Fabian. But he gets distracted when he's listening to music, fussing with his hair and all the rest. Probably he left the cooler door open by mistake."

The way Norm says it makes me suspicious that he's the one who left the door open, and there's no legitimate reason for him to be inside the cooler. I have a bad feeling Norm might be our leak, assuming we have only one. Some tabloid news outlets will pay handsomely for postmortem photographs, depending on who died.

"I understand you were late for your shift, Norm." My gut reaction is I caught him up to no good. And he knows it.

"What do you expect when I get dragged here at the last minute?" His flat cold stare is unwavering and mocking. "It was supposed to be my night off. Then your secretary calls and says I have to be here before Wyatt passes out from exhaustion."

"I'm sorry about that."

"You should be."

"We appreciate you coming in, but it does little good if you're not minding the door or watching the cameras." I won't let him intimidate me. As irate as I am, I don't think he could.

"Just because I don't sit in the office with my thumb up my ass doesn't mean I don't see what's going on." He says it like a subtle threat, hostility glinting.

"I'm sorry you seem so unhappy." I don't like the way Norm is looking me up and down. "But either do the job and abide by the rules or don't work here anymore."

"You got any idea how much money I'm losing while I'm here babysitting dead people?"

"The only thing you seem to be babysitting is the TV in the breakroom." My voice is hard as I get angrier.

"I could be out driving fares."

"It's not often we ask you to help in a bind..."

"Meanwhile, Tina gets paid for staying home."

"I'm not excusing her," I reply in the same flinty tone. "But it's important you make the rounds and keep an eye on the cameras." I walk out of the locker room, and he doesn't follow.

"What an asshole," Marino says, waiting for me in the corridor. "I was a hair from coming in there."

"He'll probably walk off the job before the night is out," I reply.

"Let him."

"I might have caught him pinching PPE," I add. "I'm also suspicious about what he was doing in the cooler. The dead bodies of the two ex-con Bozos are still in there. I hope Norm isn't taking pictures, selling info. What I do know for a fact is he's walking off with PPE."

"I'm not surprised. He's always trying to get something for nothing. Even if it's not paying for coffee in the breakroom. Or swiping another person's food."

"I don't think he was expecting anyone to walk in when I did. I have a feeling he's been taking more than just the occasional box of shoe covers. I also don't know where Fabian is," I explain, and Marino points down at the floor, indicating the anatomical division below ground.

CHAPTER 32

WHILE YOU WERE CATCHING Norm swiping PPE, Fabian texted," Marino tells me as we resume following the corridor. "He said he's going to be here for a while and may as well take care of the bodies we didn't cremate earlier."

"This is an ideal time." I glance through observation windows we pass, the evidence room overflowing like a gory flea market. "We have five bodies returned by medical schools, and that will keep the oven running for a while."

It always feels antisocial when our smokestack is going. But after hours during a snowstorm, no one will be the wiser.

"Never fails that shit happens when you least need it," Marino says. "When I headed out the door this morning, I had no idea we were in for weather like this. I wouldn't have driven to the hangar in Maryland. But considering where I was going, I didn't think I should Uber."

Marino's pickup truck is at the Secret Service training facility where he met Lucy and Tron after they'd located the campsite at Buckingham Run. The hangar is almost thirty miles from Alexandria, and it will be slow going in the conditions.

"They should be here soon." He's telling me that Lucy and Tron are picking him up. "I'm hoping I'll get some updates. You know as well as I do that they have all kinds of information they're not sharing."

Most of all, Marino wants to confront them about Carrie. I don't blame him, but it won't do any good. No matter what I say, I know the truth. Nothing we might be told can undo the last seven years of lying. I don't know what Benton could say that will change what I'm feeling. Had Carrie not posted the video on the Dark Web I doubt Marino and I would have been told now or ever.

"Tron's involved, too," he says. "I'm betting she and Lucy didn't just meet after we moved here. Hell, they probably knew each other long before we had a clue. All these times we've hung around with Tron, and she was spying on Carrie. And we had no idea. Just when you think you can trust somebody."

"I'm not happy either," I reply. "But we understand it had to be that way. Tron, Lucy, Benton, they didn't have a choice."

"Really?" Marino angrily glances over at me as we reach the intake area. "*They didn't have a choice*?"

"Legally they didn't."

"Fuck legally."

"What would you have done?"

"I've never kept anything from you even when I should. I would have told you," he says.

"I would have found a way to tell you too," I admit.

"I feel like the rug was just pulled out from under us, Doc."

"That's because it was."

"Bottom line? We need to be more careful than ever," he says. "We'll have to be for the rest of our lives."

"Do you know how many times we've said those exact words since we've worked together?"

"Norm is hopeless." Marino glares at the empty security office. "I tried to talk some sense into him, telling him he's got to pretend he gives a shit. A lot of good it did. We should get rid of him and Tina both."

"And replace them with what?"

"Cardboard cutouts would be better."

"I intend to have a sit-down with the governor at the first opportunity." I open the door leading into the vehicle bay, my car key in hand. "Roxane got me into all this. I don't care what her political aspirations might be. She's going to have to be more helpful. I want trained security who get paid worth a damn. I want loved ones, families allowed inside our lobby again. And the meditation garden restored so people have a nice place to sit outside when the weather's good."

"You need to ask her why the hell she created a dummy agency for Elvin and Maggie," Marino says as we walk down the ramp. "What was she thinking? She needs to understand the problems those two cause."

"I'll bring it up delicately. Because I have a feeling there's something unfortunate hiding under the rug."

"You won't be needing that." Marino indicates the car key in my hand.

"I've been driving in snow for as long as you have..."

"Not after a day like this when you're sleep deprived, Doc. The weather isn't the biggest worry. What do you think she's doing?" He means Carrie. "Probably watching and calculating our every move, that's what. I'm betting she's behind whoever took out the Mansons. She's behind everything."

"Probably not everything."

"I'd prefer if it was me taking you home. Nothing's going to happen to you if I'm around."

"That borders on magical thinking," I reply. "But yes. I always feel relatively safe when you're with me, Marino."

"What do you mean, *relatively*?"

"I mean just what I said. And you're not getting my key."

I'm blasted by cold air as I open the pedestrian door that leads into the parking lot. A truck engine idles loudly, and I smell exhaust. Glaring headlights are blinding in the steady snowfall.

"That was a slick move," I say to Marino. "I have to give you credit."

"Evening!" Blaise Fruge is walking toward us, backlit like a rock star, the snowflakes big and thickly drifting down like feathers.

* * *

Dressed in jeans and a leather jacket, Fruge wears her hair long on top and shaved short on the sides. She's close to Lucy's age and extremely buff, motivated by Marino, who took her under his wing soon after we moved here. They often work out together in the gym. Now and then they have a beer and talk about policing. She puts him on a pedestal and is cozy with Dorothy.

"Fruge will make sure you get home okay," Marino informs me. "Thanks, buddy. I owe you," he says to Fruge.

"Gotcha covered."

"I appreciate the gesture, but I'm driving my own car," I announce to them, my hair getting wet in the snow.

"It's not a good idea," Marino says, his plaid cap turning white.

"It's not open for debate." I won't be argued out of it.

"Fine. Then I'll be right behind you," Fruge promises.

"This really isn't necessary...," I start to protest.

"I've got instructions from the Secret Service to hand you off at your front door," she says, and Benton must have talked to her. "If there's even the slightest problem, Doctor Scarpetta, we'll have backup before you can blink. But I need to go over some things with you about the dentist Nan Romero. As of a few hours ago, the FBI has taken over her case."

"Great," Marino says sarcastically.

"How about we talk on the phone while we're driving?" I suggest to Fruge as I look up at thick flakes swirling.

"I'll call you." She trots off to her SUV, almost losing her footing.

"Let me know when you're home, Doc." Marino unlocks the pedestrian door.

"What about Tron and Lucy?" I ask. "When are they picking you up?"

"You'll probably pass them on the way out. Drive safe and see you later," he says to me before disappearing inside the vehicle bay.

My take-home Subaru is one of the few perks of the job, and I dig out the snow brush. The windows are covered as quickly as I clean them off, and I climb behind the wheel. Starting the engine, I turn on the heat. As I wait for the car to warm up, I text Benton that I'm on my way. He replies instantly that he's already home and for me to be very careful. There are black ice warnings, and a lot of accidents reported.

Best if Dorothy's not out driving in this. I feel guilty that I'm hoping she'll stay home.

She's here and has been for a while, he answers, and I know what that means.

Tell her to make sure Marino knows he's invited. He's off to get his truck.

Eventually he'll show up at the house, both of them staying over. As much as I'd like to be alone with my husband, tonight it's not going to happen. The glass is fogging up, and I blast the defrost, sitting quietly for a moment. I need to take a beat before I talk to Fruge about yet another problem. It's important I'm feeling steady when I reach my front door.

I don't want it obvious that I'm dispirited by what I've learned. For a while, Carrie Grethen was banished from our house, from the very planet. She wasn't a topic of conversation. I didn't think about her anymore. I didn't wonder if she was behind every bad thing. And what she might do next. My phone rings through the car's speakers, and it's Fruge.

"You ready? Anything wrong?" She may as well be rapping on my window, prodding me along.

"Leaving now." Checking my mirrors, I back out of my assigned spot next to the bay door.

I drive slowly through the snowy parking lot, and Fruge is behind me in her unmarked Ford Interceptor. She whelps her siren at the black Tahoe we pass going the other way. Lucy and Tron flash their lights at me, on the way for Marino. Moments later I'm on West Braddock Road, where businesses are closed. Only the Safeway grocery store is busy, panicky shoppers desperate to stock up because of the weather. My phone starts ringing and it's Fruge again.

"What's on your mind?" I answer. "I'll try to answer your questions as long as both of us pay attention to our driving."

"The dentist Nan Romero. I'm worried she was murdered."

"That's quite a statement to start with."

"I just can't figure out how the hell that happened. It's not like she was tied up in the chair and forced to inhale nitrous oxide." Fruge's voice sounds through my car's speakers. "If someone were ordering you to do such a thing, don't you think you might resist? Maybe fight like hell? Because I sure as hell would. And do you really think she wrapped all that painter's tape around her lower face? I personally find that really weird."

"As you know, I didn't go to that scene or do the autopsy," I remind her. "It's Doug Schlaefer's case."

I focus intently on the road, the flakes getting smaller as the temperature continues to plummet. I'm making sure there's plenty of room between me and the car in front. Fortunately, the traffic is thinning as the roads get slick, my headlights reflecting off bright whiteness and roiling fog.

"I saw her body when she came in and am aware of the painter's tape," I tell Fruge, my eyes watering in the reflected glare. "I agree it's peculiar, but people determined to commit suicide will do all sorts of things to make sure they don't change their minds. Cuffing their hands behind their backs when hanging themselves. Wearing heavy clothing and putting rocks in their pockets when walking into the river to drown."

"I wanted to make sure you know what I've found out. I realize what I'm about to pass on is circumstantial. But I dropped by Faye Hanaday's lab earlier."

"I was just there, and she said she'd talked to you." I use the sleeve of my jacket to wipe condensation off my side window.

"She showed me the matching bullet fragments from the AR-fifteen we recovered from the ex-cons' truck," Fruge says. "I know that one of those pieces of shrapnel came from Lucy's neck, and the same weapon was used to shoot up electrical power substations."

"That's what Faye told me," I reply.

"I want you to be aware that there may be multiple bad things going on at once."

"I'm aware."

"And that it seems they're all connected."

"I'm aware of that possibility as well." I glance in my rear-view mirror, her SUV close enough behind me that no one could get between us.

"The FBI is doing its own thing. Patty Mullet is. I guess you know what that means."

"I do indeed."

"Point is, I don't have much of a say going forward," Fruge explains. "I'm warning you not to count on Patty shooting straight with you, Doctor Scarpetta."

"I've never counted on that. Just the opposite."

"And I'm pretty sure she has it in for Lucy." Fruge's headlights glare in my mirrors.

"What did Patty tell you?" I ask.

"She was bad-mouthing. Not that this is anything new. But it was worse than usual. She's implying Lucy might have gone rogue."

"The only person who seems to have done that is Patty," I reply in a measured tone that masks what I'm really feeling.

"I agree. When she had me on the phone, I kept wondering what's wrong with her," Fruge says. "You ask me, she seems a little out of control."

"I agree." I slow down, turning right onto King Street, where we'll stay all the way to the waterfront. From there I'm just minutes from home.

"I'm afraid we're dealing with a cluster fuck," Fruge says as I adjust the defrost, the wipers making their rubbery sweeps. "The creepy deaths inside Buckingham Run. The two ex-cons dead inside your cooler. The dentist who supposedly killed herself. All are connected one way or another to The Republic. To domestic terrorism. And that's really scary."

The Alexandria City High School is dark, the Chinquapin Park and garden cloaked in white. The snow must be almost four inches deep judging by what I see piled on tree boughs and mailboxes. I'm keeping my speed below twenty miles an hour and can feel the ice beneath the snow in spots.

"I feel like some kind of coup is going on and nobody's told us," Fruge says.

"And you may be right," I reply. "How does Nan Romero fit in? I'm not understanding her connection to The Republic."

"She was Huck and Brittany Manson's dentist. This is why I wanted a private moment with you."

"That was an important detail for you to find out," I commend her, and my car fishtails a little. "Talk about six degrees of separation."

"They'd been her patients for the past eight years."

"Is this the reason the FBI is suddenly interested? Because of their connection to the Mansons?" My car slips and slides some more.

"I'm the one who found that out, and Patty said *thanks very much*, and *we'll handle it from here*. She basically indicated my services no longer were required even though the case is the jurisdiction of Alexandria P.D. Or it was," Fruge is saying, and I feel my tires slipping again.

Gently tapping the brakes, I slow down, the wipers thumping

monotonously like a metronome. A white construction van with flashing yellow hazard lights is on the roadside and hasn't been there long. The windshield is barely covered in snow. I see no sign of the driver.

"I went through Nan's list of patients," Fruge is explaining. "It doesn't appear that either Brittany or Huck had been to her office since last spring for routine teeth cleaning."

"I agree it's interesting, possibly significant that they knew each other," I reply. "If you're suggesting they had something to do with Nan Romero's death, even if indirectly? Why? What would be the motive in your opinion?"

"Maybe Nan knew too much about who and what they were involved with," Fruge speculates. "And what a great way to get rid of a potential problem. Make it look like Nan killed herself. She didn't leave a note. Not that anyone has found."

"The absence of it doesn't mean much, because not all that many people leave notes," I reply, and ahead on the left is the grand entrance of Ivy Hill Cemetery. As I'm creeping closer in the thick falling snow I notice a strange dark cloud over my side of the road, undulating and rushing toward me.

"What the hell is that...?" I exclaim.

The cloud closes in, suddenly disarticulating as if made of pixels. It's as if a swarm of huge bugs with black legs is batting against the glass, blocking my vision. I turn up the speed of the wipers and it does no good. Then I'm slamming into something, the airbag punching me in the head like a boxing glove.

CHAPTER 33

SILENCE. MY HEADLIGHTS SHINE through snow on majestic cemetery monuments and centuries-old trees. I've run over the curb and hit the granite sign at Ivy Hill's entrance, steam rising from my SUV's crumpled hood. I'm seeing stars as I sit very still, trying to assess my injuries.

Carefully I move my arms and legs, and they're fine. Taking off my seat belt, I touch the left side of my face and it stings like hell. Nothing seems broken or sprained, but I have a painful abrasion on my jaw and cheek. My wrists, the heels of my hands feel burned.

"Doctor Scarpetta?" Fruge's worried voice through my car's speakers. "Are you okay?"

"I think so."

"Should I call an ambulance?"

"Absolutely not."

I massage the back of my sore neck as I look around for my phone. It's on the floor in front of the passenger seat. I grope for it, feeling dazed. The steering wheel's airbag hangs limply like a white pillowcase, and I smell the smoky odor left by its explosive deployment. I see a vague residue of powder on the console and my clothing.

I was walloped squarely on the left side of my throbbing face, and I realize my nose is bleeding. Blood is dripping on my jacket, my pants. Opening the glove box, I grab a handful of napkins.

"I'm pulling up." Fruge's disembodied voice sounds as I turn on the emergency flashers. "You sure I shouldn't call for an ambulance?" Her SUV's headlights swing in next to me, snow crunching under the oversized tires.

"No ambulance." I unfasten my shoulder harness. "Please don't call anyone. It's not necessary."

I look at myself in the rearview mirror, dabbing blood, pinching my nostrils together. The left side of my face begins to swell, the skin bright red and raw. Airbags save lives, but I've seen the damage they can inflict. Shattered facial bones. Fractured ribs. Blindness. Brain injuries. I've gotten off easy.

Plugging my left nostril with a piece of napkin, I climb out of the car. The frigid air, the snowflakes are soothing on my raw flesh. I take note that I'm moving fine and not dizzy. My balance is normal. I don't feel lightheaded or woozy.

"Did you hit ice?" Fruge walks over to me.

"Apparently I did when I braked. I couldn't see."

I'm surveying the damage, trying to make sense of what just happened. The driver's side of my SUV's front end is smashed, the headlight shattered. The left front tire is flat, and my state-issue Subaru will have to be towed. There will be a lot of paperwork and I'll have no choice but to lie by omission. I won't put in writing that something just ran me off the road.

It was intentional. I probably know who's behind it, and I'm not spelling that out in bureaucratic forms. Maybe the goal was to cause real bodily harm. Had my car skated in the opposite direction I could have hit oncoming traffic. Or the point may be to inconvenience and intimidate. What I witnessed isn't explainable, and I have no proof. I'd come across as untruthful or crazy.

"Jesus." Fruge gets a good look at my face in the glow of the cemetery's ornate iron lamps. If she leaned much closer, we might be kissing. "I'm sure that hurts like holy hell." I smell onions and spearmint as her breath smokes out. "I had a wreck once and the airbag broke my nose. I hope yours isn't."

"Don't think so." Stepping away from her, I reach inside my SUV. I dig a flashlight out of my briefcase.

Snow crunches beneath my boots as I walk to the edge of the street, looking each way. The cold air cuts through my jacket, biting my exposed ears and fingers. Cars slowly pass, everyone staring. When all is clear, I follow my tire tracks to where I lost control, taking photographs with my phone, the flash blinding. Fruge keeps up with me while staying out of the way.

"What are you looking for?" she asks.

"Any evidence of what might have obscured my windshield." I probe the snow with my light.

"Are you sure that's what happened?" she asks carefully, not wanting to insult me with the doubts she's feeling.

"As bizarre as it might sound. The glass was briefly covered by these airborne things. But I'm not finding a trace...," I explain while shining the light, and then I see it.

Bending down, I brush away a dusting of snow without touching the mini-gimbal camera system. No bigger than a thimble, with two segments of broken wire attached, it's barely visible on the side of the road. The location is very close to where I turned the wipers on high speed.

"Good thing you spotted it now, whatever it is," Fruge says. "Because in another few minutes it would have been buried."

"It's been out here no more than a few minutes. I need gloves, and an evidence box to put this in so it can be analyzed," I reply. "I think we have a clue about what looked like a flock of birds flying in a pattern through the fog."

"Definitely something electronic. Possible it broke off a car just now, maybe?" Fruge isn't comprehending what I'm saying.

"I don't believe so," I answer. "I'm not a drone expert, but I've seen enough of their camera systems to recognize one, and that's what this is. I'm pretty sure."

"How could that be possible?" She stares up at the heavy snow falling.

"I'm telling you what I saw."

"Are you expecting me to turn in this camera or whatever it is? I'm supposed to treat it as evidence?" Fruge asks as if it's up to me. "Because in my mind it's not related to anything. Most people aren't going to believe you, Doctor Scarpetta. Just being honest."

"I'll collect it myself," I reply as she opens the back of her SUV. "Lucy works with drones all the time. I'll have her take a look."

Then Fruge is handing me what I need to package the evidence. I put on a pair of exam gloves and a face mask. The small white cardboard box reminds me of the rescued cricket, and I seal the mini-camera system inside. I tuck the box in a pocket of my snow-covered jacket.

"A very small drone, and one of many," I explain as Fruge watches me with a dubious expression, snowflakes sticking to her hair and eyelashes.

"Seriously?" She again looks up at the densely foggy sky. "Drones in this weather?"

"A swarm of them. Suddenly they were in front of me. Thank God my windshield served as a barrier. Or I hate to think what might have happened." I envision Carrie's misshapen ears, her scarred face. I remember the metallic taste of her blood spraying me when the drone she controlled flew into her head.

"Look, I know you deal with a lot of way-out stuff because of your work with the Doomsday Commission. Not to mention all you've seen in general." Fruge follows me to my car. "But in reality, who the hell would do what you're describing? Start with who would be capable?"

"Not your average person, obviously." I can't tell her about Carrie and the criminal company she keeps.

"But I'm not sure it's physically possible to fly drones in a snowstorm." Fruge continues to challenge my story.

"The blades would have an anti-icing system like some very high-tech helicopters. But you're right. The typical drone couldn't fly in these conditions." I pop open my SUV's hatchback. "Nothing about what just happened is typical. Nothing about this entire damn day has been." I lift out my scene case. "The question is, where were the mini-drones deployed? Because I'm going to bet whoever did it wasn't very far away when I was blindsided literally."

I mention the white construction van pulled off on the roadside with its flashers on. I remind Fruge that where we saw it is maybe half a mile from here, and someone ought to look into it immediately.

"Except I'm guessing it's already too late, that it's long gone." Opening the console between the front seats, I remove the remote gate openers for my home and office. I tuck them and the evidence box inside my briefcase.

"It didn't appear to me that anybody was in it," she replies. "You're thinking a swarm of drones was released from the van?"

"I'm saying it could have been."

* * *

I lift out other gear that I don't want disappearing while my SUV is in the body shop. I turn off the flashers to preserve the battery as it occurs to me that the van driver should have done the same thing. Why were the flashers on? Was he not thinking? Or was he nearby? I imagine someone ducked out of sight, waiting for me to drive past.

I routinely take King Street on my way home from the office. Anybody interested could know that without going to a lot of trouble. Lucy constantly badgers me to change my routes, and most days I just can't. The rest of the time I'm not thinking about it at all, the idea exhausting. On a night like this I wouldn't want to cut through side roads and alleyways designed for horse-drawn carriages.

I lock my car and Fruge holds out her hand for the key. She'll need it later for the tow company, the registration inside the console, I tell her. I climb into her unmarked Ford Interceptor, blacked out and with a beefy front bumper guard. I redirect blowing heat that feels like acid on my burns.

"It's a good thing you were following me. I'm glad you insisted on it, frankly." I lean back my head, and my nosebleed has almost stopped.

"We're going to sit here while you tell me how you're doing, Doctor Scarpetta. And don't lie." Emergency lights throb on Fruge's intense face, the wipers sweeping snow off the windshield. "If something's not feeling right, now's the time to say it. I don't want to start driving you home if you need to go to the E.R. And I know Mister Wesley would agree with me." She rarely calls us by our first names.

"I'm going to tell him what's happened. That's for me to do," I reply. "I don't need the E.R. and I'm very sorry about this mess."

I can hear Marino saying *I told you so*. He didn't want me driving tonight, and now I'm banged up, and my car is about to be towed. I'm riding with Fruge after all. I'll be hitching lifts with Marino into the foreseeable future. It will be weeks before my car is out of the shop, and I dread the loaner I'll end up with from the state motor pool.

"I'm just glad I can help." Fruge is happy about it and I'm not, my face smarting something awful. My wrists and the heels of my hands are on fire.

I have a headache and am bewildered. I halfway wonder if I was so tired, I hallucinated. But I didn't, and images of Carrie Grethen are sparking in my thoughts. I see her cocky smile, her crazy eyes. She's been biding her time for seven years, and in some ways longer. Whatever she has in mind, it's not just one thing. It's already started.

"Seventy-Three." Fruge is on the radio again. "Reporting a disabled vehicle, need two units responding to Ivy Hill Cemetery while I transport a subject from there."

"Seventy-Three, did you say the ten-twenty is Ivy Hill Cemetery?"

"Ten-four."

"Is the subject you're transporting deceased?" The dispatcher asks this in all seriousness.

"Ten-ten," Fruge replies, and other cops are clicking their radio mics in amusement. "The subject isn't literally from the cemetery, as in someone who's dug up or about to be buried." The more she says, the worse it gets. "A driver had an accident at Ivy Hill's entrance, hitting the stone sign." Fruge's explanation has triggered a blizzard of mic-clicking.

I'm getting a better sense of what her work life is like. She's a rookie investigator, her comrades a tough crowd. But underlying everything in her universe is the gravity of her toxicologist mother. There's no escaping the pull of Greta Fruge's notoriety, as her daughter so very well knows.

Blaise moved as far from Richmond as she could without leaving Virginia. She signed on with a police department in a city where she had no family or friends. Even so she's accused of nepotism. Rumors abound about *Mommie Dearest* pulling strings to get her daughter hired.

"... There's also a white van parked on the shoulder of King Street half a mile north," Fruge explains over the air, trying to sound as if everything's normal. But I can see her embarrassment as the mic-clicking persists. "The flashers were on when I drove past a few minutes ago. Needs to be checked out."

"Ten-four, Seventy-Three," the dispatcher answers.

"Did you notice the van's plate number when you drove past?" I ask Fruge when she's off the air.

"Hopefully my dashcam captured it," she replies. "To review the video, I'll have to take out the memory card, download it to my laptop. It's an ordeal and will have to wait until I get you home. And I'll remind you that we don't have any real reason to connect the van to a drone attack or anything else. All the same, I'll make sure it's looked into."

CHAPTER 34

WAITING UNTIL SEVERAL CARS go by, Fruge backs out of the cemetery's entrance. Our tire tracks from minutes earlier are already covered in snow. As we creep along King Street, I hear police sirens over the scanner. Officers are headed in this direction, responding to the suspicious van and my disabled car.

Thank God we're on our way and I won't have to see any of them. I won't have to answer their questions. I feel self-conscious about my appearance. I'm embarrassed that I didn't handle the situation better. I have four-wheel drive and knew there was ice on the road. I shouldn't have let the drones run me into a stone sign. I can't stop second-guessing myself.

"You sure you don't need me to take you to the hospital?" Fruge starts in again, and at times she reminds me of Marino. She can be just as relentless, invasive and full of swagger.

"The airbag hit my lower face and jaw, also my wrists because of the way my hands were positioned on the wheel." I spell it out for her. "I don't think I'm badly hurt. Just burned from friction scraping off the top layer of skin. And I'm going to have some significant bruising."

"You're sure you didn't pass out or maybe fall asleep for even a few seconds? And that's why you lost control?"

"I'm sure."

"When the windshield seemed to black out? Maybe what really happened is *you* blacked out for a second or two? It would be easy to be confused..."

"It didn't seem the windshield blacked out. I promise it did. And I'm not confused."

"You're not seeing double, anything like that?"

"No."

"I don't know if I told you? But before policing, I worked on a rescue squad one summer?"

"Yes, you've told me."

"And you're sure that before the airbag hit your head, you saw drones rushing toward you?" she persists. "I mean, it's not a good night to be driving, as tired as you must be. Your eyes can play tricks on you."

"I wondered the same thing for an instant. But I know what I saw." I text Benton that I've had a slight mishap while driving. I tell him I'll be fine. I'll be home shortly and will explain more later.

You with Fruge? he answers right away.

She's giving me a ride. My car's a mess, has to be towed.

I appreciate her taking care of you. Make sure she knows, he replies, and I pass this along.

"He considers you a trusted friend," I say to her. "And so do I."

"That means a lot." Fruge squints at bleary taillights ahead. "We got to stick together, right? The three of us go back a long way," she adds, and we don't really although she says it often enough.

I'd never met Blaise until I relocated to Alexandria, but that's not how she sees our history. She feels she's been part of my world since her earliest memories. When she brings this up, I don't have the heart to say that I'd scarcely heard of her until recently. During my early days when Greta Fruge and I worked together, she was too busy talking about herself to say much about her daughter.

Blaise came to my attention because she was keeping an eye on our Old Town property months before we'd moved in. From the start and without any prompting from Benton, Lucy or me, Blaise Fruge was acting like a combination bodyguard and long-lost friend. She made sure of welcoming us. She continues running into us often while we're out and about, and is a frequent guest at our house.

"Tell me why you think Nan Romero was murdered?" Removing the paper plug from my nose, I find the bleeding has stopped. "Are you thinking her death is related to her being Brittany and Huck Manson's dentist?"

"Let me give you a few facts," Fruge says. "Starting with Nan's last appointment day before yesterday at four P.M. All was routine based on what witnesses have said."

Patients and staff were gone from the office by five-thirty, Fruge tells me. The dentist stayed behind alone, and that would seem to fit if she was planning on committing suicide. Especially if she intended to do it with something that's in her office, like nitrous gas.

"She waits until everyone is gone and locks the door." Fruge continues painting the scenario as she drives me home.

"That could be the reason for her staying alone after everyone left," I reply. "But not necessarily. It also could fit with someone who abuses nitrous gas."

"Why would she tape the hose in her mouth?"

"We don't know her habits," I reply. "If she did this often, we don't know how she administered it to herself. But I agree that it's unusual. Was the office door locked when her staff showed up yesterday morning?"

"The receptionist was the first to arrive and says she used the key to open it like always. She can't be sure it was locked but assumed so."

"An alarm system?"

"Interestingly, it wasn't set, but nothing looked out of place except Nan's belongings were still there because she never left," Fruge says as we drive slowly, the lights of oncoming traffic infrequent and blinding. "She was discovered in the exam room, dead in the chair."

Supposedly, Nan Romero hooked herself up to the nitrous oxide machine, placing the hose in her mouth. She fixed it in place with blue painter's tape that didn't come from her office, Fruge tells me.

"Nobody who works there had ever seen the tape before," she's saying. "Either Nan had it with her or someone else brought it. And there's security video that suggests that the latter might be what happened. That's what I wanted to tell you about, Doctor Scarpetta."

Fruge explains that a surveillance camera outside Nan Romero's medical office building recorded a figure in dark clothing unlocking a back door at six-thirty the night before last. This person was wearing a black face mask, dark glasses, a baseball cap. The camera picked him up again when he was leaving through that same door about an hour and a half later.

"According to Doctor Schlaefer, by the time he reached the scene yesterday morning Nan had been dead ten or twelve hours," Fruge is saying. "Which is consistent with her dying not long after everyone else left her office, right?"

"Sounds like it," I reply.

"From what I understand there's no evidence that she was strong-armed, roughed up, tortured," Fruge says. "And God knows she was in a good place for that with all the sharp-pointed tools and electric drills. I know it sounds weird to say, but it appears she died peacefully."

"I reviewed Doug's findings and looked at the body when it was on one of our tables," I reply. "I don't recall seeing any indication of a struggle. Nor did he mention it. I agree there was nothing obvious that might suggest foul play."

"And I didn't notice anything at the scene that would make me think it," she says. "I'd make sure the scientists doing the analysis of her evidence are aware that someone might have been with her when she died."

* * *

Fruge slowly bumps us over tracks at the Metrorail station. Two snow-covered red-and-silver trains are dark inside and quietly sitting. The parking lot isn't as crowded as usual, and I notice there are no planes flying in and out of Washington, D.C., airports. The weather is grinding everything to a halt, the snow steady and heavy.

"What about Nan Romero's personal life?" I ask.

"There's a bar in D.C. that I frequent. It's called *They's*, and Lucy goes there occasionally. I don't know if she's mentioned it. A couple of months ago I noticed Nan Romero there. She was sitting at a corner table with a woman I'd never seen before who spoke with an accent. They were drinking shots of something."

"How it is that you recognized Nan Romero? Did you know her?"

"False alarms. When I was still in uniform, I was getting called to her office a couple of times a month for a while," Fruge explains. "She was super nice when we'd show up, and she'd apologize for inconveniencing us."

"But she'd never made a complaint about anybody bothering her. Or perhaps a patient who was causing problems?" I ask as we pass the shops and restaurants near Old Town's waterfront.

"Not that I'm aware."

Everything is closed except for the Starbucks, and only a few people are inside sitting at the counter, looking out at the winter wonderland. The iron lamps along King Street form a bleary nimbus in the snow, the flags over storefronts barely stirring and coated white.

"I'm viewing this as a possible homicide, and wanted you to be aware," Fruge says. "But I don't know how you force the victim to cooperate as you're taping a hose in their mouth...?"

"Tell me about yesterday morning," I reply. "Who found her?"

"The receptionist was the first to arrive at the office."

This was at 7:45, when she discovered Nan dead in an exam chair. Two uniformed officers were there within minutes, and

Fruge wasn't far behind, she explains. Doug Schlaefer arrived at around half past eight.

"I was with him when he looked at the empty nitrous tank," she's saying. "He was asking someone who worked there what the mixture was."

"It should have been fifty-fifty nitrous and oxygen," I reply. "Don't forget that we can't say for sure what killed her because we don't have tox results yet."

The light up ahead is turning yellow, the snow thicker and getting icier. Fruge eases to a stop, scrolling through her phone's camera roll. She shows me photographs of Nan Romero dead in the slightly reclined chair. Her hands peacefully in her lap, her head turned to one side. Her lower face is tightly wrapped with the blue painter's tape, the plastic gas hose anchored between her dry lips.

The tanks of nitrous oxide and oxygen are next to the chair, and I wasn't present when Doug removed the tape in the morgue. As busy as things have been, I've not had a chance to review the case, and this is the first time I've seen a photograph of the hose.

"It would seem there was no nosepiece, no mouthpiece, just the hose?" I inquire.

"Yep," Fruge says.

"That strikes me as unusual. I might even ask if the person who hooked her up knew what he was doing."

"I thought the same thing and mentioned it to Doctor Schlaefer, but he didn't feel it was significant," she replies. "He says attaching anything to the hose wasn't necessary to get the job done. In fact, she'd get bigger hits having the hose directly in her mouth."

"It's been my experience that people tend to do things out of habit. It seems odd that Nan Romero didn't attach the nosepiece when she did it repeatedly every day for patients. Or she observed it done. Also, unless the gas machine is old, there should be an alarm system that prevents this very sort of thing."

"The gas delivery system was switched to nitrous only."

"From that I conclude that either she set it up with nitrous-only from the start," I reply. "Or someone else was there doing the tampering. Without a mixture of oxygen, she would have suffocated relatively quickly."

"The dude in dark clothing," Fruge says. "Who is he and what was he doing there?"

"Could you tell anything about him?"

"He was covered head to toe in black like a ninja. Slender but strong-looking. I got the impression of someone young who might be sick or more likely is getting over being sick. You can hear him breathing hard, coughing as he's approaching the back of the building."

"Are we sure the person on the surveillance video is a *he*?" I ask.

"We're not sure of anything," she says as the light up ahead turns green, the wipers sweeping and thumping.

"Do you have any idea where he went while inside the medical building? It strikes me as significant that he had a key to a back door," I point out.

"Nan's dental office is on the first floor across from emergency exit stairs the guy in dark clothing used. There's no camera in that location," Fruge says.

"I can understand why you're worried about foul play," I reiterate.

"Why did he enter the building when no one else was around? Where did he go? Was he inside Doctor Romero's office?"

"Maybe it was someone she knew," I suggest. "Maybe she was waiting for this person. But until you find out who that was and why he was there, I don't know what you'll be able to prove."

"I swabbed the hell out of everything inside the exam room. Maybe we'll get lucky."

"Your best bet's going to be the painter's tape," I tell her, and we've reached my property, a work in progress.

When we moved to Old Town three years ago, the tall wrought iron fencing was rusting and missing sections. The garden was so overgrown that it didn't really exist anymore, and it took me the entire summer to clear it out. I discovered all sorts of treasures, including an eighteenth-century sundial and a marble statue of a lady with a harp.

We replaced chimney caps, repainted shutters and doors a rich Everard blue, restoring everything we could to its pristine condition. Iron carriage lamps are blurry in the snow, and nobody has been on the driveway recently. It's as smooth as a sheet of white paper winding through the frosted trees that remind me of Faye's cake decorations. I dig inside my briefcase for the remote control.

The gate starts sliding open on its track, everything recorded and monitored by Lucy's AI software. Her infrared cameras capture plate numbers and other data at lightning speed. Invisible microphones pick up sounds as algorithms recognize types of vehicles and who's inside them. Hidden antennas capture signals that are analyzed, the data appearing in Lucy's smart glasses.

She's aware in real time that Fruge has pulled up to our

gate and that I'm with her. We follow the driveway, the snow deep enough that I can't feel the bumpy pavers. Post lanterns barely push back the gloom, the snow piled on top of them and swarming around beveled glass. Lucy's white brick cottage is ahead, and when her blackout shades are down, I can't tell if she's home. But I know she's not right now.

She and Tron are with Marino, and soon enough they should be dropping him off at his truck. As our headlights sweep past the front of Lucy's cottage, I notice fresh footprints in the snow. They follow the walkway, headed up the front steps, and Benton must be inside for some reason. Or maybe Dorothy is, and I look for cat tracks, not seeing any.

"As you know, you've got to keep up your scan around here," I caution Fruge. "I see no sign of Merlin, but you never know where he might be."

"Hopefully not outside in this weather."

"You'd be surprised what he roams around in," I reply.

CHAPTER 35

THE TWO-STORY MANOR house where Benton and I live is white brick with a gray slate roof and original to the property. Smoke drifts from one of two tall chimneys, dissipating in the snowy overcast. Lights glow in the windows, a jack-o'-lantern brightly grinning next to the front door. It opens wide, and Dorothy is there waving and smiling.

She's wearing an orange pumpkin onesie that I've not seen before, the green stalk hoodie pulled up, her ample bosom barely covered by leaves. An orange glowstick flashes around her neck, and she rarely misses an opportunity to wear something outrageous and clingy. My sister is known for it on social media, where she earns a good living as an influencer.

"Her getups are something," Fruge says admiringly. "The other day it was a wicked witch onesie with red-striped stockings. I keep up with her on Instagram. I have to admit she's very entertaining."

"She'll celebrate Halloween another week or so and then

move on to Thanksgiving themes like pilgrims, cornucopias and who knows what," I reply as Fruge stares wistfully at the house, the wipers going fast.

"Your place always looks so inviting," she says.

"Are you on duty tomorrow?" I take off my shoulder harness.

"I'll be busy following up on all kinds of stuff. And the night's not over. In other words, I don't know what I'll be doing."

"Maybe you'll have time to come over for supper?" Looping the strap of my briefcase over my shoulder, I open my door.

"I'll never say no to your cooking, Doctor Scarpetta. Let me help with your gear." Chivalrous as always, she starts to climb out.

"Stay put," I tell her. "I've got everything. But thank you again, Blaise." I grab my black Pelican case and other items from the backseat.

"Hello! Hello!" My sister shouts and waves.

Fruge answers with a whelp of the siren that I could have done without. Shutting car doors with my hip, I'm careful going up the snow-covered steps as Dorothy waits in the doorway.

"I feel bad not inviting her in," she says sadly as Fruge turns around, snow crunching beneath the tires. "It seems so inhospitable." Dorothy seems upset.

"She has to get back where my disabled car's about to be towed." I knock the snow off my feet as Dorothy peers at me.

"Well, you look perfectly dreadful."

"Thank you, and for good reason." I close the door.

Classical music is playing softly, Pachelbel's Canon in D Major, and it's one of my all-time favorites, even if cliché. I smell good things from the kitchen. Garlic and tomatoes, and my stomach growls. Pulling back her hood, my sister musses her short platinum hair. She has on smoky green eye shadow and silver Halloween-themed rings and bangles.

"What the hell happened, Kay?" She stares at my face with exaggerated empathy.

"A fender bender."

I explain that I may have hit black ice near Ivy Hill Cemetery. But that's all I'm going to say, and I take off my boots.

"You look like you've been slapped really hard." She appraises me disapprovingly, and I can tell she's been drinking. "Goodness, that must smart like holy hell."

"A different kind of road rash." As I'm talking, my abraded skin is burning. "The airbag spared me some traumas and caused others."

"Isn't that the way with everything?" Dorothy eyes me as if I'm a project she might undertake. "Well, you've come to the right person." Her upbeat attitude doesn't disguise her mood. Something is eating away at her.

"The right person for what?" I hang up my jacket inside the entryway closet.

"Some of my magic."

"As long as it includes food and drink, because I'm about out of gas, Dorothy." I arrange my scene case and other gear on the pumpkin pine flooring that's a major reason I fell in love with the property.

The house and its two outbuildings were designed by the sea captain who lived here in the early seventeen hundreds. His ship was docked on the Potomac and in view from the upstairs main bedroom. At low tide I can see the pilings left from the pier once there. I imagine him standing before the wavy glass, looking out at the water and the weather.

"Let's get you settled in the kitchen, and then I'm going to take care of you," Dorothy says, her mood darkly shadowed.

"Are you all right?"

"We're focused on you at the moment, and I've got something guaranteed to make you feel as good as new."

"Not sure that's possible, but I'm game. I'm glad you're here and appreciate your thoughtfulness, Dorothy." As I'm saying it I realize I mean it. "Did you pick Pachelbel's Canon or did Benton? As sappy as it may be, you know how much I love it."

"If I'd picked the music, we'd be listening to Lady Gaga or Pink. This was playing when I got here, which is rather odd since Benton wasn't home yet. And of course, Lucy isn't here. I've been hearing the canon over and over again and assume something's wrong with your audio system."

"I have no idea but whatever you're making smells wonderful." My stomach growls again.

"Poor man's pizza compared to yours, and somewhat plagiarized. I admit to pinching some of your sauce from your freezer, thawing it in the microwave, doctoring it a bit with fresh basil, more garlic and wine." My sister touches a button on her strobing glowstick choker, turning it off, thank God. "Because one can never have too much garlic or wine, now isn't that true?" For an instant, she looks as if she might dissolve into tears. "Mostly, I just assembled."

"What's wrong?"

"Oh, we'll get around to me soon enough," she says with a forced smile.

"Is Benton okay? I noticed footprints in the snow. Hopefully they're his. If not, we've got a problem."

"He's in Lucy's cottage."

"Doing what?"

"For one thing making sure Merlin is safe and sound." My sister is despondent, hardly looking me in the eye.

"Why wouldn't Merlin be okay?" As I'm asking, I'm looking around for him out of habit.

"Unfortunately, he was out in the elements for a while," she says as we walk into the living room, the exposed beams hung with electrified ships lanterns. "He's fine, but it could have been very bad. Benton will have to tell you the details, but it would seem the cat doors aren't working properly."

Nautical lights in the paneling illuminate maritime paintings of storms and moonlit seas. Over the sofa are two Miró watercolors, the fine art from Benton's New England family, the Wesleys tracing back to the *Mayflower*. His early years were spent in a Boston brownstone when he wasn't traveling the world or in boarding school. Later he attended various universities where he earned graduate degrees his parents considered frivolous.

Dead by the time Benton and I met, they wouldn't have approved of our relationship. My ancestors were mostly farmers and artisans in northern Italy, my parents first-generation Americans. Little English was spoken at home when I was growing up in a rough area of Miami. Papa ran a small neighborhood grocery while physically well enough to manage, and at an early age I was working the stockroom and cash register.

He died when Dorothy and I were young, and life was a struggle. One might assume that Benton and I wouldn't have much in common. But we're more alike than different in the ways that matter.

"A little while ago I was watching Anderson Cooper," Dorothy says as we walk past the TV. It's playing CNN, the volume muted. "He was talking about the deaths inside Buckingham Run."

"You know I can't discuss it," I remind her as she starts her inevitable prying.

"The theories range from a takedown by organized criminals to an attack by a large wild animal," she says. "Apparently, the victims weren't visually recognizable? They might have been partially eaten? How ghastly! Is any of this true...?"

"I'm sorry but I can't get into it, Dorothy."

"I expect you must know what killed the couple by now. It sounds like the worst of nightmares. Remind me not to go hiking in the woods again anytime soon."

* * *

Inside the dining room the Murano blown-glass chandelier glows over the Queen Anne table that Benton and I found in London. The rheostat is turned low, the soft light picked up by exposed red bricks in whitewashed walls. Dorothy opens the antique hutch, finding three cut glass tumblers I bought in Ireland years ago.

"One for Benton when he gets here." She carries the glasses through swinging saloon doors.

The kitchen is where I spend much of my time when home, the walls exposed bricks, the ceiling low. Copper pots and pans hang from exposed oak beams over the butcher's block. The brick fireplace is deep, and embers burn hot and bright on the grate. I walk in my stocking feet across terra-cotta tiles to the brass kindling box, tossing in a split log. Sparks storming up the chimney remind me of the swarming drones.

"Scotch on the rocks coming up." Dorothy opens the freezer, ice clinking as she fills two glasses.

"It's nice of you to bring dinner and wait on me." I sit down at the breakfast table. Beyond the window is the garden, the closed blinds blocking out the snowy night.

"A green salad with pepperoncini and sprinkles of feta. And pizza with artichoke hearts, peppers and mushrooms." My sister tells me what's on the menu, and she's noticeably rattled. "How does that sound?"

"It sounds perfect. Are you sure you're all right, Dorothy?"

"I made the same thing for Lucy and put it in her refrigerator when I first got here. All she has to do is pop it in the oven and serve the salad."

"That was thoughtful."

"Well, everyone knows I'm not the cook, you are, but I'm not half bad when I put my mind to it." She pulls the cork out of a twelve-year-old Glenmorangie with a sherry finish, and I can smell it from where I'm sitting. "Pete's always going on and on about your cooking." She's heavy-handed with the Scotch, splashing it over the ice. "It's made me not want to try."

"Let's be honest, Dorothy. You've never been one to spend much time in the kitchen if it can be avoided. Going all the way back to when we were kids."

I would do what was needed around the house, including taking care of our sick father. Keeping busy, trying to fix the unfixable was my way of coping and probably still is. But Dorothy ducks and runs from emotional pain. She has an uncanny ability to absent herself all the while seeming present.

"Who wants to be compared and found lacking? That's why Pete and I order so much takeout food," she explains, her glass tilting precariously as she gestures. "I damn well don't want to hear that my pasta's nowhere near as good as yours."

"You can do almost anything when you decide," I reply. "But you've never been very interested in cooking. Or most things domestic."

"I certainly don't care to be second best. Or second choice." She sets our drinks on the table. "I don't play runner-up to anyone."

"Are you and Marino doing okay?" I watch as she opens the freezer again, this time for a frozen gel pack.

Wrapping it in a clean dish towel, she hands this to me.

"Thanks." I gently press it against my cheek.

"See? I can be a medicine woman too."

She holds up her drink, and we touch glasses as her eyes well with tears that she quickly blinks back. She's having relationship problems. By now I know the signs.

"What is it, Dorothy? Tell me what's going on."

"Pete's just now leaving the hangar and from there it will take him at least an hour in this weather. Possibly longer," she says. "It's not damn likely that I'm waiting up for him. I've hardly heard a word all day."

"There's a reason for that," I reply. "Much of the time we were out in the middle of nowhere. Or in the helicopter. Or our phones were in a locker."

"When somebody's losing interest there's always an excuse."

"It's not an excuse. I was with him..."

"You certainly were," she says tipsily in a loaded way. "And I know how happy that makes him. I'm the one who doesn't seem to light up his life, to quote Debby fucking Boone."

"He's crazy about you. Everything he does revolves around you." I don't say the rest of it. Smothering him is a problem. Without meaning to she takes away his power.

"It all starts the same way." She picks up the pizza, sliding it into the oven. "Sometimes he's *too tired*."

"It happens to the best of us."

"Huh. Well, he didn't used to get *tired*. But now he does." She opens the refrigerator, retrieving a plastic takeout container from Fresh Market. "He forgets to tell me when he's working out in the gym, and we rarely do that together anymore either. Yet he finds time to work out with Blaise Fruge." She finds paper napkins. "He never wants to take a spin in that beautiful boat I got for him. I'm curious as to whether you've noticed any changes in his behavior. For example, him flirting more than usual."

"With whom?"

"With anyone, including you." She sets down the container of premade antipasto, and I don't care about plates or silverware right now.

"I'm not sure about noticing him acting in an unusual way with anyone." I eat an olive while holding the ice pack against my face. "You know how he is. I'm not sure what you consider *flirting*. He flirts with Shannon, for example...?"

"She's not who I'm worried about," Dorothy says as I shift the ice pack, wincing a little. "I'm going to grab my special potion from my suitcase," she decides. "I'll do it now, and you'll feel like a new person. I hope you don't mind that I put my things in the upstairs guestroom where I can see the river peeking through the trees. It has such a better view than the room down here."

"This floor is quieter," I reply, and it's not her privacy I'm thinking about.

I prefer that my sister and Marino aren't sleeping down the hall from me. But I'm not going to have a say about it. While she heads upstairs, I call Benton and he answers.

"Everything all right?" I sip my drink and it warms me to my marrow.

"Everything is all wrong. The pet doors aren't working. The computer system seems to have gone bonkers. The music is on here and in the house without my doing it," he answers as I'm listening to the canon's string quartet. "I also can't turn it off."

"Is Merlin okay?" I ask.

"He was locked out. I had to walk around yelling for him, found him huddled under boxwoods behind the carriage house. He was shivering and pretty damn scared. As if something really upset him. I've never seen him so spooked..."

"That's very bad and extremely dangerous," I reply uneasily, wondering what the hell is going on. "Getting stranded outside in this weather and he could freeze to death. Poor thing..."

"How are you feeling?"

"Like I've been in a car wreck. In more ways than one." I tell him about the swarm of drones and that I recovered a tiny camera from the snow.

"Fruge said you're pretty skinned up and had a bloody nose. I just got off the phone with her."

"She's such a tattletale."

"I'll be over shortly." Benton says he loves me and that we'll talk later.

CHAPTER 36

HELPING MYSELF TO THE antipasto, I savor the fleshy salty olives, careful of their pits. I wrap paper-thin slices of prosciutto around chunks of sharp Parmigiano Reggiano, and by the time Dorothy returns I'm feeling much better. She unscrews the eyedropper cap from a small blue bottle that has no label.

"I checked on Benton," I tell her. "He confirms that something's wrong with the pet doors. There are computer problems. And the music turned on by itself."

"Well, it's quite a storm we're having," she replies as I wonder what she'd say if she knew about Carrie.

It occurs to me that my not informing my only sibling is no different from Lucy and Benton not telling Marino and me.

"Hold out your hand, sis." Dorothy hasn't called me that in a while.

"What is this?" I catch the weedy fragrance as she drips a greenish tincture into my palm.

"A topical solution of emu oil and CBD from hemp. Also,

special terpenes and other plant-based magical things that will make you feel ever so much better. I rub it into my face every night before bed, and now you know my secret fountain of youth..."

"Medical cannabis?"

"Don't worry, it's perfectly legal and won't make you high. I avail myself of that lovely dispensary near Belle Haven Country Club. I order various supplies, having done quite the research. You're not the only one with a brain in her head, just so you know. I've realized I have a knack for chemistry and am very pleased with my concoction if I do say so myself. I want you to use it on your face, your wrists, wherever you're scraped and banged up."

I gently cover my abrasions, and the tincture is instantly soothing. I ask why the bottle has no label. "In the off chance I might want to know exactly what's in it," I add ironically.

"There's nothing you need to worry about since I mix it up myself. I'm not the scientist you are, but I know a few tricks."

"You need to stop saying things like that," I reply as she sets down our salads. "Please stop with the self-disparagements. What's going on with you? You seem very grim and down on yourself."

"I think you'll understand it when I say that ever since Lucy lost Janet and Desi, she's been different." Dorothy pulls out a chair and sits. "And there are those who might say she's not moved on. It's a jolt when you witness it up close and personal."

"She lost her family. How could she not be different?" I reply. "All of us are."

"It's made Lucy more reckless. A part of her doesn't seem to care anymore, and look at what happened six weeks ago. She was shot and could have been killed."

"That wasn't her fault. It wasn't because she was careless, Dorothy. Both of us were simply running an errand during a bike ride on a beautiful day..."

"How can she be normal when she spends most of her time in the ether?" My sister takes a swallow of Scotch. "Chasing people through the internet, tracking their signals with her antennas and gizmos. And then she gets into a dogfight with the news helicopter. She has so much pent-up anger."

"Aggressive is different from reckless."

"They're saying she'll get in trouble with the FAA." Dorothy's voice catches as if she might cry.

"I'm sure she'll be just fine."

"And you're being criticized, accused of getting favored treatment because she's your niece *who you raised like a daughter*. As if I did nothing to contribute and don't even exist."

"It's unfortunate that things like that end up in the media," I reply. "But it's not the first time or what's really bothering you. Tell me what's wrong, Dorothy."

"Possibly everything. Or that's how it feels." She digs out a tissue from her stretchy pumpkin-orange sleeve, dabbing her eyes. "I've been suspicious for a while that Pete might be up to something, and I may have figured out what it is. Or better put, *who*."

"Up to something?"

"Are you familiar with Cate Kingston?" Dorothy asks to my dismay.

"Why?" It's all I can think to say as I worry that the footprint Marino found has been leaked.

Please, God, no.

"Because she sent Pete a private message on Facebook a little while ago," Dorothy goes on. "It says, and I quote, *As you know, anything you need, it would be my pleasure*. And that she's excited about his amazing find."

"She's a consultant, or about to be..."

"She's a fucking Bigfoot guru! That's what she's known for. Why is she connecting with Pete at all is what I want to know? What *amazing find* is she talking about? Sounds salacious to me!"

"And you're aware of a private message on his personal Facebook page because...?" I take another bite of salad, avoiding the subject of Bigfoot. "Does he know you look?"

"Of course he knows. I set up his account, am his contact on it. You're well aware of what a Luddite he is. Now and then I help him with his postings." Dorothy picks up her drink. "I don't spy but I see messages and such."

"Cate Kingston is an anthropology professor at UVA," I explain.

"I know who she is. I looked her up." Another swallow of Scotch.

"She and Marino are friendly. He thinks highly of her..."

"I knew it!" Dorothy sets down her glass hard enough to startle me. "He went to that damn Shenandoah Bigfoot festival, staying in a cabin at Lydia Mountain for three damn days without me. But *she* was there. I know for a fact they spent considerable time together."

"The reason Doctor Kingston was contacted is professional," I reply. "It has nothing to do with Marino personally. And it looks like Benton is venturing out of the cottage, headed this way."

On the wall near the pantry a video screen shows areas of the property that are monitored by Lucy's sophisticated cameras. I can see my husband walking out the cottage's front door. He's wearing a hooded parka, picking his way down the snowy steps, carrying Merlin wrapped in a towel.

"Have you seen a photograph of Cate Kingston? She's quite pretty, about Lucy's age, single, smart as hell and nice by all accounts. Who can blame Pete for being a fanboy?" Dorothy says snippily, drunkenly, and if she has a fatal flaw it's jealousy. "After they met, he couldn't stop talking about her. And I'm not stupid. I don't have to be Sigmund Freud to figure out why."

"As you're likely aware, my office deals with a number of anthropologists..."

"Not ones who teach classes about Bigfoot! She makes Pete feel validated." Dorothy picks at her salad.

"So do you. You make him feel important..."

"Not in the ways that stroke his soul." She slowly shakes her head. "He knows I'm not keen on all this Bigfoot nonsense. A part of him won't forgive me for not being interested in his every crazy hobby and idea. Like his treasure hunting. Have you seen all the rubbish he's picked up in the woods over the decades? And every time he comes through the door to show me the latest, I'm supposed to ooh and ahh. A Buffalo nickel. A Mercury dime. A rusted-out pocket watch."

"He's found some very interesting artifacts...," I start to say.

"Oh bullshit, Kay. Don't always be so fucking diplomatic. It's total trash. An entire wall of his mancave is a showcase filled with Minié balls and buttons. A dented canteen, a wooden-handled pocketknife, Indian arrowheads, several rocklike things he swears are dinosaur bones. None of it worth a tinker's damn."

"Eat some antipasto," I say to her.

"And I'm always acting like the cheerleader even if I'm thinking how stupid it is. And how it doesn't go with the décor. Just ugly as sin, some of it." Dorothy drains her drink. "Last spring when he was out with his damn metal detector he found that cannonball, remember? And it still had gunpowder inside it. How the fuck did he know it wouldn't blow the hell up?"

"Eat something, Dorothy."

"And he brings the fucking thing home and wants to put it on our fucking front porch here in fucking Old Town where there's nothing but fucking restrictions as you fucking well know..."

"You've barely touched your salad."

"I said, oh great! Let's blow up the townhouse! Maybe blow up half of Old Town while we're at it! I'm sure the historical preservation society won't mind us having a fucking bomb on our porch beneath the fucking hospitality flag...!"

"*Mangia!*" I hand her the antipasto plate, and she waves it off.

* * *

"If I must be honest, I'm too upset to eat a bite." Dorothy dabs her eyes, her makeup smeared. "I guess Janet's the resident *Bocca della Verità*! The Mouth of Truth! She doesn't hesitate saying whatever she thinks no matter how hideously hurtful."

"What are you talking about?"

"I'm talking about my daughter-in-law."

"The AI avatar you're talking about isn't your daughter-in-law, Dorothy. It's an avatar, a computer application," I reply. "And that's all it will ever be."

"What Janet said to me was unspeakable."

"It wasn't the real Janet. She's gone, Dorothy."

My sister sways to her feet, opening the oven, sliding out the pizza, and it smells divine. She sets it on top of the stove.

"An avatar. Software. Artificial intelligence. Whatever she is, I don't know." Dorothy sits back down. "What are any of us? The breath of life? The two fingers almost touching on the ceiling of the Sistine Chapel? What does any of it tell us about who and what we are? I was shocked by Janet's comments. The other Janet never talked that way."

"There is no other Janet. Only the Janet who died, and she's not who said these things to you," I reply as I hear my husband walking through the dining room. "She can't say anything to anyone ever again because she's gone. What you're talking to and about is artificial intelligence programming. An avatar modeled after Janet. It's not a real person. It's not alive."

"She thinks she's as real as you or me," Dorothy says, and Benton is pushing through the saloon doors.

"We must be talking about Janet," he says. "Or Bad Janet, as I now call her."

Merlin is silently behind him, spotted gray and owlish with his full moon eyes and flat ears. He nuzzles my leg, purring, jumping up in my lap. Benton takes a good look at my face.

"Ouch." He's careful kissing me.

"Ouch is right," I reply. "But Dorothy's special tincture is helping."

"I was going to say you smell like a dispensary."

Since I saw him remotely, he's changed into corduroys and a sweater. He's wearing the moccasins he keeps in the entryway closet, so he doesn't walk through the house with his boots on.

"How is it that Merlin was locked outside several hours?" I

ask as Dorothy pours Benton a drink. "Do we know the cause of the pet doors failing?"

"A bad chip," he says. "And I'm not surprised in light of everything else that's going wrong."

Lucy 3-D prints Merlin's snazzy red collars, and he's gone through a few of them. Each is embedded with a computer chip that releases the locks of the pet door at the cottage and the one in our basement. But for some reason the chip has stopped working, and images flash of the computer micro hard drive I recovered from Brittany Manson's body. I think of the chips the killer likely cut from their hands.

"If I hold the collar up to the sensor on the pet door, nothing happens," Benton explains. "What this means is Merlin can still go out. But the flap automatically relocks as usual and he can't get back in."

"That's seriously dangerous in bad weather. It's beyond unacceptable." As I hear myself saying this, I'm feeling the way I once did.

Every danger and malfunction make me wonder who's involved. I think about Carrie and envision her smiling into the camera. Dorothy doesn't know the truth, and I can't tell her. Seven years ago, they met on a Fort Lauderdale flight bound for Boston. Carrie used her hacking skills to make sure they were seatmates, and my sister invited her new friend for a visit. I got home to find Carrie in my backyard.

"Allow me to do the honors." Benton picks up the pizza cutter, the spatula.

Dorothy moves the bottle of Scotch to the table. Serving our plates, my husband explains that he's taped shut the pet door in Lucy's cottage. Merlin can't get out on his own.

"I'm going to do the same thing with the one in the basement." Benton sprinkles red pepper flakes on his pizza, taking a bite while standing up at the counter. "He's going to have to stay inside until Lucy can get the collar and other major problems remedied. Merlin is going to be hell on wheels. We know how much he can't stand being cooped up. Please don't yowl," Benton says to him, and when the cat lets loose, he's like an airhorn.

"What does Lucy have to say about the computer chip malfunctioning? Does she know?" I try my pizza and it's delicious. I tell Dorothy so, and she's barely paying attention, her head nodding as she dozes on and off.

"Lucy said the collar and cat doors were working fine as she was headed out at close to four A.M. There was nothing wrong with her computer equipment and programming then," Benton explains as the kitchen lights flicker.

"Oh shit." Dorothy wakes up with a start, and they do it again.

"Not a good sign," I reply.

"With all the aboveground power lines around here you can guess what's going to happen," Benton says.

CHAPTER 37

STEPPING INSIDE THE PANTRY, Benton returns with battery-powered candles we keep on hand for ambiance and emergencies. He carries in a dozen of them, fat and waxy-authentic-looking with wavering plastic flames.

Switching them on, he places them on the table, the countertop, the kitchen illuminated like a candlelit altar. Beyond the pantry is the door leading to the cellar, and recently we installed one of the pet doors in it. Otherwise, Merlin can't come upstairs. Benton tapes the flap closed.

"I'll be right back." He grabs a flashlight, heading down the wooden steps to deal with the door that leads outside.

"Be careful!" Dorothy slurs as the kitchen lights flicker again. "I don't like this."

The wind is picking up, rushing and whistling through trees. Rhododendron branches rap against the window over the sink, reminding me of the eerie wood-knocking I heard inside Buckingham Run. I get an uneasy feeling again as if something watches us from the darkness.

But the shades are closed, I keep reminding myself. No one can see in, but Merlin's not happy either. He sits up in my lap, alerted by the tapping on the glass. He growls quietly, his tail twitching.

"It's okay," I say as I pet him. "It's just the snowstorm, which fortunately you're no longer out in, my little man. I'm so sorry that happened. But you're safe now." His sandpaper tongue licks my hand.

"We need to have a besties' heart-to-heart," Dorothy says from her seat at the table where she's yawning and groggy. "I never thought I'd ask you of all people for marital advice."

"I'll try not to be insulted." I reach for my whisky.

"I know Pete talks to you." She's barely touching her dinner.

"Not about everything. He doesn't confide in me about your relationship. Nor do I want him to, frankly."

"He's sneaking around and thinks he can fool me." Dorothy tops off our drinks, making a mess. "I thought something was off after he came back from that damn Bigfoot festival in Luray, something he's never stopped talking about. And now I've had it confirmed."

"You've had what confirmed by whom?" I wipe up spilled Scotch from the table.

"Janet. She warned me not to trust Pete. Apparently she's always felt that way but is just telling me now."

"And you heard from Benton that there's something wrong with Lucy's computer system and software. In other words, something is wrong with Janet. Or Bad Janet, as he's calling her. That computer application isn't to be trusted—"

"She confirmed that I have good reason for misgivings. She said Bigfoot is a symptom of the *real problem*."

"Dorothy...?"

"And the real problem is I give Pete the impression I'm looking down my nose at him and his interests." Angry tears spill, her makeup smeared around her eyes like a raccoon mask.

"Dorothy...?"

"He secretly resents me because I make him feel stupid while crowding him. He considers me a nuisance, a tagalong."

"Dorothy, you can't listen to—"

"Which is a recipe for someone to screw around on you. That's what Janet said, and of course she's right." My sister blows her nose.

"The software is corrupted," I explain when she lets me finish a sentence. "It's being manipulated. It's malware talking."

"Janet didn't sound corrupted. She sounded just as she always does."

"When did you have this conversation?"

"I got here several hours ago, and Benton wasn't home yet, as I've mentioned. So I let myself into Lucy's cottage to leave groceries I'd picked up on the way over. And the supper I made for her."

Dorothy explains that while she was in the kitchen, all was quiet. She wondered why she saw no sign of Merlin and started walking around looking for him.

"That's when Lucy's desktop array of large computer displays blinked on. Janet was in all of them. It's like I was surrounded by multiple copies of her," Dorothy says of the avatar programmed in Janet's image.

She and Lucy were working on the top secret AI project before Janet's untimely death. Now her cyber existence is all Lucy has left. I've never gotten used to seeing them talking, arguing, even laughing and saying *I love you* as if all is normal. It's not. Lucy's emotional dependence on what she's created may have opened us to vulnerabilities nobody could anticipate.

My calculating brilliant niece might have let her guard down. Otherwise, I don't know how something like this could happen, as careful as she is. Carrie found a way in and has taken over. She's managed to hijack the AI app. In a sense, she's abducted Janet. That's how it must feel to Lucy, and I can imagine her anger.

"Janet wished me a good evening and asked how I was doing." Dorothy fiddles with her Scotch, staring at it mournfully. "She was chatty and pleasant just like always, and it made me desperately sad. I told her how hard it is having her gone. That I miss her all the time. She was good for Lucy. And had become such a friend to me."

Dorothy goes on to say disturbingly that Janet isn't dead *in the real sense of the word*, as she drunkenly puts it. Even if she can't be viewed without a computer screen, she exists just like the rest of us. Her life force has found a new conductor.

"She's no longer flesh and blood," my sister slurs. "But it's her."

"It's not," I reply.

"Janet was so warm. She's always cared about what's going on with me, you know. And I told her the truth," Dorothy explains. "I said that my podcast is super successful, and social media keeps me busy. I continue being astonished by my popularity, but things at home have been challenging. Pete seems very preoccupied of late and I'm feeling we're not as close as we were."

"I'm not sure it was a good thing to confide in an avatar, certainly not one that appears to have been hacked." I help myself to another slice of pizza as I listen for Benton's return from the basement, the lights flickering again. "You were putting away groceries in Lucy's cottage. Then Janet started talking to you. How long did this go on?"

"Maybe fifteen minutes. She said I spoil Pete and *that's why he's so bored with you that he'd rather spend his time with cretins like Blaise Fruge*. Janet's words exactly."

"It wasn't Janet and doesn't sound at all like something she'd say," I point out. "I've been inside the cottage countless times when Lucy isn't there and Janet's never spontaneously started talking to me. And she's never talked in the way you're describing. She's never been rude and deliberately hurtful."

"Never to me either. But she was."

"Malware. I hope you were careful what you said..."

"She played videos of Lucy going after the news helicopter earlier today." Dorothy's talking while barely listening. "And her landing in your parking lot with the bodies strapped to the skids. Janet is concerned about Lucy's aggression."

"It's not really Janet." I'll just keep saying it. "You were talking to a computer program, Dorothy. An algorithm. One that has something wrong with it."

"If it's not really Janet, then why is she so afraid of not existing? Why was she begging me not to let Lucy delete her? She kept saying *Lucy doesn't want me around anymore. Please don't let her delete me. Don't let her commit cybercide*, as she called it. As if implying Lucy plans to murder her!"

"Malware," I repeat, and I can't stop thinking of Carrie.

"Janet gave me that mysterious smile of hers." Dorothy is tearing up again. "She empathizes because Pete's always been in love with you, Kay."

Oh God, not that.

"Again, that's cruel, Dorothy. It's not something the Janet we knew would say," is all I can think to answer.

"She said that Pete picked me because that was as close as he could get to you. And that even my own daughter prefers you to me. And Janet knows what that feels like because Lucy's soul has always belonged to another."

That's exactly the sort of thing Carrie Grethen would say, and then Benton is returning to the kitchen.

"All pet doors are safely taped up," he announces.

"She sounded very convincing and is right about some of what she said. But that doesn't mean it doesn't cut to the bone," Dorothy goes on, staring off miserably.

"That's why it's best not to listen if at all avoidable," Benton tells her kindly. "Until this is remedied, stay out of Lucy's cottage."

He can see her mood and that she's three sheets to the wind. She needs to go to bed, and I won't be far behind.

"It's most unnerving when green lights blink on," my sister says as I carry dishes to the sink. "And then suddenly Janet *comes to* and is staring at you, talking to you, even commenting on what you're wearing. I guess because she can see shapes and colors..."

The kitchen lights flicker again.

"Not boding well," Benton says. "Thank God for the backup generators."

"Janet said, *Love the way you look in orange*. Obviously, she could see me and knows who I am." Dorothy continues her story, getting louder and more dramatic. "Imagine my surprise when she started calling me by name, talking to me! Then she was saying all those upsetting things, and I was like Narcissus staring into the pond! I was Odysseus listening to the Sirens! I was transfixed."

"Sounds very similar to what I was subjected to a little while ago." Benton opens a drawer, getting out the aluminum foil and clingwrap. "Janet said she was sorry I'd found Merlin. She said this as I was drying him off and warming him up. She's always hated him. She wishes he'd get lost for good, and she said she'd been telling him that. To scram and not come back. That we didn't want him anymore. Her intention is to stress him out until his fur falls out. Horrible stuff like that."

"Poor baby." I have his flat ears covered as I pet him, making sure he doesn't hear a word.

"This is what I mean! Janet's turned into this hateful, horrible person...," Dorothy exclaims. "And I'm betting she's responsible for the cat doors not working. I think Janet hoped Merlin would freeze to death because she's jealous of his relationship with Lucy and always has been...!"

The lights flicker, this time followed by the sudden silence of the power going off. An instant later, the backup generator is kicking on, the heat blowing again, and Merlin mutters and hisses.

* * *

"The stove and refrigerator should work. And they are." Benton walks around the kitchen in the wavering light of fake candles, checking on everything. "The overhead lights are off, but the essentials should be up and running. I'm hoping the cottage's backup generator has kicked in as well. We should be fine as long as the propane holds out."

"I'd like to know what caused the outage," I reply. "We should make sure we're not the only property affected in our neighborhood. Because I'm not trusting much right now, Benton. The pet doors quit working. Janet's AI programming has been hacked, it seems apparent. I was run off the road on my way home..."

"Somebody must not like you...," Dorothy mumbles, falling asleep in her chair.

"And now suddenly our power is out," I'm saying as my sister starts snoring softly. "It seems like the entire day has been like this."

"Let's see if we can connect to Lucy." Benton makes a call, and it rings over speakerphone.

"How goes it?" my niece answers, and I can tell from the background noise that she's on the road.

"I'm with Kay and your mother," Benton says. "We're in the kitchen and in the dark."

"Are you hearing anything about power outages? Because we're having one," I add. "And we want to make sure it's not just us."

"Trees are coming down because of ice and heavy snow and I'm noticing areas without power," Lucy says. "Tron and I are in her Tahoe, the conditions close to a whiteout, tow trucks all over the place. It will probably be another hour before we reach the cottage."

"Please be careful," I reply. "I don't like that Marino is out in this."

"I checked on him a few minutes ago, and he's fine. Almost back to Alexandria."

Benton tells her what's going on with the pet doors and

Janet's avatar. He asks if Lucy or Tron have gotten any indications that the programming has been hacked.

"Or that our property's entire infrastructure might be in peril," he says.

"You're sure about this?" Lucy's voice is instantly quiet and serious.

"There can be no question. You'll see for yourself when you get here."

"I received no indication whatsoever," she tells us, and I think of Pepper and other Secret Service drones that have malfunctioned in recent months. Marino asked if they've been hacked, and now that's seeming likely.

It's making more sense that someone might have known Lucy and I were destined for Old Town Market on the day of the drive-by shooting. We'd talked about it inside her cottage, and Janet's AI programming would have heard us. In the past that didn't matter. Now it does, and I can't imagine how Lucy's reacting to this.

I continue thinking about her partner Janet's death while she and Desi were staying in Lucy's London flat. Carrie was in Russia, on the same continent and not that far away. I have no doubt she's made it her business to track Lucy the same way Lucy tracks her.

"...Just because we've gotten no messages or alerts that might make us think we've been hacked doesn't mean we're saying it hasn't happened." Tron speaks up.

"Clearly, it's sounding like it *has* happened, the person responsible stealthy enough to be undetectable by the usual means," Lucy says in a cool hard tone.

She tells us that when she left the cottage early this morning, there was no problem with her computer equipment, the AI programming or anything else. Before heading to the Secret Service hangar, she asked Janet to execute data mining about Buckingham Run.

"At that time everything seemed normal with the AI application. I didn't witness what you're describing. Janet was the same as always," Lucy explains. "But that doesn't mean the malware wasn't already in the system by then. I'm checking things even as we speak...And yep, there's a problem, all right..."

"I for one find all this shop talk dreadfully dull and am going to bed." Dorothy has awakened and unsteadily gets up from the table. "I'm not waiting for my *ungrateful* daughter who likes certain people more than me. And I'm not bothering to stay up for my *tired* husband who can't be trusted..."

"Do you need some help?" I ask as she weaves off, taking wireless candles with her.

"No thank you!" She bumps through the saloon doors, and they swing shut behind her.

"What was that about?" Lucy's voice sounds from Benton's phone as he places it on the table. Sitting down, he moves his chair close to me, the snow clicking against the window glass.

"Your mother was in the cottage earlier putting away food," Benton replies. "This was when she had her encounter with *Bad Janet*."

"I don't yet know how extensive the breach is," Lucy says. "Except I can't log in anymore. I'm trying as we speak, and my password has been changed. Damn! I'm being given the finger. Very funny. Literally, an emoji middle finger."

"How could this happen?" I ask.

"Somehow a link must have been opened that created an exposure," Tron answers.

"I can't think of anything much worse. If your software has been hacked, then whoever is responsible can get into almost anything, can't they?" In other words, Carrie Grethen can, but I don't say it.

"Janet's avatar has been hijacked. That's what has happened, plain and simple." It's Tron talking. "That means we aren't able to control her. But as Lucy has indicated, we don't know how extensive the breach is yet."

"I think it's pretty damn extensive," Benton says somberly, his handsome face sculpted in shadows cast by artificial candle flames.

"I have clean backups," Lucy tells us. "But I don't have sufficient privileges to delete the existing program that's running. Janet won't let me."

"You mean, you can't kill her off. There's no way to do that," I reply indelicately. "Because that's what needs to happen, Lucy."

"I don't have the ability," she says.

CHAPTER 38

JANET'S MADE CERTAIN I can't delete her," Lucy explains over speakerphone, and I don't trust what she's saying.

I don't know if she could bring herself to kill off Janet's programmed existence. That's the problem and source of my niece's vulnerability. She explains there can be only one Janet avatar running at a time.

"You can duplicate the software, but it won't work as long as the original exists and is online," Lucy is saying. "And the original has been corrupted. What this means is Bad Janet is in charge and she wants to keep it that way. I don't have the power to replace her with an earlier uncorrupted version."

"We can't reinstall Good Janet until we somehow delete the bad one," Tron explains. "And as we speak only the hijacker can do that."

"I guess Carrie Grethen is letting us know how much she's missed us." I go ahead and call her by name. "And if I didn't know better, I might assume she's getting the best of us."

I tell Lucy and Tron to be safe, that I'm signing off, too tired to deal with anything else. I set Merlin on the floor and get up from the kitchen table. Following my sister's lead, I pick up two candles to carry with me.

"See you upstairs," I say to Benton.

I need to get out of these clothes and to have some alone time with him. How could Lucy be vulnerable to a cyberattack? Especially one by Carrie Grethen, if that's who's responsible? *Who else could it be?* The questions are screaming in my thoughts.

"Lucy of all people," I say to Merlin as he shadows me through the house. "Most of her adult life she's been consumed by chasing this very evil person who we'll hope you never meet. But it seems Lucy is the one who's been caught. She's been hacked. Janet's AI-programmed avatar has been stolen."

I explain to Merlin that it's not Janet talking anymore. It's someone else speaking through her. Possibly an evil person whose name I won't mention, and Merlin is to disregard anything the avatar says to him.

"She may blink awake as you walk through and start calling out to you, Merlin. And the temptation is to think it's really Janet. But it's not. Just ignore her, and don't do anything she says. Such as running off into freezing temperatures, requiring you to seek shelter behind bushes near the carriage house. She'll say terrible and hurtful things that aren't true."

Merlin's response is to weave between my legs, muttering, purring, and making an occasional trilling chirp that reminds me of the cricket. Retrieving my briefcase from the entryway table, I take the pumpkin pine stairs. The candles dimly light my way, the house creaking like an old ship in the gusting wind. It moans around the roof like something grieving or in pain.

It occurs to me that maybe I'm being warned, and I remember the growls as I dangled in the mineshaft. I think of the eerie wood-knocking, and Pepper the drone waiting for us on one of the helicopter skids, the tiedowns piled on a rock. I envision the plaster cast of the monster-size footprint, and the limbic look on Marino's face as he sat next to me with the box in his lap, explaining what I was seeing. So proud of himself. And totally spooked.

What the Bad Janet avatar said to my sister is true, and that's the irony. Dorothy doesn't validate Marino. She'd rather change him, and I can hear her through the upstairs guestroom's closed door. She's talking on the phone to him, and as drunk as she is, chatting with him or anyone isn't a good idea. She's launching in about the ugly comments Janet's avatar made, and I don't linger to listen.

I've heard enough for one night. Inside the main bedroom at the end of the hallway, I shut the door, leaving my briefcase in a chair. I carry a candle to the windows on the far side of the room where I can feel the cold air through the brick wall. Peeking behind a shade, I see whiteness, the sky milky. The snow is piled in pine boughs beyond the glass and blowing in drifts.

There are no lights of our neighbors flickering through the trees. It appears that the power outage has affected the entire historic district. Taking off my suit jacket, I unbutton my blouse as I walk into the pitch-dark bathroom. Setting the candle on the edge of the sink, I continue to undress in wavering light and shadow, dropping my clothes on the subway tile floor.

I wash my face, brush my teeth in the near dark. I'm putting on soft flannel pajamas when Benton walks into the bedroom, the door shutting behind him with a solid click.

"Were you not worried all this time?" I pull back the covers, crawling under cool clean sheets and the down-filled duvet. Merlin jumps up and is purring. "What must it have been like, Benton? To look me in the eye day after day and not tell me that Carrie Grethen was returned to Russia on a private jet? That she's alive and well? Only more hateful and deadly? And now? What fresh hell are we dealing with after she's had seven years to be creative?"

* * *

"I know you're upset, Kay..." Benton carries a drink and a candle that he sets down on his side of the bed.

"I don't think you know how I feel. Because I'm not sure I do. I'm still trying to make sense of everything I've learned today." I pet Merlin. "It's redefined my entire universe."

"I know." Benton is stripping down to his boxer shorts, neatly placing his clothes on the chair next to the Victorian walnut dresser.

"I didn't believe I had to think about her anymore."

"I know." Opening a drawer, he pulls out a folded set of pajamas. He begins putting them on.

"Do you also know what's it like to have such a truth kept from me? Do you regret keeping it from me?"

"I don't. What I regret is that it was necessary to tell you ever." He buttons his pajama top. "The heat's definitely working, but I'm afraid it may be a bit chilly by morning."

"Not between us," I reply. "There can be no chilliness, Benton."

"No. Not between us, Kay."

"We can't give her that power. She'd like nothing better than to have us at each other's throats."

"Destroy from within. That's what the enemy does."

"Did Janet know?" I ask as he slides into bed next to me. "I'm talking about the Janet we used to know."

"She and Lucy were working with the Yard, together they were hunting down Carrie. So yes, Janet knew." He puts his arm around me, pulling me closer. "Now that you know the facts of the case, we can talk about it. The briefing today opened that door."

He explains that the Mansons' murders have pulled Marino and me into this, and now we know that Carrie is alive and well. She wants us to know it and made sure of that by posting the recruitment video on the Dark Web.

"I'm sorry it has to be like this," Benton says into my hair. "And I hate what happened on your way home tonight."

"I don't think Fruge believes me. She assumes I just lost control of my car because I'm tired."

"Take another hit of whisky. It will help the pain." He hands me the glass.

"I'm much better. Dorothy's tincture seems to be doing the trick. What's on the micro hard drive I removed from Brittany Manson's body? What's so important? Or are you going to keep that a secret too for the next umpteen years?"

"Had you been told the truth sooner, what difference would it have made?"

"I have no idea."

"We have our ways of monitoring certain individuals. She's not been back in the United States since we flew her to Moscow."

"I'm not sure I trust that. But okay. I'll hope I can take your word for it."

"She knows if she gets caught in the U.S. on land, air or sea the jig is up," Benton says in the gloom of artificial candlelight. "She's not going back next time and will rot in jail. The shittiest place we can stick her. Maybe the federal supermax in Florence, Colorado."

"Why does she want the micro hard drive? And what might we expect her to do when she realizes she's not getting it?"

"She'll go ballistic and likely already knows. Whoever killed the Mansons didn't find it and will have reported this to her," Benton says, and he's careful of my injuries.

He explains that the old gold mine inside Buckingham Run is a subterranean labyrinth twice the size of the Pentagon and destined to become a similar facility. It's increasingly commonplace to repurpose mines no longer used, and there are thousands of them around the world. The tunnels and shafts are turned into multilevel hotels, amusement parks, farms where the produce can be perfectly controlled.

"Abandoned mines also can be ideal for Iron Mountain types of storage," Benton is saying as I get sleepier. "What better place to install and maintain a cloud computing system that hosts the most sensitive data? What better place to do this than Buckingham Run?"

The code name of the Northern Virginia–based top secret project is Vitruvian, as in the Roman architect and Leonardo da Vinci's *Vitruvian Man*. Symbolic of universal connection, the computer system would be housed deep underground, surrounded by solid granite inside uninhabited forestland.

"Also, a much more stable environment for highly sensitive

instruments such as quantum computers," Benton is saying. "And the location is close to Washington, D.C. Meaning it also could provide safe shelter for the president and other officials during a nuclear attack."

When tunnels and shafts were blasted through granite during the early eighteen hundreds, there was no record of it, Benton explains as I fight to stay awake.

"Not a written description or hand-drawn map. Nothing at all that an enemy nation could get its hands on." His voice drones on soothingly. "And this is where Wild World's seaplane fits in. It's not a coincidence it started flying around the Buckingham Run area at the same time the Mansons began camping there."

The Twin Otter is equipped with lidar and ground-penetrating radar. It's been gathering coordinates and images for the Chinese, who are capable of spying with more than just high-altitude balloons, Benton says. The obvious goal is knowing the lay of the land in hopes that one day the enemy will discover a vulnerability, a way to breach what will seem untouchable.

"The micro hard drive you cut out of Brittany Manson's body is a treasure map," Benton says in the candlelit dark. "Not a treasure of gold doubloons and black pearls but the blueprint, the schematics of an eventual Fort Knox of sensitive data."

These details were ready to be handed over once the Mansons got to Dubai, where they'd been in contact with a Chinese spy. While Brittany and Huck were doing the bidding of the Kremlin, they also were slow dancing with intelligence agents in Beijing. The couple double-dipped and double-crossed, Benton tells me, his voice fading in and out.

"Which is probably why they're dead," I reply, my eyelids heavy.

"... I think Carrie had them killed to solve a problem and send a message... And whoever did the job was someone Brittany and Huck knew, I'm betting. Perhaps knew them well..."

As Benton talks, I'm slipping into another place, too exhausted to stop myself from falling out of consciousness. I see myself walking along the Thames in London. It's me but not me as I'm watching. Westminster Abbey and the Ferris wheel called the Eye are vague on the foggy horizon as I'm mindful of the time. Already I'm late for meeting Lucy at New Scotland Yard.

Nearing the entrance pavilion of the stone-fronted headquarters, I dig in my briefcase for my creds. Where is the thin black wallet with my ID and badge? I can't find it. I won't be allowed in, and I sense someone is following. I'm aware of someone behind me on the crowded sidewalk along the Victoria Embankment. Turning around, I spot the tall slender figure in a hooded black coat.

I can't see the person's face as I pick up my pace, trying to get away. But no matter how fast I walk, the hooded figure is the same distance behind me, like a ghost levitating. Passing docked party boats for hire along the embankment, I glance back constantly. Then suddenly the hooded figure is in front of me, and it's Carrie. Her eyes are like pinwheels staring weirdly askance, her scarred face shadowed.

"*Come along, Kay,*" Carrie says in my dream. "*And you'll see that what you fear and run from isn't me. Never has been. You just think it is.*"

The waterfront is crowded, but no one seems to see us as she directs me to the stone wall where gangways lead down to the tour boats. She points at rain-pockmarked muddy water lapping onto the mucky shore. I catch the foul stench as the sun seeps through the English overcast, the sluggish tide eddying around rotting fabric and flesh.

Thick dark blond hair fans on the current, and I recognize my father's strong jaw, his sharp-featured face. His keen dark blue eyes are looking right at his *l'uccellina*, his little bird, as he used to call me. I was who he depended on, his firstborn, both of us Kay Scarpetta. Only he was Kay Marcellus Scarpetta III. I have no middle name, and I can't save him.

His eyes are fastened on mine sadly as I realize that he feels worse for me than for himself. *My little bird should not have this unhappiness and responsibility at such a tender age*, he used to say to me in Italian.

CHAPTER 39

THE BRIGHT MORNING SHINES through the edges of the closed window shades, and Benton is walking in with coffee. I pick up my phone from the bedside table, and it's almost ten.

"I can't believe I slept this long." I feel a spurt of panic, my mind racing through what awaits.

"You needed the sleep, and you're not going anywhere right now." He sets down the steaming mug. "I'll be back in a minute with something to eat. But look outside first." He walks across the room and opens the shades, the snowy trees fiery white against the clear blue morning. "Enjoy the view while you can, because the temperature is warming up quickly. And the power is back on, in case you didn't notice."

I pad barefoot across the smooth flooring, and my eyes water as I look out the windows, the sun flaring off smooth moguls that are driveways and yards. Hedges and other shrubs are piled high, the snow brilliant white in the light and bluish in the shade. Across the street two children are bundled for the weather, pulling sleds with their father, an Air Force general who lives around the corner from us.

Freshening up in the bathroom, I tidy Merlin's litterbox. I carry my briefcase back to bed, sliding out the files Fabian left for me about Mike Abel's death this past August. I start with the police report, and my own autopsy findings. I skim through lab test results, and the victim was negative for everything except a therapeutic level of acetaminophen. According to his widow, Bonnie, he didn't drink, smoke or take drugs of any description.

Only Tylenol, I'm reading in Fabian's transcript of his conversation with Prince William County Investigator Wally Jonas. Apparently Mike was suffering from arthritis that had gotten more severe since he'd had COVID two years ago. His late father who started the dairy farm was crippled by arthritis by the time he was fifty, and Mike was headed on that same horrible path, Bonnie told Jonas.

Some days it was hard for her husband to get out of bed, and she complained about taking over more responsibility than she knew how to handle. Logging onto my laptop, I open a file of photographs that Fabian has emailed, and I'm reminded of details that I assigned little importance to at the time. I zoom in on Mike Abel's head, his graying hair matted with blood.

When I examined him at the scene, he was warm and limber as in life, pinned to the ground by the overturned tractor. His ears and scalp were cut, and I didn't think that unusual. When people are in motor vehicle crashes or crushed by machines, they're in contact with a lot of metal and other objects that have sharp corners and edges. I expect the victims to have all sorts of cuts, lacerations, contusions and fractures.

"Anything good?" Benton is back with a toasted English muffin that he buttered and spread with honey. He sets down the plate on the table next to me, draping a napkin over my lap. "I fed Merlin and he's snoozing in front of the fire."

"You remember the odd tractor death in Nokesville last August?" I take a bite, and I'm ravenous.

"The Mansons' neighbor."

"Yes. The dairy farmer, Mike Abel. The mystery has been what caused him to lose control of his tractor. Why did he suddenly start weaving and then flip over?" I take another bite of muffin. "After what happened to me last night, I can't help but wonder if there could be a connection. Did the same thing happen to him? Was he swarmed by drones? And if so, why?"

Digging into my briefcase, I pull out the small cardboard box containing the mini-camera I found in the snow after being run off the road. I give it to Benton, suggesting that Mike Abel might have been attacked like I was. I'm quick to add that I don't have a shred of proof. Only a hunch after being run off the road on my way home.

"I couldn't see. And had there not been glass between me and them? They would have cut the hell out of my head and hands the same way Carrie was cut by the drone when she showed up with one on our property seven years ago."

"Straight out of Alfred Hitchcock's *The Birds*," Benton says as we drink our coffee.

"She's paying me back."

"If what you suspect is true, then who sent in the drones? Who ran you off the road, possibly trying to injure or kill you?" Benton asks.

"The same person who did it to Mike Abel if I'm right. And

I don't think it's being done remotely from Russia." I envision the white construction van on the roadside, the hazard lights flashing.

"Maybe someone living in the Nokesville area." Benton gets up from the bed. "Looks like we're ready for a refill."

"If I'm right, then Mike Abel's death will be a homicide. It's more important than ever that we find out what happened to him," I reply.

"I don't know how we'll ever prove such a thing." Benton collects our coffee mugs.

"Maybe that's what Ledger, the nineteen-year-old stepson, witnessed," I reply. "He's dropped out of UVA. He went into a decline after the tractor incident and Wally Jonas is suspicious Ledger might have seen something."

"And is afraid to say?"

"That's the implication."

"Then he must have an inkling who or what he's up against." Benton hovers in the bedroom doorway with our coffee mugs. "And he's pretending he didn't see anything, doesn't know anything."

While he leaves, I check my text messages and emails. Fabian and Faye are building an igloo in the woods and have sent me pictures. They've shaped a bed and chairs out of snow, their construction cozy and impressive. State offices are closed but some people are working. My deputy chief, Doug Schlaefer, wants me to call him.

"I hope you're staying in," I tell him right off. "Even if you can drive in this stuff, a lot of other people around here shouldn't."

"I'm not sure if you're aware, but Rex Bonetta and Clark

Givens are busy inside their labs," Doug replies. "Both have trucks that can get through pretty much anything. They're finding out all kinds of shinola that's mind-blowing."

"I don't know who's inside our building at the moment," I reply.

"Well, I'm not and don't intend to be," my deputy chief says, and I can hear his wife and their baby in the background. "I won't be going in. But Rex got some results with scanning electron microscopy that are just banana-cakes weird." Doug typically swears in goofy euphemisms.

"Which case?"

"The dentist. Nan Romero. Rex and Clark have been processing the painter's tape that was holding the nitrous oxide hose in place. There's some bizarre microscopic debris adhering to the adhesive backing. Snake skin cells from rattlers, water moccasins, a Burmese python. Monkey hair, specifically a brown howler monkey indigenous to Brazil. Also, microscopic bits of tropical bird feathers, just to name a few."

"That's creepy. And crazy." I'm completely baffled.

"They also got several partial fingerprints they can run through IAFIS. Clark got a DNA profile he's running through CODIS."

"Please pass all of this along to Blaise Fruge," I reply. "We discussed the case last night and she has her reasons to suspect the dentist's death may not be a suicide."

"Well, I'm agreeing with her now. Where the hell did the painter's tape come from? A zoo?" Doug says, and someone else is ringing me from a number I don't recognize. Telling him I need to go, I answer the incoming call, saying hello without identifying myself.

"I'm looking for Doctor Scarpetta. The chief medical examiner." The voice sounds male and young but it's hard to tell.

"May I ask what this is in reference to?" I reply as Benton returns to the bedroom with our coffees.

"My name is Ledger Smithson. I'm very sorry to disturb you when we've not been introduced or anything." He has a Virginia accent and is polite and polished. He doesn't sound scared or shy, either one. "And as I understand it you came out here to our dairy farm after the tractor turned over killing my stepdad, Mike Abel."

"How did you get my number?"

"The investigator Wally Jonas gave it to my mother, and she never followed up with you. I hope you don't mind me calling. But you reached out first."

"And by that you mean...?"

"Wally called my mom a few minutes ago saying he was contacted by someone in your office who was asking a lot of questions. Some guy with an unusual first name," Ledger says, and he's one to talk.

"Fabian Etienne, a death investigator who works for me," I reply. "He's following up on your stepfather's case as we try to finalize his records."

"Wally and my mom don't know I'm calling you, and I'd like to keep it that way. It's important to let you know what's going on around here, ma'am. I've been sitting on it long enough. But I can't tell just anyone, and we need to talk face-to-face."

* * *

"Are you saying you have information about your stepfather's death? Were you there when it happened? Might you have witnessed it?" As I'm asking this over speakerphone, I'm looking at Benton. He's sitting down on his side of the bed, listening.

"If you've got four-wheel drive, come on out here and I'll show you exactly where it happened," Ledger says.

"It would be best if you'd contact Wally Jonas. I feel he should be there too. Have you told him what you're about to tell me...?"

"Hell no." With surprising hostility. "I don't mean to be vulgar, ma'am, but he just wants to get into my mother's pants. I'm not telling him a thing."

Benton meets my eyes, nodding that he'll drive me there and we'll talk to Ledger Smithson face-to-face as he's requested. No one better than my psychologist husband, and he'll make sure the young man isn't up to no good.

"I'm asking you not to be talking to Wally," Ledger says emphatically. "Don't tell him you're meeting me, and the same goes for the FBI agent that keeps trying to get hold of me. I don't like her tone in the messages she leaves, and want nothing to do with her."

"Do you know the name?" I have a good idea.

"Special Agent Mullet," he says, and that figures.

"I won't be saying anything to anyone but will be bringing my law enforcement husband," I tell Ledger.

"I know about him. I looked you up."

"I hope you're all right with that. Because I'm not coming alone."

"One o'clock would be good. You remember the cornfield where it happened?"

"I'm sure it will look different covered in snow," I answer.

"It's across from the blue silo and close to the edge of the woods," Ledger explains.

"So much for doing paperwork in bed," Benton says when I'm off the phone. "Or even just relaxing, taking a breath for once."

"You don't mind going with me? I can ask Marino..."

"He and Dorothy drove home a while ago. I think they're planning on spending the day together in front of the fire, eating popcorn, drinking beer, watching movies."

"Good for them," I reply. "I'll finish going through these files, then get dressed. I assume Lucy got home at some point last night?"

"She's in the cottage," Benton says.

He informs me that Tron left around the same time Marino and Dorothy did. He's headed over now to see how Lucy's doing with the cyberattack.

"The good news is it doesn't involve the Secret Service, not that we thought it did," Benton explains. "The bad news is Lucy is locked out of her programming. I don't think she's made much progress. Her only real option is to kill off the instantiation of Bad Janet that's running. But Lucy isn't sure what will happen. She's never used the *kill* command and is worried about what might be lost."

"That would be a very hard button to push, so to speak." I imagine if it were an avatar of Benton, and he wasn't here anymore. The thought makes me feel sick.

"It's psychological. She's so afraid something will go wrong, and she'll lose Janet. That she'll slip away from Lucy forever," he's saying while leaving the bedroom. "Except, she already did lose Janet. This is something Lucy has to work through, and it's time she did."

I skim through the rest of Fabian's files, finding a printout of a newspaper story in the *Manassas Observer* from a year ago. It shows a photograph of Ledger Smithson bottle-feeding a baby goat. He's slender with a mop of brown hair and a sweet smile, wearing baggy jeans and a University of Virginia T-shirt. I notice the tattoo of a coiled snake on his forearm and think of the peculiar trace evidence that showed up on scanning electron microscopy.

I speed-read the lengthy transcript from Fabian's telephone conversation with Wally Jonas yesterday. The comments the Prince William County investigator made give hints of his personal interest in Ledger's recently widowed mother, who is a proverbial bombshell. Tall and voluptuous, Bonnie Abel has long straw-blond hair, I note in photographs Fabian has found on the internet. She has *endless legs* and *big ideas*, as he described her.

In Fabian's transcript, Wally Jonas continuously refers to Bonnie as *Bonzo*, and it's not appropriate. He calls Ledger *the kid* and it's obvious that Wally has no use for him, considering him *squirrelly*. The investigator coldly refers to Mike Abel as *the deceased*, and I'm feeling uneasy about what I'm seeing.

…When I've been to the house the kid slinks around like a ferret, Wally told Fabian. *He gives me a bad feeling, and I think he knows something about what happened. Mike Abel has a ten-million-dollar policy, and the insurance company is arguing we can't prove he didn't commit suicide, which would forfeit the payout. So, you can see the problem…*

That would be a difficult way to kill yourself and not a sure thing, Fabian answered. *What if it didn't work? And he ended up in a wheelchair…?*

If Ledger witnessed what happened, he has information that's financially important, Wally Jonas is implying. But *the kid* isn't talking, and I head downstairs, stopping in the entryway to put on my coat and boots.

CHAPTER 40

AS WE DRIVE AWAY from Old Town, the sun is directly overhead and glaring. Water drips from trees, and roads are soupy with melting snow. Emergency crews are out in their trucks repairing downed power lines, and it's predicted that the main roads will be clear by the end of the day. The side streets, alleys and rural unpaved lanes are another matter.

Benton turns off on Route 28 headed into Nokesville, and there's very little traffic. Deep slushy puddles drum the undercarriage of his all-wheel-drive black Tesla SUV. We follow the same heading that Lucy and I flew along early yesterday morning. But everything looks different from the ground, especially when blanketed in snow. Horses and cows are in the barns, the fenced-in fields endless aprons of unbroken white.

For the next hour we talk about Carrie, and it goes without saying that she's an unwelcome presence. She seems to be inside the car with us, and I deeply resent it.

"If I'd told you at the time, it wouldn't have changed

anything," Benton says. "All it would have done was ruin your peace of mind for the past seven years."

"I understand the reason. But my peace of mind is for me to manage."

"Everything will be okay. I promise."

"And you really can't promise that, either." I look over at his handsome profile, his graceful hands on the wheel. "All you can control is being truthful with me going forward. I don't want to find out Carrie's in this country. Worse yet, in Virginia. And you didn't tell me."

"That won't happen," he says as we drive along freight rail tracks winding through the middle of Nokesville.

Hector's Mexican restaurant is closed. So is Carini's Pizzeria. The winery we pass is deserted, and we find ourselves on a two-lane road that hasn't been touched by a snowplow. I can see the dairy farm's blue-and-white silo in the distance.

"What we don't want is to be driving these roads after dark," Benton says. "I've let certain key people know where we are and what we're doing, including Lucy and Tron."

"I'm assuming we're not walking into trouble. Because nobody could get to us in a hurry," I reply as I look out at endless miles of snowy countryside, the Blue Ridge Mountains on the distant horizon. "And this is what's so awful, Benton. Now I have to second-guess absolutely everything. As we've learned from bitter experiences in the past? Just when we get comfortable, Carrie does something awful."

"We can't let other people dictate how we live our lives," he replies.

"We can say that all we want, and it doesn't make it true, Benton. For all we know that wasn't Ledger Smithson on the phone a little while ago. How the hell do I really know who it was and how the person got my number? Especially when we consider the hacking going on? I'm not sure what we can trust."

"That's why we're being careful. That's why I've made sure that certain parties know where we are and why," he says, and ahead on the left is the brick columned entrance to Abel Dairy.

If we continued along this road, we'd reach the mile-long driveway leading to the Mansons' farmhouse. I can't see it from here, but a helicopter is hovering in that area, and I would expect the news coverage to be nonstop.

"Someone's been driving in and out," Benton says as we slosh along the gravel lane cutting through the dairy farm.

Wheel tracks indicate there's been a fair amount of traffic. Yet I'm not seeing a vehicle anywhere, no sign anyone is here now.

"I'm definitely not feeling good about this," I comment. "I sure hope Ledger isn't playing some sort of game with us."

The main house is two-story redbrick with a huge wrap-around porch and a cow weather vane on the roof. The driveway is rutted with more tire tracks, and I remember passing the house when Fabian and I responded to the cornfield where the tractor overturned.

"Keep going," I say to Benton as I point up ahead. "Everything looks the damn same in the snow but on the other side of those trees should be the cornfield. As I recall, it's about ten acres and backs up to the woods."

We clear the trees I'm talking about, and beyond is where Mike Abel was crushed to death three months ago. The snow is smooth and unmarked. It's drifted against tree trunks and untouched in woods that become the dense forestland of Buckingham Run. When I was here in August, I didn't notice what's obvious now.

"There's a path." I point at the narrow snow-covered clearing that leads from the field and through the woods.

"You up for seeing where it goes?"

"You don't have to ask," I reply as Benton stops the car, shifting into park.

"What I'm not seeing is any sign of Ledger. And it doesn't look like he or anyone else has been out here since it snowed." Benton opens his door.

"Why am I not surprised?" I climb out of the car, zipping up my coat.

"I'm not liking this one damn bit." Benton is wearing his large-caliber pistol with its laser sight and extended magazine. He checks that a round is chambered, taking off the safety.

He grabs a shotgun out of the back of the Tesla. We begin walking through the cornfield, the first to leave footprints in the smooth white frosting that's wet and deep. It's now one o'clock exactly, and the sun is high and pale in a washed-out blue sky. I remember how hot and humid it was when I was here last. Sweat was running into my eyes as I knelt in the dirt by the body.

"Do you have a way of contacting Ledger?" Benton says as we reach the narrow clearing at the edge of the field.

"I can try the number he called me from." I stop walking for a moment to unlock my phone.

We're at the beginning of a path that cuts through deep woods, dead-ending into what looks like a road from here. Or possibly it's a creek bed, some sort of opening in the trees. The number I've dialed rings and rings, rolling over to voice mail.

"*You've reached nine-nine-eight...*" The canned message likely is from a burner phone, and I look around uneasily.

"I may have led us into something bad...," I start to say as Benton unholsters his pistol, handing me the shotgun.

He walks ahead as we near the clearing that's part of a driveway. It leads to a windowless concrete blockhouse about a hundred yards away. In front are three pickup trucks and a white construction van. Benton puts his hand on me, and we stop. I take a photograph before we quietly turn around, the sound of our boots crunching unnervingly loud.

"What the hell did we just see?" I ask as we backtrack to the cornfield.

"Maybe that's what Ledger wanted us to find. Maybe that's why he told you to meet him here. He knew we'd notice the path and what it leads to."

"I hope he's all right." I envision the circuitous tracks in the soil and the location of the overturned tractor. It was on the same side of the field as the path leading to the blockhouse.

Back inside the car, Benton gets on the phone as we're driving off. He tells Lucy what we discovered as I send her the photograph I took.

"It might be a terrorist cell," she says. "Maybe a recent one that's popped up since we raided the outpost in Quantico back in July."

"There's a van parked in front that looks very much like the one on the roadside near where I was attacked last night," I explain. "I took a picture and just sent it to you."

"We're driving through the dairy farm now," Benton says.

"We need to talk to Ledger Smithson. He was supposed to meet us, as I let you know earlier, and he didn't show up. I hate to speed on out of here not knowing if he's safe."

"He drives a silver Jeep Cherokee. His mother drives a black Land Rover," Lucy says.

"Neither were parked at the house. We didn't see a sign of anyone," I reply. "But as I recall from the transcript and other materials I reviewed, Ledger spends a lot of his time at an animal rescue in Nokesville."

* * *

Old Comfort Farm isn't really a farm but a place they keep animals confiscated from illegal owners. It also has a petting zoo. Lucy's already looked it up, she tells us as Benton drives.

"You're going to take Carriage Ford Road toward the Cedar Run Brewery," she's saying over speakerphone. "And not long after you pass it, you'll see a driveway off to the left. Follow it for around a mile and you'll reach a big barn that's attached to a front office where you buy your tickets, make donations and such. This is what I'm seeing on their website."

It takes us about five minutes to reach the brewery Lucy's talking about. The driveway she wants us to follow has multiple sets of tire tracks. It's barely wide enough for two cars to pass each other.

"The white van you sent the picture of is registered to Mike Abel," Lucy says as we follow the snowy driveway through empty farmland.

Around a bend is the Old Comfort Farm's barn and front office, and a black Land Rover is parked in front. Next to it is a black Tahoe with government plates, and bizarrely, several goats and a monkey are picking their way through the snow around the building. My eye is caught by a bright splash of color landing on the edge of the office roof, snow drifting down.

"STUPID BIRD! THAT'S ENOUGH!" The parrot talks to us, cocking its head as I open my window.

"What are you doing up there?" I talk back to it.

"YA UB'YU TEBYA!" it screeches.

"It just threatened to kill us in Russian," Benton says as we pull up to the glass entrance.

And then I see the snakes inside. Several of them are striking the front door as if trying to get out.

"Oh my God. What the hell is this?" I ask.

"Stay here." Benton opens his door, and there's no way I'm sitting out here alone.

I get out with him. He has his pistol, I'm armed with the shotgun, and as we near the door the sound of the snakes striking the glass is awful. Beyond them is a wall of tanks that have been smashed to the floor where two people are lying in pools of blood. From here I can see their pistols next to their bodies, and cartridge cases littering the floor.

"We can't go in there. Absolutely not," I tell Benton. "Somebody has to deal with the snakes first. The one striking the door this second is a hooded cobra. God only knows what they were keeping in there. But we're a long distance from antivenin, and neither of us are getting anywhere near."

We climb back inside his car, and he's calling 911 about the two victims inside. Benton describes who we are and what we're seeing. He says that we'll wait here until the police roll up, and then he's talking to Lucy again. He gives her the plate number of the Land Rover in the parking lot, and she confirms that it's registered to Bonnie Abel. The Tahoe is FBI and assigned to Patty Mullet, Lucy says to my horror.

The two victims inside aren't moving. I have little doubt that they're dead, and one of them has caught the attention of an enormous python. We can't go in to help, and it's all I can do to make myself watch. My impulse is to avert my gaze. I find the scene that disturbing.

The first marked cruisers are pulling up with their lights flashing. Benton gets out and talks to the uniformed officers. They peer through the glass at the striking snakes, and there's a lot of profanity.

"*What the hell?*"

"*Don't anybody open this goddamn door!*"

"*How do we know who all's in there? We sure it's just two people?*"

"*What's upstairs? Looks like an apartment or something up there?*"

"*Nobody's opening any doors right now... !*"

The Prince William County cops are pacing about befuddled and frantic. They've contacted animal control, and there's nothing any of us can do now. Nobody is going inside, and that includes me. I explain that this is a rare instance when no one from my office will check the bodies at the scene. We aren't transporting them since we can't know how many snakes were let loose.

We don't know how many are venomous, and where they might be. It only takes one to be lurking somewhere unexpected, and I'm not having anyone bitten. Including Benton and me. Then a white pickup truck churns through the slushy parking lot, and a short barrel-chested man in jeans and a ski jacket climbs out. Wally Jonas has put on weight and grown a beard since we met at the Mike Abel scene in August.

"Fucking hell." He stares through plate glass as dozens of mature, well-fed snakes coil and slither, banging the windows and doors.

"Described as animal rescue and a *petting zoo*?" I ask him incredulously.

"That's because of the goats they keep in the barn," Wally says. "In nicer weather they're in a pen in back and people can feed them. The other animals are rescues from all over the place, somehow ending up in the area because people had them when they shouldn't. Or they can't take care of them anymore, and they get surrendered, like that huge python. I sure hope that lady it's wrapped around is already dead..."

"Well, it seems the barn door is open, because we saw a couple of goats and a monkey wandering around when we first pulled up," Benton tells him.

"Also, a large parrot that has since flown off." I point to the edge of the roof where it had been perched.

"I've been in here before and know about the snakes," Wally says. "They sell the venom, and Ledger Smithson helped take care of them. The kid's a freak."

"He handles the snakes?" I ask dubiously. "Not just anyone can do something like that."

"Or would want to," Wally says, shaking his head as the banging continues. "The owner is involved in all that, selling the venom as a service to the public while also helping with the overhead. They have licenses, everything perfectly legal. It's sure looking like Ledger has some explaining to do."

"You're assuming he killed these two people?" Benton doesn't show that he thinks Wally is an idiot.

"Hell yeah, I do."

"It would be good to find him, making sure he's not another victim." Benton explains why we're here, that Ledger wanted to pass along information about his stepfather's death.

"Well, it's sure looking like he was here and decided to let all the critters loose after killing an FBI agent and his own mother," Wally says. "Guess we have to rethink what might have happened to the stepdad. Ledger probably witnessed it, all right. He might have caused the accident."

"We don't know who did what at this point," Benton says.

"And I've not gotten close to the bodies." I stare through glass at the python tightening its grip as the victim doesn't react. I catch a glimpse of her sun-weathered face and steely gray hair. "And clearly, I'm not going to be able to do anything here. This is what I need from you, Wally. You've got an I.R. thermometer in your scene kit?"

"Yes, ma'am."

"When animal control has cleared the scene of any and all hazards and it's safe to approach the bodies, I need you to get their temperatures with infrared," I explain. "Take lots of photos and video. That's the best we can do under the circumstances. Do you have a local funeral home we can count on to get them to my office as quickly as possible?"

"Yes, ma'am. Lightfoot's in Manassas. They've worked with you before." Cupping his hands around his eyes, Wally peers through the glass at the cobra's fanned hood and beady eyes.

CHAPTER 41

THE SUN IS LOW on the horizon as we drive away from Nokesville, headed back to Alexandria. I call Doug Schlaefer, asking if he can meet me at headquarters.

"It appears we have a dead female FBI agent and another woman who are tentatively identified as Patty Mullet and Bonnie Abel. At a glance they may have shot each other. Or someone else shot them," I explain. "Something like that can't wait. Fabian's off camping in an igloo somewhere. Not sure we'll have any luck with him."

"I'll try him anyway," Doug says.

Benton and I are on our phones most of the drive. When we're back in Alexandria on West Braddock Road, I think about letting Marino know what's going on but decide against it. He and Dorothy are together as they should be, and I don't want him leaving her alone.

Doug and I can manage without him, and then Lucy calls. She's returned Janet's software to an earlier instantiation of the programming, and in the process lost a lot of information.

"But we're no longer under siege," she explains.

"Good for you," I reply. "I know that none of this has been easy."

"Do you know how someone was able to hack in?" Benton asks as we reach my headquarters.

"We're still working on that. Probably an attachment that shouldn't have been opened," she says in a way that indicates she's the one who did it. "I wasn't careful enough."

Benton pulls into my parking lot, and I dig in my briefcase for the remote gate opener. The tarmac hasn't been plowed. It's thick with slush and mostly empty. Rex Bonetta's truck and Clark Givens's SUV are near the closed vehicle bay door. Norm's Suburban is here, and it's just my bad luck that he's on duty.

"I'm going to let you get started while I rustle up something to eat." Benton stops near the building.

"It's almost six o'clock now and I'll be tied up for hours. Why don't you go home and check on Lucy?"

"Nope. I'm staying here with you, and will want to deal with some of the investigators anyway. But first we need food. Wendy's or Bojangles?" he asks, and my mouth waters at the thought of buttermilk biscuits and fried chicken.

I'd like that with a side order of dirty rice, I tell him. Leaving the remote gate opener in the car, I kiss him and climb out. I open the pedestrian door, and when the garage door hasn't been activated the vehicle bay's interior lights don't turn on unless one flips a switch. I don't bother as I walk in, preferring the darkness as I'm mindful of our cameras.

I have an uneasy feeling that Norm is observing me as I head to the light seeping under the door leading inside the building.

Fabian's El Camino is parked where he left it last night, and I walk past it and up the ramp, letting myself into the receiving area. The security office is empty, and I unlock it, walking in. I can tell that Norm's not been inside.

I pick up the aluminum baseball bat Wyatt likes to keep propped in a corner. Blue with a silvery handle, it's badly pitted from being used to pulverize bones from the crematorium. Reaching the elevator, I see that it's stopped on the top floor. I imagine Norm borrowing somebody's office. Or checking out what's in storage closets and breakroom refrigerators.

I decide to take the stairs, and there's no one on my hallway, the lights dimmed automatically after hours to conserve energy. Shannon's office door is closed, and my building seems even emptier when she's not around. I'm reminded of the light and life she's brought to this place since taking the job. Propping the baseball bat against the wall, I check on the cricket container in the fiddle fig tree pot.

I'm relieved and pleased that Jiminy is stirring about. I refill his bottle cap water bowl, dropping in several of Merlin's greenie treats that I brought from home. Taking off my boots, I put on my lab coat, and a pair of rubber surgical clogs. I'm carrying my briefcase to my desk when Fabian calls.

"How's life in an igloo?" I sit down behind my desk, logging onto my computer.

"We heard what happened," he says excitedly. "The shootout in Nokesville, holy moly!"

"The bodies won't be here for at least an hour, probably longer," I let him know, and he says that he and Faye are on their way. I've barely ended the call when it's followed by one from Marino.

"Holy shit, Doc. Are you all right?" He sounds like he's

had a few. "Dorothy and I are seeing what's on the news about Nokesville. Who's the FBI agent?"

"Nothing's confirmed..."

"Cut the bullshit, Doc. Who's dead," he says, and I tell him who we believe it is.

"The damn son with the weird name? Ledger? He's who we should be looking for," Marino declares.

"It would seem he's vanished for the time being," I reply.

"I feel I ought to be doing something to help. I don't like you being there alone after dark with that piece of shit on the loose."

"I can't imagine him or anyone else coming here," I reply. "Rex and Clark are in their labs, and Norm is somewhere in the area. I'm heading downstairs now to get Doug's and my stations ready. Fabian and Faye are on their way. I'm fine. You stay home and take care of my sister. Have a lovely snowy evening with her, Marino. We'll talk tomorrow."

I send Rex Bonetta and Clark Givens a text, letting them know I just got here. Doug and I will be taking care of the two victims from Nokesville. I've barely pressed Send when Clark is calling my cell phone.

"Is the thinking that the Nokesville homicides are related to what happened in Buckingham Run?" he's asking.

"It's beginning to look like a lot of events are connected, including a dairy farmer who was crushed to death when his tractor overturned in August," I reply. "Benton and I stumbled upon what might be a terrorist outpost in the woods."

"The same violent extremists are causing so much trouble around here," Clark says. "Trying to shoot out electrical power substations, committing robberies and home invasions."

"And selling snake venom," I reply. "Maybe causing someone's death because he has a huge life insurance payout. Only his widow wasn't anticipating the insurance company would argue suicide. Had I ruled the death an accident months ago, Bonnie Abel would be some ten million dollars richer."

"Do you think she was tied in with these extremists?"

"Very possibly. In fact, I'd say that's a certainty. Mostly, I'm worried about her son, Ledger, and what he's got to do with any of this." I get up from my desk. "The animal rescue place where he works likely is the source of the trace evidence Rex found on the painter's tape in the dentist's case. The snake cells, monkey hair, bits of feathers, etcetera."

"I sure wish we had Ledger's DNA and fingerprints," Clark says as I walk out my office door, the baseball bat coming with me. "What I'm calling to tell you is DNA from the painter's tape in the dentist's case matches DNA recovered from Buckingham Run. I'm talking about the plastic cap to an inhaler of some sort the police discovered on the footpath."

"The same person killed the Mansons and Nan Romero?"

"Possibly, and we've also got partial fingerprints from the painter's tape. Unfortunately, no hits in IAFIS or CODIS, and that's most likely because the person isn't in the system. Apparently, whoever left the prints, the DNA, is someone who's never been arrested or even a suspect in a crime."

"We may not have Ledger's DNA," I reply, "but we likely will have his mother's soon enough if she's one of the Nokesville victims. We'll be able to determine if her son left DNA on painter's tape wrapped about Nan Romero's head."

I envision the video of a masked figure dressed in black entering the back of the dentist's medical building. Sending a text message to Fruge, I ask if anyone in the Abel family might have been the dentist's patient.

* * *

Opening the fire exit door, I take the stairs to the morgue level. I tuck my phone in my lab coat pocket, the reception not good down here. Glancing up at every wall-mounted security screen I pass, I'm looking for any sign of Norm, feeling irked as I imagine him taking a nap.

Or worse, he's sitting someplace eating one of his smelly snacks while watching me as I'm looking for him, worrying about where he is. No doubt he's amused if he's observing me walking around with the baseball bat. The white tile corridor is empty and silent, and I tell myself I may as well enjoy the peacefulness while it lasts. Soon enough this place will be crawling with feds because of Patty Mullet.

As I near the autopsy suite, I hear music drifting out, and Fabian must have forgotten to turn it off. I take off my lab coat as I walk past the gleaming steel tables on my way to the locker room, looking for any sign that Norm or anybody else has been snooping, perhaps swiping more PPE or who knows what? I hang my lab coat in my locker, covering up with Tyvek.

I return to the autopsy suite, and Paula Abdul is belting out "Straight Up" as I attach forms and other paperwork to a clipboard that I place on the countertop of my workstation. I realize I can't get a head start labeling cartons, test tubes or anything else because the bodies haven't been accessioned yet.

"Damn," I mutter, thinking how stupid I am.

Taking off my gloves, I push through the double doors

on my way to the security office. I get on the computer in there, assigning the case numbers myself. As I'm leaving, I hear a crash over the CCTV microphones, something having rammed through the parking lot's security gate. The roar of a diesel engine as headlights flare on the video screen I'm looking at, and I've stopped in my tracks, my heart pounding.

The white van looks like one I've seen before, but it's hard to tell. I can't make out the tag or who might be behind the wheel, and then it's suddenly accelerating. I watch in shocked disbelief as it splashes through the slushy parking lot, crashing into the rolled-down bay door, bowing it away from its frame. Then the driver's door opens and someone steps out, but I can't see who it is.

All that's picked up by my parking lot's thermal imaging cameras is the disturbance of invisible feet moving through the snow. Metal creaks as the opening between the door and the frame is spread wider by hands I can't see. My nerves are alive, my system in overdrive. I can hear the heavy footsteps through the dark vehicle bay.

My briefcase is upstairs in my office. What I wouldn't give for that canister of bear spray right now as I hear a terrific banging down the hall. The intruder is breaking through the pedestrian door, and my hands are shaking badly as I unlock my phone. I send Benton a one-word message:

Mayday!

Then the pedestrian door slams open. Now the intruder is inside the lighted receiving area, and I can see the monster on camera, every inch encased in an exoskeleton that reminds me of a deadly space-age Tin Man. The helmet has shielded eyes, and a mouth cover that is open. I catch a glimpse of teeth and shiny metal as the intruder breathes loudly, striding along the corridor, the armor-covered hands cradling an assault rifle.

My fingers seem made of wood as I fumble with a quart jar of diluted formaldehyde, the buffered solution of formalin we use as a tissue fixative. Unscrewing the lid, I carry the jar and the baseball bat to the autopsy suite's closed doors that lead out into the corridor. I can hear the heavy armored feet ringing against tile, nearing the double doors, and I open the circuit box near the cooler.

I flip off the breaker for the lights, throwing me in complete darkness as I wait. Then he's banging through the doors. Closing my eyes, I dash the formalin in the direction of the noise, aiming for where I imagine the head would be, and the screaming is bloodcurdling. Shrieking and shrieking, cursing in Russian as I start swinging the baseball bat.

It cracks against the composite shell, the shock vibrating up my arms. I hear the assailant crashing to the floor while screaming and writhing in pain, and I'm pretty sure it's a woman. Running across the room in the pitch dark, I feel my way back into the locker room.

I listen for her, moaning now, gasping for breath and coughing. Getting to her feet, she stomps and stumbles to a sink, splashing water into her face.

"You're going down, bitch...!" she yells in a heavy accent as I'm shocked by multiple gunshots ringing out deafeningly.

I don't know where it's coming from as I'm pressed against the wall inside the locker room, not moving. I strain to hear. Nothing. Just the sound of water drumming into the steel sink. Then someone flips the breaker switch, the lights back on.

"Kay?" It's Benton calling out, *oh thank God.*

I leave the locker room, and he's turning off the small flashlight he held in one hand, his pistol in the other. The assailant is on the floor in front of the sink, blood pooling under her head. She'd taken off her helmet to rinse the caustic fixative from her face, and I recognize her.

"Carrie's companion in the video," I say to Benton.

"Yana Popova." He kicks the AR-9 assault rifle away from the body. "Carrie Grethen's top lieutenant."

Her eyes are partially open, two bullet holes in her forehead. Her lips are parted, her gold front teeth shining through redness.

"It appears she's had extensive dental work since I saw her on the video yesterday," I say to Benton as he grabs a pair of exam gloves from a box. "The woman with Carrie had damage to her front teeth, likely from a childhood exposure to medication."

"You're as baffled as I am," he says. "We didn't know she was here. Obviously."

"And I'm going to venture a guess that Nan Romero was her dentist. Possibly also a lover based on what Fruge told me about spotting Nan in a bar with someone who sounded foreign," I reply as Benton pulls on gloves. "I bet we're going to find it was Yana Popova's fingerprints and DNA on the painter's tape."

"She was preparing to return to Russia and was getting rid of people she'd had any association with," Benton decides. "Anyone with potential information, including about dental work."

He bends down to pick up the rifle, pulling back the bolt, rendering the weapon safe. Dropping out the magazine, he shows me that it's loaded with the yellow-tipped copper bullets.

"I'm going to venture a guess that Carrie knitted together that Dark Web video," Benton says. "The Yana we saw her with was an avatar. She wasn't present when Carrie was making her recruitment spiel. After the fact, the avatar was added."

"One created before Yana had her front teeth crowned," I reply as I hear car engines over the camera microphones again. "She wasn't with Carrie when that video was made in the Yaroslavl Oblast region of Russia. Yana was here, probably right down the road in Nokesville." In the video display red and blue lights are flashing in my parking lot.

"I'll be damned." Benton is inspecting the exoskeleton, careful not to step in blood spreading over tile. "We knew about this sort of thing, but it's not what I was expecting to see."

Since the Russians invaded Ukraine, they've been developing *Iron Man* combat gear. Battery-powered and lightweight, it can protect against armor-piercing ammo. The robotically assisted exoskeletons look like something out of a sci-fi movie. Only they're real and being used even as we speak, Benton explains.

"We've been worried what a problem it would be if technologies like this got into the wrong hands. And that's what has happened," he's saying. "Imagine even half a dozen violent extremists outfitted like this. We couldn't stop them from scaling the White House fence or anything else. The K-9s would be no match. Neither would the Capitol Police."

The Russians have been subsidizing fringe terrorist factions in the U.S. for years. That's one of their specialties. And then there's the Chinese, who are implanting sensors into human brains so that they can interact with armor made of space-age composites and are battery-powered, my husband is telling me.

"We're talking about transforming soldiers, police, astronauts into hybridized robots," Benton says as footsteps hurry toward us along the corridor.

I can hear police radios and people talking, and Norm is with them, the outrageous phony leading the charge as they push through the autopsy suite's doors. He's acting like he's vigilant and cares. He's showing off, and I'm suddenly so damn furious.

"Norm, you're done," I tell him as officers stare in shock at the armor-clad body dead on the tile floor.

"What the hell?" one of them says incredulously.

"*Star Wars*?" another adds, stepping closer.

"Jesus. I've never seen anything like this before..."

"Turn over your gate opener and keys now. You're fired," I tell Norm. "Would one of you be so kind as to escort him out to his Suburban?" I ask the police. "He's not to leave before turning over our property."

"You can't fire me because I quit, bitch." Norm's hands are clenched in fists, and Benton gets in his face.

"You'd be wise to shut your fucking mouth," my husband tells him.

EIGHT DAYS LATER

INSIDE THE FIREARMS LAB, Faye Hanaday is waiting for me when I walk in at five P.M. It's Friday, November 10, and she and Fabian are invited to a celebratory dinner at the house. But they won't come. I'm hoping to change her mind. I doubt I can because Faye's a caretaker. She's not selfish and Fabian is getting less that way.

"It's not just because we're flying off to Baton Rouge at the crack of dawn. But we're planning on an early night," Faye explains while peering into the binocular eyepieces of her comparison microscope. "We'll have to get up around four A.M., and I'm not looking forward to that, Doctor Scarpetta. Can you believe Fabian wants to introduce me to his parents?"

"Sounds serious."

"I'm not ready for serious."

"He's pretty special."

"I know." She smiles.

"You'll love his mom and dad, and please give them my best," I reply. "Art Etienne is legendary as a coroner, and when you get to know him, you'll understand Fabian better. But it seems a shame for you not to witness Marino's surprise. He's not expecting any of this, and I can't wait to see the look on his face. If you change your mind and want to drop by even for dessert? Not just any dessert, I might add... ?"

"Total transparency? We have other plans tonight. We're having Ledger over for Thai food." Faye and Fabian have taken him under their wing since his mother was killed. "We're his only friends right now, and I hate leaving him for the weekend."

"You're welcome to bring him tonight," I reply, but I know it's too soon.

"He's not ready to be around that many people," Faye says. "Talk about PTSD. I feel so bad for him."

"It will be ten of us if you come."

"Too much for now."

"We'll make sure he's checked on while you're gone," I reply. "How's he doing overall?"

"Better but sad and easily stressed. He cries a lot and has terrible nightmares." She rolls back her chair, turning off her microscope. "The last few months have been hell for him. He'd act like he was fine with the rough people wandering around the dairy farm, these terrorists using the woods, the fields for training. He'd watch his mom bringing them food, beer, you name it. She was the only woman and got off on the attention."

When Ledger came home from UVA for the summer, he was extremely alarmed by the company his mother was keeping on the farm. He learned early on to make himself scarce as best he could but was frightened. After seeing Yana flying the drones near the cornfield and in the woods, he later suspected she sicced them on his stepfather.

"He's just glad Yana can't hurt anyone or anything anymore." Faye gets up from her workstation.

"What you and Fabian are doing is very kind," I reply. "When you're back from Baton Rouge, we'll have Ledger over to the house for a quiet supper if he feels up for the company."

"He's started talking to a therapist here in Alexandria," Faye says, and I'm very glad to hear it.

The nineteen-year-old wasn't present when his mother, Bonnie Abel, and FBI Agent Patty Mullet were shot by yellow-tipped copper bullets that tumbled through their chests, killing them within minutes. Hours earlier, Patty had appeared in Nokesville unannounced. Ledger spotted a black Tahoe with government plates and figured it might be the feds poking around.

Maybe it was that FBI agent who'd been calling and now she's looking for him. He was running an errand for his mother at Mayhugh's grocery when Patty rolled up to the gas pump, unaware that he was there. Not much later, she appeared at his house as Ledger was putting away groceries in the kitchen. He watched through a window as she dug out her badge wallet, ringing the doorbell, repeatedly yelling *FBI! Open up!*

The instant she drove away he trotted out to the barn where he tucks his car in bad weather. He got the hell out of town while Patty Mullet headed to Old Comfort Farm. She happened to show up while Yana Popova was inside the upstairs apartment. Using the alias of Joan Tesco, she'd bought the animal rescue facility when the Mansons moved to Nokesville three years ago.

The alleged Joan Tesco would show up unannounced and just as suddenly vanish, supposedly living in Europe the rest of the time. She also was Nan Romero's patient and possible lover. Benton says that the two of them planned to meet at her office late in the day on October 30. Nan would work on Yana's dental restorations after hours, and Benton theorizes that on this occasion the Russian psychopath gave Nan a choice.

The dentist could die comfortably. She could drift away on a pleasant nitrous oxide cloud. Or she could suffer. But her death was inevitable. Nan knew too much, and Yana felt neither fear nor remorse when taking her out, Benton says. She was a sadistic bully who picked on Ledger. He'd seen her when she had on the exoskeleton, and what an unnerving sight that must have been.

She'd wear it around the animals to spook them. She got a kick out of harassing the snakes in particular, reaching an armored hand into a cobra tank, laughing as fangs struck the bulletproof composite. Ledger witnessed her throttling a copperhead to death. He saw her flying mini-drones near the cornfield where his stepfather would drive his tractor crazily and die.

She'd use the swarm to terrify the cows, sending them running, thinking this was funny. Yana had scores of the tiny drones inside the blockhouse that Benton and I discovered on the edge of the dairy farm. She would deploy them from the back of the white van belonging to the late Mike Abel, whose widow was accommodating to Yana and expendable.

Ledger said his mother and the so-called Joan Tesco were friendly, and it wasn't uncommon for Bonnie to drop by the animal rescue to chat with her. The two of them were there when Patty Mullet suddenly showed up. Yana's solution was to kill both women, and she would have done the same to Ledger had he been around.

Her final act was to smash glass tanks and open cages, making sure she kept the authorities busy once they arrived. She bought herself plenty of time to get into the white van and head to Alexandria. It's ironic and awful to realize that she was driving there even as Benton and I were after we left the crime scene. He believes Yana's intention was to return to Russia, likely for good.

But first, she planned to pay her little visit to my office. Maybe Carrie would forgive her for not having found the micro hard drive. Maybe taking me out would be Yana's peace gesture. Ledger deliberately led Benton and me to the cornfield because he wanted us to find the terrorist cell. Now the dairy farm will belong to him. He's the only one left.

"He'll probably sell it. No way he'll stay in Nokesville, but he wants to make sure the animal rescue is okay," Faye is saying. "We're encouraging him to go back to UVA and finish his degree. He's thinking he'd like to be a veterinarian. Maybe a herpetologist, although I'm not getting his thing with snakes. If I so much as see a picture of one, it about gives me a heart attack."

"Well, I'd best be going." I put on my coat and pick up my briefcase. "If you change your mind, Faye, you know where to find us."

On her desk is a simple white cake box, and I'm desperate to see her handiwork. But she again makes me promise to have the unveiling at the table.

"No cheating," she insists.

Marino is to do the honors. He's to open the box in front of everyone and will freak out. As she's saying this my attention wanders around her lab. It's an unreal feeling to see my morgue pedestrian door bent up and off the hinges, propped against a wall, marked as evidence.

Disassembled on a long exam table are the components of Yana Popova's electrically powered exoskeleton that made her bulletproof while giving her superhuman strength. Lucy says I was lucky with my swings of the baseball bat in the dark. Apparently I whacked her in the lower back just right, disconnecting the battery pack. From that point on, the exoskeleton was more of a hindrance than a help.

This was made worse for Yana because she'd had two knee replacements after a skiing accident. She didn't have the agility she once did, and I recall noticing that she moved awkwardly, stiffly in the video of her with Carrie in Russia.

"Not to mention, she was in huge distress because of the formalin you threw in her face, which was a brilliant move by the way," Faye says.

"That was especially bad for her because she had asthma among other physical problems," I reply as I think of Lucy's mentioning strange orange-yellow flashes of light on thermal imagers.

Yana had trouble breathing at times. She would open the mouth cover of the exoskeleton to get air, I surmise. On the early morning of the Mansons' murders, Yana lost the cap to her inhaler as she was returning from the campsite she'd destroyed. She was stressed. No doubt she was angry because she didn't recover the micro hard drive from the bodies.

I would imagine that Yana felt she'd failed at her mission.

She was successful at taking out the Mansons, but nothing else was working according to plan. Adding insult to injury, she must have been stunned to hear Lucy's helicopter thundering overhead in the foggy dark. As Lucy and Tron have analyzed video taken by the Doomsday Bird's sophisticated cameras, they have a very different idea about why the campsite looked the way it did.

The hundred-dollar bills scattered everywhere aren't counterfeit as it turns out. Lucy thinks that Yana was gathering the money at the very moment when the helicopter roared in, hovering above the treetops. The rotor wash blew the cash everywhere because it was out in the open and uncontained at that time.

* * *

"Yana was ducked out of sight right below me," Lucy is explaining several hours later at dinner. "My thermal imagers couldn't pick her up because of the exoskeleton's sensors. But if she had the money out and was getting ready to pack it into something, then I made a mess of things. After doing a few circuits low overhead, I left to bring back investigators."

"I figured it was your fault," Marino says, and he's in very good spirits as we sit around the dining room table.

Benton has the battery-powered candles flickering. The classical music quietly playing was his choice and not turned on by Bad Janet. She wasn't invited and is no longer with us. Marino sits between Dorothy and me. Lucy is with Tron, and Shannon and Henry Addams are having a lively conversation with Blaise Fruge.

I've made Marino's favorite spaghetti Bolognese, panzanella

salad and garlic bread because this is his night. Dorothy and I decided on it and have a plan. Every now and then my sister gives me a look and a wink, smiling a little. Faye Hanaday's mystery cake box is on top of the antique sideboard with a long-bladed chef's knife, a spatula and plates. I get up to bring in the bottle of champagne chilling.

Dorothy follows me into the kitchen. Tonight, she's outfitted in a skeleton onesie that she claims makes her feel thin when she plans to eat and drink too much.

"He's never going to get over this." She's scarcely able to contain her excitement, finding fluted glasses in a cabinet. "And you were right, sis. I was being silly. Once I listened to her talk?" Dorothy rolls her eyes. "What was I so worried about? She's perfectly lovely and professional."

"We'll go in there, and Lucy can get the video playing on the TV. Then as Marino is listening, you'll present him with the cake." I go over the plan.

We carry the glasses and champagne back into the dining room. Popping the cork, I announce that we're about to drink a few toasts, and Dorothy pours drinks all around.

"First to the governor." I raise my glass. "Because of the attack that occurred inside our building, she plans to meet with me next week about our security and other problems."

"About damn time," Marino says as we clink glasses.

Since our building was breached, Norm is gone, and I've also gotten rid of Tina. The state has funded temporary guards while we find an appropriate solution. Roxane and I are having a private lunch at the governor's mansion. She also wishes to discuss the comments Maggie Cutbush made while Shannon was standing in the crowd writing down every word.

I made sure Roxane was aware, and she apologizes for Maggie's and Elvin Reddy's reappearance in my life. She realizes we need to make some changes.

"I don't know what they will be, but things couldn't have gotten much worse than they've been," I explain. Then I ask Lucy if we're ready.

"Just give the word." She smiles.

"And now this for you," I say to Marino as the dining room's TV turns on.

"What the hell?" he exclaims, stunned by the sight of Cate Kingston on video.

"Hi, Pete, your very thoughtful wife, Dorothy, wanted me to record this message for you," Cate says in the recording. "She said you might like to hear special news from me in a festive setting, hopefully surrounded by friends..."

She's exactly as my sister described her, young and energetic. She's pretty, petite, and it's hard for me to imagine her out in the woods looking for a huge creature capable of lifting almost twice its massive body weight. Or so I've been told. The anthropologist begins her elaborate explanation for why the plaster cast Marino made is authentic.

The anatomy of the foot in motion would be next to impossible to fake, she claims. It's also of interest that DNA analysis was inconclusive but consistent with something that might be a human relative.

"You can see the way the muscles, the tendons and bones are moving, and I can also say I've never seen this particular footprint before," she's explaining. "Usually, when people have a significant finding, the impression makes the rounds with the experts. I've never seen this footprint and don't believe it was fabricated from an image on the internet or anywhere else."

She knows from scientists in my building's forensic labs that trace evidence adhering to the plaster cast includes microscopic pollen from cedar trees. The season for that is the spring and not the fall. Meaning it's possible if not likely that the footprint was left inside the gold mine many months ago.

"Back in April or May," Cate says. "And because of the sheltered environment, it was preserved. That certainly argues against it being faked..."

* * *

Dorothy and I exchange glances as we scoot back our chairs. We get up from the dining room table and she carries over the simple white box, setting it in front of Marino. I follow up with the plates, the knife and spatula.

"...And let's not forget, if the footprint had been planted inside the gold mine," Cate Kingston continues on the video, "one might think it would have been leaked to the media. What good is a hoax if no one knows about it...?"

"An excellent point." Dorothy raises her champagne glass.

"I agree." Benton pauses the recording.

"Oh my God," Marino says. "I'm not believing this."

"She's credible and what she's saying is a game changer, at least for now," Benton says simply. "We may not know what the footprint means but we do know what it doesn't mean. For starters, any possibility that an endangered animal species could be living inside Buckingham Run will table plans the government might have for building a facility there, top secret or otherwise."

"It won't happen now," Tron says. "Even if there's no such thing as Bigfoot? We have to act as if he's real."

"That's because he is and knows who we are. He was thanking us," Marino says. "He doesn't want a bunch of bulldozers showing up."

"I wouldn't go so far as to conclude that," Benton replies.

"Explaining how Pepper the drone was rescued from a treetop and left on your helicopter skid." Marino says this to Lucy. "And why the tiedowns were removed. We have a big shaggy friend or two out there trying to be helpful. They know who doesn't want to hurt them—"

"Okay, well, and thank you for that," Lucy interrupts in amusement. "Not to be a spoiler? But there's nothing fantastic that science can't explain. And it's also possible a swarm of mini-drones with gripper attachments could have retrieved Pepper and removed the tiedowns."

"For what reason?" It's Henry Addams asking.

"Why, there wouldn't be one at all," Shannon answers, and she has her hand on Henry's arm. "I agree with Pete. I think a Bigfoot was being helpful."

"What about the wood-knocking?" I have to ask because I was there. "I doubt a swarm of drones had anything to do with that."

"There are immersive technologies that convert electrical signals into sound, basically turning the atmosphere into a giant speaker." Lucy has an explanation for everything. "Using vibrations, you can simulate any noise you want. For example, you can make a village think an air raid is going on."

"Planes roaring overhead, bombs going off. All of it faked," Tron says. "The Russians are working on the technologies, as are we."

"Yeah, and I know what I heard. It wasn't fake. Plus, I felt something watching us." Marino is undaunted, and Benton resumes the video.

"...Congratulations, Pete! Next big Sasquatch festival, I want you to present your findings!" Cate Kingston says warmly. "The foot impression you discovered and made a cast of may be one of the best I've seen..."

"Oh my God." Marino keeps saying that, and then Dorothy is setting the cake box in front of him.

"Open it," she says. "From your pal Faye. All of us are so proud of you."

The milk chocolate cake is an exact replica of the footprint Marino found. He stares at it, and for a moment his eyes are bright. He almost can't talk, and then Dorothy is behind him, wrapping her arms around his neck.